THE CONSTANT NYMPH

Margaret Kennedy

With an Introduction by Anita Brookner

virago

VIRAGO

First published by Virago Press in 1983
Reprinted 1986, 1990, 1992, 1996

This edition published by Virago Press in 2000
Reprinted 2000, 2007, 2009, 2010, 2012, 2013

A CIP catalogue record for this book
is available from the British Library.

ISBN 978-0-86068-354-4

Printed and bound in Great Britain by
Clays Ltd, St Ives plc

Papers used by Virago are from well-managed forests
and other responsible sources.

MIX
Paper from
responsible sources
FSC
www.fsc.org   FSC® C104740

Virago Press
An imprint of
Little, Brown Book Group
100 Victoria Embankment
London EC4Y 0DY

An Hachette UK Company
www.hachette.co.uk

www.virago.co.uk

VIRAGO
MODERN CLASSICS
121

Margaret Kennedy

Margaret Kennedy was born (1896–1967) in Hyde Park Gate, Kensington, the eldest of four children. She was educated at Cheltenham Ladies' College and Oxford where she read Modern History. Her first published work was *A Century of Revolution* (1922), a textbook on modern European history. Her first novel was *The Ladies of Lyndon* (1923), preceding by only a year her major popular and critical success, *The Constant Nymph*. In 1925 she married David Davies, a barrister who became a Q.C., a County Court Judge and was knighted in 1953. They lived in Kensington and they had one son and two daughters. Five plays by Margaret Kennedy were produced on the London stage, of which *The Constant Nymph*, written with Basil Dean and starring Edna Best, Noel Coward and John Gielgud, won great acclaim. *Troy Chimneys* (1953) was awarded the James Tait Black memorial prize. After her husband's death in 1964 Margaret Kennedy move_____ O_____ b__ _____ __e lived until

Works by Margaret Kennedy

A Century of Revolution
The Ladies of Lyndon
The Constant Nymph
The Game and the Candle
Red Sky at Morning
Come With Me
The Fool of the Family
Return I Dare Not
A Long Time Ago
Escape Me Never
Together and Apart
Autumn
The Midas Touch
The Feast
Jane Austen
Lucy Carmichael
Troy Chimneys
The Oracles
The Heroes of Clone
The Outlaws on Parnassus
A Night in Cold Harbour
The Forgotten Smile
Not in the Calendar
Women at Work

TO

MR AND MRS ROLF BENNETT

CONTENTS

CONTENTS

INTRODUCTION

When Margaret Kennedy published her second novel, *The Constant Nymph*, in 1924, she was twenty-eight years old, well-born, well-bred, and highly educated. Although *The Constant Nymph* attained heights of best-sellerdom that few young writers dream of, let alone achieve, its success did not interrupt the even tenor of her life or its predictability. The year after its publication, she married a barrister by whom she was to have a son and two daughters. They lived in Kensington, and one might assume that in all essential respects Margaret Kennedy had the sort of life enjoyed precisely by those ladies for whom her subsequent novels were written: ladies beset with domestic problems of a kind which seems fairly beneficent by today's standards and which have to do with the organization of expansive family holidays or the incongruities that might shatter a weekend house party or the eternally refractory nature of servants, most of whom have to be replaced fairly frequently from an apparently inexhaustible supply.

The reader who is about to pick up *The Constant Nymph* for the first time should perhaps stalk its author not through her first novel, *The Ladies of Lyndon*, which is indeed obsessed with these problems, but through the novels she wrote in the 1930's, novels with stark romantic titles like *Return I Dare Not*, *Escape Me Never*, *Together and Apart*, *A Long Time Ago*, and *Red Sky at Morning*. These are generally held in low esteem, and they can be seen as the sort of drawing-room novel which could be enjoyed by women but also by men: gentle, perceptive, and feminine exercises in the middle range of fiction, not highbrow, but at the same time not for the uncultivated, and enlivened by a dash of morbidity which reveals that the author is not what she seems, that she is not only a romantic but an anarchist, and that she knows the ways of men and women very well indeed.

She is particularly good at patient husbands and virtuous wives, and she is even better at spotting what brings them down. Her wives, however virtuous, are usually rather smug and sometimes frankly tiresome. They bemoan the fact that they are hemmed in by domestic considerations; they also bemoan the fact that they have never been allowed to give free reign to that wild romantic impulse which, they are absolutely sure, lies only dormant in their well-behaved souls. While pondering infidelities, they reserve as their alibi the record of wifely duties flawlessly performed, and this record is thought to be sufficient sustenance for the dull respectable husbands to whom they consider themselves chained. But these women, who are in fact incapable of romantic folly, make a grave mistake in not recognizing the secret and painful impulses that animate a man. The lovely Philomena Gray, in *Return I Dare Not*, thinks that an *affaire* with the rising young dramatist Hugo Pott might suit her very well, but it is her husband, Gibbie, a man given to noting down the minutest sums of money disbursed (an evening paper, a tip to the station porter) who ruminates so surprisingly in the privacy of his dressing room and the silence of the night:-

> For real life, the male life which he had lived as a boy becomes with manhood too vast and bleak a thing. Humanity cannot survive without some subterfuge, some shelter from the winds that scourge it. If women were like men, he reflected, if they were not enervating and consoling, the whole race would be liable to perish from too much spiritual exposure. Only the epicene require candour between the sexes. That is why the Elizabethans, and indeed all the poets of the more virile ages of the world, were so much taken up by the idea of a woman's falseness, her "jestings and protestings, crossed words and oaths". Really they liked false women. They needed them. They could not have endured anything else. They wanted some respite from the intolerable burden of their manhood.

This passage contains an echo of the formula which made *The Constant Nymph* such an astonishing and sustained success, and which earned it so many tributes from male readers, readers who included J.M. Barrie, A.E. Housman, Arnold Bennett, John Galsworthy, Walter de la Mare, and even Cyril Connolly. Indeed, it may even be a romance for men rather than for women. There can be few women reading it even today who will not feel more than a twinge of sympathy for Florence, the very model of a prudent, elegant, worldly and ambitious wife. But by the same token, there will be few men who will not identify with Lewis Dodd, the unpredictable, undomesticated, ferocious genius whom Florence tries to turn into a husband. And I doubt if there will be any men at all who will find it in their hearts to condemn Lewis's love for the fifteen-year-old Tessa, the nymph of the title, who is every bit as unpredictable, undomesticated, and, in her own way, as remorseless as Lewis himself.

These two characters, Lewis and Tessa, are extremely serious creations. They go beyond the fact that the clever author has established in the one story both a romantic hero and a romantic heroine. Lewis and Tessa, although springing from time-honoured romantic stock, are convincing on the page. We are made to understand why Lewis is impossible for a normal woman to manage; he exasperates the puritan in us·all by failing to wear ordinary clothes or to behave with ordinary politeness to the celebrated critics and established patrons whom his wife invites to her parties, but at the same time we are made to feel the pain caused by his artless brutality, and may even long, through the character of Florence, for the means to bring about even a momentary subjugation. And yet we recognize, in the brilliant Tessa, who has a woman's mind in a child's body and who has always, and easily, possessed Lewis's love, the three tremendous forces which give the novel its power: the mercilessness of the privileged, the subversive appeal of the wrecker, and the fatality of the wound inflicted by passion.

Tessa comes with all the appurtenances that are going to bring poor Florence to grief. She is a member of 'Sanger's Circus', one of the children of a legendary composer much honoured outside his native England, who lives a gypsy life in the Austrian Tyrol. Not only is Tessa divinely unfettered, she has the benefits of hereditary genius (Sanger) and natural distinction (her mother was a Churchill). To this paradise in the Alps come various visitors, including the young composer Lewis Dodd, who is, of course, attractively dishevelled, as is everybody else on the winning side, and two luckless stereotypes, a Jew named Birnbaum and a Russian named Trigorin. Although these two characters, who are very crudely drawn, are later to play a respectable part in the story, they are initially introduced to demonstrate an innate lack of charm, in comparison with which the anarchic gaiety of the Sangers appears at its most persuasive. At this juncture of the story it cannot be said that the device altogether works.

Sanger dies. Back in England the Churchill connection is revived as the next of kin are alerted to rescue the children. Florence, the brisk and pleasing young mistress of the Master's Lodge at St Merryn's College, Cambridge, elects to go to the Tyrol to arrange her cousins' future. But the Alpine spring undoes Florence, moves her to new perceptions, new indulgences, and it is in this softened mood that she falls in love with Lewis, who, much to his alarm, marries her. This is the first surprise for the reader. The second is the passion revealed by Florence during the long summer days and nights of her Italian honeymoon. The third is the increasing ferocity of Lewis's behaviour as he finds his mind filled with images of Tessa, now a sorrowful schoolgirl in England.

Florence, needless to say, ruins her case, as she was bound to do, for she is a lady and thus no match for a woman, even if that woman is barely fifteen years old. She buys a house at Strand-on-the-Green and furnishes it 'artistically', which, in the style of the day, means that it is not very comfortable. She intends to launch Lewis on London society and arranges a concert for him. But Lewis, under duress, becomes more moody and impossible; he is barely polite, obdurate, uninterested, and dangerous. It is with a revelation of delight that he welcomes Tessa, who has run away from school, and who makes her home at Strand-on-the-Green while a grim Florence tries to arrange for her to return to a suitable educational establishment. In no time at all Tessa domesticates the house, brews up tea, welcomes visitors, and wins the admiration of her Churchill relatives. Indeed, it is Florence's own father who, perceiving the natural sympathy which flows between Lewis and Tessa, reflects:-

> [Tessa] was, probably, the only woman in the world who could manage this man; she would respect his humours without taking them too seriously, she would never require him to behave correctly, and, if he annoyed her, she would reprove him good-humouredly in the strong terms which he deserved and understood.

Only Florence is less than enthusiastic about this natural sympathy, or love, for that is what it is, and is acknowledged to be; she deteriorates into a jealous and vengeful harpy, and finally she confronts Tessa and hurls at her "a word"—we are not told what it is. The rounded picture of Florence's discomfort, her exasperation, and her fury, constitutes the fourth surprise for the reader.

And there are further surprises to come. The extraordinary, and extraordinarily rapid, denouement of the novel becomes a sort of romantic test case and may prompt reflections on the reliability of romantic passion. As everyone is bound to have some sort of opinion on this matter, it is easy to see why *The Constant Nymph* has proved to be attractive to so many people. For although the story is a simple one, it deals with matters which are effectively very complex. And it deals with them in a manner which is intellectually quite honourable, for the reader is not manipulated into sharing the author's point of view. Indeed we are not quite sure what that point of view is. The tragedy of the situation arises out of what is done, rather than what is said: there is no attempt to cover dubious actions with the sort of special pleading or high-flown discourse common on these occasions. Actions, in fact, are allowed to speak much louder than words. In this respect, the climax of the novel, and its aftermath, indicate an authorial integrity of a very high order.

There is great professional skill, too, in the manner in which the novel is so quickly and so expertly ended. Its conclusion contains that admixture of worldliness and pain which Margaret Kennedy was to understand so well and to ridicule only occasionally. It is a noteworthy performance, and one which is bound to attract new readers, for whom the title is an echo, a reminder of something familiar, but not yet a reality.

Anita Brookner, London, 1982

xiv

BOOK I

SANGER'S CIRCUS

CHAPTER I

AT the time of his death the name of Albert Sanger was barely known to the musical public of Great Britain. Among the very few who had heard of him there were even some who called him Sanjé, in the French manner, being disinclined to suppose that great men are occasionally born in Hammersmith.

That, however, is where he was born, of lower middle class parents, in the latter half of the nineteenth century. The whole world knew of it as soon as he was dead and buried. Englishmen, discovering a new belonging, became excited ; it appeared that Sanger had been very much heard of everywhere else. His claims to immortality were canvassed eagerly by people who hoped soon to have an opportunity of hearing his work. His idiom, which was demonstrably neither Latin nor Gothic nor yet Slav, was discovered to be Anglo-Saxon. Obituary columns talked of the gay simplicity of his rhythms, an unmistakably national feature, which, they declared, took one back to Chaucer. They lamented that yet another prophet had passed without honour in his own country.

But for this the British public was not entirely to blame ; few people can sincerely admire a piece of music which they have not heard. During Sanger's lifetime his work was never performed in England. It was partly his own fault since he composed nothing but operas and these on a particularly grandiose scale. Their production was a risky enterprise, under the most promising conditions ; and in England the conditions attending the production of an opera are never promising. The press suggested that other British composers had been heard in London repeatedly while Sanger languished in a little limbo of neglect. This was not quite the case. The limbo has never been as little as that.

Sanger, moreover, hated England, left it at an early age, never went back, and seldom spoke of it without some strong qualification.

Appreciation, though tardy, was generous when it came. A special effort was made, about a year after Sanger's death, and The Nine Muses, an enterprising repertory theatre south of the river, undertook the production of " Prester John," the shortest and simplest of the operas. The success of the piece was unqualified. All the intelligentzia and some others flocked to hear, and proved by their applause how ready they were to appreciate English music as soon as ever they got the chance. There were no howls of rage such as had arisen when " Prester John " was produced in Paris ; •no free fights in the gallery between the partizans and foes of the composer. The whole thing was as decorous as possible and the respectful ardour of the audience, their prolonged cheers at the end, left no doubt as to Sanger's posthumous position in his own country. They were not unlike the ovation accorded to a guest of honour who arrives a little late.

Having renounced his native land, Sanger adopted no other. He roved about from one European capital to another, never settling anywhere for long, driven forwards by his strange, restless fancy. Usually he quartered himself upon his friends, who were accustomed to endure a great deal from him. He would stay with them for weeks, composing third acts in their spare bedrooms, producing operas which always failed financially, falling in love with their wives, conducting their symphonies, and borrowing money from them. His preposterous family generally accompanied him. Few people could recollect quite how many children Sanger was supposed to have got, but there always seemed to be a good many and they were most shockingly brought up. They were, in their own orbit, known collectively as "Sanger's Circus," a nickname earned for them by their wandering existence, their vulgarity, their conspicuous brilliance, the noise they made, and the kind of naptha-flare genius which illuminated everything they said or did. Their father had given them a good, sound musical training and nothing else. They had received no sort of regular education, but, in the course of their travels, had picked up a good deal of mental furniture and could abuse each other most profanely in the *argot* of four languages.

They seldom remained more than three months consecutively in the same place, but they had, as a matter of fact, one home of their own, an overgrown chalet in the Austrian Tyrol, where they were accustomed to spend the Spring and early Summer. Sanger liked Alpine scenery of a moderate kind and chose to have some place where he could entertain his friends. He invited all the world to come and stay with him, disregarding grandly his poverty and the want of proper sleeping accommodation in his house. His habitual sociability was unbounded; he was constantly picking up new acquaintances and these always got an invitation to the Karindehütte. The chalet was often full to overflowing and, to make room for the swarming guests, the children were sent out to sleep at neighbouring farms. Odd strangers of all classes and nationalities, people whose very names had been forgotten by Sanger, would turn up unexpectedly. No visitor could be sure what queer companion might be thrust into his room, or, indeed, into his very bed. Everybody was welcome.

These tumults and discomforts were endured by the guests for Sanger's sake. In his prime the enchantment of his convivial presence drew them to the house in the mountains as often as ever they were asked. The place had a spell which no one who had been there could forget. In after years it became a legend. It was the nearest approach to a home built by this wandering star, and, dying there, he was buried under the gentians and primulas in the pleasant alp before his door.

Visitors to the Karindethal were generally obliged to spend the night at a little town in the valley of the Inn, for the last stage of the journey was long and slow. Persons coming from a distance usually arrived at this place late in the evening, and, if they could afford it, went to the Station Hotel. Not that the Station Hotel was costly, being, indeed, quite a humble little public-house ; but Sanger's guests were sometimes very poor and travelled fourth-class, all among the mothers and babies and market baskets.

Among them and under them. Lewis Dodd, travelling up the Innthal one night late in May, got so far buried beneath the other fourth-class passengers that he found it difficult to leave the train at the right station and was very nearly carried on to Innsbruck. Disengaging himself in the nick of time, he got stiffly down on to a waste of railway lines, shouldered his knapsack and made for the Station Hotel, following an elderly porter who carried two large, beautiful leather suitcases. These belonged to a first-class passenger who had left the train without difficulty some five minutes earlier and was already established at the inn.

They crossed the station yard, a small gravelled enclosure surrounded by chestnuts all in bloom, like Christmas trees, with their thick spiky candles. Tall arc lamps among the tree trunks splashed the darkness here and there with pools of white light, and painted inky shadows among the brilliant leaves. Hidden in the night, all round the little town, were the mountains. The air of the snowfields, sharp and cool, came in puffs through the warm, heavy smell of chestnut blossoms. The first-class passenger, remarking it, had taken off his hat and wiped his forehead and murmured something

4

about the heavenly-beautiful *bergluft*, before going in to his supper. Lewis also lifted up his face to the hidden ranges which, on clear nights, shut out the stars from the valley towns. He was very glad to be going back again to the lovely mountain Spring and to his friend Sanger.

Both these travellers were on their way to the Karindehütte, but they did not discover each other until next morning, when they breakfasted at adjoining tables in the bare little coffee-room. Here they waited for the eggs they had ordered and observed one another suspiciously. Their mutual impressions were so little favourable that for some minutes they hesitated glumly on the brink of conversation.

The first-class passenger was a fat fellow who spoke fluent German with a French accent. He was probably a great deal younger than he looked. His clothes were impressive. He wore a magnificent suit, cut very square on the shoulders and a trifle too big for him. There was a good deal of unobtrusive but valuable jewellery about him, and a soft black hat lay on the table at his elbow. His figure was heavy and unagile. He had thick white hands, much manicured, and wore his dark hair *en brosse*, a style which ill-suited the full, fleshy curves of his pale face. His eyes, which should have been bold and greedy, were strangely unhappy and disclosed, in their direct gaze, an unexpected diffidence, an ingenuous modesty, entirely out of keeping with the rest of him. Of this he was aware ; he seldom looked full at those people whom he wished to impress, but sometimes in his eagerness he forgot himself. His general air was excessively urbane, and he looked oddly out of place in the Bahnhof coffee-room.

Lewis Dodd, on the other hand, was a lean youth, clothed in garments so nondescript as to merit no attention. He wore several waistcoats and had a yellow muffler round his neck. He, too, was pale with the kind of pallor that goes with ginger hair. Loose locks straggled across his bony forehead and hung

5

in a sort of fringe over the muffler at the back of his neck. His young face was deeply furrowed, nor was there any reassurance to be found in his thin, rather cruel mouth, or in light, observant eyes, so intent that they rarely betrayed him. His companion, distrusting his countenance, found, nevertheless, a wonderful beauty in his hands, which gave a look of extreme intelligence to everything that he did, as though an extra brain was lodged in each finger. Their strength and delicacy contradicted the harsh lines of his face, and it was this contrast which determined the stranger to make a conversational plunge. He observed, as a cock crowed boastfully in the garden outside :

" An egg has been laid. It is, perhaps, the event for which we wait."

Lewis made an abrupt statement in such execrable German that he was not understood. He repeated it in French :

" Cocks don't lay eggs."

" *Tiens !* " exclaimed the other in surprise. " One never supposed that they did."

" Hens," pursued Lewis, " don't crow."

" *Tiens !* "

Lewis, inspired, began suddenly and with skill to demonstrate the noise of a hen who has laid an egg. His companion started violently. The landlady, hearing the din in the kitchen and understanding it as a reproach, put her head in at the door and declared that the eggs ordered by the highly well-born gentlemen were already in the frying-pan. Whereat Lewis left off clucking and began to play spillikens with the wooden toothpicks on the table.

His companion, who had never seen toothpicks put to so paltry a use before, raised his eyebrows, shrugged his shoulders, and turned away. From the leather portfolio beside him he took a fountain-pen, very much mounted in gold, a small notebook and a roll of manuscript music. This he began to cover with annotations and strange hieroglyphics, referring occasionally to the notebook. As he worked his large mobile features writhed continuously ; he frowned, blinked, snorted, smiled and raised his eyebrows in a kind of frenzy.

His activities were observed with melancholy attention. Lewis abandoned the toothpicks and regarded him closely, seized by the unpleasant idea that they were to be fellow-guests at the Karindehütte. This fat person must be going to stay with Sanger ; there was no other explanation for him. For the rest of the journey they would be compelled to travel together. They might even have to share the spare room unless Kate could be persuaded otherwise. Kate, the eldest of Sanger's daughters, was the only person in the household who ever wrestled with the problem of guests and beds. She was kind and thoughtful.

The odious possibilities before him depressed Lewis very much. He was too easily persuaded that he should not like people. His own appearance was not conspicuously prepossessing and he had no business to be so critical. While he sat wondering how long it would be before they were betrayed to each other, the landlady, bringing in the eggs, did the deed. She knew him well for an intimate of the Sangers and lingered genially to enquire after his health and send her compliments to the family, for whom she had a great liking since they brought so many guests to her house. They had only been up in the Karindethal a fortnight, she told him, and she believed that they had come from Italy. One of the young gentlemen had got lost on the way. Getting out of the train at a wayside station in the middle of the night, he had been left behind. His loss was not discovered for some hours as his family were all asleep. They had arrived in a great way about it. Fräulein Kate had wanted to go back, but Herr Sanger said that the child was old enough to look after itself. Fräulein Kate had wept and said that the poor little one had no money and no ticket

7

Gnädige Frau said that it served him right. They had argued most of the night about it, in this very room, sometimes in one language and sometimes in another, but in the end they decided to let the affair alone and went on to the Karindethal next day. The boy had turned up later.

Lewis listened and mumbled indistinct comments, aware that she had given him away. His fellow-traveller was listening eagerly, and enquired when they were alone :

" You are going to visit Mr. Sanger ? "

" Yes."

" Ach ! I also ! " The gentleman observed Lewis afresh from his yellow muffler to his ragged socks. " My name," he said, " is Trigorin. Kiril Trigorin."

He made a sort of little bow in his place where he sat. Lewis made another exactly like it. The name awoke vague echoes but he could not place it. Kiril Trigorin! The man had a box-office look, and his jewellery was of the presentation order. Possibly an operatic tenor. He became aware that the situation required something from him. He said hurriedly :

" My name is Dodd."

" Dodd ? You are English ? "

" Yes."

" Dodd ! Is it possible that you are Mr. Lewis Dodd ? "

Trigorin became radiant and turned full upon Lewis his innocent, humble gaze, crying :

" Can it be . . . can it be that I am at last to have the pleasure, the privilege, of meeting so gifted a composer ? One for whose genius I have always . . "

" Yes, my name's Lewis."

Trigorin got up, clicked his heels, and made a really deferential bow. Lewis nervously did the same but was unable to avert a flood of polite felicitations upon his work, talents and future. He learnt that Mr. Trigorin had watched his career with attention ; that he was, of all the younger men, the most

8

promising and the most likely to stand by Sanger's side; that his least popular work, the " Revolutionary Songs " for choir and orchestra, was indisputably the finest and showed a great advance upon his better-known Symphony in Three Keys; and that he must not be depressed because the public was taking a long time to discover him. With all original work, said Mr. Trigorin, this must be the case. The critics have always persecuted young genius. The plaudits of the herd are as nothing to the discerning appreciation of a small circle. Lewis found that his hand was seized and that he was being tearfully besought to rise above his own unpopularity.

" I should not mind it if I were you," ended Mr. Trigorin with great simplicity.

Lewis was not as grateful for this encouragement as he should have been. He disengaged his hand with a venomous look. It was not for the appreciation of people like this fat Slav that he had written the " Revolutionary Songs."

" In future," went on his friend, " we shall speak English. It is more better practice for me."

" All right," said Lewis.

" You have stayed at the Karindehütte before? But that is natural. You are the dear friend of Mr. Sanger."

" Am I ? "

" It is well known. And what a privilege . . ."

And he was off again, undaunted by the limitations of his English How great a genius was Sanger! Colossal! Nobody like him in the world! Lewis scarcely listened, for he had begun to remember who the fellow was. Surely his name suggested a famous ballerina. Irina Zhigalova! Of course! This was her husband, and a person of some ability if it was true that he designed all her ballets. But what on earth was he doing here?

From Trigorin's conversation an explanation of sorts was emerging It seemed that he had arranged a ballet in the

9

Autumn for Sanger's opera " Akbar," and had got this invitation on the strength of it.

" Never before have I visited here," he ended confidentially.

This was evident ; the odd thing was that he should have been invited now.

" This moment, you can imagine, my dear sir, is for me a very great one. I go to visit Mr. Sanger ; I meet Mr. Dodd. I find myself in the company of two most distinguished men all in the one time. I am amazed."

Lewis thought that he would be more amazed when he got to the Karindehütte. But he said nothing.

" Of what," demanded the innocent creature, " does the family consist ? "

" Who ? The Sangers ? You've not met them all ? "

" Only Mr. Sanger. At Prague he was alone. I think it is a large family."

" Oh . . . well . . . yes . . . pretty big."

Trigorin wished for more details which Lewis was most reluctant to give. At last he said :

" Well, there's Madame."

" Madame ? " said Trigorin dubiously. " You would say . . . Mrs. Sanger ? "

" Yes," exclaimed Lewis, as though he had suddenly discovered a relieving explanation for Madame. " And then there are the children."

" Many children ? "

" Oh, yes. A lot of children." After a pause for thought he stated : " Seven ! "

" Seven ! And all the children of Madame ? "

" Oh, no ! Not all." There was another pause and then Mr. Dodd repeated : " Not all. Only one."

" Ach ! Then the other six . . . they have had another mother ? "

" Mothers."

10

"Mothers ?"

"He's been married several times."

"So !"

"The first wife," said Lewis very glibly, "had two; the second four; and the third one. That makes seven."

"Please? Not so quick !"

Even when it was repeated more slowly Trigorin took some minutes to assimilate it. Then he said :

"And this Karindethal? How do we come there? By the road ?"

"By the mountain railway," said Lewis. "It takes us up to the lake, where we get the little steamer across to Weissau. From there we drive four or five miles up the Karindethal to the foot of the pass. Then we get out and climb."

"Climb !" cried Trigorin, sweating a little at the mere thought of it. Lewis grinned and said with energy :

"Oh, yes. It's quite steep; several hundred feet. Too rough for driving."

"Ach ! And our gepacks? We must carry them ?"

"Quite so. I hope you travel light, for your own sake."

"And the train? When does it go, Mr. Dodd ?"

"Oh, in about an hour. I'll meet you at the station. I have to go into the town to buy a . . . a razor . . ."

And Lewis made his escape, rather pleased to have got off so easily. Trigorin finished his breakfast and strolled out into the garden which was full of little tables under the chestnut trees. He sat down at one of them and began a letter to his wife, writing in French which was most commonly used in his household. He described his journey, as far as it had gone and observed :

"I sit here amid the most exquisite scenery. Spring has already come to this charming valley, and the meadows round me are full of . . ."

11

He had a look at the meadows round him, but could not determine what it was that filled them. There were a lot of blue flowers and some yellow, but as these were neither camelias nor gardenias he could not put a name to them. He compromised :

" . . full of a thousand blossoms of every colour."

With an oath he brushed a chestnut flower off his page. They drifted down everywhere, settling on his straight, upstanding hair and on the backs of the hens pecking about in the grass. They were a plague. He continued to write :

"Around me, on every side, rise the mountains, still crowned with Winter. Behind these grim ramparts, nursing his genius in solitary grandeur, dwells The Master. I go to him by the train in an hour's time."

He knew that his wife would not really find this very interesting. But he was suffering from such an *épanchement de cœur* that he had to write it all to somebody and there was no one else. He described his meeting with young Dodd :

"Need I tell you that something in the air of this savage youth immediately attracted my attention ? I studied him secretly, as yet unaware of his identity. 'Here,' I said, 'is genius ! I divine it in every gesture.' Presently he introduces himself in his simple English way. He is Lewis Dodd !"

At that moment the savage youth himself strolled round the corner of the house. Catching sight of Trigorin he retreated hastily and went to talk to a man who was watching a cow graze in a field. He was less afraid of this kind of person than of any other, and was almost affable to it. The conversation lasted until it was time to catch the train.

Trigorin was a little surprised that any gentleman should desert him for a cow-herd, but he was not resentful, since this was Lewis Dodd and The Great have queer ways. He wrote :

12

"Lewis Dodd travels like one of the people, his knapsack on his back. He is even now talking to a poor peasant with the greatest cordiality. With me, I must confess, he was a little abrupt (*un peu bourru*), but I set it down to nervous sensibility. I did not let it trouble me."

This was a good thing since Lewis was not the first of his kind to snub Mr. Trigorin. They often did. But he did not deserve it. Indeed, he merited their pity, if all were known.

He had entertained in his early youth an ardent desire to compose music. He could imagine no keener joy. But his gifts were not upon a scale with his ambitions. He could write nothing that was at all worth listening to, and, being cursed with unusual intelligence, he knew it. So he gave it up and took to arranging ballets, a business at which, almost against his will, he was eminently successful. He had a choreographic talent which hardly fell short of genius, and which was at first something of a consolation to him ; though it was poignant work interpreting the music of other men. Falling in with La Zhigalova he designed for her a series of surpassingly beautiful ballets. She was a fine dancer, but no artist, and it was he who discovered to her the full possibilities of her own person and talents. Out of gratitude she married him, a little to his astonishment, and secured his services for life.

While thus saddled with a profession which he had not entirely chosen, Trigorin still thought sadly sometimes of his dead hopes, worshipped his flame in secret, reverenced deeply all composers who came in his way and persisted in seeking the company of musicianly people. Unfortunately they seldom took to him, regarding him as something of a mountebank and undeniably vulgar. They were deceived by his air of metropolitan prosperity ; he looked too much like the proprietor of an Opera House. They could not see into the humble, disappointed heart beneath his magnificent waistcoats, or guess

13

how sacred was the very name of music in his ears. Moreover, he was never at his best in their company; he lost all his impressive urbanity in his eagerness to be liked, talked too much, and, betrayed by his ardent heart, often appeared ridiculous.

Sanger, however, had reason to be grateful to him. They had met in Prague, in the preceding Autumn, while the composer was staging his opera "Akbar" and driven to the verge of insanity by the stupidity of producers. He confided his difficulties to Trigorin. He had intended to present the dawn of Eastern history, young, primitive and heroic, in contrast to the splendour of its mysterious decay. Nobody could be made to see this; the ballets were languid and decadent with a stale aroma of the Arabian Nights. Conventional odalisques were introduced everywhere, even into his spirited hunting scenes. Could Trigorin help him? Trigorin could. He designed dances and a *décor* which caught that inflection of buoyancy suggested by the music. Sanger was charmed. He borrowed fifty pounds from his new friend and invited him to the Karindethal next Spring.

The delight of Trigorin was unbounded. This was the first advance ever made to him by a composer of importance. He accepted in a passion of gratitude. When the Spring came he had some difficulty in persuading his wife that he must be allowed to go, for she rated musicians a little lower than dressmakers. She would only permit it on condition that he would make Sanger write a ballet for her. Though doubtful of his ability to make such a request, he was so anxious to go that he was really ready to promise anything. He now added a postscript to his letter:

"Rest assured, my angel, that I am not forgetting your ballet. But it is better that I do not immediately importune Mr. Sanger with these requests. It is not that I forget but that I am tactful."

14

CHAPTER II

LEWIS found the journey up to Weissau better than he had expected. His companion was indeed horribly talkative, making intelligent comments upon the grandeur of the scenery all the way, but in the choice of his topics he showed a certain respect for Mr. Dodd's nervous sensibility. They agreed that the chestnut and oak of the valley had now given way to pine woods, and discussed the names of some of the peaks towering above them. As the little train panted its way into the Alpine pastures, Lewis was even so affable as to point out several waterfalls to his companion.

After a stiff ascent the line ended by a lake and they found a little steamer waiting for them. Mr. Trigorin said that the expanse of water lent an agreeable perspective to the mountains rising sharply on the other side. Mr. Dodd said that it was so, and that when they got across they would find the same thing to be true of the mountains on this side. Mr. Trigorin said he supposed so, and became a little silent and unhappy. They crossed the lake without further conversation.

When they had almost reached the hamlet of Weissau, Lewis exclaimed suddenly :

" There they are, some of them ! "

" Please ? " said Trigorin anxiously.

" Two of Sanger's children. On the landing-stage."

He pointed to the little group of peasants waiting for the boat. Two young girls, standing rather apart from the crowd, had already recognised him and were waving vehemently. As

15

soon as he got off the boat they flung themselves upon his neck, kissing him with eager delight.

"Oh, Lewis!" exclaimed the smaller. "We never expected to see you at all. Only some one is probably coming by this boat so we thought we'd come in and buy some sweets and get a ride back."

"Yes," said the other. "Sanger got a letter to say this person was coming. And you should hear how he goes on about it. He says he never . . ."

"I expect it was Trigorin," interrupted Lewis.

"O—oh, yes! That was the name Sanger said, wasn't it Lina?'"

"Well then, this is your man. Mr. Trigorin. Miss Teresa Sanger; Miss Paulina Sanger."

Trigorin put down his suitcases and bowed low, beginning:
"I am most delighted . . ."

But Teresa cut him short.

"Lewis! Have you got . . . you know what?"

"What? Oh, I know. Yes. I have it in my knapsack."

"That's all right. We'd have lynched you if you'd forgotten. But you've been the hell of a time fetching it. We've only got three days; his birthday's on Thursday. And he won't like it unless it's properly done."

"Three days will do if we work hard," Lewis assured her.
"Look! Have you ordered a cart or anything? Because, if not, one of you must leg it up to the hotel and ask for one."

"Oh, we've got it. It's just behind the shop. It's got a pig in it that Kate told us to bring up. It's quite a quiet pig. It's dead."

Teresa looked at her sister and they both giggled.

"Can he eat bacon?" whispered Paulina in an audible aside, with a glance at Trigorin, who was waiting patiently beside his suitcases until somebody should take notice of him. "He looks a little like a Jew. We had an awful time once when Ikey

16

Mo's uncle was staying with us and we had nothing in the house . . ."

"If he can't eat bacon, there'll be nothing else for him to eat," said Teresa. She turned to Trigorin and enquired baldly : " Are you a Jew ? "

" No," he said, a little stiffly. " I am from Russia."

" Well, there are Jews in Russia, aren't there ? " she argued.

" They are not as I," Trigorin told her.

" Really ? " she said derisively. " We've all got something to be thankful for, haven't we ? You have got a lot of luggage. I hope there'll be room for us all in the cart as well as the pig."

" It's a very heavy pig," supplemented Paulina, exploding again into suppressed laughter. " Tessa and I had to drag it all the way from the slaughter-house."

They turned towards the little village shop which stood close to the landing-stage. Lewis walked in front with a girl hanging lovingly on either arm ; Trigorin toiled in the rear with his suitcases. Behind the shop they found a very small carriage shaped something like a victoria, and, at the sight of it, the mirth of the children became almost hysterical. They had hoisted the gutted carcase of the pig into an upright position on the back seat. Draped in a tartan rug and crowned with Teresa's straw hat, it was a horrible object but not unlike a stout German lady, when seen from a distance. The children, who thought it irresistibly funny, demanded eagerly if Lewis did not see a resemblance to Fräulein Brandt, the celebrated contralto.

" Perhaps," said Lewis. " But do you expect us to sit on these cushions ? They are all over pig."

" Your clothes won't spoil, darling Lewis."

" They are all I have, darling Tessa. And what about Trigorin ? He's a gentleman."

" I shall go on high with the driver," stated the gentleman firmly.

17

"Then," said Paulina, "Lewis and Tessa can sit on the back seat, and I on Lewis's knee, and we'll put the suitcases in front of us with Fräulein Brandt on top."

With some difficulty they were all packed in, and the little cart started off up the valley at a great pace. Soon the village was left behind and their way lay through pine woods, along a rough, green track. In front of them a straight wall of stony mountain shut out the sky, and they seemed to be driving to the very foot of the barrier.

Teresa and Paulina Sanger were at this time about fourteen and twelve years of age. They were the children of Sanger's second wife, who had been of gentle birth; from her they had inherited quick wits and considerable nervous instability. Both these qualities were betrayed in their eager, stammering speech and in the delicate impudence of their bearing. They had pale faces and small-boned, thin little bodies, fragile but intrepid. They had high, benevolent foreheads from which their long hair was pushed back and hung in an untended tangle down their backs. Teresa was the fairer and the plainer; her greenish eyes had in them a kind of secret hilarity as though she privately found life a very diverting affair. But she had begun lately to grow out of everything, especially jokes and clothes, and she really saw no prospect of getting new ones. Still, she laughed pretty often. Paulina was less inclined for compromise, a brilliant child, sometimes tempestuous, sometimes vividly gay, never sensible and always incurably wild. She had an extravagant and untutored taste in dress, and wore on this occasion a ragged gown of a brilliant red and green tartan which she had somehow managed to acquire. It was much too long for her, so she had kilted it up at intervals with pins, and in front it hung in vast folds over her flat little chest, being cut to fit a full bust. She used the space as a sort of pocket, stuffing in apples, sweets and handkerchiefs, which gave her figure a very lumpy look. Teresa wore the peasant dress of the country, a yellow frock, brief and full, with a square cut bodice and short sleeves. This she had touched up with a magenta apron. Both girls were barefoot. Both contrived to have, at unexpected moments and in spite of their rags, a certain arrogance of demeanour which proclaimed them the daughters of Evelyn Sanger, who had been a Churchill.

They chattered incessantly all the way up the valley, and Paulina, producing peppermints from the bosom of her bright gown, refreshed the whole party, including Trigorin on the box.

" You heard about Sebastian getting lost on the way up ? " she said. " You know at the place where he got left behind he met some Americans. And he told them he'd been kidnapped by anarchists and that he was really a Russian prince. I don't expect they believed him. But they liked him. He said they kept telling each other how cute he was. They brought him on with them to Innsbruck, and he had a lovely time stopping with them at their hotel. When he got tired of it, he went to the manager of the Opera House, who's a friend of Sanger's, and borrowed enough money to get on here."

" And what did the Americans say ? "

" Oh, he left a note behind to say he'd made a mistake about who he was, but he'd had a blow on the head when quite a child which confused his memory. .He said it had come to him all of a sudden that he was the son of Albert Sanger, and that he'd gone home. By the way, you didn't see Tony anywhere in the town did you ? "

" Antonia ? No I didn't. Is she there ? "

" We don't know where she is," said Teresa. " She's been gone nearly a week now. She left a note to say she was going to stay a bit with a friend, but she'd be back for Sanger's birthday."

" We can't think what friend she can have gone to," added Paulina. " Sanger is quite annoyed about it. He says he'll belt her soundly when she gets back."

19

" And Linda says that if Tony gets into the habit of going off like this, it's odds she'll be bringing him home a grandchild one of these days," pursued Teresa. " And Sanger says she can take herself off for good if she does as there's quite enough to support in our family as it is."

" He doesn't mean half he says," commented Lewis.

" I know," said Teresa, in a slightly lower voice. " He says he won't stir out of his room while that fellow up there," she nodded at Trigorin's broad back, "is in the house. He says that he never thought the fool would be such a fool as to come."

" Linda may like to talk to him," suggested Lewis.

" I do hope she won't," whispered Teresa. " Because that might make him stay. But if nobody takes any notice of him he might go away pretty soon. Why ever did Sanger invite him ? "

" Oh, you know what he is ! He'd invite the Pope if he met him after dinner."

" Yes, I know. But the Pope wouldn't come."

" What is this guy anyway ? " asked Paulina.

" He dances in a ballet," Lewis told them.

This they took as a tremendous joke, but he assured them with gravity that it was so.

" Well ! I've heard of dancing elephants," declared Paulina at last.

She poked Trigorin in the back and he turned round, smiling benignantly down at her.

" He says," she pointed at Lewis, " he says that you dance in a ballet. Do you ? "

" Ach no ! I cannot dance."

Both children turned indignantly on Lewis, crying :
" Liar ! "

But he, quite unabashed, declared that he had confused Trigorin with La Zhigalova, conveying an impression that

Sanger's unwelcome guest had been invited solely upon her account and could lay no other claim to distinction. Trigorin said nothing and turned away from the group in the carriage, not without a certain grotesque dignity. The children, aware that Lewis had scored in some way, and regarding this as the first step in the routing of an interloper, exchanged gleeful glances. Teresa's mirth, however, was a little forced; she found herself wishing, absurdly, that Lewis had been kind to the poor fat person on the box. As if Lewis was ever kind to anybody!

With a sudden spasm of alarm she stole a look at him, and saw that he was smiling sleepily to himself. Paulina, tranquilly sucking a peppermint lozenge, was curled up on his knee. Thus often, in thoughtless security, had Teresa sat, when she was a little girl; when, with a child's hardness, she found his cruelty funny and saw nothing sinister in his perversities.

Now she was afraid of him, apprehending dimly all that he might have it in his power to make her feel. And yet she loved him very completely—better than anyone else in the whole world. An odd state of things! She was inclined to regard these uneasy qualms as peculiar to her age, like the frequent growing pains in her legs which made her quite lame sometimes.

They drove out of the pine woods into an open meadow which formed the end of the valley. It was an almost circular space of short grass enamelled all over with little brilliant flowers. Many cows strayed across it, and the clear, sunny spaces were full of the music of their bells. An amphitheatre of mountains rose upon every side, shutting out the world behind stony walls. At the further end of the meadow a low ridge with a faint bridle track zigzagging across it marked the pass.

The Karindehütte was just visible about half way up;

a long, low chalet built upon a flat shelf which caught more sun than fell to the share of the valley meadow.

They drew up at the foot of the pass beside a little group of herdmen's huts. Lewis and the girls jumped out at once and began to climb the mountain track, leaving Trigorin to pay for the carriage and arrange with a cowherd for the transport of his suitcases and the pig. He then followed pantingly, finding the sun very hot, his clothes very heavy and his boots very tight. As he toiled round each bend of the zigzag path he saw the others well in front of him, the little girls skipping over the rough stones on their hard, bare feet, and Lewis swinging steadily forward with his knapsack hitched up on his shoulders. They got past the good shade of the trees into a region of scorching, blue air where the wind blew warm upon them, smelling of myrtle and Alpine rose.

At length the party in front, rounding the last corner, reached the ledge of meadow where the Karindehütte was built. They paused for a moment to look over the valley and saw empty air in front of them, and, far below, the tops of trees and little cows and their carriage crawling back along the valley road. Cow bells rose very faintly like single drops of music distilled into this upper silence.

"I suppose," ventured Teresa, "that we ought to wait."

"He's getting very blown," said Lewis, going to the edge to look over at Trigorin on the path below.

Teresa hallooed kindly to the labouring figure and told him that he was very nearly at the top. Her brother Sebastian, who had joined them from the house, added encouraging shouts and besought the stranger to take it easily.

"Is he this person Sanger said was coming?" he asked his sisters.

Teresa nodded.

"His name's Trigorin," she said.

Sebastian was the youngest of Evelyn Sanger's four children, and possessed the largest measure of good breeding. Though entirely graceless, he was often very gentlemanly in his manners. He was ten years old, but looked younger, being very small and fair, like his sister Teresa, with grave, green eyes and a great mop of hair. He now thought it his duty to go down the hill a little way and welcome his father's guest.

"How do you do," he said politely. "We are all so pleased that you have been able to come."

Trigorin stopped and wiped his forehead with a silk hand-kerchief. He perceived that this courteous urchin must be another of Sanger's children. It looked more propitious than the other two.

"This hill," he gasped, "is terrible!"

"It's a bit steep when you aren't used to it," agreed Sebastian. "But we've got a nice view at the top. I'm afraid my sisters came up too fast for you. Women, you know," he added confidentially, "are inclined to run up hills. I've noticed it."

When they reached the level sward where the others waited for them he handed the guest over to his sisters with a great air, explaining:

"I'm afraid I can't come in just now. I have an engage-ment with this fellow."

And he pointed to a small peasant boy, rather younger than himself, who had been lurking in the shadow of the house. It appeared that they were going to look at some badger holes and the girls immediately demanded to be taken too. All the children set off hastily down the hill again, leaving Lewis and Trigorin alone on the Karinde Alp. Lewis said sulkily:

"Well, I suppose we'd better go in, as there seems to be no one about."

They went round to the front of the house, which had a long veranda looking over the valley. Here they came upon a massive but very beautiful woman fast asleep in a hammock.

23

"Madame," murmured Lewis, and they stood looking at her, uncertain what to do.

Linda Cowlard, for she had no real right to Sanger's name, was an exceptionally lovely creature, a vast dazzling blonde. Her origins were obscure, but it was believed that she had once been the daughter of a tobacconist at Ipswich. She had a magnificent constitution, no nerves and very few ideas ; was, indeed, splendidly stupid. Sanger could not have found a more suitable companion. She had lived with him for eight years and showed, as yet, no signs of exhaustion. Her placid animal poise was, if anything, nourished by his insane jealousy and the violent quarrels which occasionally broke out between them. She was incapable of sustaining any severe shock, having the rudimentary nervous organisation which relieves itself in distress by loud, immediate outcries. Her indolence was terrific ; she lay dozing all day and seldom finished her toilet before the afternoon. The management of the house she left to Sanger's daughters.

One child of her own she had, a little girl of seven years, whom Sanger had insisted upon calling Susan. Linda had modified this to Suzanne as being less common. The rest of the family derisively nicknamed their sister "Soo-zanne" in order to show their contempt for her. It was a wholesome, plebeian-looking brat, pink and formless as a wax doll, garnished about the head with tight clusters of yellow curls. Linda was very fond of it, dressed it in white with pink ribbons, and defended it sourly against the animosity of Sanger, who declared that Susan was a posturing little monkey and should have been trained for a tight-rope dancer. The child did, in fact, look something of a stranger among the others ; her healthy inferiority especially distinguished her beside the brood of the ill-starred Evelyn, with their intermittent manifestations of intelligence and race.

The two young men looked at Linda and listened to a series

24

of repeated hoots, going on inside the house, which Lewis identified as Kate practising her head notes. A full morning sun blazed upon the woman in the hammock but could hardly outshine her beauty. She wore a white dressing-gown, flung carelessly about her, and beneath it some flimsy under-garment all lace and ribbons. Trigorin, always susceptible, gaped at her, his eyes nearly popping out of his head. Her superb bulk was entirely to his taste, but he had not expected somehow to find anything like her at the Karindehütte. Part of his nature resented her intrusion there ; he suspected that she might disturb him when he wanted to talk about music to Sanger. Still he could not but feel that she was the most desirable woman he had ever set eyes on.

Lewis also stared down at her, with a wry smile, as if he had swallowed vinegar. Then he looked away, looked at the blue static mountains across the valley, and looked back again at Sanger's mistress, and finally, catching sight of the perspiring Trigorin, burst into loud laughter

Linda opened her eyes, which were the colour of the gentians in the grass. She yawned, stretched her supple limbs like a large cat, and sat up.

"If it isn't Lewis," she exclaimed. "Well, you are a stranger. Albert never said you were coming. Have you brought a friend ? "

The blue eyes slid round to Trigorin.

"Mr. Trigorin, Mrs. Sanger," muttered Lewis.

"Pleased to meet you," said Linda, offering a large cold hand. "We knew you were coming. Kate's been getting a room ready. Sit down won't you, Mr. Trigorin. And you too, Lewis."

They sat down and she took leisurely stock of the stranger. Usually she found the Karindehütte very dull. Albert's guests were not always amusing. Too often they were like Lewis, whom she detested. This one, however, might have possibilities. He wore expensive clothes and his bulging eyes proclaimed him a conquest. She began, in her sleepy voice, to make remarks to him, punctuated by slow, evasive smiles. Trigorin, lost in the flame of those blue eyes, stammered replies in English which emotion had made almost unintelligible. He was as helpless as a swimmer swept away in a strong current. Lewis, nursing his knapsack on his knee, observed them and smiled to himself. Occasionally he got from the lady a glance which was by no means friendly and which hinted that he might remove himself.

She had not always disliked him so bitterly. Once, some years ago, she had felt very kindly towards him and as good as told him so. But he, in spite of her conspicuous attractions, of which he was fully sensible, rejected her advances with some brutality. He did not think her worth a breach with Sanger. She concealed her fury as best she could and continued to treat him civilly, at least in public, in the hope that Sanger might one day become jealous and forbid him the house. Sanger saw through her manœuvres and, in his turn, did not consider her worth a quarrel with Lewis, whom he valued beyond any woman in the world. But she persisted in the stratagem, being too stupid to devise any other method of attack.

Presently Lewis bethought himself that he had better see Kate soon, if he wished to secure a bedroom to himself. He got up and was moving into the house when Linda called to him, over her shoulder :

" Oh, Lewis ! "

He waited.

" You didn't see Antonier anywhere on the way up, did you ? "

" No."

" God knows where she can have got to," piously commented Linda. " Albert seems to think it's my fault, if you please !

26

I tell him if he wants those girls looked after he'd better put them to school somewhere. Not that any decent school would keep them a week ; but that's another matter."

" A young lady is lost ? " enquired Trigorin, who was a little fogged. " One of your family ? "

" One of Albert's children," replied the lady. " Not mine, you'll please to remember, Mr. Trigorin."

" She'll turn up," said Lewis at the door. " These children all fall on their feet. Look at Sebastian ! "

" She's not a child ; that's just where it is. She's sixteen past," retorted Linda, adding ruminatively : " Dirty little cat ! "

Lewis left them and went into the large open hall which served the family as dining-room. Through it a door led into the music-room, an almost empty chamber with a dais at one end and a grand piano. Here Kate stood before an open window, her hands held out before her and lightly clasped, while she took in deep breaths and let them out in long, high notes. They were full, clear, honest notes, very like Kate herself, who was the most honest thing alive. Her mother, Sanger's first wife, had been Australian—clean, respectable, middle class, hard working and kind. Kate persisted in being all these things, in spite of her upbringing. She had none of the wildness of her half-brothers and sisters. She had rosy cheeks and neat, brown hair, was trim and comely, and wore shirt blouses. Her voice was promising and she worked strenuously, hoping, with her father's backing, to succeed some day upon the operatic stage. She also ran the household and did all the work which the single manservant could not do. Every one respected and liked her. She was a little obtuse, but this was probably the salvation of her, since it enabled her to disregard the inconsistencies of her own life. A more perceptive young woman could hardly have gone on being so modest, sensible and affectionate without a little encouragement from her surroundings.

27

Lewis listened for a few seconds and called down the room :
" Very nice indeed, Kate."

" Oh, it's you ? We'd given up expecting you. Have you got the thing for us to act on father's birthday ? "

Kate and her brother Caryl gave their father his proper title. It was only Evelyn's children who referred to him carelessly as Sanger.

" I finished it this morning," said Lewis. " We can begin rehearsing after lunch."

" But the tiresome thing is that we can't begin without Tony, and we don't know where she is. Didn't you hear ? "

" I heard she was off somewhere."

" I hope she's all right," observed Kate, looking anxious. " I don't like it. You know, she's awfully silly sometimes."

Lewis did know, and secretly thought that Antonia was bound to get into a scrape sooner or later. But he did not wish to distress Kate by saying so, and, to change the topic, remarked :

" By the way, I brought a fat Russian ballet dancer up with me. I picked him up in the inn at Erfurt."

" Mr. Trigorin ? Yes, I know. Father invited him in the way he does, you know. I do hope he'll be civil to him. He's so furious with him for coming. He couldn't remember who he was at first, when we got the letter. Where is he now ? "

" On the veranda."

" Oh ! Is Linda there ? "

" Yes."

" Oh."

Kate grew pink, but all she said was :

" Then I needn't bother about him. What is he like ? "

" He looks," said Lewis viciously, " like one of those men who exhibit performing fleas. And that's all he is ; on a wider scale of course. He's done well out of it. Linda likes his clothes."

"Oh, dear! Perhaps he won't stay long! Father is fearfully busy writing a new last act to 'The Mountains.' Often he's up all night and Caryl too. Caryl's had to put all his own work aside, poor dear. And the worst of it is, father's too ill to be working at all. I'm sure he is, and so is Caryl. You'll be shocked when you see him. He looks all wasted and shrunken up sometimes, and his eyes so yellow and bloodshot. He gets queer, giddy turns, but he says it's only because he's thirsty!"

"Can't you make him see a doctor?" asked Lewis anxiously.

"No. He says perhaps he will when we leave here, if he isn't better. He's very difficult. Men are really perfectly impossible sometimes."

"Yes, aren't they? I quite agree. But look here! Where am I going to sleep? Who else is here?"

"Nobody. But the family is spread all over the house, and father turned Linda out of his room the other night and said she could go and sleep by herself until he had finished 'The Mountains.' I've put Mr. Trigorin in the spare room. Of course it's got two beds in it . . ."

"No, Kate. I'll sleep on the doorstep, but not with the flea trainer. Is there nowhere else?"

"Well, there's the little room in the annexe. It's very small and it's never been disinfected since Tony and Tessa had scarlet fever there two years ago. I meant to burn a sulphur candle but I forgot. Do you mind?"

"Not a bit. Germs are better than Trigorin any day."

"And it's tiresome going out there if it rains. However, if you don't mind . . . Let's go across and have a look at it."

They went out and climbed the hill at the back, a little way to a second hut. The lower part was used as a store-house and the two bedrooms above were reached by an outer stair and balcony. Kate led him into a tiny room with two camp-beds

29

in it and nothing else. Floor, walls and ceiling were of wooden planks and smelt of the forest. A dusty rosary hung from a nail by the door and the walls above the beds were covered with childish writing, for Teresa and Antonia had enlivened their scarlet fever by scribbling rude remarks about each other. Kate glanced at them and blushed. She did not like to think of Lewis reading these sisterly pleasantries, and determined to send Caryl at the first opportunity with a plane to plane them off.

"This is very nice and quiet," said Lewis.

"Of course it is that," agreed Kate. "I'll bring in Roberto's chair and table. Come and help me fetch them."

They went into the larger room next door which belonged to Roberto, the Italian manservant. It had a bed, a table, a chair and a yellow tin trunk. On the trunk lay Roberto's bowler hat, and on the chair, a cherished testimony to his peasant blood, Roberto's umbrella, which, on the finest Sundays, went to Mass with him.

"I don't see why we should take the poor fellow's only chair," observed Lewis.

"Oh, he doesn't sit on it. He has no time to sit. He only uses it for keeping his umbrella on. We always take it if we want it."

They carried the furniture next door and Kate made up the least rickety of the camp-beds, saying :

"You can use the other for putting things down on. Is that all, Lewis ? Then I'll be off as I've a lot to do. Father often has his meals upstairs, which gives extra trouble. You're quite fixed ? *Mittagsessen* will be . . . when I've cooked it . . soon . . ."

She gave him an amiable smile and ran off. She was the only person in the family who had no positive feelings, one way or the other, towards Lewis. She just regarded him as one of the many people who depended upon her for comfort. He, for his part, liked her very much, was grateful to her, and was generally both obliging and civil in his dealings with her. She let him alone, and that was a thing which very few women could do, seemingly, in spite of his plain face and unmannerly ways.

When she was gone he threw himself down upon the newly-made bed and pulled from his knapsack the MS. score of a one-act opera called "Breakfast with the Borgias," which he had promised the Sanger children to write for their father's birthday. It was to be acted by the family, who could most of them sing in tune, and by any guests who happened to be about. He began to read it through, correcting it in places with a stubby pencil, and writing in fragments of libretto as a guide to the performers, who were to compose their own words when they had learnt their tunes and got the hang of the plot.

Presently he let the music slip to the ground and lay back on the hard little bed, smoking and dreaming. Through the window he could see the cloudless sky and a piece of bright pink mountain. Very far off a cow bell tinkled drowsily and he meditated upon the peculiar, unearthly quality of a sound that comes up from below. He felt so tremendously high up ; almost half-way to heaven. Turning his head to the wall he read :

"My sister Teresa is a little . . ."

And a half-hearted attempt at erasure, as though even Antonia could occasionally feel ashamed of herself.

CHAPTER III

In spite of Sanger's contempt for England, the mothers of the children at the Karindehütte had all been British. Vera Brady, his first wife, had been the leading lady of a third-rate opera company of which he was *chef d'orchestre*. He was then quite a young man and remarkably unsuccessful. They had gone on tour in the Antipodes, were married at Honolulu, and knocked about the world together for a good many years. She was an excellent woman, with a fine voice and extreme powers of endurance ; her devotion to Sanger kept her beside him through misfortune, hardship and neglect. Of her children none survived their precarious infancy save the two youngest. These were born during a period of comparative prosperity when Sanger, who had begun to attract attention, held for a short time a permanent post in a German town with a famous Conservatorium. Vera was able to quit the stage and set up the respectable household for which she had always craved. All her instincts were domestic and she was very happy for a time, bustling round her little flat and passing the time of day with congenial housewives at church and market. Caryl was born and she was able to rear him in peace and decency. She believed that her other children had died because she had been forced to work so hard in those nightmare years when she had nursed her babies hastily, in draughty dressing-rooms, awaiting her call. Caryl lived, and grew plump and strong, and was a comfort to her.

This interlude was brief ; new troubles soon gathered round

her. Sanger's infidelities had become almost a commonplace in their wandering life, but she had always been able to fly from gossip and at least she was sure that each episode must be brief. Once or twice he had run away from her, but he always came back. Now that she was planted in one town she could no longer ignore the scandalous legends which collected round his name. It was hinted to her that the place would soon be too hot to hold him, and though she persistently shut her eyes and ears she could not help knowing all about Miss Evelyn Churchill. The entire district was ringing with it.

This young lady was Sanger's pupil. She had come from England to study music and report had it that she was of very good family. She was talented, beautiful, and Sanger's junior by twenty years, but she had lost her head and her heart and she was advertising the fact in the high-handed way peculiar to women of breeding who are bent upon flying in the face of accepted convention. The affair became an open scandal and the Churchill family threatened to come to Germany and stop it. The young lady replied by going to Venice, taking Sanger with her.

Poor Vera, brooding in the little home where she had expected to be so happy, began to decide that life was altogether too hard for her. She was not proof against this last blow. Sanger's women were not, usually, of a calibre to occupy him for long, but Miss Churchill was a rival of a different order. She was exceptionally intelligent, her health and beauty were not impaired by long years of hardship, and she loved him to distraction. With such a mistress he had no further need for Vera, and the thought broke a heart which should by rights have cracked some fifteen years before.

Yet he did come back, upon the day that Kate was born. He had left a number of manuscripts in his wife's keeping and wanted to collect them from her. She told him, not unkindly,

33

that she was dying, and it soon became clear that she spoke the truth. Her constitution had been undermined by past privations ; she had made up her mind, fatally, that she should not survive the birth of her baby. She spoke of Evelyn without rancour.

" That young lady," she said, " will you marry her when I'm gone ? "

Sanger, looking rather foolish, said he did not know.

" Well, then don't, Albert," whispered Vera. " Promise me that you won't now ! "

" All right," he said agreeably.

" I've never known you keep a promise yet," the tired voice toiled on, " but I'm glad to hear you say it. Not that she wouldn't be good to my babies ; I feel somehow that she would, which is more than I'd say of many women. But she's no wife for you, Albert. She's been bred soft, poor thing ! And I don't wish her harm. I forgive her. I'd be sorry to think she should come to any harm. Mind you're not to marry her, Albert."

The good creature died and Albert immediately broke his promise. He married Miss Churchill in a very few weeks in consequence of a certain pressure from her brothers, who had come out to put an end to the affair and who stayed to pay Sanger's debts and hurry up the wedding.

Evelyn, whose chief merit was a kind of reckless generosity, readily undertook the charge of Caryl and Kate and continued to love them when her own children came. She was indeed heard to regret that she could not pass off Antonia and Kate as twins ; the six months which divided them made it just not possible, and strangers asked so many questions and were so stupidly slow in grasping things, that it would have been convenient. This was how she faced life in those early days— meeting her problems with an audacious levity. Sanger had lost his work, but they had not yet got through all her money.

34

In the course of time she stopped making jokes. Her lot was the harder because she had been, as Vera put it, bred soft. But she met odds with an uncomplaining courage and always recognised that she had only herself to blame for the dishonour, poverty and pain which were her fate. In a multitude of disasters she revealed a constant fortitude, and to the end, though a little battered by ill-fortune, she never quite lost the carriage of a gentlewoman. After bearing four children in six years she contracted heart disease and died rather suddenly upon the eve of her thirtieth birthday.

The household entered thereafter upon a period of storms and changes until Sanger fell in with Linda, who looked like a permanency. She had the strength of mind to ignore completely her six step-children, and for Caryl she even entertained a vague sort of affection. He had grown up into a handsome boy, very like his mother and sister in temper and complexion. His disposition was excellent ; from an early age he managed all his father's business and financial affairs, kept him out of debt as far as possible, and transcribed his manuscripts. In his rare intervals of leisure he wrote music on his own account, but very little attention was paid by the family to his career. He and Kate propped up the crazy household between them and were privately agreed as to its dreadfulness. Linda was grateful to them and tolerated the others.

Lately, however, a new cause for disturbance had arisen. Linda had begun to feel aggrieved at the ripening beauty of Antonia and disliked having to go about with her. This eldest of Evelyn's children was by far the most handsome ; she was born before retribution had fully overtaken her mother, and did not look as delicate as the rest. She was full of a changeful colour and brilliance, though her bloom was but just beginning and she had still the colt-like movements, the long limbs and loose joints of a very young creature. To the experienced eye her promise was infinite. She had a lovely

35

vivid little face, with strange greyish eyes, sulky brows and a white forehead. Her mouth was childish and unformed, but the long curve of cheek and chin, the tilt of the nostrils, and the smooth modelling of the temples revealed a finely constructed skull, a beauty which was bone deep and which would survive the loss of youth. In character she also resembled her mother : was unbalanced, proud and at times impossibly generous. But she lacked Evelyn's courage and was reckless rather than intrepid. She could only take a risk by deceiving herself as to its issue, and confronted by a reality she always went to pieces. She cried when she could not get what she wanted, boasted when she was frightened, and was, like her sisters, a deplorable little slattern.

She turned up at the Karindehütte on the afternoon of Trigorin's arrival in a very uncertain state of mind, having been absent for a week. Unsure of the attitude of her family, she would not go in by the veranda for fear of meeting Linda. She slipped round to the back of the house and climbed through a window into the music-room, where she found Teresa and Paulina sitting on the dais step and devouring cherries. Immediately she put on a kind of defensive swagger and strolled carelessly across the room as though she had never been away at all. Her sisters opened their eyes very wide indeed and asked where she had been.

To give herself time she sat down beside them, snatched a handful of cherries from the basket, and stuffed them into her mouth. Then she mumbled.

" Oh . . . in München."

" München," cried the others. " Who on earth did you stay with ? "

She spat out her stones and would not answer ; but, when they asked incredulously whether it was Ikey Mo, she nodded.

" Himmel ! " gasped Teresa and Paulina together.

They referred to a young man, a friend of Sanger's, whose

real name was Jacob Birnbaum, but whom they had christened Ikey Mo on account of his nose and his shin bones. To this nickname he had not submitted with the best grace in the world. He was, for reasons of his own, naturalised a British subject ; he dressed like an American, and talked four languages correctly but without much command of idiom. He belonged to an immensely rich family and had no regular profession, though he dabbled a good deal in finance. The reigning interest in his life was music ; he sometimes acted as a sort of *entrepreneur* in the arts, financing genius if he thought it would repay him. It nearly always did, for his admirable taste was supplemented by the sharp, forcible intelligence of his race.

His connection with Sanger, however, had brought him no financial profit ; he had even lost money over his friend's productions and he was quite content to do so. For he had his ideals. He almost worshipped Sanger ; regarded him as the greatest musician of the century—as one of those magnificent, unique figures which do not inspire every generation.

In appearance he was not pretty, being short, fair and very stout. But he had benevolent little eyes, and a fine, thoughtful forehead. The Sanger children knew him very well, for he had a flat in Munich and often came up to the Karindehütte. Also he had spent part of the Spring with them in Italy, giving Sanger advice about some copyrights. Teresa, casting her mind back, remembered that he had looked a good deal at Antonia as he sat entertaining Linda in their Genoese garden.

Paulina was asking :

" Did you have a good time ? "

" O—oh, yes ! A lovely time ! Anything I said I wanted, Ike got it for me at once. He just gave me anything I asked for. We used to go along the street and look at all the shops, and if we came to a flower shop he took me in and ordered all I wanted. And once in a sweet shop there was a basket in the window, all made of chocolate with marzipan fruits and gold ribbons ; and I said I'd like that. And he said all right, and got it. And then, just to have him on, I said I wanted an enormous wedding cake in three tiers. But he said : 'Oh, if you want it you can have it. It will be very . . .'"

She broke off and bit her lip.

"Did you bring any sweets back with you, Tony ? " asked Paulina eagerly.

"Little greedy ! No ! I ate so many I got sick. So I gave them all to some children in the cellars. But Ike would have given me more if I'd wanted. He'd have given me anything. And we had lovely meals ; sometimes in restaurants and sometimes sent in. Last night we had a *vol-au-vent*, and asparagus, and lobsters and an iced bomb and peaches, and Ike had a saddle of mutton as well. And we had champagne. I was drunk every night."

"Well, I don't wonder he's so fat if he eats all that," jeered Teresa.

"That's what I told him. I used to say, very loudly, in restaurants and places, 'Now I know why you are so fat.' And all the people laughed. I said it in every language I knew. He got quite annoyed. He doesn't like jokes about his figure."

"I wonder he kept you then," said Paulina.

"Well, I said to him : ' If you don't like what I say I'll go home. I can go this minute if I want to. Nobody can stop me.' So of course he had to put up with it."

"Did he give you that hat ? "

Antonia wore the very ragged cotton gown in which she had left her home. But she had acquired a fine, flimsy town hat made of black lace with a wreath of gold flowers.

"No," she said. "I bought it with my birthday money. Do you like it ? "

"It's rather vulgar," said Teresa "But it suits you."

Antonia took it off and pinched the tawdry flowers lovingly. Her sisters exclaimed in excitement :

" Why, you've got your hair up ! "

" Yes," she said carelessly. " Ike said I'd better."

She had drawn it all off her forehead and pinned it at the back of her head. It was a style which revealed the subtle shadows and curves of brow and temple, giving her an appearance of character and intellect which the low-brimmed hat had destroyed. The calm, youthful beauty of her forehead contrasted strangely with the evasive defiance of her eyes, heavy with the weariness of a week's frantic dissipation. She sat for a while making nervous grimaces, and then announced :

" We went to the opera every night."

" Oh ! Was it tolerable ? " asked Teresa, with very fair imitation of Lewis in his least agreeable manner.

" Of course it was. It was very beautiful music. Only Ike has strange tastes. Just fancy ! He likes Wagner ! I told him that we don't. I said that all savage races like loud noises."

She paused to laugh heartily at this jibe, and Paulina asked in a puzzled voice :

" But what did he have you there for if you were so rude ? I don't understand. What did he get out of it ? "

" You'd never take him for a lover," cried Teresa ; then, catching sight of her sister's face : " Oh, Tony ! You didn't ! "

" Yes I did," said Antonia, adding hastily : " Do you know he says I've the loveliest voice he's ever heard in his life ! He says I'm miles better than Kate ; he says I've got more temperament than Kate and my interpretations are more sympathetic. So that's one for Kate isn't it ? Always stodging away ! She'll never do anything very much I expect."

" He was just making fun of you," said Teresa. " Or else he's as mad as you are. Because no sane man, even if he was your lover, could think that you sing better than Kate. But I wonder at your taste, Tony. He's so fat ! "

39

"Why shouldn't he be ? There isn't any law that the first lover anybody takes has to be thin is there ? "

"N—no," said Teresa with a rare blush. "You know you'll have a terrible time with Sanger. He said he'd beat you when you came back ; and I don't know what he'll say when he hears what you've done. What will you tell him ? "

"Nothing, or Linda either. I don't think he'll ask. He never asks questions unless he's sure he's going to like the answer."

This was true and the little girls nodded. She went on :

"I expect it will be all right. Ike came back with me, you know. He's up with Sanger now, and he brought him some cognac for a present. That ought to put him in a good temper. I advised him to bring it and he said it was a good idea, but he was still afraid that Caryl might call him out. So I said : ' Caryl never does silly things and that would be silly. Because if he started fighting over us his life wouldn't be worth a sick headache by the time Soo-zanne's grown up.' And Ike said that was probably true. I told him I didn't wonder he was frightened, for he'd make a splendid target. And Caryl's a good shot. If he fought anybody he'd kill them, I think. I shouldn't like poor little Ike to be killed. But I don't see why Caryl should mind, do you ? It isn't as if I was likely to have a baby or anything."

They rather resented the swagger with which she made this assertion and Teresa said crushingly :

"Did you walk all about Müchen with that enormous hole in your stocking ? I wonder Ike put up with it ! "

Antonia turned over her little foot and looked at it. Most of her pink heel stuck out of her stocking. She said instantly :

"Ike gave me stockings. He gave me twelve pair, all silk and all different colours."

"Fancy taking clothes from him ! "

"I didn't. I threw them out of the window. I asked him

40

what he took me for. And they all got caught in the telegraph wires, and the people in the street looked so surprised. It was windy, you know, and they waved about like little flags. I laughed till I nearly fell out of the window myself."

"Liar !"

"I did. It's true. I said to Ike : ' If I have a hole in my stocking, what's that to you ? My clothes are my own affair, I should hope. If I'm not grand enough for you to take me out, leave me alone and I'll go home.' And he said I could throw them out of the window if I liked. So I threw them. And he said he didn't mind. He said he wouldn't mind if I threw all my clothes out of the window. He said . . ."

She pulled herself up with a little gasp as if she had again stumbled upon a recollection which terrified her. But she went on, boastfully elaborating the details of her escapade, and heaping insults upon Birnbaum as though by abuse she could revenge the humiliations of her surrender. She seemed to be bent upon representing him in as ridiculous a light as possible, and Lewis, who joined them in time to hear some of her most highly-coloured sallies, was struck by their apt cruelty—at the edge which this episode seemed to have put upon her somewhat primitive wit. He sat on the piano stool, applauding her waggery and encouraging her to fresh efforts until something in her desperate spirits made him uneasy. He observed her more closely, got a glimpse of the disaster in her eyes, and laughed no more ; turning round abruptly he began to play the piano and ended the conversation. The girls, immediately silent, listened to him with the grave attention which his music merited. He played sitting very stiff and upright, staring thoughtfully at the notes with a faint, preoccupied smile. The immobility of his body seemed to contribute somehow to the violent activity of his hands as he flung them about the keyboard. He had charged into the last movement in the Appassionata, and for some minutes the room was full of its resistless, onward sweep. Then he broke off, commanding Paulina, with some irritation, not to breathe down his neck.

"Finish it, Lewis," cried Antonia. "Play the Presto bit."

"I can't play that piece," he demurred. "It's too difficult."

"Oh, Lewis! How can you? I've often heard you."

"Well," said Teresa maliciously, "I must say I've heard it better done."

He spun round on the music stool as if somebody had stuck a pin into him, and looked at her. She gave him such an innocent little grin that he could not help laughing. He said that they had better lose no time in rehearsing "Breakfast with the Borgias" now that Antonia was back, and went off to fetch it. Paulina said:

"He didn't like you saying that you'd heard the Appassionata better done, Tessa."

"Well, he shouldn't have said it was too difficult for him in that silly voice. It was just to show off. I can't help teasing him when he asks for it like that."

"I wish," said Antonia with a shiver, "that he wouldn't look at a person as if he saw all in one second everything that had ever happened to them."

"It doesn't matter," stated Teresa. "He only thinks of his own concerns. The other things he hastily forgets, so they shan't get on his mind."

Lewis reappeared with the score, which he propped up on the piano, saying:

"Now I propose to play over the tunes to you until you know them and you can supply your own words. Who will be Cesare Borgia? He's a tenor."

"Roberto," said Paulina. "He's got the best voice here."

"And Ikey Mo must be Pope," broke in Antonia. "It will suit him so very well."

"Oh! He's here is he?" asked Lewis.

"Upstairs with Sanger."

42

"Good ! He can double the parts of Pope and Friar. They don't come on together. Then the flea trainer . . what's his name . . . Linda's follower . . . Trigorin . . . he can be the servant, Scaramello. It'll be just the part for him. He has a good deal of business with a poisoned tooth-pick. Just fetch him, Tessa ! You'll find him, I expect, on the veranda. And you, Lina, produce Roberto for me."

Teresa ran out and found Trigorin engaged in desultory conversation with Linda. He was looking a trifle crestfallen and uneasy ; he had been disappointed not to see Sanger at lunch. Lewis and Kate had discussed " The Mountains " across him, without taking any notice of his attempts to join in. Their conversation reminded him of all his joyful anticipations as he drove up the valley and roused him from the brief delirium occasioned by Linda's blue eyes. He had not climbed this heavy hill merely to make himself agreeable to a fine woman. She would be very well anywhere else, but here she was not seemly, and to become entangled with her would be to profane the dreams which he had woven about this visit. She found him much less promising after lunch.

He jumped up with alacrity when he heard that Lewis wanted him and followed Teresa as she skipped back into the house. He was radiantly at their service, but his face fell when he heard that they wanted him to sing.

" It is impossible," he exclaimed. " I cannot sing."

" Everybody has got to," said Lewis. " You needn't be a Caruso. No ! None of your modesty ! Here, sing this ! "

He played the opening bars of Scaramello's song. Trigorin stood, fat and mute, spreading out hands of deprecation

" I cannot," he repeated.

" Sing this then," commanded Lewis, playing the first bar

Trigorin produced a voice so small and reedy that Teresa and Paulina rolled on the floor with laughter.

43

"No, you're quite right, you can't sing," said Lewis crossly. "But who is to take the part then?"

"I could play?" suggested Trigorin diffidently. "Then you, perhaps, shall sing."

"Play? I doubt it. It's all in pencil and vilely written at that. It would be sheer guess work."

"To me it will be clear," Trigorin assured him. "Often I must read such scores."

And, sitting down, he began to play the little overture with great smoothness and spirit, interpreting the scrawls which stood for chords without much difficulty. Lewis listened impatiently and then said:

"Yes, that'll do. But don't play it as if it was Chopin!"

Trigorin began to play much louder, as the only amendment he could think of. Teresa, who had been admiring the excited agility of his fat hands, put an arm round Lewis's neck and drew his head close down to hers.

"Lewis," she whispered, derisively confidential, "sometimes, you know, you talk . . . poppycock!"

He pulled her ears and called her something unrepeatable, but he went over to Trigorin and told him how much obliged they all were for his timely skill in playing for them. Trigorin beamed and played louder than ever.

"Now," said Lewis. "I'll be Scaramello. So we needn't rehearse the opening song. Where's Roberto?"

"Please?" said Roberto, who had been waiting politely by the door until called for.

He was a small, thin Italian, clad invariably in blue linen overalls. He had a brown, good-natured face, with a little beard and moustache. He was devoted to all the Sangers. He did the whole work of the house and undertook any odd job that turned up, darned Sanger's socks, prepared Linda's bath, and interviewed the Press. Sanger asserted that he had once acted as accoucheur when Sebastian arrived rather unexpectedly

44

into the world, but this was so long ago as to be almost
legend.

"Listen, Roberto," said Lewis. "Can you act?"

"*Scusa!*"

"Which of you girls can talk Italian? Tony! You
explain to him what he's got to do. You, Trigorin, play him
his tune. Get him along to Lucrezia's entrance. It's marked
on the score, there. Where's Kate? I want her. She must
be Lucrezia."

"Oh, Lewis! Let me be!" cried Antonia. "Kate
can't act."

"She can sing. I won't have my music spoilt. No, Tony."
He went to the door and shouted for Kate.

"But she'll ruin the part, Lewis."

"Not a bit of it."

"She can't interpret. She's got no temperament."

"All the better," said Lewis drily. "Temperament is
like vinegar in a salad; a little goes a long way. I'd sooner
have none than too much. Kate! Where are you?"

"Oh, Lewis, do let me be. I can sing! I can really!
Everybody says I've come on a lot."

"They may, Tony. I don't say you sing badly. But Kate
sings better."

"Oh, well then! I hope she'll spoil your silly old play.
Standing stuck in the middle of the stage looking like a sofa
cushion like she always does. I never heard anything funnier
in all my life than Kate trying to act Lucrezia Borgia."

"Birnbaum as Pope will be much funnier. No! Kate
must be our diva. You must be her victim; a beautiful
creature who is poisoned and dies writhing. You'll like that
won't you? You can work off a temperamental contrast to
Kate's stolid villainy."

"Oh, well," said Antonia, somewhat mollified. "But
what will Tessa and Lina be?"

45

"Tessa must be the confidential waiting maid and Lina and Sebastian are to be pages. They've a duet."

"And what about Suzanne? Had you forgotten her? Oh, that doesn't matter. We don't want her."

Lewis clapped a hand to his head in dismay and exclaimed :

"If I hadn't forgotten Soo-zanne. Will your father . ."

"Sanger won't mind her being left out," Paulina assured him. "He nearly is sick when she sings and so are we."

"Very well. There isn't time to alter it, anyhow. Kate!"

"She cook supper," volunteered Roberto. "She say she come after or you get nothing to eat."

"What a plague! Well, I'll take her later, and Caryl too. He is our heavy bass. We must do what we can now without them. Come, Tessa! You and I have a love scene together. If you'll come down to the end of the room with me I'll hum you the tune and we'll concoct the words, while Trigorin coaches Roberto."

They went and sat in a distant window, composing their libretto with a good deal of hilarity. She supplied the rhymes, while he attended to the metre, and they soon became very ribald indeed. Presently Roberto, who was getting hold of his part, struck a tremendous attitude and burst into his first air. As he sang he stalked about the stage with fiery Italian gestures.

"There," said Lewis. "That is exactly what I want. You will all of you observe that this is a very Latin piece. This fellow does it to perfection. Copy him and you'll please me. That'll do, Roberto. Up with you, Tessa, and we'll sing our duet."

They mounted the dais. Trigorin's hands softened on the keys as Teresa's little treble and Lewis's inconspicuous baritone rose through the room. Neither had much voice but they sang with spirit, and it was obvious that Teresa was straining to do her very best. In that house she could do no less. Music there was a sacred thing ; perhaps the only sacred thing. Even in

46

an absurd charade like this it might not be cheapened by carelessness or economy of effort. The Sanger children were ignorant of obedience, application, self-command or reverence save in this one cause. And of Lewis the same thing might have been said.

He was looking wild and weary. His red hair, damp with sweat, was pushed up into a crest on the top of his head. He had flung aside all his waistcoats and the muffler and was directing the rehearsal in his shirt sleeves. Having Teresa in his arms, he was making love to her with a business-like competence which showed that he had quite forgotten for the moment who she really was. He was busy listening to the effect of the duet and considering the sequence of this song with the next; in his preoccupation he hardly remembered that she was not the Roman waiting wench for whom he had written the part. His eyes were grave and intent, and saw nothing at all, but in voice and gesture he was using the absent-minded mastery of a practised lover. Teresa did not like such handling; she was no actress and could not throw herself into her part sufficiently for its demands. A certain stolidity in her, an absence of the invariable response, brought him to himself with a start; he remembered that he had got poor little Tessa and not the full-blooded contadina he had framed. He laughed at her reassuringly, and finished the scene with a kind of bantering gaiety which put her at her ease.

They worked away until Susan, sidling round the door, told them that supper was ready. Very hungry and happy they all trooped into the hall, where Kate, flushed and dishevelled, was helping soup from an enormous tureen. Linda, already seated at the table, had begun her meal. She raised her eyes contemptuously to look at the musicians, but at the sight of Antonia she remained fixed in a stare.

"Oh!" she said slowly. "So you've come back?"

"Yes. I've come back. What soup is it, Kate?"

" We mayn't ask where you've been, I suppose," asked Linda.

" I've been on a visit."

" Oh, indeed ! I hope you enjoyed yourself."

" Very much, thank you."

" You never know," murmured Linda thoughtfully. " Sometimes girls don't enjoy visits as much as they think they will. Sometimes they come back . . quite changed."

" Will Sanger be down to supper, Kate ? " interrupted Lewis hastily.

" Yes," said Kate. " Jacob Birnbaum is with him. I went up to tell them and they are just coming down."

" Jacob," stated Linda, " came the same time Tony did. You'll tell me, I suppose, that you didn't travel together."

Antonia took no notice and began to eat her soup.

" She's been stopping with 'im," piped Susan. " I heard her telling Tessa and Lina. Ah . . . oh . . Mammy ! Tessa pinched me ! "

" Oh, God ! Will you leave the child alone ! " exclaimed Linda, angrily leaning forward to box Teresa's ears. " Come here, Suzanne, and tell us what you heard."

" Tessa and Lina was eating cherries and they wouldn't give me any and shut me out of the room. So I climbed up into the balcony and listened to everything they said to spite them. And Tony came in and said she'd been stopping at Ike's flat . . ."

" Yes ? Be quiet, Lewis, please ! I want to hear this. Kate ! I wonder at you, interrupting in that rude way. You can tell Mr. Trigorin about the landslide afterwards. Just all of you be quiet and let me hear this. Go on, lovey ! What next ? "

" She's a filthy little liar ! " burst out Antonia. " I never said anything of the sort, did I girls ? "

" No ! " asserted her sisters loyally.

48

"Didn't you? We'll see. When Suzanne's finished telling me all she heard she can repeat it over again to your father."

At that moment Sanger appeared at the head of the stairs, an enormous, infirm figure. His son Caryl supported him. Jacob Birnbaum strolled thoughtfully along the passage behind them and peered over their shoulders at the scene going on in the hall below. Linda rose and pointed at Antonia.

"Look at her, Albert!" she bawled. "Just look at her. She's come back, if you please. D'you want to know what she's been up to?"

Sanger descended the stairs with difficulty, leaning heavily on Caryl's arm and preceded by Gelert, his boarhound. Birnbaum, looking a trifle nervous, brought up the rear of this procession. Lewis and Trigorin forgot Antonia and her troubles in the shocked surprise with which they viewed their host. In the months that had elapsed since they saw him last, disease and decay had made rapid advances. His huge frame looked shrunken : the flesh sagged heavily on a face half hidden by grizzled hair. The splendid vitality of the man was gone, leaving this mountainous wreck, blinking at them with dim, bloodshot eyes.

When he reached the hall his mistress began to upbraid him and Antonia, calling them by every discreditable name in her very extensive vocabulary. Lewis and Birnbaum, used to these scenes, greeted each other with long faces and tried to create a diversion by announcing that the corkscrew had been lost. But Sanger paid no heed to any of them ; he continued to stare at his daughter as if waiting for her to speak. She had gone very white, but was steadily drinking her soup as if nothing had happened.

"Well, my girl," he said at last. "I had intended to beat you when you got home. But it's too much trouble ; too . . . much . . . trouble. Besides, I'm hungry."

49

And he collapsed into his chair at the head of the table.

"When I'm less busy," he promised Linda, "I'll institute a disciplinary system. I'll thrash all the girls for half an hour every morning, including Susan."

And he shot a ferocious look at his youngest, who shivered in her chair, though, as a matter of fact, she was the only child in the house who escaped his blows.

"Thrash all the girls every day?" asked Sebastian, who had joined them in time to hear this remark. "What for?"

"For their incontinent behaviour," replied their father. "Beating, Sebastian, is the only remedy. You can beat Susan if you like."

"I would like," said Sebastian.

"If the men of this family co-operate, we may manage to introduce a little order into the household. Caryl shall beat Kate."

"Kate doesn't need it," said Sebastian gravely.

"I daresay not. But a little undeserved beating does them no harm. Kate will be all the better for it."

And Sanger looked affectionately into Kate's distressed face and asked her for some soup.

"You'd better let Jacob beat Antonia," said Linda sourly. "He's been keeping her this past week."

"Is that so?" Sanger shifted his morose regard from his daughter to his friend. "Is that so, Jacob?"

"I hope that you have no objection," said Birnbaum, with as much effrontery as he could muster. "Some day, perhaps, some more of the children will come down. We amused ourselves so much. But Tony was anxious to be at home for the birthday."

Sanger sighed gustily and said:

"Very friendly of you, Jacob!"

At which Birnbaum looked uncomfortable. Antonia, lifting her head for the first time, looked at her father and then at her lover with stony, scornful eyes. In the uneasy pause which ensued the voice of Trigorin was heard in a speech which had gone on, unheeded, ever since Sanger appeared on the stairs.

"There is no privilege," he was saying, "which I have more desired than to be a guest at this house."

"Bless my soul! Trigorin!" exclaimed Sanger. "I'd forgotten you were here. I must apologise. But you're a family man yourself, I believe, so you're probably accustomed to this sort of thing. I hope Kate is making you comfortable. Look! Have you met Birnbaum?"

But Trigorin did not want to talk to Birnbaum, who was, obviously, no musician. And Birnbaum did not want to talk to anyone. He occupied himself sulkily in pulling corks and glancing furtively at Antonia. Sanger was very silent and ate little. He sat staring at his plate in such a moody abstraction, heaving such melancholy sighs, that nobody liked to speak to him. Lewis talked to Caryl in undertones, the children giggled at their end of the table, and Trigorin was thrown once. more upon the melting glances of Linda.

The gloomy meal proceeded calmly enough save for a scene in which Paulina and Sebastian were ordered from the room for spitting at each other across the table. But even this was accomplished without the tumult and gusto of other days. Sanger had lost his love of life. He was a sick man, absorbed in his last desperate struggle ; too ill to resent the conduct of his children and his friends. He saw the looks which Linda cast upon Trigorin ; he guessed that Birnbaum had seduced his daughter, but he could not rouse himself to any protest. Towards the end of supper, however, having drunk a good deal of the cognac which Birnbaum had brought him, he brightened up a little. He began to tease Lewis about the "Revolutionary Songs," and told how at an early rehearsal the tenors had taken their first lead a bar late and how they had remained a bar late throughout the piece, whereat Lewis determined that it sounded better that way. Later in the evening he became very good company indeed and told them funny stories about Brahms. For an hour he was himself again, and his friends forgot their gloom ; they caught the old sense of space and heroic joviality —felt that they were assisting at something epic and earning a sort of immortality simply by listening to Sanger and laughing with him. But as the night advanced he became less intelligible, and when Caryl and Lewis took him up to bed he was speechless. Trigorin and Birnbaum, who did not find much to say to each other, retired to the spare bedroom which they were to share.

CHAPTER IV

JACOB BIRNBAUM stood behind a screen which formed one of the wings in " a room in the Vatican." His intelligent forehead was smothered beneath three tea cosies, placed one upon the other, to form a papal crown. The rest of his person was muffled in an ancient Spanish cope. He made a sufficiently impressive Borgia. Upon the stage the Dodd opera was in full swing and Trigorin was rattling away at the piano. Antonia was dying in as Latin a manner as she could compass, her long hair trailing over the shoulder of Roberto, who made a most polite little cardinal, in Kate's red dressing-gown. He supported the poisoned lady as she swung through her final swift, suave, heart-rending air, and when she had breathed her last put her on the floor almost at Birnbaum's feet. She lay there very pink and pleased with herself, her eyes tightly shut in an innocent attempt to look convincingly dead.

The man in the wings stared down at her sombrely, his mind ranging back unhappily over all that had befallen the pair of them since that day, scarcely a month ago, when he had looked at her picking freesias in the garden at Genoa and discovered, with a sense of dazed shock, the enchantment of her loveliness and youth. That day had been the beginning of his madness. At the thought of the havoc she had made in his peace of mind he could almost wish that she was really lying dead at his feet. If she were dead she could not be more lost to him. Should this sweet, tormenting thing, that had been his, die and be buried, be thrust away under the mould, he might forget her. But

53

while the living, revengeful spirit which had eluded him gazed upon him with her eyes and mocked him with her tongue he could never hope for tranquillity.

Because she had seemed to promise Paradise, and because he was accustomed to get what he wanted, he had persuaded her, with promises of lavish entertainment, to come to Munich. The rest of the business had been most pitifully easy. Only, in return, she had made a fool of him ; she had opened his eyes so completely to the illusion of all possession that he doubted if he should ever again enjoy anything without an after-taste of bitterness. She had given him none of the bliss he had anticipated ; and long before the end of the week he knew that he had made an irremediable mistake, that his need had been for some moment of shared passion, some appeasement of his loneliness, some sign that she returned his feeling. He would gladly have relinquished his brief, unsubstantial victory, if that were possible, for some hint that he was in any way necessary to her happiness. But an implacable remorse told him that by his own folly he had lost her.

Upon the stage Scaramello, the servant, was being instructed to throw her into the Tiber. He picked her up and carried her behind the screen. When he had set her carefully upon her feet she opened her eyes with a laugh which ended abruptly, since she found herself so close to Jacob Birnbaum. Shrinking back she eyed him defiantly, and he, stung by a sudden, unendurable pain, returned her glance with a smile of deliberate insolence which sent her pale with fury. Lewis, watching them, thought that they made a pretty pair ; he shuddered a little at them. He did not like to think what dark things must have passed between them at Munich that they should still choose to remain in each other's company for the sake, apparently, of mutual torment. He turned his back on them and, since his head that day was completely in the clouds, he soon forgot them.

The even flow of his own music pleased and soothed him, but he found that he could not listen to it in a spirit of intelligent criticism. A strange helplessness had come upon him ; he knew it for the first stage of a violent seizure of mental and spiritual activity. Very soon he would be thinking desperately, but at the moment he was obsessed and baffled by a vague conception, a form, the outlines of a new thing in his mind. While this veiled idea disturbed his peace he could not think connectedly upon any subject, since he must needs reject every image which was not the right one. He brooded absently—anxious, yet afraid of the moment when his thought should take shape.

Presently Birnbaum had to leave them and join the group on the stage. Lewis, standing with Antonia behind the screen, was jerked out of his absorption and exasperated beyond all reason when he discovered that she was in tears. He whispered fiercely over his shoulder :

"Stop making that noise, can't you ? "

She felt herself that he ought not to be disturbed when he was listening to his own music, and with a meek gulp she replied :

"I'll try. Can you lend me a handkerchief ? "

He thought he could. He searched his raiment and at last discovered a very dirty red cotton object which he gave her. Then he turned his back again while she quietly mopped her eyes, until the end of the piece set her free to run away and howl as loudly as she pleased.

He took his call, lost still in his uneasy preoccupation. He climbed on to the stage and bowed to an audience composed of Linda, Susan, Sanger and the village schoolmaster. They crowded round him, and Linda said that she hadn't known he could write anything so pretty, and Sanger said that he was an amusing fellow. Trigorin clasped his hand in a couple of wet white ones.

" It is admirable," he gasped. " You say it is to imitate the Italian opera ? I say not. It is inspired by that school . . yes . but also it is original. My dear sir, it is a work of genius ! "

" Very good of you to say so," replied Lewis, trying to release himself. " You played well, Trigorin. I don't know how you managed to make out my scrawls."

" It was a pleasure . . . an honour. I like it so much. It is so beautiful, that little work. It has the true melody . . ."

" Is it an advance on the 'Revolutionary Songs'?" asked Birnbaum, who was listening.

" But no," said Trigorin, shaking his head very seriously. " That I cannot say. This I like so much ; but the others I like better. They also are the work of genius, but more heavy."

Lewis looked very much pained and intimated that he himself was inclined to consider " Breakfast with the Borgias " as the most profound effort he had yet made. It was a blow to him, he said, if Mr. Trigorin thought it superficial. He had succeeded in reducing his fellow-guest to a perfectly speechless condition of embarrassment and mortification when Linda was heard to ask, in no mean voice, why a part had not been written for Susan.

" The child can sing in tune," she asserted. " And I'd like to know why she's been passed over."

" My dear Linda," expostulated Albert, " one must keep the thing even. We like a high standard in our family productions, but Susan's level is beyond the rest of us."

" I don't know why you should have such a spite against the poor little thing, I'm sure," complained Linda, fondling Susan. " As if it matters how a kiddie of that age does things ! I don't see anything so wonderful, come to that, in the way that Lina and Sebastian sang their parts."

" There was nothing wonderful," said Sanger wearily,

56

"except that they had the grace to take pains. If either of them had dared to set up the confounded little pipe which we hear from Susan I'd have stopped the piece. You never did, did you ? I dare say not."

"I can tell you, Albert, there's plenty of people think differently. There was a gentleman down in Genoa that heard her sing and he said she was wonderful for her age. He said she'd inherited her talent, and he'd know her anywhere for Sanger's daughter. He said she'd go very far."

"Sanger's daughter ! Heaven and earth ! Sanger's daughter ! Isn't it bad enough to have begotten anything like Susan ? I'm ready to swear I never did. And now a gentleman in Genoa says she takes after me ! An intolerable insult ! Birnbaum ! Will you listen to this ? A gentleman in Genoa who heard Susan sing . . . have you heard Susan sing, by the way ? You haven't ? Well then you shall. Pop up on to the platform, Sue, and give us a song. Let me see . . . what did you sing to the gentleman in Genoa ? The flower song out of 'Faust' ? I might have known it. Sing that ! I dare say Trigorin will be able to play it for you."

"That's right, dearie, it's your turn now to sing a bit," said Linda, who could not believe that anyone should hear Susan sing and not find her very sweet.

Susan needed no encouragement. She was delighted with any sort of notice. She climbed on to the dais, pushed back her yellow curls, and began to warble in a shallow, sugary treble. Her facility, self-confidence and inaccuracy were on a level with the amazing vulgarity of her performance. She paraded every cheap effect, every little trick, most likely to outrage the pure taste of her relations. And yet there was a certain dash and assurance about her which explained the prophesy of the gentleman in Genoa. Sanger himself was inclined to fear that her push and her unscrupulous showiness would carry her further than the others and establish her as the star of the

57

family. Hence his animosity; he could not bear that she should eclipse the patient, industrious talent of Caryl and Kate, or the fine brilliance of Evelyn's children. He scowled heavily all through her song.

But she, with a persistent, babyish simper, ignored this, and ignored also the loud retching noises whereby her younger brother and sisters indicated their nausea at the style of her performance. At the end she acknowledged the slightly ironic applause of her elders as though conscious of popularity, jumped down and ran to hide her face in her mother's lap, a pretty gesture which they had rehearsed in private.

"Little monkey!" observed Sanger wrathfully. "That's what I have to put up with. And she'll disgrace us on every platform in Europe before she's done. But I shan't know it. The worms will have me before then, thank God."

He relapsed into gloom for a little while, and then said :

"Kate, my dear! Don't be shy. We're an indulgent audience and won't expect a second Susan of you. Couldn't you oblige us a little? We've not heard as much of you to-night as I'd like."

"I'm sorry," said Lewis. "I'd no idea Kate was turning into such a prima donna, or she should have had more songs of her very own. Do sing, Kate!"

Kate sang and they were all delighted with her. She sang one song after another to meet every taste, and ended with a somewhat ambitious composition of Caryl's, a setting to the lines :

Du bist wie eine Blume!

which was received by the family with varying appreciation since its sentiment was practically incomprehensible to most of them. At the end of it Lewis began to congratulate Caryl with such fulsomeness, so palpably in imitation of Trigorin, that all the children began to giggle. He was enlarging upon his privileges in being allowed to listen to a first performance of this detestable little work when Sanger, who felt that things were really going too far, went across to Trigorin and began to be civil to him. He praised his reading of the pencil score and explained how much obliged they all were. Trigorin beamed. It was the first conversational opening given to him by Sanger during this whole visit.

"It was easy," he said. "Often I must read music that is so badly written. It is very nice, this piece? Yes?"

"Humph!" said Sanger. "Very pretty fooling. It suited the cast, which was all that was required."

Trigorin, who had had a cross letter from his wife that morning, thought he saw an opportunity and rushed upon his fate.

"It is a diversion to write for an artist, sometimes. It is amusing. My wife, she hopes that you will one day write a ballet for her . . a little thing . . ."

Sanger stiffened and shot up his eyebrows.

"I'm honoured," he said. "But I don't suppose I could write a ballet that would suit Madame to save my life. Why not get Birnbaum here to write one? It's much more in his line."

"I did not know . . ." began Trigorin doubtfully, looking at the young Jew.

"You didn't know that he wrote music? Well, he hasn't written any yet. But he should. He should! And he owns several theatres. Look here, Birnbaum! Here's Trigorin wants one of us to write a ballet for Madame. I tell him you'd better do it and produce it at one of your places."

"I think that Madame Zhigalova would not be pleased with my work," said Jacob. "Why does he not do it himself?"

"I cannot write music," said Trigorin sadly

"Perhaps you could, if you tried. It is quite easy, is it not, my friend?"

"Quite," said Sanger, returning his grin. "Yes; it would

be an excellent speculation to write all her ballets yourself, Trigorin."

"Don't listen to them, Mr. Trigorin," whispered Linda, behind him, "they're just laughing at you."

The baited man turned round and looked at her and remembered how much kinder she had been than anyone else at the Karindehütte. She dropped her large white eyelids and made a place for him beside her on the window seat. For a second he wavered, looking towards the piano where Sanger, Lewis and Birnbaum were talking together ; but he knew that they did not want him, so he sat down and surrendered himself to her. She could at least help him to forget his mortification, to his sorrowing spirit she brought an easy forgetfulness, she stirred his pulses and provoked no ideas either of good or of evil.

They embarked upon a whispered conversation full of long significant pauses, as a pair of chess players will hesitate and ponder over the moves of a game. Their common goal was oblivion, escape from their several sorrows. For Linda, despite her placidity, had a sorrow—a sort of composite dread of poverty, insecurity and increasing flesh ; a fear of the future which was creeping over her life like a chilly fog ; a vision of herself as an enormous old woman, starving to death.

The company meanwhile was breaking up. The schoolmaster took his leave and Lewis, attracted by the moonlight outside, strolled a little way down the hill with him. Sanger and Caryl went upstairs to begin on their night's work. Birnbaum, straying unhappily through the house, was looking for Antonia, though he did not in the least know what he wanted to say if he found her. He stumbled over the two little girls sitting on the top step of the stairs and asked if they had seen her.

"She's in our room, Ike," said Paulina. "Crying like anything. She's been crying all the evening."

"Crying," he repeated, startled, yet a little hopeful. "That's a pity."

"She often cries," said Teresa without much concern.

"She's a regular cry-baby," added Paulina.

"So are you ! " Teresa was moved to retort. " You both of you roar and yell at the least little thing."

"What is she crying for ? " asked Jacob anxiously.

"Because Lewis wouldn't let her be Lucrezia Borgia," they told him. " She was dreadfully hurt because he despised her singing."

"So ! " he exclaimed in some disappointment, and took himself off to bed.

"It's no use us going up till Tony's quiet," said Paulina.

Teresa said nothing but crouched at the top of the stairs, brooding disconsolately, her thin arms round her knees. Suddenly she had become intensely miserable. She stared down into the darkness of the hall, cut in two by the moonlight which streamed in through the open door. She could not bear it. She jumped up with a little cry of exasperation.

"Oh ! " she exclaimed. " How I hate it all ! "

"Hate what ? " asked Paulina mildly.

"Everybody ! Everything ! I hate the whole world ! "

"Everything does seem horrid this year," agreed Paulina sadly. " We don't seem to have the fun we used to."

"Good-bye," said Teresa, setting off down the stairs.

"Where are you off to ? Are you going out ? "

"Yes ! I must get out of this . . ."

She ran out to hide herself in the mountains, frightened and furious, pursued by a desolate foreboding which seemed to fill the quiet house. As she stumbled up towards the pass she kept murmuring to herelf :

"I wish I could die ! I wish I was dead ! "

She knew that she did not mean this ; she was not in the least anxious to die. But the violence of such a statement seemed to satisfy her, just as it was a relief to run up hill.

61

CHAPTER V

THE top of the pass was such a quiet place that Teresa very
soon recovered her peace of mind. She could see nothing of
the trees or the world of men, since the valley leading down to
Weissau was full of clouds. Above and around her was the
sky, empty save for the moon. Mountain peaks stood up in
that space, bare to the light. She was at a point where the
track balanced itself for a moment on the ridge and then dived
into an inky valley on the far side. From that blackness rose
the echoing murmur of many waterfalls, so that the pit of night
was full of sound. She stood, looking down, already calmer.

By the path was a small wooden Calvary marking a spring,
and near it a grotto of stones built the year before by Paulina
and Sebastian. They had said it was for prayer and meditation,
which was strange, for neither of them was much given to this
employment; but the building had kept them happy for three
weeks. Winter storms had blown it down, and it lay now a
tumbled heap of stones beside the crucifix with its penthouse
roof. Teresa thought how nice it would be to build, not a
grotto, but a little house where she could live always, watching
the blizzards blown across the pass, and the snow melting, and
the flowers of Spring pushing up through the grass. And in
the Summer she would have a cornet, and, hidden in the
mountains, she would play lovely tunes and give terrific shocks
to lonely travellers toiling over the pass with their knapsacks.
For nobody should know of the little house.

She climbed a knoll, the highest point near by, and stared

round her. In every direction she could see for miles and miles, but the view was simple, a succession of serene ranges sticking up into emptiness. The moon had painted them all a uniform black and white, and the sky was no colour at all. It was a simplification which delighted her ; she needed it. There were, usually, too many things. The people and colours and noises crowded her mind with ideas and confused her. Often she felt that she saw nothing clearly, but here, where there was so very little to see, it might be managed. She turned round to the Königsjoch, which hung almost above her, and took a good look at it. Its stony crags, its snowfields, and the smooth, bare outline of its summit seemed almost near enough to touch, yet she knew them to be miles away. She stared hungrily, trying to stamp this image on her mind and thus secure it for ever and ever. She became entranced with it. As she looked she had an idea, a passionate hope, which took her breath away. If she could ever see but one thing properly she might quite easily see God.

The thought so moved her that she flung herself down on the short wind-blown grass and gazed up into the sky above her, waiting, rigid in an effort to reach singleness of mind. Nothing happened. In a few minutes she became painfully exhausted and very cold. The wind in her hair came straight off the snowfields. She began to think more kindly of her exasperating family down at the Karindehütte. She would go back to them.

She pulled herself together for the descent, aware that a frightful weariness was aching in all her bones. Glancing down towards the path she saw that a man was standing there, staring at the mountains in a kind of lost trance, as if he had discovered the secret thing which had escaped her. It was Lewis. She blew a loving little kiss at his unconscious figure thinking how well she was acquainted with the shape of his head at the back. She could have drawn it with her eyes shut ;

63

she had sat so often watching him while he conducted symphonies to which she did not always listen. And in this place he did not look more solitary than he always seemed in crowded concert halls.

Presently his vision seemed to break up, and he took to walking about, in a distraught frenzy, stumbling sometimes, and often almost running. She knew what ailed him and was very sorry. Living in a family of artists she had come to regard this implacable thing which took them as a great misfortune. Oddly enough it had missed her out ; alone of the tribe, she was safe from it. She did not believe that she would ever be driven to these monstrous creative efforts. She desired nothing but to be allowed to look on at the world ; and the result of her observations had been that she rated the writing of music as an atrocious and painful disease. She pitied her friend when it assailed him as much as if he had fallen down and broken his leg. To her the thing was a hidden curse, a family werewolf, always ready to spring out and devour them all. It was at the bottom of most of their misfortunes. Its place in her scheme of things was approximate to the position which the devil might hold in the mind of a better instructed little girl.

" Poor Lewis," she murmured. " I thought as much ! He's been looking like a broody hen all the week."

She guessed that he must not discover her and was for stealing off down the far side of the hill when he caught sight of her. Immediately he hailed her, bounding up the slope very quickly, so that she could not get away.

" Tessa ! What are you doing here ? Aren't you cold ? "

He spoke almost mechanically, as if he hardly knew what he said. She saw that he was shaken and unhappy at being caught off his guard. She said that she had come up to look at the moon, and he smiled rather sourly.

64

"It's a pity to go moon gazing at your age," he told her.
"But I suppose it's a symptom."

"What of?"

"The green sickness."

"What's that? It sounds very disagreeable."

He looked as if he meant it to be disagreeable. He insisted upon explaining himself with a bitterness which said to her, as plainly as possible, that she was not to suppose he was come to these moonlit mountains because he found them at all beautiful, or that he had any regard for the feelings of anyone else who might happen to think so. She felt that he deserved to be teased a little, and when he had done she said:

"What a ray of sunshine you are! It was the green sickness, I suppose, brought you up here. I thought at first you'd come to look for that sixpence we lost two years ago. I saw you running round in rings."

"How long have you been up here?" he asked suspiciously

"Longer than you. You disturbed me."

"Why didn't you say so?"

"I didn't want to be disturbed. I was busy thinking I was just going off quietly to a less crowded part of this mountain when you must needs interrupt me."

She was edging away from him. He saw suddenly that she was really afraid of him. Something that he had said must have hurt her. He laughed and asked what she was thinking of, whereat she took to her heels, ignoring his shout that she should stop. Wildly she fled down the hill, terrified, hearing him gain upon her, and seized by the primitive panic of the hunted. When, quite soon, he caught her, she screamed loudly.

"Damn you! Why can't you stop when I call?" he panted. "Now tell me . . . My God, Tessa! What's the matter?"

"Go away!"

65

"Have you got a handkerchief?" he asked presently. "Because I lent mine to Tony, who also needed it to-night."

At the mention of Tony her tears ceased abruptly. She turned away from him with a slight, wounded gesture, and was silent.

"This seems to be a habit in your family," he jibed. "If you've got a handkerchief, perhaps I'd better retire."

But he did not offer to go. He stood still, watching her intently, full of a sort of compunction. She was nearer than he liked to the rocky edge of the path, which dropped away to a sea of clouds below. He had an apprehension that she might spring over if he moved or touched her. He waited and was startled to hear her speaking in a low voice, almost to herself :

"Tony's been crying all the evening."

"Oh, Tony !" he exclaimed impatiently.

And he took a short turn along the path, away from her, as if he was afraid that she would force upon him some piece of information about Tony. He did not want to hear anything about Tony. She was a white flower, cast into the pit. He had been very fond of her when she was a little wild thing, like Tessa, a delicate, audacious creature, trapped now in the inevitable mill. No man endowed with heart and imagination could care to contemplate such a spectacle.

Lewis had both these commodities in a distressing degree. He spent his life in running away from them, and his cruelty was a kind of instinctive defence which he had set up against them. His refuge had been a sombre arrogance which denied to the rest of the world capacities for suffering equal to his own. He hurt his friends by way of demonstrating for his own satisfaction their comfortable insensibility. He really wished to convince himself that the majority of mankind is too stupid to apprehend anything keener than physical pain, and he nourished this illusion by a perverse frequenting of the company of people who were, for the most part, more brutal than himself.

Even so, he was not altogether safe. On the occasions when, despite his resistance, some sorrow of the outer world pierced the armour of his egotism, he was, out of all proportion, disturbed, simply because he would not admit that tears are the common lot. He fled from his own compassion.

He had done his best, of late, to avoid Antonia, and, if it had been possible, he would have avoided Teresa while she was thus shaken with the reverberations of her sister's evil fortune. Only that he could never fly from Teresa. She was a darling, simply, and must always be comforted, even though his own ineptitude had done the damage. She was the sweet exception to all the young, fierce generalizations with which he dismissed the world. He came back to her and took her arm and began to walk her up the hill again, consoling and protesting rather incoherently :

" Don't worry about Tony, my dear love. She'll be all right. She'll settle down. She's . . . she's just growing up. That's not comfortable. But it happens to everybody   God help them ! "

· Teresa seemed hardly to listen, but his last sentence caught her attention and she asked curiously :

" Do you believe in God then ? "

He thought about it and said that he did.

" Though I'm blest if I know what I mean when I say it. What do you believe, Tessa ? "

She hesitated and then told him how, a few minutes since, she had felt herself to be on the brink of a discovery.

" I didn't see anything," she said sadly   " That's because I'm so very ignorant. When I say God, I don't know what I mean. If I was Roberto I'd be better off, for I would know. I'd mean that God up there."

And she nodded towards the Calvary, standing out clear against the sky above them, guarding even in this lonely place the secret of man's eternal pain.

67

" You don't mean Him ? " she asked Lewis rather doubtfully.

Lewis replied, almost furiously, that he did not. He hurried her past the place and they wandered away, round the corner of the hill, to a sort of platform where they could look across at the Karwendal ranges, distant, icy, inhuman. Here, if anywhere, dwelt the divinity which they both worshipped. They sat down together on the grass and fell to talking in hushed tones as if afraid of disturbing the silent immensity of the night. He told her a number of things, he hardly knew what ; small, absurd things which he had seen and done in his wandering life. They caught her attention and soothed her distress. Soon she was laughing, and when at last they set off for home -she was skipping along beside him with the light-heartedness which usually belonged to her.

He had always thought her the pick of the bunch. She was an admirable, graceless little baggage, entirely to his taste. She amused him, invariably And, queerly enough, she was innocent. That was an odd thing to say of one of Sanger's daughters, but it was the truth. Innocence was the only name he could find for the wild, imaginative solitude of her spirit. The impudence of her manners could not completely hide it, and beyond it he could discern an intensity of mind which struck him as little short of a disaster in a creature so fragile and tender, so handicapped by her sex. She would give herself to pain with a passionate readiness, seeing only its beauty, with that singleness of vision which is the glory and the curse of such natures. He wondered anxiously, and for the first time, what was to become of her.

He knew.

He had always known, and until to-night he had taken it for granted. She was barely two years younger than that sister whose history she would inevitably repeat. Paulina, too, was fashioned for the same fate. Unbalanced, untaught, fatally warm-hearted, endowed with none of the stolid prudence which had protected the more fortunate Kate, they were both likely to set about the grimy business of life in much the same way. He knew what company they kept ; lust, a blind devourer, a brutish, uncomprehending Moloch, haunted their insecure youth, claiming them as predestined victims.

And to-night he discovered that he could not accept this He had always supposed, vaguely, that Teresa would spare his feelings by growing up quite suddenly of her own accord ; leaping into an experienced maturity which should demand no compassion. Now he grasped disturbing possibilities. While she was still so childish, so liable to be hurt, she ought to be safeguarded. She must be . . . she must be shut up. There were too many Birnbaums about. He scowled so dreadfully and marched her down the hill at such a pace that she wanted to ask him what was the matter now. He could not know that he was humming that song which Caryl had written for Kate, since he had heartily abused it. Yet the tune of it was on his lips :

Ich schau dich an und Wehmuth
Schleicht mir in's Herz hinein.

He need not have distressed himself so violently on her account. She was guarded by the constant simplicity of her young heart. He was himself the only man who could ever betray it, and she had been his, had he known it, as long as she could remember. Her love was as natural and necessary to her as the breath she drew, which is, perhaps, the reason why he divined nothing of it. And if he had known he would not, probably, have thought her fortunate. He would have wished her a better fancy. As it was, he thought that if she were his little girl he would put her into a convent. He knew little of convents, but he imagined that they were safer for girls than Sanger's circus. Lina, by way of precaution, ought to be in one too. It would be dull, perhaps, but there were, on the whole, worse things than dullness. He wondered whether he could, as an intimate friend, persuade Sanger to take some steps about it.

They parted at the house door and he climbed up to his room in the annexe. Teresa danced away to the girls' bedroom and remembered on the threshold that Antonia might still be crying there. She put her head round the door and saw that the room was empty. It was a large barn of a place with very little furniture. There was one bed for Kate and Tony and another for Tessa and Lina. Kate's clothes were packed away in a painted chest under the window, but the entire wardrobe of the other young ladies lay about permanently in heaps on the floor amid books, music, guitars, cigarette ends, cherry stones, and dust. Entering hastily, Teresa began to pull off her clothes and fling them down about the room as she promenaded in the moonlight, humming gaily her little duet with Lewis in "Breakfast with the Borgias." An old pair of Kate's stays lay across a chair and she tried them on, observing with dismal accuracy how far too ample was their fit.

"Yet Kate's not fat," she reflected, "it's I who am such a scarecrow. I wish I was Caterina."

This was a sister of Roberto who had helped with the house work in Genoa and who, at fifteen, possessed a figure which was the secret envy of Teresa and Paulina. In their eyes a southern richness of outline was the height of beauty and they deeply deplored their own angular contours. Teresa was still sitting in her brief chemise wondering sadly how to grow fat when Paulina sauntered into the room, and, after glancing twice behind her in a nervous way, began in a scared whisper :

"I say . . . Tessa . ."

"Yes ?"

Paulina shuffled her feet, unable to proceed.

"Yes ! What is it ?"

70

"Oh, Tessa !" cried Paulina with a little gasp.

" *Espèce d'imbécile !* What's the matter ? "

Paulina came quite close and clutched her arm.

" I'm frightened," she said in a very low voice.

" What ? Lina, what is it ? "

" Will you come, please ? "

" Come ! Where ? "

" Tony and I are frightened . . . at a very funny thing."

" A funny thing ! Where ? "

" In . . . in Sanger's room."

" Were you in there ? "

" No. We heard it. Outside the door."

The sacredness of Sanger's room was an unbroken law. No child ever ventured there without express permission.

" What did you hear ? "

" A funny noise. Do come, Tessa ! "

Teresa got up and made for her father's room.

" Is Caryl there, Lina ? "

" No," panted Paulina, still clutching her arm. " He's gone down to the valley to help Kate carry up the milk."

They climbed the stairs to the top landing, where they found Antonia and Sebastian listening intently outside Sanger's closed door.

" It's nothing ; he's just snoring," asserted Antonia.

" Listen, Tessa ! " commanded the boy.

She listened and wondered that the whole house did not tremble

" He's not snoring," she said. " He's sort of groaning. We ought to go in. He must be ill."

" Oh, we can't," objected Antonia. " Think what a to-do there was last time we did."

" Well then, get Linda. She doesn't mind annoying him."

" I thought of her," whispered Antonia. " I went to her

71

room to fetch her. But I didn't like to go in. She . . she's got somebody in there. I heard them whispering."

They waited some seconds longer and then Teresa, mastering her panic, stole downstairs to Linda's door and listened. She could hear nothing at first and was just going to knock when she caught a stifled laugh and knew that Tony had been right. She crept away, up to the others, who were waiting outside a room which was now dreadfully silent.

" It's stopped," breathed Paulina.

They clung together, straining for the least sound, and all started violently when a padding footstep crossed the room.

" That's Gelert," said Sebastian reassuringly. " I heard him whining a minute ago."

The dog whimpered faintly and gave two short yelping barks, ending in a long howl. Paulina whispered that it was funny that Sanger did not swear at him. But no voice came, only a furious scratching at the door and another appalling howl.

" I'm going in," Teresa stated. " Something funny must have happened. Somebody ought to go. I don't care if there is a row. Will you come, Tony ? "

But Antonia drew back crying that she was afraid. Teresa opened the door and was nearly flung down by Gelert, who bounded past them and fled howling along the passage. Sebastian pushed in front of her and advanced into the room, remarking :

" I'll come with you. I expect you'd like a man."

The lamp showed the floor all covered with sheets of music, and an overturned ink-pot and their father sprawling across the table at which he sat, his face hidden.

" He's fainted," suggested Teresa. " We ought to give him brandy."

Sebastian tugged at the heavy body, trying to turn it over, his white face flushing with the strain. They both pulled and the chair with Sanger in it toppled over and went thudding to the

72

floor. She bounded towards the table for a brandy flask, but her brother, looking at the face which gaped up at them, said :

" It's no use. He's dead."

" Oh, no ! No ! "

She knelt beside her father, pouring brandy into his mouth and over his face and over the music on the floor until Sebastian took the flask from her and led her from the room, repeating :

" It's no use, Tessa. He's dead. We must get people. I'll go and look for Ike. You fetch Lewis."

" Oh, Lewis . . . I must get Lewis . . ."

She whispered his name to herself as she crossed the moonlit space between the house and the annexe. She had to walk rather slowly because of the ache of terror which seemed to numb all her limbs. The stairs to his door seemed difficult to climb. She stood, fingering the latch, telling him what had happened. And Lewis, who had been lying half-dressed on his bed, jumped up and began to put on his boots. His coat he wrapped round Teresa, for she was shivering, and he took her back into the house. Her father's room was full of people. Roberto and Birnbaum were there, bending over Sanger's body, and Sebastian was trying to mop up the ink on the floor. They were all dazed and silent until Linda, in a pink silk wrapper with all her yellow hair blazing on her shoulders, burst into the room. Trigorin followed her. When she saw what had happened she turned a queer chalky white and burst into noisy, unrestrained weeping. Her loud cries rang through the stricken house so that Caryl and Kate, coming up from the valley, heard and knew that calamity had overtaken them all.

BOOK II
NYMPHS AND SHEPHERDS

CHAPTER VI

THE news of Sanger's death was received with concern everywhere but in England. Even there, however, the fact of it was reported in the newspapers. " Our Austrian Correspondent " wrote a little paragraph to say that Albert Sanger, by birth an Englishman and well known in Germany and elsewhere as a conductor and composer, had died at his residence in the Karwendal mountains. His best-known works were " Akbar," " Prester John," " Barbarossa," " Susanna," " The Mountains," etc. It was thus that the news of the calamity reached the Churchill family.

The unfortunate Evelyn had possessed two brothers, both distinguished scholars and both a good deal older than herself. Of these Robert, the least brilliant and the most commercial of the family, had become the principal of a flourishing university in the Midlands. Charles had never got further than being the Master of St. Merryn's, Cambridge, a position which half of his friends did not consider nearly good enough for him. The other half held that it had become important simply by reason of his holding it. He had a finger in a good many pies. He was acknowledged to be a great man by most of his generation : he looked so like one that he would probably have been able to impose himself on the world even if he had not possessed so many and such solid attainments. His gifted brother Robert could never succeed in looking like anything but an unsuccessful housemaster in a second-rate public school—a grey, harassed, precise gentleman, an invincible pedagogue, but without any of the more endearing traits of erudition, its antique polish or its unworldliness. He was always neatly dressed by the best of wives. Charles was the butt of a hundred caricaturists ; his large, unwieldy body, his little legs, his small eyes twinkling behind enormous glasses, and the grey, bushy hair which fringed his bald crown, were known all over the academic world. The contrast presented by his somewhat gross person and the fine delicacy of his wits formed the theme of endless anecdote. Being a widower he wore his clothes until they fell off him, for no better reason than that he liked them, had got used to them, and objected to change. His beautiful daughter, who kept house for him, indulged him in this and in every other whim. Early in her teens she had especially studied the business of being " the Master's daughter " and she did it very prettily, calling him " Sir " after the manner of a junior member of the College.

It was Charles who first discovered the paragraph about Albert Sanger. He came upon it at breakfast and read it through twice over with close attention. Then he took a large bite of hot buttered toast and glanced across the table at his daughter, announcing :

" Albert Sanger is dead, my dear Florence."

" Albert Sanger ? " said Florence, looking up absently.

She knew perfectly well who Albert Sanger was, but she was reading an article in her part of the paper on Poor Law Reform and she did not like to be interrupted.

" Your poor Aunt Evelyn's husband. My brother-in-law. Your uncle."

" Oh, yes," said she, with her eyes wandering back to the paper in her hand. " What about him, did you say ? "

" He's dead."

" Oh ! More coffee, sir ? "

" Not yet, thank you. I'd no idea he'd written so much. Just listen to this ! "

And he read the notice aloud to Florence.

"Susanna!" she said with some disfavour. "I heard it once, in Dresden. I didn't like it."

"No, my love. I daresay not. I never heard that Sanger ever wrote anything in the least like 'The Magic Flute.'"

Florence ignored this jibe, which was quite unjust, and proceeded to give reasons for her opinion of "Susanna." She invariably supported all her opinions with excellent reasons.

"I don't like subjects chosen from the Bible."

"The Apocrypha, Florence."

"Is it? Well, but it's the same *genre*. These semi-sacred operas are nearly always treated with levity and bad taste, I don't know why. They've no dignity."

"Not a very dignified theme," mused Charles.

"And it's dreary music. Ugly, you know, and noisy."

"Dear! Dear! Times change! Your aunt didn't find it ugly. She thought the world and all of him, poor girl!"

"That was a very odd affair," she commented thoughtfully.

She remembered her aunt very well. Nobody who had known the brilliant creature before her sudden and complete disappearance could possibly forget her. She played so beautifully. And she had a dashing, daring way with her and left vivid impressions of laughter and excitement and people crowding round to hear what she said. Her low voice and enchanting, husky laugh always seemed to inspire other people to make a noise; the dullest gathering, when she joined it, would gaily begin to sound like a party.

Florence was sometimes told that she resembled her aunt, but she could not feel it herself. She enjoyed a conspicuous popularity of her own, being clever, good-humoured, an excellent dancer and competent at games. And in appearance she was, perhaps, not unlike; she had the same clear, glowing brown skin, aquiline features, fine eyes, and neat, dark little head. She had the same choiceness of dress. But she lacked that overwhelming power to charm which Evelyn had possessed independently, as it were, from all her other qualities. Her simple, tranquil gaiety of manner, though pleasing, could never enslave a crowd. She was at her best in a small circle, while no stage had been too large for Evelyn in her prime.

Yet all that beauty and fascination had been squandered. There had been a time when Charles and Robert had hurried off to Germany, a discomposed interlude, full of telegrams and discreet family conclaves behind closed doors. Florence, a schoolgirl, could only guess at what had happened. She did not learn the full history until some years later, when she was considered old enough to hear it. By then it was too late to come at the whole truth. The runaway aunt had become crystallized into a legend, a subject for stock sentiments She was 'your poor aunt'! She had married the man Sanger, borne many children, had been, mysteriously, very unhappy, and died. That was all, and it gave very little food for the imagination. She remained, for her niece, a vital, audacious memory, an unlucky star which would not remain fixed in any charted constellation, but went streaming off, like a lost meteor, into the void.

"Poor Evelyn! Poor girl!" muttered Charles into his coffee cup. "That fellow was a brute."

"I expect," said Florence aggressively, "that she got a little bored with polite society. The world's a big place."

"So it is! So it is!" agreed Charles with a chuckle "And plenty of fine things in it. She needn't have selected a dustman with a turn for music."

He found it uncommonly difficult to keep a straight face when his daughter instructed him as to the size of the world. It was a point which had but recently attracted her attention, and, in his opinion, she had taken her time about coming to it.

"He had more than a turn for music," she said rather grudgingly. "What was the matter with him? What sort of class?"

"Upon my word I don't know. He was no class, as my old bedmaker used to say. No class at all. A perfectly uncultivated savage, that's what he was."

"A child of Nature?" queried Florence, who was really very curious about Sanger.

"Why yes! That's more like it. 'Red in tooth and claw.'"

"I think I like children of Nature."

"You never met any. I, for my sins, have met Sanger. I prefer a child of grace every time."

> "*Ne me laisse jamais seule avec la nature,*
> *Car je la connais trop bien . .* "

quoted Florence sapiently. "But I daresay he was encouraging after a surfeit of clever young men. I'm getting very tired of clever young men myself."

"You cannot possibly be more tired of them than I am," replied the Master. "But when you are my age you'll know that stupid young men are very much worse because there are more of them."

Florence was nearly twenty-eight. She referred to the fact continually, for she had begun lately to take her age as a serious matter. She had quite suddenly grown out of a lot of things which had till then contented her.

"It doesn't say if he's left a widow," said Charles, returning to Sanger. "But he's bound to. Some sort of a widow. And children! He had children of all kinds, as you might say. Some of them are your cousins. I hope they are all right! Remind me to write to your uncle Robert about them. We ought to make enquiries, I think."

He got up, folded the paper, and brushed the crumbs off his waistcoat. At the door he turned to say:

"Oh . . . and the bishop will be here to lunch. And I'm dining in Hall."

Florence, having finished her breakfast, went about her

81

household duties with the methodical but unenthusiastic efficiency of a woman who is too intelligent to neglect such things. Then she put on her hat and went out to practise string quartettes with some friends. Unlike the rest of her circle, she had no profession, but she was a busy young creature. Since she left College there had been so many attractive things to do, books, music, exciting vacations abroad, eventful terms, full of political meetings and Greek plays, charming friends and, above all, so much to discuss that she scarcely noticed the flight of time. But it had gone on quite long enough. Sometime, quite soon, she meant to put an end to it. She would settle down to some serious work, or, if she could find a man to her taste, she would marry. At present her most favoured cavaliers were in their sixties, and for a husband she wanted somebody younger than that.

As she sauntered along Chesterton Lane, lugging her unwieldy 'cello and nodding to acquaintances, she thought curiously about her aunt, and wondered if it was just mere boredom which had prompted her to fling her bonnet so effectually over the mill. She had abandoned this delightful existence for another, unimaginably remote. Was it possible to presume that she had grown tired of the refinements, the endless demands of civilization? Or had there been a force more potent than mere discontent? There had been, of course, the musical dustman. They had gone to Venice, which sounded the right sort of place, but it was difficult to guess how they had occupied themselves. They did not discuss architecture or pictures because Sanger was an uncultivated savage and could not, presumably, discuss anything. Florence actually paused in her walk, trying to figure out what one would do in Venice with a savage. Even supposing an ungovernable passion had brought them there, it seemed that they must have been without occupation for many hours, compelled to row about silently in gondolas.

And then it was impossible to guess whether Evelyn had ultimately repented of her bargain. The family assumed that she did, but, all things considered, their grounds were slender. It looked as though they found it more decent to suppose that she regretted her conduct. They had never been able to forget that the wedding had taken place after the Venetian expedition. But Florence, who was nothing if not broadminded, took little exception to that. The only really inexcusable thing that her aunt had done was to call Sanger a great musician.

Still, there must have been more in him than was apparent to Robert and Charles since Evelyn had chosen to remain with him. A lady of such spirit would not have done that unless she had continued to be satisfied with him. So thought Florence, who had never herself gone anywhere without a full assurance that she would be able to get back. To her it was clear that Evelyn had been happy, content in the life she had chosen, finding romance in it perhaps—a splendid quality, dark and violent and exciting, like a Russian novel. Indubitably the family must have been wrong.

A week later she found her father tearing his hair over a bundle of letters.

" Florence," he said, " you never reminded me to write to your Uncle Robert about those children."

" What children, sir ? "

" Your poor Aunt Evelyn's children."

" Oh, yes ! I'm so sorry. I forgot all about them."

" Well, I'll have to write now, for it's obvious that something must be done. I've a letter here from one of Sanger's other children. A nice fellow he seems to be, too nice to be a son of Sanger's I should have thought. The old rascal left nothing but debts, and our children—there seem to be four of them, all under sixteen—are left to starve, unless something is done for them."

And he handed her a letter from Caryl, an excellent letter,

deferential but independent. He had thought it right, he said, to discover the views of the Churchill family before making arrangements for his young half-brother and sisters. It appeared that he and Kate had got employment and were willing to contribute towards the support of the others if no other help was forthcoming. They would all be staying on in the Tyrol for another month, should Charles be disposed to communicate with them.

"Poor little dears," exclaimed Florence. "How old is he, do you think, and sister Kate ?"

"I should imagine that they are all short of twenty. But just read this ; it's amazing !"

He handed her a letter from Jacob Birnbaum, who began :

"As a very old friend of Albert Sanger I take the liberty of writing to you. He has left four children who are, I think, related to you. Sir, you may not be aware that his death has left them penniless. The eldest is now sixteen. They are not able to support themselves without help. A brother and sister they have who are able to work, and they have said that what is possible they will do. But these, too, are very young, and I hope you will agree with me, sir, when I say that it is too much for such young people to support the whole family. I do not think it possible. I do not know if you are able to help these children, but it is right that you should know how they are left. Before arrangements shall be made, your wishes should be asked. I have wished to pay for the little boy, for five years at a school. Also I will pay something if you should think of placing the young ladies in an establishment. I would like to do this ; I have loved their father."

"Well ! That's generous !" commented Florence.

"Humph ! I'll believe in his money when I see it," grumbled Charles. "I distrust the common sense of anybody who could be fond of Sanger. I shouldn't worry to read the next letter, if I were you. It's very long. It's from another friend of the family who writes the most surprising English. Very flowery! He condoles with me, in two pages, upon the loss of a unique brother-in-law, spends three more in explaining what a blow it is to the whole world, and ends up with his own bereavement and the privileges of knowing Sanger. At the end, just before sending me his distinguished sentiments, he mentions that he will subscribe £500 if anything is to be done for the children. He's crazy!"

"Where do they all write from?" asked Florence, looking at the postmarks. "All posted from Weissau! Is it a sort of settlement, do you think?"

"Heaven knows! One of us will have to go and find out They seem to be uncommonly free with their money. Personally I favour the gentleman who wrote the postcard. He's the only one who professes no regard for Sanger."

Florence looked at the postcard, which said :

"Are you thinking of taking the girls away? Somebody should. If money is short, I could let you have £50. That is all I've got, but I daresay I could send you some more some time.—Yours, etc., Lewis Dodd."

"Dodd!" she cried, in great excitement. "Lewis Dodd! Why! That must be the man who wrote the Symphony in Three Keys! You know, father! I'm sure you've heard me speak of it. I heard it last time I was in Germany. It's so unfair of you to accuse me in that wholesale way of not caring for modern music. Nothing could be more modern than that symphony, and I felt quite transported when I heard it. Fancy his being a friend of Sanger's! His music is immeasurably better. The second movement is quite beyond praise. It opens with a twenty-bar theme for strings which . . ."

"I know, my dear, I know. He seems to have got fifty pounds out of it anyhow."

"And he wrote this postcard!" she said, looking at it respectfully.

"Rather uneducated handwriting," was Charles's comment.

Florence turned it over. On the back of it was a picture of a bright blue lake surrounded by very black pines and pink mountains. A small blotchy steamer was crossing the lake in the middle of the card. Along the azure sky Mr. Dodd had written a postscript, an afterthought :

"It would be a good thing if they were put into a convent."

Charles was saying :

"But who can go? Somebody must. Somebody ought to be on the spot to settle things. And, as you know, I can't get away with this Commission coming next week."

"Of course you can't. But I can. I'll go at once and bring all the poor little dears back with me."

"Well, my dear, I'm not sure if I ought to let... "

"I assure you I can manage it perfectly. I'm not a child. I'm twenty-eight."

"I doubt if any woman could tackle it alone. We must see if your Uncle Robert can't go."

"Uncle Robert?" Florence looked very doubtful. "Do you think he would be any use at all?"

Charles began to laugh.

"Robert!" he shouted. "Ho! Ho! Poor Robert!"

Florence also laughed. It was their custom to be amused at Robert, who was supposed, in Cambridge, to be incapable of making or seeing a joke.

"No, it's not Robert's job," conceded Charles with a subsiding chuckle. "He was pretty well at sea, I remember, when we went out to look after your poor aunt. But this I will say for him : he has a good head on his shoulders where money is concerned. He'll deal with these philanthropic friends and their cheques."

"But really I think a woman ought to go. He won't know

a bit what to do with all these little girls. They are probably very startling children. There may be all sorts of things to be settled on the spur of the moment."

" Well then he can take your Aunt May with him, and she can deal with any widows there may be around."

" Widows ? "

" As I said, there is bound to be at least one. More probably there are half a dozen, if I know Sanger. But we'll hope they will have taken themselves off before Robert and May arrive."

"Oh, I should like to go !" cried Florence with sparkling eyes. " I should love to see Uncle Robert confronted with the widows. And I'm sure Aunt May won't go, for Hilda and Betty have the measles. If she can't, I think I really must."

" I don't like it, my love ; I don't like it. You'll have plenty to do later, when we get the children over here. I think Robert had better go by himself to fetch them."

" But I should enjoy going. I've always wanted to see the Tyrol in the Spring. And I'm so much intrigued by all these queer friends and . . . and their postcards."

" It's these queer friends and their postcards that I don't want you to see. I know what Sanger's queer friends are probably like. You may depend upon it, they aren't fit for a decent young woman to associate with."

" My dear father ! Do you really think I can't take care of myself ? After all I've been about a good deal, and I've met some pretty odd people. I don't suppose I shall be nearly as shocked at the widows as Uncle Robert will be."

" I daresay not. I'd rather you were more shocked. But you've lived a very protected life . . ."

" Father ! "

This was an unendurable accusation and she looked very much hurt.

" But you have, my dear ! And I can't help remembering

87

how my poor Evelyn—I was very fond of your aunt, you know, Florence . . . she was younger than you, of course . . . but . . ."

"That was quite different. I don't see what can possibly happen to me if Uncle Robert goes too."

"Well, well! We'll see. But you must really be careful in your dealings with any boon companions of Sanger's you may meet. They are probably the sweepings of the earth. Give me that postcard."

"All we know at present," she said, taking another look at it before she gave it up, "is that they are generous."

"On paper, Florence, on paper!"

"Really, sir, I think you are being unjustly suspicious. You are prejudiced because of Aunt Evelyn. But you know, I often wonder why you take it so for granted that she was miserable. We can't know. That sort of life is attractive to some people. There is something rather fine, when you come to think of it, about an uncompromising demand for freedom. Our life is, in a way, so cramped . . ."

He looked at her. From infancy she had always done exactly what she pleased with a persistence which belied the sweet placability of her manner. In the face of criticism or protest she exhibited none of Evelyn's flaming defiance, only a pleasant disregard which had always vanquished him. Sometimes, viewing her unswerving pursuit of a chosen course, he was compelled to liken her to something slow, crushing, irresistible—a steam-roller. Already he knew that he would have to let her go to the Tyrol, and she talked about her life being cramped!

"I think, my angel," he said, rather testily, "that you scarcely know what you are talking about."

CHAPTER VII

It was eleven o'clock in the morning and Kate was busy chopping suet in the kitchen when Lewis poked his head round the door. He asked if there was any breakfast left in a tone which suggested that he did not suppose so. He knew that she would not let him starve, but he wanted, if possible, to feel aggrieved.

"Of course there is," said kind Kate. "Come and sit by the fire while I make you an omelette. I hope this means you've had a better night."

"No," he said gloomily. "I slept a couple of hours late this morning, and that was all. I was dropping off just when it was getting light, and then those bloody cow bells roused me."

"Oh, yes ! They are driven up to pasture every morning at sunrise. We get used to it. Poor Lewis !"

"I've tried going to bed drunk, and I've tried sober. I can't sleep either way."

"It's shock," said Kate placidly, as she broke eggs into a pan. "Your nerves got upset when Sanger died. It's the same thing that makes Tessa and Sebastian sick. They've been sick, off and on, you know, ever since that awful night."

"I do know," he said with distaste. "It's impossible for anyone in this house not to know how sick Tessa and Sebastian have been, off and on."

She dished up her omelette and gave it to him. Then she said, as she brewed some coffee :

"It's been very upsetting for all of us. Now I do hope

89

you'll take a day off. You can't work while you are in this state. If you try, you'll only have another sleepless night."

" I can't stop in the middle of a thing."

" You'll do no good at it."

" Mind your own business, Kate."

She excused his incivility on account of his interrupted work and bad night. He was plainly exasperated. Sanger's death had thrown him off his balance, a thing which happened easily at any time. There was nothing to be done for a man in this state. Her father had always been like this, possessed by a furious despair, when any unlucky accident pulled him up short in the evolution of a new idea ; and her father had been serenity itself beside Lewis. She went on with her work, while he devoured his omelette, a savage, baffled expression on his white face.

Presently she said :

" I wish I could mind my own business. Here's Schenck wants me to join the company at once. I don't suppose he'll keep the place open for me. But how can I go until something's been settled about the children ? "

" Wouldn't be a bad thing if you didn't go. It's not a good enough show for you. Chorus work will spoil your voice."

" It's the best I can get," she said with a sigh, " and I must do something. I'll risk its harming my voice. With luck it won't be for long. Schenck has promised he'll give me something better the minute it turns up."

" I daresay ! He'll forget you in a fortnight. You see ! "

" Jacob will jog his memory, if he does."

" Jacob takes a brotherly interest in you, doesn't he ? " said Lewis sourly, as he scraped his plate with a piece of bread.

He was determined to break down Kate's obstinate good temper, and observed with pleasure that this last taunt had wounded her. She flushed, and he felt better.

" He's not a bad sort, Jacob," she pleaded. " He's been

very kind since father died. You know I think he's really worried about Tony, and sorry too."

" Sorry ! What for ? "

" He is anxious about what is to become of her."

" It's perfectly obvious what will become of her. Why couldn't he think of that before ? "

" Why not ? Oh, Lewis ! As if any of you ever did ! "

" I don't know what he thinks he's after now," complained Lewis. " I know they make the house intolerable. What with Ike and Tony sparring in one room, and Linda throwing fits in another, and Tessa and Sebastian finding themselves unexpectedly indisposed everywhere, the place isn't fit to live in."

" Well, then, why do you go on living in it ? "

" Me ? Oh, I stay here for safety's sake. There are no opportunities for folly on the top of this mountain ; and I'm just ripe to make a fool of myself if I get the chance. I'd better keep out of harm's way."

" Well, yes, perhaps," she said, considering his case.

" And I'd like, you know, to see Tessa safely settled somewhere. And Lina and Soo-zanne, of course. It would be a weight off my mind."

" Oh, what is to be done about them ? Some sensible person must take charge of them. No, Susan ! I can't have you bothering in my kitchen. Run along back to your mother."

" Mammy said I was to come down here for a bit," whined Susan. " She's getting up, and she's got Uncle Kiki in there, talking to her."

" Has she ? Well, you can go and tell her that I won't have you here, and the sooner she takes herself off, and you, and him, the better pleased we shall be. She's no business here."

Such an explosion was unusual in Kate, but she was indignant at the relations between Linda and Trigorin and their prolonged sojourn in the house. Linda was in no hurry to depart, as long as somebody else could be prevailed upon to feed her. She meant to remain until she was turned out, and she kept Trigorin, now hopelessly subjugated, at her side in case of need. They were resented by the whole family, but Caryl, now the master of the house, was too much harassed and preoccupied to meddle with them, and was, moreover, a little embarrassed by Trigorin's generous offers of money for the children. Kate said to Lewis :

" It's a bit too much the way he's always in her room ! "

" It keeps him out of all the other rooms," argued Lewis. " And that's something. For my part, she can have the flea-trainer as a gift, if she wants him."

" If only . . . Oh, Caryl ! Is that you ? Just come in here for a moment ! Here's Schenck written to say he wants me at once. What am I to do ? How can I leave the girls ? "

" Oh, that's all right," said Caryl cheerfully, waving a letter in his hand. " That's quite all right. You can go as soon as you like. There's a lady coming."

" A lady ! "

" Yes, and a man too. The children's uncle."

" I know," said Lewis. " The Master. The man we all wrote to."

" Did you write ? " asked Caryl in some surprise. " No. It's not him, but his brother. He writes this though. It's most liberal. He will take the children, Kate. He says we aren't to worry."

" But the lady," said Lewis, " is the wife of . . . which ? "

" Neither. She's one of their daughters By what I can make out they are coming quite soon."

" But is she married ? "

" How should I know ? He doesn't say."

" Because," said Lewis dubiously, " if she's only some one's daughter she may be quite a young lady. I wonder if she'll do."

" He seems to think so," said Caryl, glancing at the letter. " He says she'll advise about the girls' education. He says he recommends a good English school, but we must discuss it."

" A good English school ! " exclaimed Lewis. " That would be better even than a convent, I expect."

" But you say they are coming soon ? " began Kate. " They are never coming here ? Not here ! We've no room, for one thing."

" The man can have father's room. And if you are gone, the lady can have your place in the girls' room," said Caryl.

" Oh, no ! " Kate, thinking of the dirt and confusion in the girls' room, was positive that she could not put the lady there " And Tony has taken to having nightmares ; she screams and kicks anybody in the bed. They really can't come here, Caryl."

" Put the lady in Sanger's room," suggested Lewis, " and let the uncle share with Ike, and put Trigorin into Linda's room for good and all. That would be quite simple."

" Oh, but we couldn't . ." began Kate, solemn and shocked.

" Of course not," put in Caryl with a frown. " Linda must go. She must go at once before this lady comes. And then Trigorin will go too and we shall have lots of room."

" I wonder how much it will cost you to get Linda out of the house," speculated Lewis. " A good deal, if she guesses you have reasons for wanting her gone in a hurry. She . ."

" Look out ! " whispered Kate, " that child . . ."

But Susan had already slipped off to report the news to her mother. Lewis consoled them by saying that even if Linda did demand a bribe they could always borrow it off Trigorin.

" It's certainly a difficulty, their coming so soon," said Caryl. " But I shall be glad to see them. I'll hand the children over and get off. And Kate can go as soon as she has packed her things."

93

Kate went next day. To the last she was very much distressed to think of the discomforts which the lady would have to bear. She left a thousand instructions with Roberto, who gathered that Miss Churchill would want cups of tea and large cans of hot water every two or three hours. Caryl, who was much grieved at parting with his sister, decided to accompany her as far as Munich, where he would spend the night and return next morning. Lewis and the children came down to Weissau to see them off and the parting upon the landing-stage was very affecting. Kate broke down suddenly and began to sob with the strangled, speechless grief of a placid person tried beyond endurance. She stood, neat and stalwart, hiding a very red face in a clean pocket handkerchief, and grasping in her free hand a dress-basket and umbrella, until the boat came up and Caryl gently propelled her on board. He took her down to the little cabin, where she might recover herself, and neither was there to wave when the boat made off again across the still lake waters.

The children, contrary to their custom, did not cry at all. Kate's tears, the premonition that this tender and loving sister had abandoned them, shocked them too deeply. They watched the departing boat in silence, looking so small, pale and forlorn that Lewis, who was in a particularly vile temper, began to swear at them. This revived them wonderfully. They went and bought bulls'-eyes at the village shop and then demanded that he should take them for a row on the lake, which he did in an old boat almost as big as the ark. They paddled about in the sun, tried to race the steamboat on its return journey, passed the time of day with all the other pleasure parties, and finally took a bathe in full view of the chief hotel and the high road leading along the lake. To Florence, who was sitting on a bench by the waterside, they afforded much amusement, for they artlessly bathed in their skins and got dry in the sun.

" And one of them is quite a big girl too," she thought, as

94

Antonia climbed into the boat. "But it seems to be the thing here. And they look very charming, I'm sure."

She had just driven up from Erfurt with her uncle because the little train was so full that they could not get into it. Weissau was full of merry-makers as it happened to be a holiday. Along the lake road came a continual stream of people, all enjoying the lovely air. There were parties of sunburnt young men with knapsacks and ice-axes, and stout Germans in blue linen coats, and peasant girls in bright aprons and boys with flowers in their hats. Florence, who hated bank holiday crowds in England, loved this one; she could even tolerate the Innsbruck shop people drinking beer under the trees in the hotel garden, because they looked so new, and were all so happy, and the day was so fine. Nine out of every ten who passed were carrying great bunches of wild flowers. The noise they made, the guttural, good-humoured shouts of laughter, the twanging of zithers and snatches of song from the boats on the lake, were enchanting simply because they were strange, and not the high-pitched cockney and the mouth-organs of Hampstead Heath.

Though rather tired with her journey, and glad to sit still, she was completely happy. Robert Churchill had gone into the hotel to order lunch and enquire the way to the Karindethal, and she was pleased to be rid of him. He did not share her enthusiasm for this beautiful place. All the way from England he had grumbled at an enforced uprooting in the middle of term, and more than once he had tactlessly expressed a wish that his wife had been able to come with him. The crowds were, to him, a final source of irritation. The drive from Erfurt, through endless, mounting pine woods, had seemed most vexatiously slow and expensive. Now he only wanted to get on to their journey's end, transact their tiresome business, and have done with it.

Florence, on the other hand, was continually blessing the chance which had brought them. Her joy had begun early in the morning when she woke up and looked out of her window and saw, through the chestnuts of the garden, the flowery meadows of the Innthal, flanked by far blue mountains. They woke in her an expectant rapture which was crowned by this vision of the lake. She could not look at it long enough. Sometimes the water was so still and translucent that the boats, hovering over their reflections, seemed to float on green air ; and then an unexplained wind would brush it all silver, blotting out the lovely pictures of mountain top and sky which had rested for a moment on its clear, profound surface.

She hoped that the Sanger affairs might turn out to be unexpectedly complicated so that she might have to stay for a long time.

Presently she recognised, in a party approaching her, the delightful bathers in the old boat. They were walking up to the hotel, but there was no mistaking them. In their clothes or out, they attracted attention. Though dressed like peasants, they looked wilder than the wildest mountain people, and they were so much thinner. The young man was as lean as a scarecrow, and the children were mere shrimps. They walked, too, with lightness and pace, unlike the heavy-booted trudge of the Tyrolese. As they passed her she heard with surprise that they were talking English. The smallest of the girls was saying :

"Sebastian thinks he's going to be sick some more."

"Poor Sebastian," thought Florence. "He stayed in the water too long. Oh ! Sebastian ! Four of them ! It must be ! "

She started to her feet and pursued them, crying :

"Oh, I beg your pardon, but are you Sangers ? "

The five of them turned, gaped, but at last admitted that they were.

"I'm your cousin," she explained. "I'm on my way to see you. Didn't you get our telegram ? "

They shook their heads, perfectly dumb with surprise. She was, to them, a strange type, from her neat grey travelling hat and veil to her comfortable, expensive, low-heeled shoes. The children had never spoken to anything like her in their lives, and to Lewis she was an envoy from the past, the sort of lady who had domineered over his infancy but who was never allowed to interfere with him now. Sebastian was the first of them to recover. He gravely bade her welcome, and explained that they had been expecting her though they had received no telegram. Then they all shook hands.

"But how many of you are my cousins?" she enquired, looking them over and liking what she saw.

"All except him," calculated Antonia with a nod at Lewis.

"And you are . . . Caryl?" Florence spoke a little doubtfully, for as she framed the words she thought he looked rather too old to be Caryl.

"Oh, no!" he said hastily. "I'm no relation. Just a friend."

"Oh, yes . . ." she murmured in a tone that was a trifle chilly and yet not unfriendly.

"Mr. Dodd, Miss Churchill!" said Sebastian suddenly, recollecting the formula.

"Oh!" She sparkled and ceased to be chilly. "Is it Mr. Dodd? I think my father heard from you."

"Yes, I daresay he did," said Lewis, turning very red. "He . . . he hasn't come with you, has he?"

Florence suddenly remembered Robert and thanked heaven in parenthesis that he had been inside the hotel when his nieces were bathing in front of it. She explained where he was, and suggested that they should all lunch together before driving up to the Karindehütte. They moved along the path, still rather shy and embarrassed The children could not believe that they were really related to such a marvellous creature. They stared expansively. Lewis also took her in, a little more furtively, and she was put to it not to glance at him rather more than was necessary when she remembered that she was walking and talking with the composer of the Symphony in Three Keys.

"Bitter looking," she thought, ". . . and ugly . . . and so ragged! But what a charming voice! And very fond of the children, I think. Sixteen, isn't she? She doesn't look it. One must get rid of all one's prejudices, to understand them. I do believe he's shy!"

He was desperately shy. But he was making a great and unaccustomed effort to be agreeable because he was anxious that the strange lady should be pleased. On inspection he had decided that she would be a most excellent person to have charge of his friend Teresa. At first he had thought that somebody less young and charming would better fill the part; but the efficiency and ease of her manners, the elegant common-sense of her dress, soon convinced him. Only it was a misfortune that she should arrive plump into the middle of them like this. He had meant to urge the girls to comb their hair before she came, and now it was hanging in a dripping tangle down their backs. And Caryl and Kate were away. And, when they got up to the house, there would be Linda. He could not think what Miss Churchill would say to Linda. She might, possibly, be so much scandalized that she would pack up her gear forthwith and return to England without the girls. So he did his best to entertain her and make a good impression, speaking very quickly and stammering slightly as was his habit when particularly bashful. He explained how Caryl and Kate had gone to Munich.

Just before they got to the hotel he caught sight of two stout gentlemen coming posting along the valley road, who looked, as they got nearer, uncommonly like Trigorin and Jacob Birnbaum. They seemed to be in a great hurry and much agitated. He detached himself from the cousins and joined them.

"A telegram came, after you had all gone," panted Jacob

" We thought we should open it. And then we thought we should at once come down and tell you. These English cousins . . they will come to-day. We thought it might be better if we could warn you. You can tell them that they shall stay at the hotel."

" Too late," said Lewis. " They've come already. We've just met Miss. There she is."

" Ach ! " said the other two, surveying the distant Florence in alarm.

" And she intends to come up to the Karindehütte after lunch. She says so."

" Can we not say that there is no room ? "

" Sebastian told her that there was plenty of room. His neck ought to be wrung."

" Ach ! "

" What about Linda ? " asked Lewis anxiously. " Does she know ? What has she done ? "

" She has a headache ; she has gone to bed," Jacob told him.

" I think she will stay there. One cannot be so barbarous as to pull her out, unless the English uncle will attempt it."

" Then let her stay," advised Lewis. " They won't know she's there. To-morrow, when Caryl comes, somebody can take the lady a walk to look at the scenery, and we will eject Linda."

Uncle Robert had come out of the hotel and was being introduced to the children. Trigorin, who had been taking stock of the group, now broke in, exclaiming :

" But . . . but that young lady is clearly of the *beau monde !* *Femme parfaitement comme il faut !* It is unmistakable How is it possible that she should stay at the Karindehütte ? "

The other young men shook their heads. It scarcely seemed possible that she should. The prospect filled them all with a sort of panic.

CHAPTER VIII

FLORENCE found the young Sangers quite charming. Uncle Robert did not. The beauty of the Alpine Spring had not, perhaps, moulded his mind sufficiently ; he showed no signs of sharing the gay serenity of mood which enabled her to find everything at the Karindehütte either delightful or funny. His new nieces especially appalled him ; several times during that first lunch he had looked at their dripping hair and shuddered. And he had blenched at some strong expressions used by them when they burnt their mouths with hot soup. On the way out from England he had talked a good deal of inviting them for the Summer to his bungalow at Tenby, that they might have the advantage of association with his daughters, Hilda and Betty. But Florence doubted whether this invitation would now be given. He admitted that the Sangers were handsome children, that they looked intelligent and enunciated their words very well, but that was the best he could say of them.

Nor was he moved towards the three young strangers, who looked, to his mind, very like a trio of young ruffians. And in this she was more inclined to support him. Even in her eyes the magnificence of the scenery did not perfectly excuse the raffish vulgarity displayed by Birnbaum and Trigorin. They were, she knew, the types of which she had undertaken to beware. Their disrepute was written all over them, and, remembering her father's warnings, his absurd apprehension that she might be in danger from such people, she hardly knew whether to be amused or impatient.

Mr. Dodd she placed rather differently, though he was, in

appearance, the least presentable of the three. The Symphony in Three Keys gave him the right to look like a tramp if he pleased. She could, however, understand why Robert had condemned him as the worst of the lot. He had been ostensibly rude, while the others were only too civil. His eagerness to conciliate the lady did not carry him as far as politeness to the old gentleman, and Robert Churchill's manner to a young man did not recommend him to one who had thrown off all authority at the age of sixteen. To Florence he remained courteous, and when she relieved his worst anxieties by a timely chuckle at Paulina's language, he gave her a swift smile, so intimate and brilliant that it startled her. Then he turned grave again and offered her salad in his shy, hesitating voice, so that she hardly knew what to make of him. Yet the charm of that smile remained the most real thing in an amusing but very unreal day. After lunch they drove up to the Karindehütte and were regaled, almost immediately, with another meal, a sort of supper, which was eaten in an atmosphere of tense, strained embarrassment. Every member of Sanger's circus, from Roberto to Susan, had become aware of the necessity for good behaviour. Their desperate efforts were rather exhausting and Florence retired early to sleep, in tolerable comfort, in the room which had once belonged to Sanger.

She awoke next morning in a mood of remote, impregnable happiness and, while she dressed, she looked out, in the pocket Shakespeare which always travelled with her, that passage in " A Winter's Tale " beginning :

Thou'rt perfect then our ship hath touched upon
The desarts of Bohemia ?

The desarts of Bohemia was an apt description of the place as seen by poor Uncle Robert. For herself the wilderness was flowering like a garden. The words of the scene still ran in her head when, standing at the top of the stairs, she looked down

and saw Lewis and the children eating their porridge in the hall.
She remembered the warning :

> Go not too far i' the land !
> This place is famous for the creatures of prey
> That keep upon it.

The mysterious lady who lurked in her room with a headache
was very possibly a creature of prey. Nor did the term sit
badly upon the two fat youths, the Jew and the Russian. But
these amusing, pathetic children, this mild and bashful young
peasant, with his wonderful talent and his gentle voice, were
surely a nicer kind of inhabitant. They were with her inside
the magic circle where all the world was gay and innocent and
funny.

She had forgotten that creatures of prey have often an
engaging appearance. Nor did it occur to her that their charm
was largely due to the simplicity of their ideas. She, shackled
in every thought by traditions, ideals and scruples, was scarcely
safe among them. For if beasts of prey are rapacious, so were
these ; if they are unmerciful, so were these ; if they know no
law save their own ungoverned appetites, neither did these.

If she had come down a moment earlier she might have
heard some pretty language, for Lewis was out of humour. He
had passed a bad night, his head ached atrociously, and he had
come to breakfast in that sort of mood which always roused
Teresa to call him their sunbeam. He succeeded almost
immediately in making both the girls cry and even drew oaths
from the placid Sebastian. But it is to his credit that he
endeavoured to pull himself together when their lady cousin
appeared. He talked to her quite politely if a little morosely,
and presently began to explain the difficulty of producing
Sanger's operas, a subject which greatly interested him. The
general atmosphere of the breakfast table brightened and grew
more cordial. Florence knew a great deal about the difficulties

of producing opera.   In some ways she knew more than Lewis.
She told him all about a new scheme for the State financing of
British opera.

"I wonder that you had not heard of it," she exclaimed ;
and then, after a slight hesitation, she added : " It was started
by my friend . . . Sir Bartlemy Pugh . . ."

She had many distinguished friends and she always introduced
their names in this fashion in order, perhaps, to warn people
that they must be careful what they said.   But here her
caution was wasted ; Lewis, who shared Sanger's opinion of
Great Britain, showed no signs of having ever heard of Sir
Bartlemy Pugh, though as a musician he certainly ought.   Nor
was he quite as attentive as he should have been when she
explained the scheme for endowed opera.   He was just going
to be rather rude about it when Teresa averted the catastrophe
by breaking in and asking, with derisive solicitude, after his
dreadful headache.

Florence did not altogether like being interrupted.   She had
a good deal more to say and this untimely intrusion of a child's
banter broke up the conversation.   Before turning to another
topic she took silent stock of her young cousin, looking her up
and down, and, for the first time, mentally separating her from
the rest of the family   Decidedly she was the least attractive of
them ; in feature and person she might almost have been
called ugly, though improvement was possible if, on a richer
diet, she should take it into her head to grow.   The meagreness
of her under-nourished body contrasted ill with a certain
amplitude of scale in her face, which was round and firm, with
a finely curved chin and large, wide set eyes.   Her mouth was
small, and, though the fullness of her lips gave it generosity,
there was a sardonic turn about it which Florence did not like
to see in so young a girl.   And her tone, when she asked after
Mr. Dodd's headache in that pert way, was a great deal too
assured and intimate.

It was a pity that he had a headache. Florence was very sorry to hear of it and recommended that he should dose himself with aspirin and lie down in the dark till it was better. This he agreed to do, but first he strolled out with her upon the mountain side in order to put in a good word for the girls. He informed her diffidently that they needed looking after.

"Oh, but that's obvious," she agreed with a laugh

"It's not their fault, I mean," he said eagerly. "This house and the way they've been brought up. If you think at first that they are a little wild, you mustn't mind."

"Of course not. I think them such dears ! They shall all come back with us and I'll find a nice school for them and for Sebastian too. What a funny little boy he is !"

"Sebastian ?" He looked blank "A school for him ?"

"He wants looking after quite as much as the girls."

"Perhaps. But schools ! Some boys can't do with them. I doubt if he could. At the school where I was . . ."

He broke off, and she asked in amusement if he had not been able to do with his school. He told her that he had run away and that he believed Sebastian would do the same. He told her of Sebastian's recent excursion, which amused her very much, but she would rather have heard how old he was when he ran away and what he had done since. She steered the conversation in that direction and learnt eventually that he had been rather older than Sebastian, sixteen, to be exact, and that he had maintained himself by playing the cornet in a circus band.

"Afterwards," he said, "I wrote some pieces for that band to play. Circus music is a fine thing to write. Sanger says my style bears traces of it still."

"Like journalism," said Florence. "It will out, in an ex-journalist's work, however literary he is."

"I daresay," said Lewis, looking frightened.

He was not used to these parallels and hastened away lest she should try his wits too highly, with a headache and all. He spent the rest of the morning swallowing aspirin in a darkened room and thus missed the thrilling departure of Linda, Susan and Trigorin, which shook the rest of the house like a tornado.

Caryl, on his return, was much shocked to discover that the English relations, upon whom so much depended, had arrived with so little warning. Linda obstinately guarded her room, and it was Birnbaum who hit upon the strategem whereby she was finally ejected. He suggested that Trigorin should be asked to go, opining that Linda would incontinently follow rather than let him slip through her fingers. Caryl accordingly interviewed Trigorin and suggested, very civilly, that he might go down to the hotel since they were rather crowded by the unexpected arrival of the Churchills. It was a difficult thing to say, for they were all very much indebted to Trigorin, who had produced ready money, whenever it was required, all the time that he had been there. No one else had any, except Jacob Birnbaum ; and he, though he could be generous on a large scale, had a curious dislike of parting with small sums. Trigorin had provided them with food ever since Sanger's death and he had lent Kate her fare to Leipzig. But he was most considerate and agreed to go at once, with many polite regrets that he had, perhaps, already stayed too long. Before he went he sought out Uncle Robert and handed him a cheque for £500, insisting that it was a privilege to do anything for Sanger's children.

"Never again," he said sadly, "shall I have a friend like Mr. Sanger. It is a great sorrow for me that he has died so soon when I come here. We have no time to speak of music, as I have hoped. This shall be my return for the happiness I have had that he should ask me here. I cannot do anything else for him."

And he turned away, so much overcome that Robert did not like to argue the question any further with him.

Jacob was right. Linda no sooner heard the tidings than she sprang from her bed, declaring that she and Susan could not

105

possibly stay in a house where they were not wanted. If Caryl insisted on turning her out she would pack up and go. And pack she did, in a kind of cyclone which ravaged the house and left it strangely bare. The family were so much relieved by these symptoms of exodus that they never enquired what she took with her, and it was not until much later that they discovered all that was gone. She took several valuable autograph letters, a presentation clock, a gold cigarette case given to Sanger by Wagner, and every small article of value that came in her way, including all the spoons and forks. Two men, summoned from the valley, staggered off down the hill with her heavy boxes on their shoulders and, half an hour later, she quitted Sanger's house for ever.

She came downstairs just as Trigorin was taking leave of the family in the hall. She had dressed herself in the deepest black ; a long veil hung from her hat and hid most of her yellow hair. In one hand she held Susan, who was all tied up with black ribbons, and in the other she displayed a handkerchief with a black border. Roberto trotted apologetically behind her, bearing a green leather dressing-case. She looked so majestic and so mournful, so authentically widowed, that even Robert Churchill had a qualm of uneasiness and wondered if they were not treating her barbarously in insisting that she must go.

" Come Kiril," she said to Trigorin. " Let's go. If I'm turned out, I'm turned out, and there's an end of it. I'm not going to make a fuss, though there's some that might."

She had determined, apparently, to take no direct notice of the Sangers or the Churchills, and when Susan gave a loud sniff she said to nobody in particular :

" She's crying for her daddy, poor little mite ! You wouldn't think, the way she's treated now, that she was his favourite child. Come, lovey ! We aren't wanted here. Will you carry my dressing-case down the hill for me, please, Kiril ? Roberto has it."

Trigorin looked doubtfully at his own suitcases, but made an effort to comply. He was wrestling with the problem of picking up all three at once, and Linda was half out of the door when the scene began. Antonia darted forward crying :

" You mustn't take that ! It's my dressing-case."

" What's that ? " exclaimed Linda coming back. " You give it here *if* you please. It's mine. I've had it these five years."

" 'Tisn't yours," cried Antonia, snatching it up and dodging round behind Birnbaum. " It ought to be mine. It was my mother's."

" What's that got to do with it ? " retorted Linda. " It's mine now. Your dad gave it to me. You give it back directly ! "

" I won't ! You're a thief ! " screamed Antonia. " He never gave you my darling mother's things. You stole them."

" Tony ! Tony ! Let her have it," whispered Birnbaum. " It is old . . not worth fighting for. I will give you a better one."

It was indeed old—a perfect derelict of a dressing-case—so stained, scratched and battered that no self-respecting woman would have cared to claim it. There were marks on it of every haphazard journey taken by Sanger's circus for the past seventeen years. But, as Antonia held it up for the others to look, there was discernible a faint E.N.C. stamped on the side.

" Evelyn Napier Churchill ! " she said. " That's my mother."

Robert remembered it. He and Charles had given it to their sister on her twenty-first birthday ; he recalled, with a curious pang, the shop where they had bought it, and how they had decided that the clean, plain beauty of ivory fittings would suit the fastidious Evelyn better than the glitter of gold or silver.

" Yes, it is hers," he said. " But it must be quite worthless by now. Let her have it, Antonia ! "

107

He wanted, at any cost, to end an intolerable situation. So did everybody but the chief combatants. Antonia clung to the dressing-case and cursed Birnbaum for interfering. Linda, having worked herself up into a fine rage, was prepared to let them have a piece of her mind.

"I don't leave this house without it!" she shouted. "You call me a thief? What are you, I should like to know? You turn me out. You treat me as if I was a tart. What better are you? Tell me that. And what better was your mother? Think I don't know. . . ."

"Tony! Don't listen to her! Don't answer her!" exhorted Florence, for Antonia was preparing to fly at Linda. "Come away!"

"Don't you worry with her, miss," advised the woman. "She's not fit for you to touch, not by a long chalk. She's an artful little bitch and no better than what she should be. You ask Mister Birnbaum there if . . ."

"Here's the bag," cried Caryl, snatching it and hurling it at her, while Florence and Birnbaum forcibly held Antonia down. "Take it and go for goodness sake! You'll miss your train."

"Yes, madam! You'd really better hurry," advised Uncle Robert, who, watch in hand, was trying to be impressive and gentlemanly.

"Go?" finished Linda. "Yes, I should think I am going! I wouldn't stay here for anything in the world, not with all I've seen going on. But if you're all so particular I wonder at you for bringing the young lady here, for it's nothing better than a dirty case house and never was."

And with that she took herself off. Trigorin, after some frenzied antics, managed to pick up all the baggage and followed her without further farewells. Three times during the first hundred yards did he drop one of his burdens, while the family, utterly shattered by the storm which had gone over them, watched him from the window. Sebastian remarked with some glee that he had panted and puffed a good deal when he first came up, but that he would find going down even more strenuous. Linda's black, fluttering draperies disappeared round the first corner and a sort of sigh passed through the group of children. The resolute enmity died out of their faces; they had detested her for eight years and were now prepared to forget her in as many minutes. When, for the fourth time, Trigorin dropped something, kind Caryl would stay no longer; he went out and carried the disputed dressing-case to the bottom of the hill where a peasant's cart was awaiting the travellers. On their way down Trigorin said several times how sad it was to end a visit which one had greatly desired to make.

Up at the house Florence was the only person who could not share in the general rejoicings. She was conscious of having lost a little of the morning's enchantment. She could not be quite sure, now, that everything at the Karindehütte would invariably amuse her. The struggle over the dressing-case had been rather horrible in the light which it cast upon the more intimate history of Evelyn Churchill. Nor was there anything funny in the reflection that Evelyn's children had grown up under the dominion of a foul-tongued harpy. It was no wonder that nice Mr. Dodd felt anxious for them; she began to understand his assurance that " the household " was not their fault

But the harpy had now flapped her black wings and sailed away and the creatures of prey about the establishment were fewer by two, not counting Susan, who was obviously a harpy in embryo. The young Jew remained, but he was not really so bad, and was, moreover, quite genuine in his offer to pay for Sebastian's education. It was determined, in a consultation among the elders that afternoon, that the four children should be removed immediately to England, and, in the Autumn, should be put to school. Robert could recommend very highly a small preparatory school for Sebastian, and Florence was all for sending the three girls to Cleeve Ladies' College, where she had received her own education. Robert had his doubts about the wisdom of this, but, since his chief objection was that no reputable establishment would take them, he was overruled. Florence knew Cleeve ; she vowed that, as nieces of Charles Churchill and daughters of a musician of dawning fame, they would be welcome at her old school. Cleeve, she said, would overlook a great many shortcomings in such a case and her father would use his influence. There seemed to be more real difficulty in the task of persuading the girls to go. They pulled very long faces when they were told of the arrangements which had been made for them.

" But you will enjoy it," said Robert encouragingly. " You will make plenty of little friends and you will learn how to play games."

This mystified them very much ; it was the last thing they would have expected to hear of any school. They explained that they knew how to play games. He tried to convey to them some idea of the importance of games in an English school and they became very dismal indeed. Antonia stoutly declared that nothing would induce her to play games. Her sisters, being children, might submit, but she was grown up and would have everybody know it. She was too old to go to school.

" In England the big girls all play," Robert assured her. " My little daughter, Hilda, is older than you ; she is seventeen. And she loves her school and doesn't want to leave it. She is captain of the school hockey."

The four looked at each other, and though they were too courteous to say so they feared that their cousin Hilda must be a terrible simpleton. Sebastian said at last :

" Well, thank you very much. We'll think it over. I suppose it will do if we let you know by to-morrow ? "

" Let us know ! What ? " asked Robert gaping.

" If we want to come. Of course we see it's most kind of

110

you to think of it, don't we girls ? But we'd like a little time
to consider it, you know."

" If you want to come ! My dear boy ! You'll do what
you are told, let me tell you. It's no question for you to
decide."

" I think it's more important to us than to anybody else,"
argued Sebastian. " We may not like going to school."

" That will be excessively foolish of you, but I doubt if it will
otherwise have any importance whatever."

" We don't belong to you," stated Sebastian, still pleasantly
reasonable. " I mean, there's no law, is there, to give you
power over us ? Nobody made you our guardians, did they ? "

" Er . . . hmph . . um ! " snorted Robert, who had no
answer ready.

Florence stifled her laughter with a violent effort, for she
knew that this question of legal guardianship was, to his cautious
mind, a grievous problem. She made a sign to him and said :

" Yes. Talk it over and we'll discuss it again to-morrow."

" We'd like to consult our friends," explained Teresa.

" Your friends ! " exploded Robert. " May I ask what
friends are those ? Mr. Dodd ! He has nothing whatever . . ."

Again Florence checked him.

" I expect you'll find Mr. Dodd thinks it a very good plan,"
she said. " But do ask him."

Later she said to her uncle :

" It's much better to avoid trouble if possible. They'd
better think that they are going to school of their own choice ;
it will dispose them to try and adapt themselves. And it will
do them no harm to talk it over among themselves."

" I don't agree with you, Florence. It's high time they
learnt to do what they are told without cavil or question. They
haven't the slightest idea of discipline."

" They'll learn all that at school, poor dears ! They don't
recognise the shades of the prison house yet ; they think they

111

are their own masters. It will come by degrees. I don't want any battles till we have got them all to England."

"I never saw more impudent, ill-mannered, disobedient young people in all my life. It's not their fault of course. But their language, my dear Florence, is outrageous ! And what morals can they have growing up in this place ? 'Pon my word, I doubt if we are justified in turning them loose in decent schools. I wouldn't have Hilda associate with that girl Antonia for the world."

"She struck me as no worse than the others. Now Teresa . . ."

"She's the eldest. And she's spent her life in the society of depraved people. You heard what that woman said."

"That woman," said Florence with a shudder, "was a horrible, obscene creature. I don't think you need quote her."

"It's quite probable that she spoke the truth for all that. Look at the sort of people the poor child has knocked about with. This Dodd . . "

"I think better of that young man than you do," said Florence. "And I can tell you this. He's most anxious that they should go to school. I'm sure he'll advise them sensibly about that. He's devoted to them."

And she was right, for he did advise them very sensibly. They had, however, no opportunity for consulting him until late in the evening, for he was away all day in the mountains trying to walk off his sleeplessness. When he came back he brought with him a little Persian kitten which he had bought at a farm as a peace offering to the girls for his recent ill-humours. They were in bed so he took it up and gave it to them.

"Oh, Lewis," began Teresa at once, "wait a minute ! We want your advice. Florence says we have to go to school in England."

He sat down on the edge of the bed where Teresa, Paulina and the kitten lay curled up in a little heap.

"I expect you'll like that," he suggested.

"Oh! Do you really think we shall? Tony! Do you hear that? Lewis thinks . . ."

"Yes, I heard," mumbled Antonia from the other bed. "I don't want to hear what Lewis thinks, or what you think, or what anybody thinks. I shall decide for myself."

And she hid under the bedclothes.

"I think it would be a very good thing," Lewis told them. "Perhaps you won't like it at first. You may find that you are a little different from the other women, but you must try to get on with them! You must indeed. It's a good thing, you know, to be like other people if you can manage it. It's happier . . ."

Teresa thought this such a mighty odd thing for Lewis to say that she sat up and kissed him, murmuring:

"Who'd have thought it!"

He sat a little longer, stroking her fair hair and feeling suddenly quite wretched at the idea of parting with her so soon. He had not thought of separation in his anxiety for their welfare. But perhaps he might come to England and pay them a visit. He suggested this and they brightened up: school as he described it did not sound so very bad after all. In another half minute he was meaning to go across to his room in the annexe and begin upon his arduous night's toil. But he kept putting it off, though all the time, as he solaced himself with Teresa's company, his mind was circling round the labour to which he must shortly address himself. To stay and stroke her hair was a little respite. He was still there, staving off the evil hour, when Florence came with a candle to bid her cousins good-night. She heard him say:

"And then I expect they'll teach you needlework. And you'll make yourselves the most lovely dresses."

"Oh, Florence," cried Teresa. "Here's Lewis says we must certainly go."

Antonia poked up her head in order to see what was happening. She had a faint idea that Florence might not be pleased to find Lewis there, although he was giving them such good advice. But of this there was no sign ; Florence opened her eyes for a second or two and then smiled at him very kindly. He, on the other hand, was visibly deranged. Antonia observed with amusement that he was staring at Miss Churchill as though he had never seen a young lady in her dressing-gown before.

And it was improbable that he had ever seen one quite like that. She was lovely. Her dark plaits, her mocassin slippers, the Paisley shawl flung round her blanket-wise, all gave her a boyish look, like a decorative, fairy tale Red Indian, scarcely older than Antonia. Lewis was positively frightened. He had thought her beautiful before, but he had thought it without emotion. Now he was aware of a most disturbing revolution in his system ; it was as if the terrific energies scattered by the shock of Sanger's death were again focussed upon a single object, as if the storms of the past weeks had been but the prelude of this significant event. The thing took him perfectly unawares. He jumped up, stammered a good-night to them all, and withdrew hastily before his confusion should be betrayed.

That night he did no work, though he flung up and down his room for hours, endeavouring to think of his lost Concerto and haunted instead by quite other visions. He wished that he had gone away before this cousin of Tessa's had come to disturb him. He had told Kate that he was just ripe for folly ; at no time in his life had he been overwise. But never, never had he fallen a victim to so inconvenient an obsession as this.

CHAPTER IX

FLORENCE woke every morning, rapturously, to the tune of cow bells. For a few minutes there was a great din all round the house as the beasts were driven up to pasture, and the shouts of the herd boys echoed across the clear dark air in the valleys. Then the scattered tinklings grew fainter as the cows strayed across the mountain.

She had dragged her bed close to the window, and from her pillow she could see the pale pink tops of the range opposite and the long shafts of light which the rising sun sent down their steep sides, spearing right down into the hidden mysterious night below. Day began at the Karindehütte a full hour before it visited the valley farms.

Never, since her childhood, had she lived so completely for the present, grudging every passing moment that brought her nearer to the inevitable return.. It was an interval of utter contentment which seemed to have no relation to the rest of her life. She had a curious feeling as though this sensation of exquisite irrelevance was the result of living so high up ; she was beautifully isolated on the top of her mountain. When she went back to England she supposed that she would take up again the threads of her real life, her elaborate interests and pursuits, just where she had dropped them. She could not hope to take back with her the inconsequent gaiety, the freedom of spirit, which had come to her as she sat by the lake at Weissau. They belonged to the place. Nor did she contemplate a return, another year and in other company ; some joys can never be recaptured. She was so much aware of the impermanence of her pleasure that she was no sooner awake than a longing would seize her to jump up and run out into the mild warmth of the early sun. She was often dressed and ranging over the pass before Roberto, crying ' *Scusa !* ' burst into her room with the enormous tea-pot which he believed Kate to have said that the English lady would require every morning at seven o'clock.

She was preparing to begin the day with one of these early expeditions when Antonia knocked at the door and asked if she might come in and talk a little.

"What lovely brushes !" she said, inspecting the dressing-table. "You do keep your things nicely. Linda had gold ones, but she never washed them. Listen, Florence ! I don't mean to go to school. Why should I ? I'm grown up."

She was wearing a very short and ragged nightgown and looked anything but grown up, but Florence was too wise to say so. She agreed sympathetically that it would be more difficult for Antonia than for the others.

"Lewis says we'll like it. But what does he know about it ? He's never been to a girls' school himself."

"What sort of people does he belong to ? " asked Florence, who could not resist an opportunity of finding out more about him.

"Oh, I don't know. He never speaks of them. I only heard him speak of his home once, and then he said they had boiled mutton and caper sauce every day there. I expect that wasn't true."

"Still, even if they had it every other day, it might seem rather intolerable to a budding ascetic . ." mused Florence.

"A budding . . . ? " began Antonia.

But she did not ask what an ascetic was, in case Florence should say she was ignorant and needed to go to school. Instead she cried appealingly :

"You know . . . I should just hate to play hockey."

116

"Well, my dear, if you really hate it very much, we might arrange something else for you. But I think you must go somewhere to learn to earn your own living and be independent. It's not easy for unqualified women to get posts."

"Why should I earn my own living ? " asked Antonia in great astonishment.

Florence, with considerable delicacy, brought her to understand her penniless and dependent situation. She became very thoughtful and then asked slowly :

"But who will pay for us at school ? That will cost a lot."

"Mr. Trigorin and Mr. Birnbaum have been very generous. . . ."

"Ike ! " She swung round in amazement. "He's paying ? " "Ike ? "

"Jacob Birnbaum. We call him Ike. You say he's paying ? "

"Yes. For your brother . . and for you, in part, as well."

"Christ ! I won't have it ! "

"My dear child ! What do you mean ? "

"I won't go to England if Ike pays. I won't swallow any food that Ike pays for. I'll starve. I'll . . ."

"What has he done ? "

"Done ? It's what he is ! He's a stupid beast. He's cruel ! "

"Why, Antonia . . ."

"I hate him. I wish he was dead."

"Has he . . . has he treated you badly in any way ? " asked Florence very gravely.

Antonia pulled herself up and said loftily :

"Oh, no ! He couldn't. He's too stupid. But I won't have his money. He's a dirty Jew."

"But why are you so indignant ? He was your father's friend."

117

" That's nothing. So was Sanger a beast . . . often. And I'm not indignant. He's beneath my notice. I never think of him at all. When I look at him I just laugh."

" Well ! You're a difficult girl to understand."

" He thinks I ought to go to school, does he ? " stormed Antonia. " He thinks I don't know enough and ought to be taught some more ? He thinks a deal too much. He's a walking mountain of impudence, that man ! He shall hear what I think about it before he's an hour older. School ! "

She made for the door, but Florence held her back, exclaiming :

" My dear Tony ! He's probably asleep at this hour."

" Oh, no ! He gets up early and helps Caryl and Lewis sort Sanger's papers."

" Well then, do put on some more clothes, if you must go and insult him."

" Clothes ? I've got a nightgown."

" That's not enough. Really and truly, Antonia, you must be rather more decent in your language and deportment. He'll only tell you that you are an ignorant little girl who needs to go to school because she doesn't know how to behave."

Antonia was struck by this view. She marched off to the girls' room and, to the astonishment of her sisters, made an elaborate toilet. She scrubbed her face and hands and combed her hair. Then she selected from the common wardrobe on the floor a passably clean frock and apron. Jacob, who was alone in Caryl's room when she came to him, was as much surprised by her inordinate neatness as by her offering to address him. For some days past she had refused to answer when he spoke to her. She began, as carelessly as she could, balancing on the table and swinging her long legs :

" Well, Ike ! I hear you think I need to be sent to school. That's lovely and generous of you, but as it happens I didn't ask for your kind charity. You can keep your wonderful money,

118

that you think such a lot about, for some other girl. And be careful how you go spending it, for it's the only thing that makes anybody look at you."

" You will go to school if your uncles wish it," he said in a surly voice.

" I tell you I'd sooner be dead than kept by your money, so there ! "

" And you shall tell this to the English uncle ? " he jeered.

" I will."

" He will say, but why is that ? "

" I'll tell him. I'll tell him everything."

" Then he will send you away, as he sent Linda. He will throw you out of the house. Your lady cousin also . . ."

Antonia turned pale. She still, despite the warnings of experience, believed what was said to her. She said, a little uncertainly :

" I'll tell them it wasn't my fault. I'll say you made me so drunk I couldn't help myself. You know you did."

" Did I force you to stay a whole week, eating, drinking, spending my money ? That was your own wish. You could have left me at any time. They will ask why you did not."

" I stayed just to show you how little I cared . . ."

" Tell them that ! And see what he will say."

" I don't mind if he does throw me out. I hate everyone here."

" How will you keep yourself ? Will you work ? I think not. You will starve."

She had a private idea that she could without difficulty become a famous prima donna. But the constant raillery which her family poured upon this ambition had taught her to keep it to herself. She was tired of hearing Kate exalted. She said at once the thing which she thought most likely to torment him :

" I shall get another lover and live with him."

Jacob, his large face pale with fury, was silent for a few

119

seconds, hesitating between a choice of outrageous replies. Then he said with a sort of anguished bitterness :

" You will run away from him after a week ? "

" No, I shan't. I'd have stayed longer with you, only I wanted to be back for Sanger's birthday. I was enjoying myself."

" But were you ? Yet you would not come back ? " he cried, catching at a new idea.

She said instantly that she would, mocking his self-flattery in supposing that she hated him. No ! She would not run away again, unless she met somebody nicer. That might, of course, be soon.

He reflected that if she came to him a second time she would not run away because she would have nowhere to go. Sanger's circus, her only home, was breaking up. She would be, this time, defenceless and altogether at his mercy. He could make her pay a little for her insolence. Since she would not love him, he might find some relief in seeing her suffer. The idea of all that he could do to her filled his imagination with a dark happiness. He turned his back and began tying up bundles of papers, afraid to look at her lest she might read his purpose in his eyes and run away.

" I would rather be with you than in England," she said.

" That is well."

" And I like München."

" You will not go there ; it is too near. Your uncle might follow us. This Summer I go to Smyrna and you shall come with me."

He stole a glance to see how she took this, but was obliged to turn quickly away, she looked so young and so white.

" Oh, yes . . ." she agreed in a very little voice. " You're sure that . . . that it would be quite convenient to you ? "

" I wish it," he said grimly.

" Because . . . if it wasn't . . . I expect I could get work or something. I'll only come if it's convenient to you. I don't want charity. I should think I'd be rather in your way in a place like Smyrna. What did you say?"

He had thrown down his bundle with an oath of renunciation. For he could not do it. Two minutes was the longest space of time in which he could really wish to treat her unkindly. Struggle as he might, he could not help but love her dearly. He gave it up. Cruelty was not natural to him, in any case, and he could often have wished himself a baser man than he was, bewildered by the strife between his appetites and his intrinsic benevolence.

For an instant he stood quite still, regarding curiously the abyss which had for a moment invited him, as a man on the edge of a precipice will play with the idea of a plunge and pass on unscathed. Then he wrenched his mind away from it and forgot it. He said :

"We will not go to Smyrna. You must not think that your uncle will turn you out of the house. I was laughing at you. You need not be afraid ; he will protect you. And your cousin will be sorry for you, I think."

"Fool !" taunted the almost vanquished devil within him. "Imbecile ! You have lost her."

"I should advise," he continued valiantly, "that you confide in her. It is a pity that you had not such a friend earlier."

"Florence !" cried Antonia, blushing as red as a poppy. "I couldn't possibly tell her."

"Then tell him. He will never turn you out. I am the person whom he will blame."

"You ? Aren't you giving him a lot of money for us ? I don't see he'll have any business to be blaming you."

"He will think that I am a villain. And that is right. I have seduced you."

"Really, Ike, you mustn't talk like that. I don't blame you for that, indeed I don't. There's quite another thing that I can't forgive you for ; not that. You mustn't worry."

121

"I thought," he said, almost to himself, "I thought, if it was not I, it would be some other man. I never meant you harm. How could I know that Sanger would die and leave you with no home? Now what is to be done?"

"There's nothing to be done. It's no concern of yours, Ike. It wasn't your fault that Sanger died."

"But it is my concern. I wish that you would go to England as your uncles have decided. It is safer . . ."

"That's what Lewis says. But I can't let you pay . . . after . . ."

"Why not? How shall I ever understand you?"

She was silent, but she looked more friendly. He still had a hope that he might persuade her to go to England. He shyly ventured to assert a fact which had dominated his horizon since his first conscious thought.

"I have so much money!"

"Have you always?" she asked with vague interest. "Or only sometimes, like us. I know you had a lot when I was in München."

"Always," he said, solemnly. "More than I can spend."

It meant very little to her. He had seen that in Munich, and it had continually exasperated him. For though she had snatched at the good things he gave her, he could not persuade himself that he had bought her. She would take nothing away with her, scorning his lavish offers of clothes and jewels. It was the Sanger spirit of conviviality which brought her. She would have been quite as ready to enjoy herself if he had been a poor man; if he had lodged her in a garret and taken her to the cinema instead of the opera.

It was this lordly relish for life, a fiery abundance of spirit enriching everything in its orbit, which had first attracted him to Sanger. He now saw it repeated in Sanger's children. To himself money had always meant too much; it pervaded his entire existence, intervening and robbing him of the full fruits of experience. It had furnished him with all his assets, his pleasures, and the position which he held in the musical world. In moments of depression he was inclined to fear that it had provided his friendships ; he used to wonder how many people would have tolerated him without it. He had the instincts of a patriarch and would have liked to beget children and found a family, a household, but he had purchased so many women that he despaired of finding one who was not venal. His short association with Tony had taught him that she was neither sensual nor mercenary, and that, in her least thought, she was guided by an impulse which had been denied to him. She demanded only to feel ; she asked of life only that it should play a tune to her dancing. A queer wife she would be ! A darling wife ! The dearest company in the world for the man who could win her love. To have her confidence, to cherish and protect her and give her everything she wanted, to set safe-guards about her incautious, headlong career, seemed to him a most satisfactory ambition for a man. His own money would be a benediction, if he could spend it so.

" You should get a husband who will be kind to you," he told her. " You must not waste your beauty always upon lovers. You should have a home and little babies of your own."

She gave him a quick look under her eyelashes, but said nothing. She had fine, slender hands like her mother. He stood looking at them now. In many ways she was like Evelyn ; she had that spark which sets men aflame. It was not only in her beauty, it was in her voice, her laugh, her smallest gesture. It was her portion in that dower of genius which belonged to all her kindred ; she carried it like a torch. Beside her he felt like a senseless clod of earth, lacking life, for she was like fire, wonderful, dangerous, necessary. He thought of the children he desired and it seemed to him that they, too, would be dull creatures unless they were also hers. He was wearied of his life. He was no longer young, now that his friend Sanger was dead. He had exhausted the distractions which wealth could bring him ; he had nothing to contemplate now but the things that he could never do, the limitations which age would increase. She seemed to offer him escape. He wanted to make her his wife and get children by her, new patterns of his youth, bolder creatures than himself, who would accomplish things that were beyond his striving. Yet she hated him. He had wronged her. The love which should have saved him had made him wretched. He said imploringly :

" Could you not marry me ? Indeed, I love you. I would try to make you happy."

" Ike ! " She sprang off the table. " What's come over you ? Are you drunk ? "

" I am not. I mean it. I want you for my wife. Marry me, and then you need not go to England. You cannot wish to go to England. I would give you . . ."

This invincible instinct for a bargain betrayed him ; he knew it, almost as soon as the words passed his lips. Quick alarm leaped into her eyes and she moved away from him, asserting :

" I want to go away and never see you again."

" Oh, Tony, tell me ! You torture me. Why are you still so angry ? You say that you can never forgive me ; and then you say that I must not blame myself. Why can you not forgive me ? "

" For being such a fool ! " she said furiously. " For being so stupid. Couldn't you have seen . . ."

Her lovely eyes filled with tears. She wept for a few minutes, quietly and bitterly, almost with resignation. He would have soothed and comforted her if he had known how, but he dared not touch her lest she should turn on him. He watched her with a torn heart as she sobbed, a little turned away from him, her face hidden in her apron. Presently she made an end of it and looked round, exclaiming in surprise :

124

"Why, Ike! Are you crying too?"

He discovered that there were tears on his own face, and, producing a silk handkerchief, he mopped them up in some embarrassment.

"What's the matter?" asked Antonia tactlessly.

"*Du lieber allmächtiger Gott!*" shouted Jacob. "Have I not said? You torture me. Always you are angry and you will not say. How shall I know what you are thinking? You drive me mad."

"Really you are very stupid! Listen! I'll tell you. When we were down in Genoa, and you asked me the first time to come to live with you, I said I wouldn't. You remember?"

"I remember."

"And then I said I would. Do you know why? Because you looked so very sad. I was very fond of you, then; I wasn't going to have you as unhappy as that. You really looked as if you didn't know how to get on, unless I came. That made me more fond of you; I mean, that a very clever person like you with everything so grand as you have things, should need anyone like me to look after him. Do you understand that? But then you annoyed me by boasting about how wonderful everything was at your house and all the things you'd give me. You didn't think that I was going to give you anything; you didn't seem to think I could love you. Really, I might have been Linda! You quite disgusted me. I thought you didn't deserve I should come. And I meant to tease you a little before I had it out with you."

She looked ready to cry again. Jacob, seeing dimly the quarter whence the blow was coming, sat down by the table and hid his face in his hands, bidding her, in a muffled voice, to continue.

"I thought . . . I thought I'd stay a week, and to punish you I'd never be at all kind until just the end. And the last day, when you would be thinking I was going away, and would be very sad, I'd tell you quite suddenly that you were my dear lover. Then you'd know better for ever afterwards. I planned I'd tell you when we were out shopping or something, quite casually, so you'd hardly know at first whether to believe it I thought it would be such fun. But . . . you spoilt it all."

" I understand."

" You see, I quite trusted you. I thought you'd wait till . . . till I was ready. I never thought you would play me a trick as you did. It was horrible of you. You couldn't have loved me."

" I did love you. I do now. I always shall."

" If you had, you'd have known. You'd have waited. I can't forgive you for being such a fool. I loved you. I came to München because I loved you. And all of a sudden you turned into an enemy ; it nearly killed me."

He said nothing, but stared at her in such palpable misery that she could not endure it. She continued consolingly :

" I'm not angry now. I see you're sorry. You can't help being stupid. I know you didn't mean to be unkind." And then, a little anxiously : " Don't look like that ! It's worse than when you were in Genoa. Let's quite forget it."

" I cannot."

" Well, don't look so dreadfully unhappy ! "

" There is cause," he stated.

" There's no cause, silly ! I've forgiven it."

" I do not forgive myself."

" You can't really be trying then."

" How can I ? Consider ! I love you. And you have told me how by my own folly I have lost you."

" Soon you'll forget me."

" Never in life."

She looked him over doubtfully and said, after a long pause :

126

"I believe you're right. I can't bear it ; you shan't go on looking like this. Would you like it if I married you ? "

" If I would like it ! But you must do what is best for you. You should, I think, go to England with the uncle."

" But Ike, I don't want to go to England with the uncle."

" That name ! Must you call me by that name ? I detest it."

" Very well then, Jacob ! I don't want to go to England with the uncle. I'd rather stay here with you, because when you start looking as if you'd got toothache I feel as if I love you too much to leave you. Now try to look pleased. Haven't I said enough ? What more do you want ? "

" You have said quite enough."

But he took a little time to cheer up and explained to her, after a pause, that his head was thick and resisted a new idea. Also they had traversed so many emotions in half an hour.

" Methought I was enamoured of an ass," she quoted fondly.

" You were. You are. You must never expect too much of him. I will interview the uncle immediately."

" Well, don't boast," she advised him, " and perhaps he'll believe you. Herr Je ! This has been quick work ! "

They had certainly accomplished a great deal in a short time. Gradually he got more accustomed to these strange, new altitudes which they had achieved, where Tony, with the adaptability of her sex, was already trying her wings. Her delightful security cheered him up, and by the time that Lewis came in, bearing another basket of unsorted letters, he looked like a happy man. Lewis gaped at them, muttered an apology, and was for withdrawing, but they called him back and informed him of their betrothal. He thought that they must have gone out of their senses and was, moreover, much irritated by their complacent appearance so that his congratulations were not given with much warmth.

127

His own infatuation gathered strength with every day that passed, and with every faint attempt to get the better of it. There was nothing to soothe it in the spectacle of Birnbaum kissing Tony. He stalked off, back to the annexe and the Concerto in which he seemed to be stuck fast as in a frightful quagmire. Very bitter were his inward comments upon the folly of Jacob in thus sacrificing his independence for the sake of a chit not worth the little finger of Florence Churchill. It was absurd to marry Tony. For the other lady such a sacrifice might possibly be considered, though the idea was a wild one. Something must be done to abate this fever, for he was beginning to fear that he might go clean distracted. He was ready for a desperate remedy.

He had asked himself more than once if it was possible that she should be accessible on any other terms. And always he decided that it was not possible, though she was ready, surprisingly ready, to make herself pleasant to him. He could have sworn at times that she was no better than the others; that behind her gentle affability there lurked a discreet invitation. But a certain unfamiliarity in the style of these veiled signals disconcerted him and caused him to doubt his own perceptions. It was in fact the first time that he had been pursued for his intellect rather than his person, and the shy creature scarcely knew what to make of it. He wondered if she would have him, if he proposed marriage to her.

" It is better," he said to himself, " it is certainly better to marry than to burn, as Moses puts it."

He was rather pleased with this quotation, dimly recalled from his childhood when he had been made to attend a Sunday school. And of the party at the Karindehütte it is probable that only the despised Robert could have corrected his impression that Moses said it. For Florence had not, unfortunately, read her Bible with quite the same intelligence and attention which she accorded to other and inferior books

128

CHAPTER X

LATER in the day Antonia sought out her uncle and confided to him all those circumstances which delicacy had prevented her from mentioning to Florence. The ensuing uproar took some days to subside, for the Churchills were divided in their view of the affair, and Charles, in England, was written to passionately by both parties. Robert was the least surprised of the two ; he was scandalized but resigned. An hour with Sanger's circus had put him in a frame of mind to expect any sort of discovery. Having enquired into the circumstances and intentions of Jacob Birnbaum, he was disposed to make the best of a bad business and consent to an immediate wedding.

Florence, on the other hand, was astounded but inclined to be compassionate. Jacob was clearly an unprincipled scoundrel and poor little Tony a victim, undeserving of the punishment implied by so iniquitous a marriage. She should be taken to England and helped to live it down.

But Antonia blankly refused to go to England. She persisted in saying that she loved Jacob, and that she wished to marry him in spite of his villainy. No persuasions had any effect on her.

" He's not a bad man, really he's not," she protested. " You don't understand, Florence. He meant no harm. He thought that if it wasn't him it would be somebody else."

" Tony ! How can you ? "

" Well, that's the way he looked at it. You don't understand the way things have been in our family. He thought it might as well be him as Lewis, or anybody else staying here . ."

" Lewis ! "

" Of course it wouldn't be Lewis, as a matter of fact, because he's different ; I mean we've known him so long he's almost like our brother.   But what I mean to say is, that Jacob is no worse than heaps of other people."

" Yes, I should have thought Lewis Dodd was different," mused Florence in a low voice.

" It's Tessa he belongs to," Tony informed her vaguely. " And, of course, Tessa's too young really to have a lover.   At least, she's only just grown up, you know."

Florence smiled to hear the infantile Teresa described as only just grown up.   The halo which, for her, illumined the name of Lewis Dodd glowed a little brighter at this artless testimony. Antonia continued, by way of explanation :

" Linda tried to get him once.   We all saw.   And when he wouldn't have her she was so spiteful.   I think he despises love, though of course . . ."

She checked herself, which was, perhaps, a pity, for Florence was left with the impression that this young St. Anthony, despising love as it was known at the Karindehütte, had eschewed it : a regrettable error.   Antonia had been about to outline his sentimental career, so far as she knew it, when a most ill-timed discretion shut her mouth.   She had not meant to praise him when she said that he despised love ; friend though he was she considered such an attitude to be very shocking.   She was convinced, though she could not put it into words, that no sort of love ought to be despised, since, in spite of its rude beginnings, it is the first source of civility.   But then, civility was, to Florence, a commonplace ; while to Antonia it was a thing rare and admired, so beautiful as to cast a radiance upon its own base and humble origins.   Only she could not explain herself.

And Florence, for her part, could not have understood.   She had for the shortcomings of humanity that universal, almost scientific toleration which is based upon wide reading. No previous experience helped her to understand Antonia's point of view. She listened with growing bewilderment to an unskilful account of the visit to Munich, the quarrel, and the reconciliation. Being herself temperamentally chaste, she had no rancour against people who were not, and regarded them with a sort of uncomprehending pity. But this affair implied an equation which was outside her knowledge. It was with a gesture of puzzled resignation that she yielded at last, when Charles telegraphed his consent to the marriage.

She could, in any case, spare little time to Antonia's problems, for her own life was proceeding at such a pace that she could scarcely keep up with it. One or two attempts she had made to ignore the thing that was happening to her, or to give it a rational interpretation. It was possibly the mountain Spring which had invested the world with this new glory and freshness. It was the escape from a life which had begun to confine her. It was anything but the company of Lewis Dodd. So she reasoned until, suddenly, he took his departure. For three days he went away, flying to Innsbruck in a final attempt to break the disastrous spell which had bewitched him.

Florence, who thought for sixty hours that he had gone for good, found that all the beauty round her had become, in the twinkling of an eye, most intolerably sad. She was astonished, humiliated almost, at her own pain, and unable, any longer, to blind herself as to its cause. She was in love ; her happiness was gone with him, and she would leave the Tyrol with a wounded heart.

Then, as suddenly, he reappeared. He had not found it possible to remain away and so came back with the single intention of possessing her at any cost. She was amused at her own joy and relief ; amused, too, when she reflected that for a year or more she had quite earnestly wished to feel all the pains and anxieties of a serious love affair. Her only care now was to drill herself into the thought that he might not, after all, have returned to woo her. Yet she knew not how otherwise to interpret the absent-minded persistence with which he followed her about. Sternly she forbade to herself the pleasure of romances woven for the future ; hourly she broke her resolution. It was so impossible not to make plans. Because, of course, she had determined to marry him.

He belonged, probably, to a different class. But she could put up with that, and if her family minded it they must learn better. Like her Aunt Evelyn, she was very democratic. He was a great genius and that ought, surely, to be enough for them. His manners, though primitive, were simple. She tried to imagine him in dress clothes ; he would look odd, but not like a waiter. Charles would have to see that she could not be expected to marry anybody ordinary. And for him, if she could but bring him to her views, so much might be accomplished. She had a feeling that he might at first be restive, he was so wild and shy. She believed that he loved her, but she had an idea that the thought of marriage had not, so far, entered his vague head. She would have to put it there. Later on, when his music had been heard rather more, he would need a wife with a certain social standing. She had influence ; she knew people. Married to her, he also would know people.

Only one person at the Karindehütte was in the least aware of the state of things between these two. The household, for the most part, was entirely absorbed by the undetermined fate of Antonia. But Tessa, at this time, grew very pale and melancholy. She feared that her friend meant to entangle himself with the English cousin, a piece of folly in itself, and likely, as she thought, to involve them all in the most serious consequences. It would be a climax of the disasters which had befallen them since Sanger's death. She unburdened her mind to Paulina one day, as they lay out in the forest. They had been discussing Antonia's marriage and Paulina was saying :

"I think it's an excellent idea. Couldn't we all marry somebody and then we needn't go to England?"

"Sebastian couldn't."

"No, but if we were married women, he could come and live with us. Let's get married, Tessa! I'll marry Roberto. I'm sure he'd be quite pleased. He's very obliging."

"Twelve is too young."

"Soon I'll be thirteen. Juliet was thirteen. She was married."

"She was Italian."

"So would I be Italian if I married Roberto. People always take their husbands' nationalities."

"Imbecile that you are! That's got nothing to do with it."

"Don't be a wet blanket! We'd much better both get married. I'll ask Roberto and you ask Lewis. What have you gone so red for? He's very nice; I'd ask him myself only he loves you best."

"I'm too young."

"Not a bit. You can ask him anyhow."

"Oh, I couldn't! I'm too old."

"Too old! I thought you said you were too young!"

"So I did. Dear me! I'm both. I'm at a perfectly horrid age. I'm too old to say what I think. And I'm too young for anybody to want to marry me."

"There now, you're blushing again! You'll be worse than Kate soon. She used at least to blush regularly; I mean always at the same sorts of things. But you've taken to blushing at nothing at all. You're dreadful."

"You wait till you are my age. You will too."

"Still I can't see why you should think you are too young for Lewis. You'd suit him much better than an ordinary woman that expected him always to be bothering about her. . . ."

"Would I? Look!"

133

They were sitting at the edge of the forest, near the bottom of the mountain. Teresa pointed to the field below them where two figures were strolling intimately. Paulina took them in and asked anxiously :

"Do you think he wants her ? "

Teresa nodded.

"But he wouldn't marry her ! " protested Paulina.

"Yes, he will. She'll make him."

"He's never married anybody before."

"Yes, but she's a lady. If it's anybody like Florence, they have to marry them. Look at Sanger and our mother."

"But she won't have him," persisted Paulina hopefully. "Why should she ? Think of all the grand people she knows. She's just being nice to him, like she is to everybody."

"I wouldn't mind his getting her," said Teresa sadly, "if that was all there was to it. But that will only be the beginning, you see ! She'll want to take him off and live at that place in England where she comes from, Cambridge. He won't be happy."

"I think it'll be a shame if he gets her. She can't have seen him drunk."

"Of course she hasn't. He's not been drunk since she came."

"And she can't have seen him in a temper. Really in lots of ways he's worse than Sanger. He's not so good-natured, for one thing. Tessa, do you think we ought to tell her ? "

"Tell her what ? "

"That it wouldn't do at all. There are heaps of things . . . ."

"I can't," said Teresa, who had gone very pale.

"Why not ? If she knew . . ."

"I don't know why not. But I couldn't."

"Well, it would be rather like telling tales. He belongs to us, really, more than she does. Perhaps she'll find out herself."

This was said in a very low voice for the pair were quite

134

close to them. They were picking flowers of different sorts and saying at intervals that they had got enough, and then crying out over a good one that must be picked.

"Oh," cried Florence, flinging herself down on the grass beside the girls, "did you ever see such flowers ? They beat even the Academy pictures of ' Spring in the Austrian Tyrol.' "

"What are you going to do with these little things ? " asked Lewis, dropping gentians into her lap, one by one.

"Put them in a dish of moss on the hall table."

"Very tasteful ! Tessa ! Why have we never put dishes of gentians on the hall table before ? "

"Because we don't want them," said Teresa coldly.

"And," Florence was saying, "I must take a lot of roots home. Why is that cow bell sometimes A and sometimes A flat ? "

"It isn't the same cow," he told her. "There are two cows on that little hill, but you can't see one because it's behind a rock. If you'll move a little this way I'll point it out to you."

"I'll take your word for it," she declared lightly, moving a fraction of an inch further away from him. "How lovely the cow bells are ! I love waking in the morning very early and hearing them all round the house, don't you ? "

Lewis was about to agree fervently when he caught Paulina's eye and remembered that he had in her presence expressed himself very freely about the cow bells which woke him early in the morning. He subsided and lay back, flat on the grass, staring up into the sky and smiling. Florence continued to talk. She said how the silent nights impressed her. A distant waterfall was the only thing to be heard in the hushed spaces round the Karindehütte after the cows had been shut up.

"And running water is an enchanting sound," she said. "The most beautiful in the world, don't you think ? "

"When I was a boy," said Lewis abruptly, "I used to sleep out on some cliffs in Cornwall. And there were some birds, whole flocks of them, I d—don't know what they were, used to fly out to sea just before it got light. I remember I woke up once, when the moon had set and it was quite d—dark, and all the air was full of them. I couldn't see them. I heard wings. . . ."

Teresa, on the grass at his side, stirred a little in response to the excitement behind his hesitating, drowsy voice. She knew that some impulse had prompted him to tell them of a supreme moment, one of those instants, rare and indescribable, when the quickened imagination stores up an impression which may become a secret key to beauty, the inspiration of a lifetime. Her mind swung back to meet the mind of that lost boy who had lain awake upon a high mysterious cliff, beside a whispering sea. She, too, heard wings.

Florence was interested, also, and asked if he had lived in Cornwall. No. He had gone there in the holidays. Did he live in the country?

"N—no. In Bayswater."

He got up. It was evident that he did not like being asked about his childhood, so she desisted. She rose too, and they made their way up the hill towards the house. The girls remained sitting on the grass, occupied with rather gloomy thoughts. At last Paulina looked sharply at her sister and said :

"There's no use crying about it."

"No use," agreed Teresa.

But the tears poured down her face, whether she would or no, until she conceived the happy idea of trying to water a primula with them. Immediately the flood was dried, after the manner of tears when a practical use has been found for them.

"And it would have been interesting," said Paulina sorrowfully, "to see if it would have made any difference to the primula."

CHAPTER XI

It was discovered that Jacob and Antonia would have to be married in Vienna, owing to their complicated nationalities, and they would have to stay there at least a fortnight before all the preliminaries could be got through. Robert Churchill considered that it was his business to escort them.

"Though it will be very disagreeable," he said gloomily to Florence. "But I feel I must go. I don't altogether trust that young Jew. I must make sure that he really does marry the girl this time. But it keeps us here so long ; that's the worst of it. And I don't like leaving you here alone. When is that fellow Dodd going to take himself off ? I wish Caryl would give him a hint."

"He's quite harmless."

"I don't know so much about that. Personally, I've taken a great dislike to him. A very great dislike. He's the worst of the ragtag and bobtail we found hanging round here. The other two, the Russian and the Jew, I can place. They aren't Englishmen, and they aren't gentlemen, and I don't particularly take to either of them, but they are types I can recognise, and it takes all sorts to make a world. Now what I can't stand in this Dodd is that he fits in nowhere. He's got no ties . . . no laws. A disagreeable brute ! What's an Englishman want with this sort of life ? "

Florence smiled. It was so typical of Robert to despise a man because he resembled nobody else. She felt that it was perhaps time that she should break a lance in her lover's defence

"I find him very interesting," she said. "He's strange. I've been wondering about his origin. He speaks like a . . . like an educated man. I'm inclined to think that he's of humble birth, a peasant, perhaps, but that he's mixed a good deal with cultivated people all his life. He must have raised himself. . . ."

"*Raised*," said Robert. "He looks like a scarecrow! What on earth do you see in him that you could call raised?"

"Well . . . there are his wonderful gifts. . . ."

"Presumably he had those to start with. I should have said that they didn't seem to have raised him at all. You can't be serious, Florence! The fellow is a most terrible boor . . ."

"In a way . . . he's an ascetic."

"Humph!"

"Asceticism and Bohemianism are very much alike," she told him with energy. "St. Francis of Assisi was a true Bohemian. Great simplicity of mind is almost incompatible, in a way, with a high degree of civilization. I was thinking, only last night, of that story about Shelley, I think it was Shelley, walking stark naked into a house and through a room with a dinner party in it, because he had lost his clothes out bathing."

"Well," said Robert, "from the point of view of the dinner-party I can't see that it mattered whether Bohemianism or asceticism prompted Shelley to do that."

Florence was so sure that he never made a joke that she failed to catch the gleam in his eye when she told him that, from the point of view of literature, it mattered a great deal.

"Maybe!" he said. "But even if Mr. Dodd does resemble Shelley in that respect, I doubt if my nieces will be any the better for his acquaintance. However, I'm taking Antonia with me, and she is our heaviest charge."

She could not help being sorry for him, foreseeing an uncongenial fortnight in Vienna. The party set off next day and were accompanied by the whole family as far as Innsbruck. The children, with misplaced cheerfulness, had taken it into their heads that this was an occasion for rejoicing ; as Sebastian put it, the Sangers did not often have weddings. They insisted upon all kinds of hilarious celebrations and the day had a sort of opera-bouffe atmosphere which made it particularly trying to their uncle, who saw nothing festive in this tardy removal of a blot from their scutcheon. They began by narrowly missing their train down to Erfurt, owing to a scene with Teresa and Paulina over their toilets. They had discovered a number of black garments, inexplicably left behind by Linda, and had thought that they might as well go into mourning for their father. They appeared, after everyone else was ready, dressed like little widows, with skirts down to their toes and long crape veils floating from their hats. They were immensely pleased with themselves, twirling this way and that, to exhibit their draperies, but the rest of the company did not receive them kindly. At length they were forced into other clothes and the whole party ran irritably down the hill to Weissau.

By the time that they were sitting at lunch in Innsbruck Florence felt that the expedition had already lasted a week. Her heart sank when she contemplated all the hours of noisy junketing still before them, for they were to see the travellers into the Vienna train at two o'clock, and their own return to Erfurt was timed for six. She could not imagine how they were to spend the intervening hours ; the day was scorching and the change from the upland air oppressed her. Glancing at her companions and aware of the wild effect they all produced, she wondered whether her own father would have recognised her, meeting her thus. But she need not have been alarmed. There was nothing of the travelling circus in her own appearance. She was, as always, neat and charming. Her dress was admirably chosen to stand the exposures of such a day, being plain, cool, and of a soft cream colour which showed no dust. To Lewis, staring at her furtively between each mouthful of soup, this trim freshness was a mystery. He did not trace it to her clothes, but only knew that she looked as different as possible from the Sanger girls. Tony, for all her unquenchable beauty, looked bedizened and outlandish. Her silk frock was much crushed and her hair hung down in wisps under a magnificent new hat. As for her little sisters, they might have been pulled through a hedge backwards.

The meal was long, and the children ate a great deal and drank freely, and became increasingly noisy and ribald. Uncle Robert at length put an end to it. He cut short their final, rather tipsy attempts to toast the bride by declaring that the train would be in, and hustled them out into the suffocating sunshine of the street. Once in the shelter of the station he was able to detach himself and register luggage in seclusion. His feelings were thus spared during the final scene, for the children no sooner saw the train which was to take their sister away than they set up a loud howl at being parted from her. Antonia also wept, but more quietly and with a remarkable effort at self-control ; she was really anxious to do right in the eyes of her cousin Florence, for whom she had conceived an ardent and humble admiration. She kissed all her family very often and promised to send them a picture postcard from Vienna. She kissed Lewis and invited him to come and stay with her as soon as she had a house of her own. Finally, and with a certain shyness, she kissed Florence, murmuring :

" Dear Florence ! I'm so sorry to be saying good-bye to you. And I'll try to remember what you said about not swearing, only in my bedroom. . . ."

She and Jacob hung out of the train, waving gaily as it rattled out of the station, while Uncle Robert hid in their compartment, feeling for them all the bashfulness which was not included in their natures.

The rest of the party felt decidedly flat after their orgy of emotion. They straggled out into the station square and the children began to demand that they should all go to the cinema. This was, to their minds, a good finish to a joyful day, but their elders did not agree with them. Caryl, perceiving dismay in the face of Miss Churchill, tactfully proposed a separation. Lewis should show her the sights of the town while he escorted the children. They could all meet again for the six o'clock train. This idea was warmly seconded by Lewis, who relished the prospect of an afternoon alone with his lady and was impatient to begin it at once. But Florence felt a little sorry for Caryl when she thought of the probable atmosphere of the cinema and the unruly state of the children's spirits.

" That is really an excellent young man ! " she commented, looking after them.

" Excellent ! " said Lewis. " Where shall we go ? "

She unfurled her parasol and said that she would go anywhere cool. The day was too torrid for intelligent sight-seeing Were there no shady gardens where they might sit ? Lewis said he thought not. He said that they might have a look at some churches if she liked. He thought that a nice empty church would suit him better than a public garden, though, even if he succeeded in finding one and luring her into it, he was at a loss how to proceed. He had never imagined that any woman, especially one so kind, should be so difficult of approach. Her virtue frightened him at every turn, and he was beginning to wonder desperately if she would go away back to England, beyond his reach, before he should have plucked up the courage to make love to her.

Occupied with these reflections he walked moodily beside her while she steered herself and her parasol through all the glaring, crowded streets. She was intensely interested in all she saw, stooping to peer into courts, and up at archways, and asking him all sorts of questions which he could not answer.

But they got at last into a quieter thoroughfare, and he, seeing a promising looking church in front of them, pointed it out to her, saying that it was, he believed, an interesting old place. She was surprised, for it looked dull.

They passed into its cool gloom and wandered about, staring at tinsel bedecked shrines. He exerted himself to talk in the hope that two women kneeling before the Altar of the Sacred Heart would take it into their heads to get up and go. He discovered an ancient screen carved with figures of local saints and began feverishly inventing legends about them. She listened attentively, wondering why it was that he should suddenly know so much. But he kept it up until one of the women had left the church and the second was on her feet, collecting an umbrella and a string bag full of parcels. She stumped away down the aisle, and Florence was preparing to follow when he caught her arm, declaring that she had not yet seen the font. He tried to lead her up towards the high altar.

" But is it up there ? " she asked in astonishment. " I thought it was always down the other end of the church."

The woman had splashed herself with holy water, and crossed herself, and was out of the porch. Her footsteps rang on the pavement outside and died away. Lewis was left at last alone with Florence in the dark, silent church. He wished, in despair, that she was not so good. His methods were swift and a little arbitrary, but he had never met with any serious resistance. He looked at her doubtfully. She was asking what there was, specially, about the font.

" I l—love you ! " he exclaimed nervously.

She started and looked at him in grave inquiry. Then she smiled enchantingly and said :

" I'm glad to hear it. I love you."

" Oh ! " he said, rather taken aback.

For the candour of this unsolicited avowal he had not been

prepared. His own statement had been made as a sort of preliminary explanation, paving the way for an embrace. Her response, though it might be called encouraging, was so unexpected as to chill him a little. But having cleared his first fence he had better go on. He took her in his arms with a roughness which testified at once to embarrassment and unschooled desires.

In the desert emptiness of her mind, whence thought and sensation had retreated like an ebbing tide, a single bleak idea stood forth, a rock till then submerged and now revealed, for a timeless instant, to the daylight. It was an understanding of his essential hardness, a knowledge that this man who held her so close was indeed no tender lover but a stranger, as cold as ice and harder than a stone. Then her true self, her generous love, returning, flooding her soul, bore down upon that frightful image and drowned it in night for ever.

She heard fresh footsteps in the porch and tried to release herself, with a faint sigh of protest. He let her go. She sank upon a bench and hid her face, for a moment, in her hands.

Lewis picked up her parasol and her gloves and her handbag and placed them carefully on the bench beside her. He was cursing his folly for beginning this business in so inconvenient a place, where they were liable to constant interruption. A woman had come in and was doing the Stations of the Cross, so there was little hope that they would be alone again. He should have curbed his impatience. He thought of solitary places in the mountains behind the Karindehütte and marvelled at his own imbecility. What was he, now, to say or do?

He sat down beside her and waited for a lead. Presently she turned round and smiled at him. She had recovered her poise and her regard was clear and happy. Again he was smitten by a profound uneasiness. She was so astonishingly honest. She was like nobody else. She seemed to have no scruple in hiding what she felt, and he realized that she had

143

been speaking the truth when she declared that she loved him. And because of that she would believe anything that he said.

"She's like a child," he thought amazedly. "She's like my poor little Tessa."

This was nonsense. He knew that she was not in the least like Tessa, save for a look in the eyes which had disarmed him. But, in his mind, certain ideas were always connected with his friend, thoughts of kindness, pity, and obligation, which now came over him. This woman, because she loved, was innocent, sincere and defenceless, like Tessa; she was insecure, like Tessa. All that he felt for Tessa seemed to stir in his heart, forcing him to an extreme compassion for Florence. He swore to himself that he would never make her unhappy, and knew in the same instant that he was bound to do so. He had already discovered that he could not leave her. He fell back upon the only solution which occurred to him, a course which he had already contemplated in some awe and dismay. He said in great haste:

"How soon can we be married?"

He would marry her and he would always be kind to her. That was the best he could do. What was she laughing at?

"I'll marry you," she said, "whenever you like. Lewis . . . tell the truth . . it had only just occurred to you, hadn't it?"

"Oh, no," he declared untruthfully. "But I ought to have mentioned it earlier. Florence! As soon as we possibly can."

He took her hand and kissed it. His boats were burned.

Once outside in the sunlight and traffic he could hardly make out how it had happened. The thing was absurd, unforeseen and unreasonable. But irrevocable now, and, on the whole, very pleasant. He was betrothed. Also he was very thirsty and was on the point of suggesting that they should go and have a drink somewhere when it occurred to him that

144

she probably took tea at this hour. With a first conscious effort at adapting himself to the demands of a new life he took her to the restaurant where they had lunched and ordered coffee.

" Have some cake," he urged. " Have one of those pink cakes."

He was so nervously eager to offer her the right thing that she laughed. She was sure that he had never fed a young lady with pink cakes before, and indeed he never had. Their coffee came, and she took off her gloves and poured it out, sitting opposite him, smiling her happy, tranquil smile at him across the table. He gave her back a glance which he felt to be very domestic and husbandlike. He felt as if he had been married already for quite a long time ; as if his old, untamed existence was so long ago as to be almost legend. But a little bit of the legend was still alive, as he soon discovered, when he caught the eye of Minna Gertz, who was drinking with some students in the corner by the door. Minna was an old flame of his, the daughter of an innkeeper at Erfurt. Two years ago, when she served in her father's house, Lewis had been used to spend many pleasant hours in her company. Now she had migrated to the town and wore very fine hats and long boots buttoned up to her knees. She remembered him quite well though, because he had given her a pair of garnet earrings, and because he generally was remembered by people who had come across him, sometimes kindly, sometimes not. Minna was kind to everyone, but she despised him a little for being so poor. Seeing him now in the company of so beautiful, so obviously well born a lady, she opened her eyes very wide indeed and grinned at him expansively behind the lady's back. He nodded an amiable greeting. Florence turned round to see what he was smiling at, and looked a little surprised. He explained :

" That's Minna Gertz. Her father keeps an inn between Erfurt and Weissau. I've stayed there."

Florence bent upon Minna that serene, interested scrutiny

which she accorded to every new thing, observing her predecessor as if she had been a piece of architecture or an Alpine plant. She had the clear impersonal vision which is the fruit of an unshaken sense of security. Untouched, as yet, by any of life's betrayals, she could observe the world around her with a detachment impossible to her young cousins. They, with senses quickened to danger, would demand, of every strange thing, if it could hurt them and whether they wanted it.

She did not form any very favourable opinion of Minna, and thought she should have stayed in her father's inn. But she said:

" It's a pity they are giving up the peasant dress ; it suits their build. That girl in Tyrolese dress must have looked comely, but in that hat you see all the coarseness of the peasant type without its rustic charm. But I suppose, to her, it's progress of a sort."

Lewis said that he supposed so. He did not feel equal to discussing Minna's progress. He was busy proving to himself that marriage with Florence would not greatly derange his life. He did not want much ; he could live quite contentedly anywhere. To make certain of this he announced that they would live in England when they were married, because it was a part of the world which he had formerly avoided.

" If you like," she said. " Your . . . your people live in England, don't they ? "

" My . . . Oh, yes ! " he agreed, looking startled.

" In London you said ? "

" Yes."

" I don't want to bother you to tell me, if it's difficult. And nothing can make the slightest difference. But it's better for a wife to know, don't you think ? "

" Know what ? "

" What sort of people her husband belongs to. I haven't the vaguest idea about yours, Lewis, and you know all about mine."

" My family are very disagreeable."

" Yes ? "

" That's all."

" What do they consist of ? "

" I've a father and a sister. My father was a school inspector.
Now he's a Member of Parliament. And he writes books.
Two a year. Little text books and outlines of things, for
schools and working men who want to educate themselves.
Science and English literature and our Empire and those
things."

" Oh ! Can he   . Is he . . . any relation to Sir Felix
Dodd ? "

" He is Sir Felix Dodd."

" W—what ? "

" He is Sir Felix Dodd."

She was petrified with astonishment and could only sit gaping
at him.

" Know him ? " he asked pleasantly.

" My father knows him."

" I'm sorry for your father then."

She knew that Charles hated Sir Felix Dodd; he was
always abusing him. They sat on many boards together, for
he school inspector M.P. was a power in the educational world.
Charles had dubbed him Fulsome Felix and avoided him as
far as possible.

" Good heavens, Lewis ! " she stammered, " I can't . . .
I never . . . how very strange ! I never knew Sir Felix
had a son, at least . . ."

She remembered now that she had heard of a son who was a
terrible scamp, and must not be mentioned in the presence of
anybody connected with the Dodds. What nonsense people
talked !

" I mean I never knew his son was you."

" Why should you ? "

" Oh, it's the sort of thing one ought to know. You see, I'd heard your Symphony ; but somehow I'd never connected . . ."

" It's natural. They don't boast of me, I imagine."

" But . . . but . . . I know your sister then, by sight, anyhow. Millicent, isn't she ? She was at college with me ; but not my year. She sings, doesn't she ? Gives ballad recitals ? "

" She may. She always fancied her voice."

" And then she married . . . oh, who ? . . . Somebody in the Foreign Office . . . Simnel Gregory . . . Oh, Lewis ! How extraordinary this is ! I never thought . . ."

Lewis, for his peace of mind, did not grasp the full significance of it. It did not seem to him very important that Florence already knew all about his people. He said impatiently that he had quite lost touch with them and she wisely let the subject drop. Later on she would make him tell her what the trouble had been. And then, when they returned to England, she would smooth it all out. They must be brought to forgive him, whatever he had done.

For herself this news was a great blessing. She would not after all be forced to scandalize her family. She was radiant, as they set off for the station, feeling that life had been very good to her.

" I'd have married him," she thought, " if his father had been the hangman ; but this does make a difference . . ."

Charles would not be overjoyed to hear that she had selected Fulsome Felix for a father-in-law, but he would prefer him, surely, to the hangman !

They met Caryl and the children waiting for them on the platform. Lewis, still intent upon glueing his hand to the plough, informed them cheerfully that he was going to be married. Their faces fell, and Paulina at once exclaimed :

" You won't marry Florence ! "

148

"Yes I shall," he said, too wise to ask why not, in case she might come out with any of the obvious objections. "Yes I shall, shan't I, Florence ?"

"It looks like it," agreed Florence.

She flushed a little under the dismayed stares of the Sanger family. She could have wished that Lewis had not announced the engagement in such a hurry. Caryl was the first to recover, after an ominous pause. Rather faintly, he hoped they would be happy.

"But are you sure it isn't a mistake ?" began Sebastian. "All right, Caryl, you needn't kick me ! I wasn't going to say anything. All I mean is, don't do it in a hurry. Hadn't you better . . ."

"That's our train," interrupted Caryl. "Let's make a move. Come, Tessa ! What's the matter with you ? Have you got a stitch ?"

Teresa was sitting on a bench, apparently in great pain. She was rocking up and down with both hands over her heart. When they asked what ailed her she lifted a face so blanched and drawn that she looked like a little old woman. With some difficulty she pronounced the words :

"Too . many . . ices . . ."

"You poor little dear !" cried Florence, bending over her in concern. "Where's the pain ? In your chest ? Can you manage to get home, do you think ?"

"No," said the rude Teresa, pushing her off. "I'll have to . . die . on this bench."

"She gobbles them so," explained Sebastian. "I knew she'd be sorry after the ninth."

Between them they got her into the train and stretched her out on the seat of a carriage. When she was thus comfortably arranged, she sighed and fainted. The train started before they could bring her to.

"She's very blue," said Florence anxiously. "It looks more

149

like shock than anything else. But I suppose nine ices would account for it. Put the window right down, Caryl, so that the air blows in on her. Nine ices!"

"I'm very sorry," apologised Caryl. "I didn't know it was as many as that. Ike gave them money just before he went."

He had his own opinion, which was, by the way, the opinion of Paulina and Sebastian also, as to why his sister had turned blue. But the experience of a short and eventful life had taught him to hold his tongue.

"She'll have to be carried up the hill to the house," declared Florence. "She can't possibly walk up after such a bad faint. What a day!"

CHAPTER XII

JACOB and Antonia did not consider that Uncle Robert made a very good third upon their wedding trip. His inconvenient sense of decency threw a guilty gloom over the whole affair. He insisted that Jacob should put up at a different hotel, and he could not stomach the idea of any combined pleasure parties.

A growing partiality for his niece did nothing to mend matters. He had always been kind to her, and the pretty creature had taken it into her head to behave so charmingly to him that she was fairly irresistible. At the moment she was all for copying her cousin Florence, so that her manners in public did not shame him as much as he had feared. Her dress was neat and quiet, she drank little, laughed with circumspection, and took real pains not to talk with her mouth full. Robert was no longer tortured by the idea that she might be taken for his daughter ; at the·end of the fortnight he might almost have liked it. She had a way of crossing the crowded lounge of their hotel which might have deceived an expert, it was so quietly and competently British.

Nothing occurred, however, to make him grow fonder of Jacob. On the contrary, since it was impossible for a man of Robert's mind to be lenient towards the pair of them, every passing grace exhibited by Antonia threw a blacker shade of villainy upon her lover. Social intercourse between the three was in consequence very uneasy. Robert held himself ready to escort his niece upon shopping expeditions, and even showed an inclination to visit the opera, but he did not ask

Jacob to come with them. Yet, as the pair were officially betrothed, it was but reasonable that they should occasionally be allowed to meet. Antonia was, therefore, permitted to entertain her cavalier at tea in the afternoons, while her uncle went for a walk by himself—a compromise which interpreted Robert's notion of reasonable chaperonage.

"But it's stupid !" said Antonia the day before the wedding. "Why can't we all go about together and enjoy ourselves ? We could have such fun."

"He cannot endure the company of a wicked man like me," said Jacob gloomily, searching his pockets for the brooch that he had bought for her that morning.

He had nothing to do in the mornings except buy gewgaws for his love and every day he offered her something to console her for the tediousness of this interval.

"He's no business to then," said Antonia, bridling at any criticism of her property. "He hardly knows you !"

Jacob laughed and produced the brooch, which he pinned into her dress with a display of sentiment which would have been very distasteful to Uncle Robert. Everybody else in the hotel lounge knew at once that the pair were betrothed, and that the young Jew had brought a gift for his bride, but Tony was not so English that she minded this.

"I do think," she said, "that he might let you come when we go buying clothes. You will have to look at them, when I wear them, so I think you ought to choose them."

"And I am paying for them," he reminded her.

She did not object to his paying for them now they were to be married. Nor did she wince at his frequent references to the fact. She just took it as one of the sort of things that Jacob was liable to say, the sort of thing that so palpably upset Uncle Robert.

"Yes," she said. "But he doesn't know that."

"That is very simple of him," observed Jacob. "Who

152

should pay for them ? He knows you have not a krone of your own."

"Florence gave me some from her father. And he has no idea of the value of things. I told him I had enough to buy all the things on the list she gave me, and he swallowed it."

"Your cousin has made you a list ? " asked Jacob eagerly. "That is good ! She has style. Until you have more experience you cannot do better than to copy her. Later, I think, you should not dress quite so quietly. I shall take you to Paris in the Autumn and have you dressed in the way I should wish. Have you the list there ? Let me see it ! "

"I began it," said Tony, "and then she looked it over."

She gave him the list, which began in her own childish scrawl and was finished in the neat, scholarly script of Miss Churchill. He chuckled when he saw that his bride had intended to buy "six or seven hats, one gold evening dress with a train, and shoes with red heels," but had overlooked the need for any underclothing. Florence had modified various items and added a detailed catalogue of lingerie.

"Is two dozen chemises enough ? " he asked, planting a fat forefinger on the list. "When my sister married I remember hearing them speak of twelve dozen. You must have what is correct."

"She says it's enough for an English girl."

"She should know," he agreed.

And he continued to scrutinize the list, making very frank comments, until Uncle Robert wandered unhappily into the lounge, a grizzled, meagre presence, exhaling that mixture of superiority and suspicion which mantles some Englishmen abroad. Antonia, prompted by some sprouting social instinct, no sooner caught sight of him than she snatched the list away from Jacob with a hasty warning in a slang which Robert could not possibly understand. But their chaperon was too much disturbed to be aware of any byplay. He even forgot to be

153

cold and stern to Jacob. He had found awaiting him, on his return from his walk, a letter from Florence which had upset him so much that he felt compelled to go and tell somebody about it, even though it should be Birnbaum. He lowered himself solemnly on to a sofa beside his niece and exploded his bomb.

"Here's a pretty state of things ! Florence writes that she's thinking of marrying this fellow Dodd."

"Florence !" cried Antonia.

"Dodd !" cried Jacob.

If Robert wanted to startle them, he succeeded. They both turned perfectly pale with astonishment and dismay, and sat looking at each other while he rambled on :

"I can't think what her father will say. If he's got any sense, he'll forbid it ! He'll forbid it ! But I suppose he'll blame me. How could I have prevented it ? How could I have foreseen it ? Who could have thought that Florence, FLORENCE, a sensible woman like Florence, not quite a young girl either, would dream of doing such a thing. A delicate-minded, well-bred girl, to take up with a wretched mountebank, a disagreeable, ill-conditioned young cub, with the manners of . . . of . . . well, he hasn't got any manners. And goodness knows if he ever washes."

"Oh, but he does !" interrupted Antonia, recovering speech. "I'm sure he does, Uncle Robert. I've seen him. . . ."

"Well, he doesn't look as if he does. A shoddy Bohemian ! One of these bad-blooded young ruffians who defy decency and call it art. No better than a hooligan ! Oh, yes, I daresay he has done some very fine work, but that's no reason why she should want to marry him. Good heavens ! Isn't it enough to have had one of them in the family ? Couldn't she have been warned ? I should have thought the look of him would be sufficient ; a sulky, impudent-looking fellow, who's probably sprung from the gutter, without a single. . . ."

"You are mistaken, Mr. Churchill," put in Jacob. "I think that his family is very good. His father is Sir Felix Dodd. You have heard of him . . . yes ? "

"Dodd ! Dodd ! Good God ! " spluttered Uncle Robert.

Jacob hastily produced all the details in his possession which could cast any light upon Lewis's early career. Uncle Robert continued to call, at intervals, upon Dodd and God.

"But what on earth can they think they are doing ? " asked Antonia. "They must be mad. Florence is so clever. And Lewis isn't, a bit. And she's very good too . . ."

"But," broke in her uncle, "but, to my mind, this about his family makes it worse. Much worse ! There must have been some very grave scandal before an English family would cut off . . ."

"I do not believe there was a scandal," said Jacob, "and I think that he cut them off. I have never heard that it was their wish. He ran away because he did not like his father. He has lived a wandering life, but I think there has been no disgrace. I know he played the cornet once, with a circus . . . but . . ."

"Completely *déclassé*," groaned Uncle Robert. "No ! I think his possessing a family makes it worse. I remember now, I did hear that old Dodd had a scamp of a son who had run away from school. A tramp ! A circus band ! You tell me that he had the education and opportunities of a gentleman, and threw them away to play the cornet in a circus band ? Then there's nothing to be said for him, as far as I can see. I shall go out and telegraph. I shall wire to Florence that I don't approve at all. I shall entreat her father to come out and stop it."

Tea hardly pacified him. He swallowed a little and then bustled off to despatch his telegrams. Jacob and Antonia mournfully discussed the event.

"She can't know what he is really like," said Antonia.

"It is madness," agreed Jacob. "He has cut himself off from her world because he will not endure it. Will he now

155

return to it ? Or does he think that she will share his life ? "

Antonia conjectured that Florence did not know very much about his life. She remembered a conversation in which his name had been mentioned and said :

" I think she rather admires his character."

" Admires ! "

" Yes. She said he was . . . what was it ? An ascetic ! What does that mean ? "

" It means a man who will practice a life of austerity for the cause of some great ideal," he told her.

" O—o—oh ! But . . ."

" You would say that this does not describe Lewis ? "

" I never knew him go without anything he wanted."

" Nor I. It is true that he does not want very much. Perhaps she admires him for that. A wild savage would want even less than he does, yet she would not marry a wild savage. In some ways Lewis is not so much to be admired as a savage."

The wedding came off next morning at an early hour. Uncle Robert departed immediately afterwards, for he was in a hurry to catch a train back to Innsbruck and put an end to all this nonsense of Florence and that fellow Dodd. The wedded pair saw him go without much regret for, unceasingly distracted by the indiscretions of his nieces, he had assumed a most aggrieved air. Throughout the ceremony he stood over Jacob like a gaoler, as though he suspected him of refusing, at the last moment, to make an honest woman of Antonia. When it was over he kissed the bride with a sort of grudging melancholy and wished her happy in tones which prophesied inevitable calamity. He shook hands with the groom, averting his eyes, and popped into his taxi.

Antonia and Jacob returned at their leisure to the opulent hotel where they intended to begin their honeymoon. After

156

the constraint of the past weeks they felt very much like children on a holiday.

" Do you know," said Jacob, as he hooked up his wife's dress that evening, "I think that I am a little grateful to your uncle. It is so interesting that I have not seen any of these lovely dresses before. No ! Do not wriggle ! That is quite correct, how I have done it. I shall not get you a maid just yet ! We shall do very well without one, for a little, *nicht wahr ?* "

" I'd be frightened of a maid," she said quickly.

But he said, with some firmness, that she must have one, to keep her clothes in order. She wore black lace, which was a little old for her ; in her desire to look like Florence she did not consider that sixteen should not dress like twenty-eight. But the gown gave her height and dignity, and Jacob felt very proud indeed as he followed her into the restaurant, and saw how men at other tables turned to gape enviously at her slender, delicate beauty.

It was, perhaps, from her mother that she inherited her capacity for looking aristocratic. He had never felt more strongly this sense of having married his superior. She sat opposite him, gravely and slowly eating her dinner and looking so stately that he did not dare to press her foot under the table. Yet this was the barefooted gypsy who had conquered his heart in Genoa ; the swaggering, brazen little creature whose ragged clothes had so greatly discomposed him in the Munich streets. She was, in these days, rather silent, and often he would have liked to know what was in her mind. He could never guess. He sat and watched her now, a little miserable for all his possessive pride, as she sipped her wine, thoughtfully, and with downcast eyes. The long lashes on her cheek, the soft curve of her neck, her white fingers, drumming on the table, with his ring shining upon one of them, all were like tiny stabs. His love could show him these, but he had no clue to her prisoned thoughts. If he asked her, she would say lightly that she was thinking of nothing at all. Or she would expound to him a long train of amazing, childish reflections. Only one thing he knew : she did not think of him as persistently, or as unhappily, as he thought of her.

After dinner they went to the opera, there being nothing else to do. He could have wished that it had not been " Otello," which they had heard in Munich. Echoes of their first disastrous adventure continually haunted him. But Tony seemed to have forgotten all about it, and enjoyed herself with energy. That earlier evening had passed so completely from her mind that he could not help wondering if she had been too drunk to remember anything. He hoped so ; it was better that she should forget. He must remember, bearing the burden of it for both of them, how he had sat beside her, savagely counting the slow minutes, while on the stage an appalling drama of conquering hate swung on to its dire climax. He became so gloomy that she asked him, at last, if he was worried about anything. He assured her, instantly, that he was the happiest man in the world.

And he was. At times he was almost bewildered by his own bliss in being there, with Tony, so terribly dear, beside him ; really his own for the rest of his life. It was not her fault if the insatiable sorrows of an unequal love tormented him, the hungry demand for more, for a fuller return, for a feeling which it was not in her nature to give. As she leaned forward, absorbed in the passions staged beneath her, he felt suddenly that their box contained just himself and a wraith, a ghost ; as if the real Antonia, whom he loved, was an imagined woman living only in his sad fancy.

She saw that he was troubled. She took his hand and held it, glancing at him sometimes with an exquisite, gentle compassion which mitigated that solitude of spirit which she could not share. In the last *entr'acte* she said :

"What will Tessa and Lewis do, if he marries Florence ? "
"Tessa ? "
"Yes. She loves him."
"I never knew that."
"Didn't you ? Just think."

He thought and decided that she was quite right. In the light of his own trouble he was very sorry for Teresa, robbed thus of her friend by the lady from England. He said so.

"Florence hasn't taken him away," said Tony decidedly. "Nobody could do that."

"But Tony . . . this must be the end of it, for Lewis and Tessa. It will part them."

"Never, while they live. But Florence will be rather a complication. Listen ! "

The lights went down and the first bars of the Willow Song, a plaintive murmur of warning, stole out into the dark house. Antonia sank back into a dream. Jacob, still inattentive to the fate of Desdemona, reflected throughout the last act upon the encounter of this strange three . . . Lewis . . Tessa . . . and Florence, their wild history still before them, their tragedy still unplayed. It seemed to him possible that they might never meet. So many perils threatened this crazy marriage and any one of them might wreck it.

He sighed deeply, being in the mood to be sorry for everybody. His sigh was echoed by Tony, since the tragic loading was over. The Moor, dying, had in his arms the fair woman he had destroyed—was taking his last, sad kisses. The curtain, slow and silent like an approaching fate, slid down over the love, the mad despair, and the whispered cry : ' *Un bacio . . . è un altro bacio !* ' Violins swung through their final poignant arpeggios, and the lights went up. Jacob said :

"I give it a year."

Antonia, pale, rapturous and blinking, had to be reminded ; she was still contemplating a mock death bed.

" Florence and Lewis ? " she said. " Do you think as
long as that ? "

The night was fine and they walked home. She was still
dreamy and excited, and at every crossing she shook his nerves
by a total disregard of the traffic. The Sangers were like that,
he remembered ; they always did their best to get themselves
run over after a concert. Himself, he never suffered in that
way, even though, at the performance, he might have shed
tears of delight.

When they got to their hotel she went straight up to bed,
but he paused to get a drink. There was, in the vestibule,
a flower stall and he bought a handful of roses, stiffly wired
into a bouquet, before proceeding to the oppressive gorgeous-
ness of their bridal suite. The lift was lined with looking
glass, so that as he shot upwards he got an endlessly re-
duplicated vision of himself, stout and nervous, a light cloak
flung over his shoulder and white flowers in his hand : an
infinitely long row of gentlemen carrying offerings to an
unforgiving past.

BOOK III
THE SILVER STY

CHAPTER XIII

CHARLES annoyed Robert by talking as though the worst part of the business was the bond which Florence had forcibly established between himself and Fulsome Felix.

"Now I shall never be able to get rid of that fellow and his confounded cordiality," he complained. "My son-in-law, by your account, is an unprepossessing rascal. But Florence, not I, will have to suffer for that. As is perfectly proper. I could have endured him very well if he had been the son of another father. As it is, my daughter's marriage will be the cause, I can foresee, of great personal inconvenience to me."

Which Robert thought very flippant. Privately he regarded himself as the chief victim in the affair, for Florence and Lewis, having got themselves married with all possible speed, stayed behind in the Tyrol and left to him the appalling task of escorting the three children back to England.

The whole family had urged Charles to go out in person and forbid the banns. But he, knowing his daughter, refused to give himself so much useless trouble. He sent a few remonstrative telegrams, so wise and so witty that she quite disliked having to tear them up. And, for a long time, he unobtrusively held himself in readiness to rush off and fetch her home at an hour's notice, should she summon him. But no message came. During the first month of her married life she wrote every week to say how happy she was ; then, for a time, her letters came almost daily and he interviewed the idea of going to her without waiting for any direct appeal. But in the Autumn she seemed to settle down. She wrote less often and more tranquilly.

Lewis, it seemed, was at work again on that Concerto which Sanger's death had interrupted. They had migrated to a little fishing village on the Mediterranean where he could be quite quiet and finish his work in peace. Later, they were to return to England, move into the house which Florence had bought, and launch themselves upon musical society in London.

This house now filled up all her letters to her father. It was at Strand-on-the-Green, and had belonged to one of her many school friends. She had always thought it the most delightful house in the world, and, hearing that it was for sale, she wired to Charles to secure it for her. He bought it about three weeks after her marriage. She was quite sure that it would exactly accommodate herself and Lewis. It was easily accessible, and yet sufficiently out of urban distractions. When their position was quite assured they might live right out in the country, and people should come and stay with them, but at present it was advisable to be near the scene of action. It was a very old house, with a romantic history dating back to Charles II, and a walled garden with a mulberry tree. In this garden a large studio had been built, connected with the house by a covered passage ; this was to be the music-room, where Lewis was to exist, beautifully undisturbed. Also there was a long, lovely chamber on the first floor, looking out over the river, which was to be the drawing-room.

Florence knew every hole and cranny of the building and had already furnished it completely in her mind's eye. For this occupation she had plenty of leisure, for Lewis left her alone a great deal. He was working with as much ease and regularity as he had ever achieved in his life. Marriage seemed to have restored his scattered wits. He had recovered completely from the shock of Sanger's death, was able to sleep soundly at night, and could think of nothing but his Concerto. Florence was delighted. This work was as important in her eyes as it could be in his ; nor did she feel herself neglected, for he was perfectly affectionate when his mind came, as it were, to the surface. She liked solitude and the company of her own thoughts ; at this time she almost craved for it, feeling a need to consolidate and preserve that separate and individual outlook on life which even a wife should have, and which often grew shadowy in their unreal, happy hours together. She wanted to get rid of a new uncertainty, a sensation of never knowing her own mind about anything.

Sometimes he would leave his work and they would wander over the terraced hills at the back of the little town ; he idly enjoying himself—she attempting continually to build up a solid foundation of understanding between them. She could have wished that he would be a little more interested in the house. She described to him the charms of the district, the delightful cottages tucked away under Kew Bridge, the towing path, and the barges and the swans and Zoffany House. But he persisted in saying, a little absently, that he didn't mind where he lived. They might have been doomed to Queen's Gate.

" Do you really not care what sort of place you live in ? " she asked him once.

" I like this place," he replied, " as well as any."

They were sitting on the stone parapet of a vineyard, high up on the hills, a low wall covered with mosses and small flowers. She had taken off her hat and flung it some yards away on the grass. The southern breezes, warm and aromatic, ruffled the soft hair on her forehead, but she looked, as always, very neat and trim. Lewis was perched on the wall just behind her, his feet dangling over the edge. He was busy throwing little pebbles to see how far they would bounce down hill. Beneath them were the huddled yellow walls and roofs of the town and a few fishing boats drifted over the dazzling bay waters. All was as still and brilliant as a mirage.

" Oh, yes," she said. " This is the South. I know. But it's poppy and mandragora, you know."

" It's what ? "

" It makes one lazy. The long sunny days here induce a feeling of leisure which we northern people can't have. I'm sure our efficiency and all that sort of thing is due to the shortness of our daylight. We know our days are limited. The night is such a deplorable waste of time, don't you think ? "

" Not always," observed Lewis, hurling a pebble which broke the record.

" But it is," said Florence earnestly. " Think how much of our valuable lives we waste in sleeping ! "

Lewis rejoined with a comment which made her blush, just a little. He came round and sat on the wall in front of her, to see her doing it. He liked to say things which put her out of countenance, and did so infrequently enough that she was always taken by surprise.

The contradictions of her temperament were a perpetual source of amusement to him. She still had sudden alarmed withdrawals which delighted him and provoked him to experiment. She was so responsive and yet so shy, combined so much candour with such reticence, that he seemed to pursue long after he had captured her.

She picked a sprig of thyme off the wall, rubbed it between her fingers, and sniffed at it as she reverted to the house.

" Moving in will be simple," she told him, " for I know exactly what I want, down to the last window curtain."

" Can you always get what you want ? " he asked in some amazement.

" Oh, yes ! It's simply a matter of being firm. In the drawing-room I want the brightest colour to be those lustre jugs I told you about. The permanent decorations ought to be subdued, because the light. . . . Lewis ! Stop throwing stones ! I don't believe you've listened to a single word I've been saying ! "

" Yes, I have. You were talking about jugs. I'm

listening. I'm listening to you and a dozen other things as well."

"There aren't a dozen other things. There's only . . . the chapel bell, and some men shouting in the boats down on the quay . . . and a dog barking, and some ducks in the garden below."

"Not bad ! You've missed about fifty larks in the sky, and the grasshoppers all round us, and a car changing gear on the hill, and the oars in the rowlocks of that boat putting out, and the children playing, and the goat bells away on the hill behind us, and I think I can hear a smithy."

"What a babel it sounds ! I'd have said it was a quiet evening."

"So it is. It's so quiet that you can hear every sound in it. Generally there's too much noise for that. But come along, my girl ! Put on your hat ! The sun is setting and one of these short nights we have here is about to begin."

"Oh, dear ! I don't want to go down. This place smells of myrtle and our inn smells of garlic."

He went and picked up her hat and clapped it on her head. They began to pick their way down the hill, arm-in-arm.

"I used to wonder," she said suddenly, " what Albert Sanger and my aunt used to talk about, that time they ran away to Venice. Do you think they counted up the number of sounds they could hear ? "

"Sanger ? Oh, I shouldn't think so. He always maintained that women were three-quarters deaf."

"He couldn't have thought that of her. She was very musical."

"Oh, musical ! " said Lewis vaguely, as if this had nothing to do with the discussion.

His memory cast very little light on the career of Evelyn Sanger, though Florence had questioned him more than once. What he did say was disappointing. Evelyn had not impressed him. He did not think her beautiful or brilliant or fascinating. But he admitted that she was clever at getting Sanger out of scrapes and putting a good face on scandals. She was not as able as Linda, however, in dealing with duns. She had dwindled, it seemed, into a small souled, careworn creature, overburdened with children and defeated by the petty, material side of life. Perhaps her vision was not quite wide enough ; it had failed, anyhow. But then, Sanger was a brute. Even Lewis said so.

"If it had been me," thought the niece indignantly, "I should have left him. I wouldn't have dreamt of putting up with it. It's . . . it's degrading . . . clinging to a man who behaved like that. She could have had no pride."

In the streets of the town it was already getting dusk. They went carefully through smells and refuse, down the steep hill and under massive archways, to their little inn just above the quay. In the dark of their room they found letters from England awaiting them, glimmering whitely on the dressing-table. Lewis took his out on to the balcony where the last gleams of daylight lingered. He had a fat envelope with two letters inside it and he laughed aloud as he scanned the first :

Dear Lewis,

Will you please come and take us away from here ? It is a disgusting school and we have endured it as long as we are able. Really and truly we've tried to put up with it, because Tessa said one ought to give everything a fair trial, but it doesn't and we can't. It isn't like what you said it would be. We would never have come if we had known what it would be like. We shall kill ourselves if we are not soon taken away ; we cannot exist here, it is insufferable. The Girls are hateful, they say we don't wash and are liars. The governesses are a Queer Lot and not fitted to be teachers I'm sure. They think of nothing but games. Why should we have to play games if we don't like ?

Would you like it ? Work is sensible, we don't mind that. It was your fault that we were persuaded to come, so you will be a murderer if you don't take us away before we end our miserable Lives. When Florence wrote to say we must stay because it's good for us our hearts broke and all the house rang with our frantic lamentations. Could you come and take us out to tea ? They'd let you if you said you were married to her. And then we could all go to the Station and take some train that goes a long way off. We have nobody to help us only you, and as the Poet says : On some fond Breast the parting soul relies ! Do, *do*, DO come, DEAR Lewis. You will not be sorry when you hear our joyful ejaculations.

Your Sincerely friend,

PAULINA ELOISE SANGER.

PS. Probably we shall hang ourselves.

PS. Tessa says I'm to say she won't She says that I can if I like, but she won't on any account because it is a Mug's Game. But it's not as bad for her as she doesn't have to play this hellish hockey because she has a valvular lesion. They found it at the medical inspection, so she has to go for walks. I forgot to say we hope your having a nice time and like being married. Tony does. She is coming to England this winter. She sent us a picture postcard that the Girls said was common. Caryl did too. He is playing in a cinema.

When Lewis had finished reading this letter he swung round to call in through the window to Florence that the girls were unhappy at school and must be removed. Then he remembered that Paulina had said something about Florence having written. It was the first he had heard of it ! Queer ! He looked at the letter again and saw that the envelope contained another from Teresa. He began to read :

Lina threatens to write, so I think I'd better take up my

pen too, that I may warn you not to pay too much attention to her. I don't think she will kill herself, she is not nearly brave enough. Reflect upon her character and consider if I am right ! You need not worry to come and take us away if it's inconvenient to you, since no fatal consequences will befall.

But I must confess that we don't find ourselves very comfortably situated in this school. We don't mean to stay for another term. But I think we can endure it till Christmas. There are a lot of people here who I think you would laugh to see. I do often. But it's really a waste of time for us to be here. We would learn more in some other place where they didn't play games perhaps.

I can't write very well, because I'm frantic, because a girl called Mary Marlowe is in this room playing *Jardins sous la pluie* FFFFF ! This isn't her fault, because no person is allowed to play anything properly in this school. If they do, Miss Somers says : What are you putting in the expression for ? You can't put in the expression till I've told you what to put. In the room next door another girl called Naomi Hooper is playing the Sonata Pathétique. She is putting in the expression, and I wish to God that she wouldn't. The noise is filthy and infernal.

They hate us, and we hate them. When we come in, they all stop talking and whisper. We don't ever get away from them. A person has to be alone sometimes, but truly the only place where you can be alone here is the lavatory, which is not very comfortable, and they come rattling at the door if you stay there too long. We go there when we cannot conceal our tears. Our chief business is to be always running as there is some place, on a time table, that we must be in *every minute of the day*, and these places are often far apart, and no allowance is made for transit. I know now why you ran from your school.

With kind regards,

Your Very Dear TESSA.

170

It had grown so dark before Lewis had finished reading that he could scarcely decipher the last words. When he had done, he stood for a moment with a perfectly blank mind, staring out to sea. This unstudied letter had brought her so forcibly to his imagination that she might almost have stood beside him. She had breathed a hasty confidence into his ear, a caressing farewell, called herself his very dear Tessa (and she was ! God knew how dear !) and then, suddenly, she was quite gone, vanished into the shadows.

He leant over the balcony and looked fixedly into the odd, ill-kept little garden beneath, as though amid its tangled thickets and the blackness of its cypresses he might catch the whisk of her petticoats. But he saw nothing and heard nothing save the sea whispering on the beach. And he became aware that the gathering night was inexpressibly melancholy—empty. He was desolate because of the vast, aching sorrow of the water, pale as mother-of-pearl, smooth as glass, where a few black boats still hovered. On the horizon purple clouds collected slowly, and from the stumpy tower at the end of the quay a yellow path of light came to him across the dim expanses of the sea. It was all sad. In the whole of this cool, limpid evening there was nothing of her and he had been bereft, robbed. Her letter, crushed in his hand, was a dead thing, powerless to charm her back Florence called, in a clear low voice, from the room behind him.

" Did you speak, Lewis ? "

He thought that he must have exclaimed. Perhaps he had called on his friend, a little imploringly, in the darkness.

" No," he said confusedly. " No."

And he went back into the room.

His lady wife sat in front of the dressing-table, where two tall wax candles burned on either side of the looking-glass. She was brushing her hair with soft, rhythmical movements and did not at once turn round. All that he could see was a fine dark cascade of hair, touched at the edges to a golden haze by the candle light. It hid her face and shoulders. Presently she glanced at him and asked in surprise if he had seen a ghost. He said that he had not. But his look of blank discovery did not immediately disappear. The dressing-table was all covered with little boxes and bottles and brushes and her rings, winking in the candle light. She took them off, when she did her hair, all except her wedding ring, which shone, bland and smooth, on her left hand. He looked at it, and at her, as though he saw them for the first time. She was so solid, so inevitably established there, that she seemed to deny the memory of the little wraith on the balcony.

"I've had a letter . . ." he began.

"So have I," said his wife. "From your sister."

"Millicent?" His brow grew dark. "Again?"

"Again! Then you did get it?"

"Get what?"

"Her first letter. She says she wrote in June, when she saw our marriage in the paper. But as she got no answer she fears it never reached you."

"Yes, it reached me. I tore it up."

"Why?"

"I don't want to have anything to do with her."

"I don't think that is very reasonable. Her letter to me is very friendly. She wants us to come and see her when we are in England. Read it."

He took the note, disgustedly, and read it through.

"She's up to no good," he commented. "But I can't quite see what she's after. What does she get by this sudden friendliness?"

"Couldn't it be genuine good nature?"

"No, it couldn't. She never had an ounce of it in her life. But why can't she leave us alone?"

He simply could not understand these advances. He had

172

married Florence without ever formulating to himself any clear idea as to her social position ; at first he had thought of her as Tessa's cousin, and, later, as the object of his own desires, but never as a Churchill and the daughter of the Master of St. Merryn's. In his simplicity he supposed that she was not grand enough to be an asset to anybody. She talked a great deal about her friends, but they all had names unknown to him, and he did not realize that Millicent might have found them impressive.

Florence herself had vague suspicions of the truth, but, in her anxiety to be reconciled with Lewis's family, she preferred to ignore them. Already she had managed to forget that at college she had avoided an intimacy with Millicent Dodd with very considerable difficulty. She said firmly that she should answer the letter, and his expression, on hearing this, goaded her to carry the battle a step further.

" I think you should have told me when first she wrote. One acquires an interest in relatives, when one marries."

" Is that so ? " he took her up quickly. " You don't tell me when Tessa and Lina write to you."

" My dear Lewis ! That's a perfectly different case."

" How is it different ? "

" Teresa and Paulina," she said with a flush, " write very silly letters which, for their own sakes, I should be sorry to show to anybody."

" I'll engage they write better letters than Millicent. You can get the truth out of them, at least . . ."

" Not always, I'm afraid. The world in general finds that they . . . shall we say . . . exaggerate a little."

He stated his opinion of the world in general, rather forcibly, in terms which she had never heard used before. She asked, in some bewilderment, what he meant. Then she grew angry.

" There is no need to be so violent," she said.

" Why have you sent them to such a . . . such a . . ."

173

"What!" she cried, enlightened. "Have they written to you? Little monkeys! May I see?"

Smiling, yet a little displeased, she held out a hand for the letters, and, after a brief hesitation, he gave her Paulina's. She laughed, quite kindly, as she read it.

"Poor darlings! It's rather hard, I do admit. But they must learn to put up with it. They must become civilized beings, you know, if they are to live in a civilized world. And this process, though painful, is probably as quick as any."

"Why should they live in a civilized world, as you call it?"

"Don't be unreasonable. You know as well as I do that an uncivilized world is no place for them. Think of Tony!"

He found this unanswerable. Thinking of Tony, he had formerly given them advice which he now regretted. It was true that he had himself encouraged them to go to Cleeve. Florence was demanding to see Teresa's letter, in a determined way.

"Oh, well," he mumbled, withholding it, "it says the same thing."

"I'd like to see it, please."

He gave it up. She frowned over it, but gave it back quite safely with the comment:

"Not quite so artless, I'm afraid. Paulina is at least sincere, don't you think?"

"So is Tessa sincere."

"Not altogether. She pretends to be writing to tell you not to come. Why does she write at all then? She knows she's no business to do it. I'm sure that Paulina never thought that she oughtn't. But Teresa has some feeling in the back of her mind that she wants to hide."

"Has she?" asked Lewis, beginning to re-read the letter with interest. "I don't think Tessa could hide anything."

"I think," she suggested, "that I wouldn't answer them if I were you. Or just send them a cheery picture postcard."

"I shall do no such thing," he exclaimed, angrily aware of a hint of coercion in her manner. "I shall write and advise them to run away if they don't like it."

"Don't be absurd! I must ask you not to do anything so silly. I've taken the responsibility for those girls and I'm sure my father would agree with me. They oughtn't to be encouraged to feel sorry for themselves."

"I can't help what you and your father think. I knew Tessa and Lina before you did."

"Still, they can't be so much to you that you would deliberately go against me in this matter? Because, you know, I shall feel it strongly, very strongly indeed, if you insist upon writing to them after what I've said."

Something in the gentle decision of her tones had a dreadful effect on his temper. They were both very angry, for behind the dispute lay deeper issues than they cared to admit. Teresa aroused in him a devotion, and in her a dislike, which neither fully realized. At last, with a furious exclamation, he seized his hat and flung out of the room, slamming the door behind him. It was their first quarrel.

For a few minutes she was quite dazed. Then she smiled and murmured to herself:

"Dear me! What a hullabaloo!"

And soon afterwards she said firmly:

"He'll have got over it when he comes in."

She finished brushing her hair and sat still, thinking. It was really time that she took stock of herself and her position. This explosion was significant of a sort of uncertainty, a hesitation of mind, which had grown on her in the past weeks. She must think; she must think about herself and Lewis. Only that was difficult when he had so completely mastered her imagination. Always he was in her mind, but not rationally; the idea of him had grown so large that it blotted out everything else. Before they married she remembered that she used to

175

think about him a great deal. She had seen him clearly though mistakenly. Since then he had changed into quite another person and she saw him clearly no more. Their closer intimacy had brought about a regrettable want of focus. Her old values were lost, her sense of proportion submerged by the cataclysmic new things that had happened to her, and she would have liked ideas of some sort to follow upon this process. But she had none. It was as if he had picked her up and carried her off to some strange place where there were no standards left by which to judge him. Nor did she rebel against this, when they were together ; in his arms she could see her lost world crumble away and remain serene. But, in her hours alone, she would search, rather frightened, for a new self. Once she could say very confidently why she loved him. Now she was hardly sure of anything about him, or about herself, save that he had possessed her. This isolated fact was so absorbing that she could not see round it.

As she slowly dressed for supper she told herself that, for both their sakes, she must recover some measure of poise and detachment. She must get rid of this pliant languor which had in some ways made their relations so easy, but which was a bad foundation for rational partnership. A determination seized her to get back to England as soon as possible. In England she would be reinforced by her own background.

She waited for him and, as he did not come, she went down and ate her supper alone. Then she came up and sat for a long time on the balcony listening to the sea. Quite late, when she was thinking of going to bed, she heard him come in, and called to him. He came out at once and stood beside her, leaning on the edge of the balcony. In the pale starlight he looked strange, wild, almost exhausted, but she did not think that he was still angry. He put a hand on her shoulder and asked in a low voice :

"Well ? What have you been doing ? "

" Listening to the sea," she said.

He listened too for a few seconds. Then he shivered and exclaimed almost in a whisper :

" It's cold. Come in ! "

" I'm not cold. Have you caught a chill ? "

" I hate this balcony ! "

Still grasping her shoulder he leaned forward and looked down into the garden. An owl hooted in the thickets and he jerked back, his nervous clever fingers tightening their clutch. For all those hours he had been thinking of Tessa, away in England, shut up, beating her untamed little spirit against prison bars. Soon he was going to England himself, near to her. A conviction that he had better not came upon him so strongly that he exclaimed aloud :

" Don't let's go ! "

" Go where ? What do you mean ? "

" England. Let's stay here. We'd better not go."

" My dearest boy ! I've bought the house ! "

" Couldn't you get rid of it ? "

" Lewis ! You're moonstruck ! It's quite impossible ! "

" Oh, very well ! " he yielded with an odd defensive gesture. " It's your doing. Come in ! Come to bed."

She did not reopen the question of the children's letters since that might sound like nagging. So she left it, almost sure that he would not write. And in this confidence she was justified. Perhaps he forgot, or perhaps he did not know what to say ; but Teresa and Paulina awaited his answer in vain, shedding many salt tears, night and day, in their bitter exile at Cleeve.

CHAPTER XIV

THE music-room was the most important of all the rooms in the new house. Here Florence put a beautiful piano and a good writing-desk and comfortable chairs and a waste-paper basket which Lewis never used. Then she turned him loose into it, with an assurance that it should be entirely his own, and that nobody should ever clean it. For this he was not properly grateful, having forgotten the ways of housemaids.

" Clean it ? " he said. " I should hope not ! Roberto never cleans anything."

Good little Roberto had attached himself to Florence and Lewis when Sanger's circus was broken up. During the honeymoon he had gone on a holiday to see his relations, and then he came to England to do the housework at Strand-on-the-Green. He was, so Florence said, more useful than three maids put together and much pleasanter to deal with. He did all the work, with the help of a charwoman who came in the mornings.

" He's exactly the kind of servant I've always wanted," said Florence. " Really feudal. He gives the right tone to the house."

" The right tone ? " said Lewis in a puzzled voice. " Scaramello ? I don't quite see what you mean, but he looks very fine now you've cleaned him up."

" He's the sort of servant we ought to have. He goes so well with the sort of effect I want to produce."

" Why should you want to produce any sort of effect ? "

" One does produce a definite impression on people, whether

or not one makes any conscious efforts about it, so one might as well take pains, and think a little. I want this house to look like us . . . pleasantly Bohemian . . . a sort of civilized Sanger's circus, don't you know, with all its charm and not quite so much . . . disorder."

Lewis looked very doubtful.

" I don't see how you're going to do it, Mrs. Dodd, and anyhow it's a queer ambition for a respectable married woman."

" You think of nothing but respectability these days."

" I daresay," he said lightly, " I'm a reformed rake."

And he fled to his music-room, leaving her to do what she liked with the rest of the house. It seemed to him that she was oddly changed since their return to England. It had begun on their journey home ; as they sped northwards she had become more assured and domineering with every mile. She grew brisker and more decisive ; she spoke more quickly. Still, she was very good to him. She took charge of everything, protected and shielded him in all disturbances, and provided this charming room where he could retreat from the racket which went on in the rest of the house. Here he worked through the shortening autumn days, emerging at intervals for food, to find his wife, competent and commanding, generally at the top of a stepladder. They went sometimes for little walks along the towing-path or to Kew Gardens, and he admitted that Strand-on-the-Green was really a delightful spot. But of his new quarters, as a whole, he took so little notice that he sometimes lost his way about the house. He was quite unable to describe it to the Birnbaums, who had taken, for the winter, a large furnished house in Lexham Gardens. He went to see them as soon as they arrived and sat with them for a long time, smoking Jacob's cigars and exchanging gossip of the Sanger world in which this young pair had been cutting a great figure. Antonia was most anxious to know how he did with Florence.

" Very well," he told her. " She's a model wife."

179

" Have you quarrelled yet about anything ? "

" Oh, no.   I'm so firm, you see."

They laughed at this and asked what he was firm about.

" Well, there's the little question of my family.   She's strangely anxious that we shall all be brought together, and since we came home she's struck up a sort of friendship with my sister.   Ever met my sister, Ike ? "

" I have not had that pleasure, I'm afraid."

" Well, that's natural, for she's your social superior ;   a knight's daughter and married to a baronet's heir.   But you needn't regret it, for she's as ugly as sin.   Toothy, you know, and pop-eyed.   And a tongue like a horse radish, as Florence will discover before she's much older.   Anyhow, over that I've been firm.   I won't have her in the house.   If I receive her, I don't know what lengths they might go.   It might be my father next ! "

" Your father !   Does he clamour to be received ? "

" Well, not exactly," confessed Lewis.   " But Florence has seen him, and she tells me that I'm in danger of his free forgiveness if only I'll apologise for my language last time we met.   So you see the ice is thin ! "

" What occurred when you last met ? " asked Jacob, who had always been curious to know.   " Did he oppose your musical career ? "

" Oppose it ! " cried Lewis.   " I wish he had !   No, it was his encouragement that drove me into being a prodigal."

" I see.   He knew too much about it ?   That happens sometimes."

" He knows too much about everything.   He had to, I suppose, being a school inspector.   But I didn't object as long as he left my department alone.   I could put up with his bloody little text-books and what his dear friend, the archbishop, said to him coming out of the club, as long as he didn't interfere with me.   When he did, I had to go away."

"He has written your pieces for you?" asked Jacob with a grin.

"I declare I wouldn't put it past him! But he didn't get as far as that. I made my protest when he had the amazing impudence to purloin a thing of mine and show it to Simon, for his opinion, apparently! Simon!"

"Simon! You mean Lucius Simon?"

"But certainly. There's only one of him, I should hope."

"One is too many," said Jacob gloomily.

Thus they dismissed a man who was still the most renowned of British composers. In their circles, however, Lucius Simon was hardly considered worth a malediction. He was, perhaps, the wrong age.

"Simon," Lewis explained, "was one of my father's friends. Bound to be! An obscene, loathsome, complacent, self-advertising maggot if ever there was one! Just the sort of fellow my father would take to. Plenty of them at our house; and all so hearty and gentlemanly, don't you know, all busy building Jerusalem in England's green and pleasant land, and doing well out of it. No, don't laugh, Tony! You think that's Ike's job? I tell you, you've no idea what these people are like. I hadn't noticed the thing was gone from my room (it wasn't much of a thing, you know, only boy's work) till the old man sent for me one evening, and there, in the library, I found Simon puffing at his cigar and digesting his dinner. I nearly vomited at the sight of him. And then I saw my manuscript in his pudgy paws, and my father said : ' I've sent your little Sonata to Mr. Simon, Lewis (he was mister then) to see if he could make anything of it for you. You'll find his suggestions very helpful.' Simon! And they handed it back to me with his filthy scrawls all over it, as if they were giving me a thousand pounds! And Simon said I had some powers and a gift for melody. Simon!"

"So you have," said Jacob. "But you are afraid of it.

Before I have always wondered why that is. Now I know that it is Simon. You were foolish, Lewis. He could have done so much for you. I suppose you insulted him ? "

" Of course he had influence. My father knows nobody who hasn't. No. I kept my temper remarkably well. I merely threw the thing into the fire and walked out of the room."

" Just quite quietly, like that," explained Tony, and Lewis had to laugh, remembering how he had stalked off, with all the fiery, outraged vanity of art and youth combined, and slammed the door upon two flabbergasted gentlemen.

" Next day," he said, " I spoke my mind. I'd been wanting to do that for seven years. Then I ran away."

" And that is the story of your life," murmured Jacob. " I have often wondered. Your wife . . . does she know ? "

Lewis reflected and said that he did not think so.

" If she knew, she would tell you, as I do, to be wise and forget it. Now he is willing to forgive you. Why is that ? "

" Oh, because I've married so well. I never realised, you know, that he'd be so pleased. If I'd known . . . oh, well, I'd have done just the same I suppose. But it riles me to think how he's probably going round telling everybody that he always knew I would sow my wild oats and settle down. But he shan't set foot in my house, unless it's over my corpse."

" I thought it was Florence's house," said Tony, puzzled.

" Oh, well, it is really. But I'm master in it."

" What is it like ? Is it as nice as this ? "

" Oh, well . . ." he looked round at the disordered magnificence of the room where they sat : " No, it's not as grand as this."

" Can I come and see it ? Shall I come to-morrow ? "

" No, don't come to-morrow. Come sometime when she's at home. She's gone away to Cambridge, to her father."

" Gone back to her father ! But not for always ? "

"Oh, no? Only for a week end. We've not parted."

Antonia, who still could not believe that Florence and Lewis were really happy together, looked dubious. She said :

"Tell me when she comes back and I'll go and see her. And she must come and see me. Do you like this house? Jacob took it. It belongs to a friend of his ; he collected all these Gainsboroughs. But I don't like having a house. It's a bother. You can be just as comfortable in your own suite in an hotel. But we thought we'd better because I'm going to have a baby in the Spring. Did you know?"

"That's excellent news. I congratulate you, Tony."

"You'd better congratulate Jacob. It's as much his doing."

"I congratulate you, Ike."

"Have a cocktail !" said Jacob expansively.

"He says," murmured Antonia, "that a boy with my brains and his money may get anywhere."

"My cherished one ! I said your father's brains."

"Yes. But that's not tactful. Myself, I feel I might have a daughter with Sanger's disposition and Jacob's appearance."

"These," said Lewis, "are morbid fears natural to your condition. You must get rid of them. I'm drinking his health !"

Until dusk he lingered with them, enjoying the stuffy comfort of the room, with its rich heavy hangings and soft carpet and chairs like little feather beds. He told them about his new Concerto and offered to send it to them. But they, who preferred listening to reading, made him play some of it to them. Their approval seemed to please him very much.

"Florence thinks it a great advance on the 'Revolutionary Songs,'" he told them.

He added, seeing that they were amazed at this quotation of an alien opinion :

"She's very interested in music, you know. Really, she seems to have heard a lot."

" *Du lieber Gott !* " exclaimed Jacob, when Lewis had left them. " Tony ! What is to become of that poor fellow ? When did one hear Sanger quote the opinion of any of his women ? "

" My mother was musical," said Antonia thoughtfully.

" Musical ! "

Jacob again called upon the God of the Patriarchs to witness the accursedness of ladies who were musical. It was a pity that Florence could not hear him.

" Your father," he said, " made a mistake when he married your mother. He was caught as Lewis is now caught ; his appetites were stronger than his common sense. But he broke through all that ; he had so much brutality. Lewis will not treat this woman as Sanger treated your mother. He is not brutal."

" Isn't he ? He's insanely cruel sometimes."

" Cruel ? Yes ! That is a different thing. Clever people are cruel. Stupid people are brutal."

" Sanger wasn't stupid."

" He was not clever. His strength was that ; it made him so different ! And, for a man of genius, little heart, he was wonderfully insensitive."

" And I can't see that Florence has done Lewis any harm. It's lovely, this Concerto he has written."

" It is good, yes!" mused Jacob. " Something has happened to him in this year. ' Breakfast with the Borgias ' was the beginning. We thought that was a joke, but it was a sign. Always, before that he had a . . . how would you call it ? . . . . a gêne . . . a constraint . . . almost a terror, of his own power to write melody. He could do it, and he would not. It seemed sad to me, for those who could do that have been so few . . . not half a dozen . . . "

" Sanger stopped him."

" I know. It was a pity, your father's influence. While he

184

was your father's disciple he would never obey his own nature. He was a *revolté* and Sanger's was the music of revolt. Now he is becoming free of all that."

"Well ! Florence isn't stopping him."

"Nothing will stop him. I think that he should have a hearing in this country. Sanger will soon be popular. Then also the early work of Lewis. The Symphony in Three Keys ! This year we will have that, and next year the new Concerto."

"You will see about it ? " cried Tony.

"I will think of it. This Concerto is good, but until now I had never thought of his future. He has fought himself."

"He's a good conductor. Better than Sanger was."

"That is so," agreed Jacob. " I will see him some time and ask him if he would like a concert."

Antonia looked very pleased, for if Jacob said that anybody should have a concert, they generally had one. And a year ago she was sure that he would never have thought of risking money on Lewis. She planned to tell Florence all about it.

Lewis jogged home, through the wintry twilight, on the top of an omnibus. He was feeling rather lugubrious for he expected his house to be chilly. The boards were too bare and the furniture too hard and sparse ; there was none of the fat comfort and untidiness that make for warmth. When Florence was there, of course, it was different. She made a sort of glow in it. But she had fallen out with him and was gone to sulk at Cambridge. That was the truth, though he had been so light-hearted about it at Lexham Gardens. She had asked Millicent and her husband to dine with them, and he, when told of it, had demanded that the invitation should be cancelled. They had come to terrible grief. Florence said that there were some things which nobody could do ; he had replied that there was nothing that he could not do, and that he would write Millicent himself if she did not. Also that his letter, if written, would probably be the ruder of the two. She had commanded and implored him. She had said that it was very humiliating for her, and that she would not submit to it. She had frozen him for three days and then, finding it, as he suspected, difficult to keep up, went off to Cambridge. He had no doubt but that she was fortifying herself by pouring out the whole shocking history to her father.

Meanwhile the innocent wretch had left him alone, with no better chaperon than Roberto, in a neat, cold house which always smelt of furniture polish, cheered by the bleak hope that on Monday a neat, cold wife might return to him. He wished that he could have stayed all night with the Birnbaums. He wanted company and distraction, for he had practically finished his Concerto and there was nothing in his head ; a dangerous time, when, formerly, he would have gone to stay with the Sangers.

The omnibus came to Kew Bridge and he got off. He whistled as he hastened down to the river and picked his way along the narrow path, in front of the little quiet houses. The river gurgled against the wooden groynings, and across the water he could hear the pulsating throb of a power house. He stood still for a moment, listening with the absent, instinctive concentration that was his nature. Tall thin chimneys stood up against the winter sunset. Presently the " Mary Blake " came chugging down stream, with a string of barges in tow, and he turned to stare after her, kicking little bits of gravel into the water.

" Tide nearly high ! " he observed, to the frosty air.

On the railway bridge just below his house a District train flashed jewelled windows into the river and he thought, rather wistfully, of all the clerks rushing to their supper and the evening paper in crowded little homes at Richmond or Kew. He felt still more reluctant to eat his own meal alone in an empty house, but he dragged slowly along, humming to himself with a grim chuckle :

" *Se vuol ballare, signor contino !* "

He opened the small iron gate in front of his house, and started backward with a cry as three people rose up from the deep shadow of the portico above. They had been sitting in silence on his doorstep.

" It's Lewis ! " breathed a voice, and he was nearly throttled by a small pair of arms, flung round his neck, and half a dozen frantic kisses.

" How . . . who . . . why ! Paulina ! " he stammered. " Sebastian ! How did you get here ? "

" We've run away," said Paulina. " We had to. Sebastian ran away from his school, so we thought we'd better too."

" We found your house all shut up," continued Sebastian more calmly. " So we sat on the doorstep and waited for somebody to come."

Lewis looked up at the third person on the step above him. She hovered, a little uncertainly, in the shadow.

" Tessa ! " he said eagerly. " Is that Tessa ? "

Then she came down to him and he caught her up and turned her face to the last of the daylight, to make sure that he had got her. He heard her laugh and say :

" Yes, it's me ! I've come to lay my bones among you."

" Oh, Tessa ! This is splendid ! How long it's been ! "

Yet she hardly seemed real. She was so pale, like a shadow, and in his arms she seemed to have no weight at all ; she had alighted there as some fragile, snowy flower might drift down to the grass of an orchard upon a windless night in May.

" Look up ! " he commanded. " Lift your head up, Tessa, and kiss me ! "

She tilted her face up and they kissed, a clinging embrace that was more like a farewell than a greeting. To her that instant brought a pang, a dim echo of times past ; to him, an apprehension of change, a foreshadowing of loss and grief to come. They drew quickly apart and she said :

187

" Are you going to let us into your house, Lewis ? "

He pulled a latchkey from his pocket and, unlocking the door, he lifted her up and brought her into the hall. The others followed and the door shut with a clap which resounded through the empty rooms. He stood still in the darkness for a moment, reflecting, asking himself what sort of parting they had had, six months ago. Strange that he could remember nothing of it ! He supposed that it was some time in June, somewhere in the Tyrol, but it seemed that he had let her go without a thought, robbed, surely of his wits, by some foolish preoccupation. Then he remembered that he had been getting married. He switched on the light and saw her again, close beside him, young and round-faced, blinking a little in the sudden brilliance.

Two telegrams lay on the hall table. They had arrived during the afternoon and Roberto had put them carefully into view before going out. Lewis opened them. The first said :

" Sanger sisters disappeared this morning last seen 9 A.M. are they with you will not inform police unless hear from you have also wired Cambridge Wragge."

The next, which was from Florence, said :

" Wire received here saying Sebastian has run away if he turns up at the Green keep him and wire me."

These telegrams Lewis read out, and Teresa commented :
" Sanger sisters sounds like a music hall turn."

" Well," said Lewis, determined to be practical and efficient, " we must wire to Florence, and all these schools, to say that you are safe. Come into the music-room."

They were much impressed by the music-room, and Sebastian immediately began to play the piano while Lewis concocted the telegrams which he was to send. The girls, sitting on either arm of his chair, made suggestions and alterations. The finished product to Florence ran :

" All children here have wired schools don't bother to come back your loving husband."

In the messages to the schools they were anxious to be as abusive as possible, but Lewis, with some remnants of prudence, insisted upon censorship. Eventually they compromised with a brief intimation of Sebastian's whereabouts, in the case of his school, and, to Cleeve, the message :

" Sanger sisters safe they are not coming back to your school Dodd."

" Because we can't possibly go back," insisted Paulina. " We bore it in silence. . . ."

" No," said Teresa sadly, " not in silence. . . :"

" I did," said Sebastian. " Nobody has ever heard a word of complaint from me."

" What made you run ? " asked Lewis.

" They said I was to be in the school choir ! " Sebastian told them, with calm indignation.

And he began to play a Beethoven Sonata, op. 111, very solemnly, as if its shocked sevenths gave point to his feeling of outrage. Soon he was making a considerable noise, and the girls, screaming over the din, gave an account of the elope-ment. Sebastian had objected to many things at his Preparatory. He did not get enough time to practise, he had an inadequate piano with three notes broken, and an instructress who knew nothing about it. His life there was clearly a waste of time and this business of the choir had been the last straw. He had taken advantage of a half holiday and a paper chase to slip off and get to the station. Here he caught a train which went to a Cathe-dral town not ten miles from Cleeve, where his sisters were ; so he thought he might as well pay them a visit before going on his travels. He pawned his coat and cap, bought others, had a meal, and went on to Cleeve, feeling that he had covered his tracks very successfully. Late in the evening he presented himself boldly at Farnborough Lodge, the College boarding house where Teresa and Paulina were incarcerated, and asked to see them. He told the lady who interviewed him a very plausible tale of an uncle who had brought him to Cleeve and who was coming next day in person to take the girls out. She never thought of disbelieving him, for it is not usual to suspect such small creatures of so much villainy. She summoned the girls and left the three together. He, finding them unhappy, persuaded them to run away too. Then he left them and spent a very uncomfortable night in the garden of an empty house, fearing the questions that might be asked if he took a room anywhere. Next day the girls put all their money in their pockets and hid themselves in a dressing-room until the whole of the College was assembled in the great hall for morning prayers. Then they put on their hats and walked out of the building, knowing that their loss would not be discovered until the house assembled for lunch at one o'clock. It would be presumed, in the classes where they should have been, that they were absent through illness.

Sebastian met them at the railway station, whither they got themselves in some trepidation, and they took the next train to London. Having found their way to Strand-on-the-Green, they had spent the rest of the time sitting on the doorstep.

"If we'd known how simple it would be," said Paulina, "we'd have done it long ago. Only we didn't know where to run. Why didn't you answer our letters, Lewis?"

Lewis looked uncomfortable and said he had forgotten.

"Tessa said you wouldn't answer."

"Did you, Tessa? Why?"

"Because you have a forgetful nature."

"No, I haven't."

"Yes, you have."

"I think I heard Roberto come in. Listen!"

"Roberto !" they cried. "Is he here?"

And they rushed out to embrace Roberto. In the kitchen there was little trace of Florence. All was a lovely confusion. Roberto could not make a pudding without using every bowl in the house, and never washed a dish until all were dirty. A grand washing up took place every two or three days, and one was evidently almost due, for dirty crockery was piled high on the chairs and tables and even on the floor. Tomatoes, spilling out of a paper bag, splashed the room with colour, onions hung in strings from the ceiling, and the whole place smelt gloriously of garlic.

"Oh !" cried Teresa, with her arms round Roberto's neck, "this is like getting home !"

Lewis pitched a ham off a chair by the fire and sat down. He pulled Paulina on to his knee and began to fill his pipe.

"We'll have our supper in here," he said. "It's warmer."

"It certainly is the place for us," said Teresa.

CHAPTER XV

Two letters had come for Florence by the early post next morning. Paulina picked them up from the mat under the letter-box in the hall and brought them to Lewis, who was eating his breakfast in the kitchen.

"They've both got the Cleeve post mark," she said, "and one is from Miss Wragge. I expect she will explain how she came to mislay us. Do open it and see what she says."

"That I can't do," said Lewis. "It belongs to Florence. She wouldn't like it."

"Couldn't you steam it open?" she suggested. "Then you could shut it up again and she won't know. We do so want to hear what's in it ; and she won't tell us perhaps."

"These things," said Lewis grandly, "are not done."

"He talks like a book, so he does," commented Teresa.

"And he's quite right," said Sebastian. "She wouldn't do it to his letters."

"I can't think who this is from," said Paulina, peering at the other envelope. "It's typewritten, I think."

Teresa turned quite pale and got up to look at it too. She suggested that it might be from Miss Butterfield.

"Oh, Tessa? Do you think so?"

Paulina also looked frightened and Lewis asked who Miss Butterfield might be. They told him solemnly that she was the head-mistress.

"Then what is Miss Wragge?"

"Only the house-mistress. There are twelve of them, you know ; one to each house, and one for the day girls. But Miss

Butterfield is the head of the whole College. She lives in a house by herself. They must have told her about us."

"Well, naturally, my good girls! Two pupils couldn't very well disappear without her hearing something of it. Marmalade, Sebastian? What was this lady like, that you blanch at her very name. Did she birch you?"

"No—o! Oh, no!"

"Did any one birch you?"

They shook their heads.

"What did they do to you when you were naughty?"

They seemed at a loss to explain, but they intimated that it had been something awful. It was not so much what was done as what was said.

"I know what it was," put in Sebastian wisely. "They said, 'Naughty girl Sanger! Don't do it again!' And you cried for the rest of the day. That's the way they do at girls' schools."

Teresa and Paulina looked very indignant, but they had to admit that it was something a little like that. Sebastian exchanged a glance with Lewis, a grin of amused contempt at women and their ways. Lewis said :

"But go on about Miss Butterfield. Was she old?"

"Not particularly," said Teresa. "She was called Miss Helen Butterfield, M.A. And she used to read prayers in the morning in a black cloak, with a queer blue thing round her neck. And she had a most beautiful voice ; quite different from Miss Wragge, who used to read prayers at the house in the evening and sort of barked them. And she saw people . . . bishops and parents and people . . . and she saw the girls if anybody had died, or if they'd done anything perfectly dreadful. And she used to give addresses to us on Fortitude and Friendship and things like that. She was very nice looking, and had lovely clothes. She very nearly knew our names." This was said in a tone of modest pride. "We once had a

193

lecture on music from a funny old granpa . . . I forget who he was . . . but I met her showing him over the College next day. And she put her hand on my shoulder and stopped me and said : 'This is Esther Sanger, one of Albert Sanger's daughters. I think I told you that we have two of them here in the College.' And he said : ' How are you, my dear ? How are you ? ' I could see he knew Sanger and was trying to figure out who my mother probably was. I was so startled at Miss Butterfield speaking to me that I couldn't say anything ; so I just made a curtsey ! . . . And she laughed and said : 'You can see that Esther has been to school in Germany. Run along, my child ! We mustn't keep you.' I'd forgotten that in England it isn't manners to curtsey when an old gentleman takes notice of you."

Lewis gaped at this recital and said at last :

" Do you know, I think it was high time you came away. I don't quite like the sound of Miss Helen Butterfield."

"Oh, but she was wonderful ! " insisted Teresa. "Really she was. Everybody thought so. I'm sure, whatever happened to her, she would always know exactly how to behave."

"Tessa didn't hate it all nearly as much as I did," Paulina explained.

"Didn't you, Tessa ? " asked Lewis jealously. "Why not ? "

"Oh . . . it was interesting in a way. It was new."

"Still, you ran away. You came here."

"Yes, because the others did. I barred being left there by myself. I didn't like it well enough for that. Look, Lewis ! We haven't seen your house yet. You've got some more rooms, I suppose, besides what we've seen ? "

"Oh, yes," said Lewis. " I'll show you the whole concern."

He took them first to the dining-room, which was washed white, with an oak cottage dresser and blue plates. There was a gate-legged table, polished almost black, with a lustre dish on

194

it full of golden oranges. The chimney piece was bare save for a Russian ornament of brilliant enamels which blazed through the sombre-tinted room. Lewis mentioned that Florence wished her house to look like the Karindehütte; an idea which puzzled the children very much. They thought this a poor, bare sort of room, not worthy of their lady cousin. Paulina asked hopefully if the pewter flagons on the sideboard were silver.

"Imitation," Lewis told her sadly.

"Oh, well," she consoled him. "They look almost real. You might never know."

They came into the hall, where drawings by Florence's friend, Mr. Argony, hung on the yellow walls. Lewis was humming a little tune which somebody, his mother most likely, had taught him before he was out of petticoats. It had just come into his head :

> "There was a lady loved a swine,
> (Honey ! says she.)

" Come upstairs, girls ! Our best things are in the parlour.

> " ' Pig hog,' she said, ' wilt thou be mine ? '
> (Hunks ! said he.) "

They went up to the drawing-room, which was a worse shock than ever. Teresa made an effort and said :

"Well, I think it's nice. You wouldn't expect Florence to have a lot of heavy sofas and things, would you ? "

"But still, she's married," objected Paulina. "Married ladies always have sofas. Has Tony got one, Lewis ? "

"Hunks ! said he. Tony ? Oh, she has half a dozen."

"What did I say ? Ike knows. I don't call that a sofa."

She pointed scornfully to a divan in the window, piled high with beautiful cushions.

" But it's pretty, Lina," insisted Teresa.

" A drawing-room," said Sebastian, " doesn't want to be pretty. It ought to be rich and grand."

The young Sangers had but a small experience of drawing-rooms. But their general notion of respectability implied a good deal of upholstered mahogany, ormolu, and many small tables with mats and albums. They approved, however, of their cousin's bedroom, to which they were next conducted. It was a fine orderly place, full of her plain, beautiful personal belongings. It was like no lady's room that they could ever have imagined. No powder was ever spilt on the looking glass, no petticoats hung on the door, no stays were flung over chair backs. The chests and wardrobes smelt faintly of lavender. Paulina looked at the twin beds, side by side, with blue linen covers worked all over in patterns of flowers and leaves in bright wools. She asked in some awe :

" Does she let you sleep in here ? "

Lewis nodded. He still found it a little surprising himself, and woke up of a morning feeling that he must have got there by mistake. A burst of music took him, and he broke into the second stanza of his nursery rhyme :

> " ' I'll build for thee a silver sty
> (Honey ! says she.) "

" Where do you keep your clothes ? " asked Teresa, peeping into a wardrobe.

" Oh, they aren't here. They're in my dressing-room."

" Oh ! Do you have a special room to dress in ? Has Ike ? "

" I don't know. I expect so. His house is bigger."

" I call that unsociable," said Paulina. " When you're washing and dressing, that's just the time you want somebody to talk to. Is she cross when she wakes up in the morning, Lewis ? "

Lewis considered, staring at her bed. He could not re-

196

member, somehow, what she was really like. He was never very good at imagining people when they were not there, and just now his mind was confused between two Florences, and the astounding reflection that he was married to both. He had begun to show the house in a spirit of marked rebellion against the domineering stranger who owned it ; but the comments and conversation of the children, their very different conception of their cousin, brought him back to an earlier idea of her. He remembered her suddenly as the beautiful, kindly, rather defenceless creature that she had been when last they were all together. There was certainly a pathetic quality about her then, which had affected him very powerfully. But since they came to England it had all melted away like snow in the sunshine.

All the morning he was musical and inclined to exclaim " Hunks ! " at intervals. Also he learned, in the course of the day, many details of the girls' life at school which amazed and perplexed him. They had, it seemed, gone there with every intention to be good, prepared for inhumanly strict teachers and a great deal of hard work. They were really anxious to be educated and might have done well if the place had not been utterly beyond the scope of their imagination.

Cleeve College was very large and very modern. It had been built up, in the last quarter of the nineteenth century, by a famous pioneer in women's education, a hard bitten lady who apparently believed that a uniform and most desirable type can be produced by keeping eight hundred girls perpetually upon the run. The young creatures, under her rule, were kept most wonderfully busy, and in their subsequent careers they did her credit. Her traditions hung heavy upon Cleeve, long after her departure. Miss Helen Butterfield, her successor, modified the syllabus and shortened the hours of work, but the girls still ran.

The staff were not at all strict ; for the most part they were lively young women, fresh from the University, with a strong faith in hockey and the prefectorial system. The earnestness which the Sangers brought to their school work won them little favour in that quarter, as long as their manners remained so casual and their laziness upon the playing-field so unconcealed. But, as was natural, their failings brought them into collision with the other girls rather than with authority. They would have suffered in any school ; but at Cleeve, which was admittedly democratic, their personal habits and their ready mendacity made them the butt of every amateur reformer. The business of baiting them had a moral sanction behind it. They were persecuted for their own good and the honour of their school until they scarcely knew if they could call their souls their own. They could discover no smallest loophole of respite or escape ; in class, at games, at bed and board the tyrannical, many-eyed mob were always with them.

Paulina, describing it, was impetuous and violent. Teresa was sardonic, and as often inclined to laugh at herself as at the school. She perceived a certain humour in some of the situations that had arisen, and she persisted in saying that she would have stayed there a little longer if Sebastian had not turned up. Lewis did not like this. He wanted her to say that she had run because she could not help it. He was not at all satisfied with her this morning. Undeniably they had succeeded in changing her at that horrible place. In six months she had grown out of all knowledge ; she was sturdier and rather clumsy sometimes ; there was a new, thoughtful hardening about her eyes and mouth. Perhaps it was her neat, well-made school clothes that made her look so odd. He had never seen her respectably dressed before. And what was this horrid fair braid that slapped her back whenever she moved her head ? He had to pull the ribbon off and burn it on the kitchen fire. But even when her hair hung loose on her shoulders it

198

looked sleek and heavy, not like the wind-blown locks he used to twist and play with.

They were at tea, toasting muffins in the music-room, when Florence returned, cold, tired, anxious and very much put out. She had received their telegram that morning and had hastened back immediately. Her first impression, as the party round the fire rose to greet her, was that she was an intruder. The children flung themselves upon her with every appearance of joy, but, for the fraction of a second, she knew that their faces had fallen. She tried to be stern and displeased, and said coldly as she got away from them :

"Well, children ! What is the meaning of this ? "

Lewis was waiting rather shyly until they had done with her, and she, conscious of their inquisitive eyes, went and kissed him on the cheek exclaiming : "Well, Lewis ! " in almost exactly the same tone. But, as if bent upon disconcerting her, he responded with a cordial hug which dissipated all her airs of distant dignity. She exclaimed, flustered and at random :

"Oh, I am so tired . . ."

They were pulling up a chair to the fire for her ; and Teresa was taking off her furs, and Paulina was bringing her a cup of tea, and Sebastian was toasting a muffin for her. Lewis, with quick, deft fingers, was pulling the long pins out of her hat. Then, somehow, he had banished the noisy trio from the room and she was alone with him in the dusk and the quiet firelight. She leant back in her chair, quite exhausted.

"I sent them to the kitchen," he said. "You're tired. You don't want to be worried with them. Have some tea ! "

When she was fed and rested he brought her the two letters from Cleeve, which were full of explanations and proposed plans of actions. He told her that he had wired to both schools. "That was sensible of you, dear boy ! "

She gave him an approving look, and he came and sat on the arm of her chair, saying affectionately :

" You needn't have hurried back like this, you know."

" Oh, I had to. They must go back on Monday."

" Go back ! Florence ! Are you going to make them go back ? "

" Of course I am."

" Is it worth while ? It's almost the Christmas holidays."

" They mustn't be allowed to think this sort of thing pays."

" I never thought you'd made them go back," he said slowly. " In fact, we said in the telegrams that they wouldn't come back."

" You said . . . What on earth made you say that ? " She sat up indignantly.

" But you won't make them stay another term, surely ? "

" I shall indeed."

" They'll only do it again."

" That's nonsense. They'll learn the folly of such escapades. If we give in this time . . ."

" They were miserable . . ."

" It was their own fault."

" It was not. This Cleeve ! A filthy place by all accounts. They were right not to stand it."

" My dear Lewis ! It's the best school in England. I was educated there myself. I know all about it."

He had nothing to say to this. So he pleaded :

" At least don't make Tessa go back. It's different for Lina."

" Lina has been loudest in her complaints."

" I know. But it's done most harm to Tessa. She was very nearly perfect before she went there . . ."

" *Teresa was very nearly perfect !* Lewis, what do you mean ? "

" She's too old for that kind of school."

" Old ! She's ridiculously young for her age. Are you out of your senses ? She isn't sixteen. And she needs badly to find her own level. What sort of school do you recommend ? "

" How should I know ? Some place where they won't change her. A quiet sort of place."

" Cleeve turns out a splendid type."

" Oh, Christ . . ."

He became too much exasperated even to swear. He flung down the length of the room and back again while Florence repeated in unquenchable amazement :

" But to say that Teresa . . . Teresa ! Is nearly perfect ! "

" Was."

An obscure relief stole over her. She lay back in her chair again and continued in calmer tones :

" She's getting to the awkward age. They'll both do that. Of course, they'll lose some of their charm ; they are bound to become duller for a time. English schoolgirls are not interesting. But on the whole it's best. They were very insecure, poor darlings . . . so childish . . . so impressionable . . ."

" Yes ! Yes ! That's it. Florence, I do entreat you not to send them back ! "

" I must. I think it best for them, and so does my father. If we think that, there's no choice about it."

He collected himself for a final appeal.

" Have you written to Millicent yet . . . about that dinner ? "

" No. Not yet."

" Couldn't you . . . couldn't we come to some agreement ? "

" I'm quite ready for a compromise. You know that."

" I know. Well, listen ! I'll give in about it ; you ask her and I'll be civil. But won't you . . ."

" Won't I . . . ? "

" Keep them here a bit . . . the children . . ."

" I'd like to, but I couldn't. It wouldn't be fair to make their future a bargain for my own convenience. I really think that they ought immediately to go back. It's not caprice."

" Very well.   I've made you a fair offer."

She was much tempted to agree, for she did not like the idea of forcing the children back.   But her conscience forbade it. On Monday morning, however, she got from both schools a definite refusal to receive the young Sangers again.   Their impertinent, unruly ways endangered discipline, and their strange oaths were likely to become the scandal of many respectable homes during the Christmas holidays.   Their elopements had been sensational and a bad precedent ;   the authorities considered that they had better be forgotten as soon as possible.   It was clear that they must remain in Chiswick until new establishments could be found willing to take them, and under these circumstances Florence had no scruple in making a bargain.   She would keep them till Easter if Lewis would be polite to Millicent sometimes.   He agreed and endured the dinner party with surprisingly good grace.

She did not suggest that he should apologise to his father. Save for the look of the thing she had no particular wish for a reconciliation with Sir Felix.   Charles Churchill laughed at him.   His influence was, she knew, due in a great measure to his own self-importance and effrontery ;   she was not prepared to stand patronage from such a man.   Millicent was different ; she clearly wished to meet, at Chiswick, those elusive people all known to Florence, whom she had so far failed to secure. She would behave herself.   To have her there sometimes would look well and create an impression that Lewis was on good terms with his family.

" I'll ask her to tea when you're out," she told him.

" That's all right.   It's your house."

" Now don't talk nonsense.   It's just as much yours."

" ' Honey !   Says she.' "

" What did you say ? "

" Nothing.   A song.   An echo of my infancy."

CHAPTER XVI

FLORENCE was not long in discovering that the Sangers in London were more formidable than the Sangers in the Tyrol. In their house she had never felt so much of a stranger among them as she did now in her own ; they seemed to have become, as a family, so much more corporate and definite. Christmas was scarcely over before she began to be aware that she had imported, not three friendless orphans, but an alien community, foreign and inimical to her way of life. She began to be very eager to get rid of them.

Of the three she liked Sebastian the best because his manners were always so charming. And he was talented ; of that there was no doubt. After listening to some of his performances on the music-room piano she fully admitted his right to take his own career very seriously. She talked to him about it and was amazed at the calm certainty of his ideas. Pending some permanent settlement he agreed quite cheerfully to attend a small day school in the neighbourhood, for the benefit of his general education.

She wished that she could be as certain of her own future. She had, as yet, done nothing to attract the public attention to Lewis. For all the notice that anyone took of him he might never have married an influential wife. This was entirely her own fault for, with half a dozen strings within her reach, she had not made up her mind which to pull. His waywardness unnerved her, and all the complications with the children had taken up time. She must bestir herself and do something.

Early in February she made up her mind that she must give a party ; not a large affair, but very choice. As the first move, it had great strategic importance. She was sure now that she had better not drag her shy young genius to other people's drawing-rooms. He could not be trusted to behave ; he must be allowed to have a solitary and retiring disposition. Those who wished to know him must come out to Chiswick where he could be seen to advantage. He needed his own background. The lovely little house which was to have the charm of Sanger's circus without its drawbacks, the river, Roberto, the mulberry tree and Lewis's many waistcoats were all part of the picture. Her business lay in building the thing up, and in after years she often told herself that she could have done it had it not been for the children, the constant dragging, hostile influence of the enemy within her gates which made of every struggle with Lewis a battle with a group.

To her first party she only meant to invite people whom she knew rather well, and these were to be chosen upon two grounds, music and influence. Also they were all to be nice people who could enjoy each other's company. The whole thing was to be intimate and very pleasant. But she was a little troubled, because she thought that Millicent should be invited and she feared the effect upon Lewis.

She had found it difficult, in the first place, to make him listen to any of her plans. He had agreed readily enough that she should give a party and even seemed prepared to hand coffee cups if she would like. But he did not grasp its real importance. He showed much more interest and concern in a piano sonata which Sebastian was to play at a concert given by his little school. The fuss which they made over the selection of this piece, and the hours of practice which it seemed to require, were an annoyance to Florence. Once, after a meal at which they had all discussed nothing else, she said impatiently :

" What on earth does it matter if he plays the Mozart or the

204

Haydn? You say the Fantasia isn't good enough? They may thank their stars for getting anything as good."

"Indeed, they may," agreed Lewis. "But it's a trifle beyond his mark, I think."

"It's only the boys and their parents," she pointed out. "They won't know . . ."

She stopped, biting her lip, aghast at what she had said. Lewis and the three Sangers were looking at her in a way she did not like; they made no comment, but their contemptuous surprise was galling to her. It was impossible always to remember how seriously they took themselves. Her own standards were high, but they were perfect maniacs. It was one of the thousand small occasions upon which she was made to feel that four people in the house were united in a point of view which was, to her, partially incomprehensible. She was still a little vexed about it, when, later in the day, she courageously approached Lewis upon the subject of Millicent's invitation.

"I don't want to offend her," she said. "She carries a good deal of weight in some quarters. It wouldn't be at all difficult for her to put a spoke in your wheel."

"I haven't got a wheel."

"She has contrived to get her opinion respected upon musical matters. I can't think why. I don't like her voice."

"A filthy rat squeak!"

"Still, I'd like to ask her."

"Then do! It's only for once."

"And I'm asking the Mainwarings . . . my cousins, you know. They're quite harmless. He's in the city, but he knows a lot about music. She's very nice. And then, if he'll come, I want to get Sir Bartlemy Pugh."

Sir Bartlemy Pugh had written a quantity of church music and some choral pieces in a melodious, old-fashioned style which Lewis heartily despised. He made some strong remarks about it, but showed no other objection to the proposed invitation. Florence said serenely :

"You never heard any of it, dear. He's a charming old man. I've known him since I was that high. Then Dr. Dawson. He's another old friend I'd like to have."

Distinguished old men who had rocked her cradle were to be very much to the fore at these early parties. She used all her pretty ways to induce them to come. Dr. Dawson, who was a fine conductor but a terrible bear, said when she tackled him :

"Don't make eyes at me, Florence Dodd ! I'm coming because I want to meet your husband."

Whereat she almost kissed him.

Lewis was quite pleased at the sound of his name, but looked less agreeable when she said that she wanted the Leyburns. He demanded who they were.

"Oh, you know ! She's a very fine singer. She used to be the wife of Jimmy Jansen, but it didn't work. They run the Guild of Beauty, she and Edward Leyburn, I mean."

"What is the Guild of Beauty ?" he asked unpromisingly.

"Those people who give those concerts down in the slums. You must know ! They have quite a good choir ; and they practically run the 'Nine Muses.' Their idea is to educate the popular taste in the Arts, beginning with the proletariat ; that's such a much more promising field than the middle classes. They try to give the people really good music. That concert we went to at Notting Hill Gate was got up by them."

"Call that really good music ?"

"N—no . . . It was a good level for amateurs, and . . ."

"Amateurs," said Lewis, pronouncing the word as if it made him a little ill, "have no business to have a level. Is this Leyburn an amateur ?"

"Don't talk in that tone of voice about amateurs. I'm one myself. Yes, he is. He sings very nicely too. And he's done a lot of splendid work bringing music to the people."

" What's he want to do that for ? "

" My dear Lewis !   Why do you write music ? "

" God knows ! "

" Don't you want to give pleasure to people ? "

" No."

" That's a pose."

" It's not !   I'll swear it's not.   I tell you this, Florence. The sight of a lot of them listening to my work, or Sanger's work, or anything decent, makes me sick.   I swear then I won't write another note, if that's what it's for.   Sanger too ! I know how he felt.   Once I remember they made a demonstration round the door of a hall when he came out, shaking hands with him and so forth, and an old fellow came up and said : ' Mr. Sanger, I'd like to tell you of the pleasure that you've given to a poor working man.'   ' Oh ? ' said Sanger. ' I suppose you think I ought to want to please every son of a bitch who can pay for a sixpenny ticket.' "

He paused to laugh at this retort, but Florence was not amused.   She said, rather angrily :

" That was abominable, and not at all funny.   Not a bit. It's a thing I can't understand in you, Lewis, the way you repeat the perfectly disgusting things that Sanger said as if they were good stories."

" They are good stories."

" It was particularly odious to say that to a poor man."

" He'd have said it, just the same, to a grand duke.   I wish it had been my father that he said it to.   No, but you miss the point.   That's how Sanger felt about pleasing people.   And I think I feel in much the same way."

" It's quite the wrong attitude.   I hope you won't say that sort of thing to the people at my party."

" Write down beforehand what I have to say and I'll learn it off."

She was reassured, a little, by his manner of saying this. To reward him she asked if there was any guest he wanted.

"Yes," he said. "I'd like to ask Ike and Tony."

"Ike and Tony?" She was very doubtful. "Do you think they would enjoy it?"

"Tony loves any sort of party. And Ike would enjoy moving in such high circles. I want him to meet Millicent. He might give a cheque to the Guild of Beauty."

Florence shuddered

"You know," she said, "I'd love to have them. But at this particular party they might feel just a trifle out of it. Every one who is coming knows every one else rather well."

"Then I shall feel out of it, and so will the children. It would be nice for us to have the Birnbaums to consort with."

Florence explained that the children were not to be there and they wrangled over this for several minutes. At length they compromised ; he would ask Jacob without Antonia, and later on he would give a party himself for the Birnbaums and the children. Florence was most cordial over this idea.

"I'll have Nils Stavgröd," said Lewis. "He's coming next week for a season here."

"You know him?" cried Florence. "Of course we'll have him. Why didn't you suggest him before?"

"I didn't mean your party, I meant mine."

"Ask him to both."

"I doubt if he'd like yours. He wouldn't get on with Millicent. It isn't his line."

"There's no privilege in meeting Teresa and Paulina."

"He's met them. He knows them. He's like me and prefers them, I expect."

"You're very arrogant."

He said nothing.

"And small minded."

"Yes," he said complacently.

208

Exasperation almost choked her. For a few minutes she could say nothing ; she sat still, wondering dumbly how much longer she was going to put up with their crazy ways. Not any longer, it seemed, for as soon as she had got her breath she heard herself proclaiming instructively :

"Your attitude is completely wrong. You put the wrong things first. Music, all art . . . what is it for ? What is its justification ? After all . . ."

"It's not for anything. It has no justification. It . . ."

"It's only part of the supreme art, the business of living beautifully. You can't put it on a pedestal above decency and humanity and civilization, as your precious Sanger seems to have done. Human life is more important."

"I know. You want to use it like electric light. You buy a new saucepan for your kitchen and a new picture for your silver sty. I've seen it. My father's cultured. He . . ."

"It's a much abused word, and one is shy of using it. But it means an important thing, which we can't do without."

"Can't we ? I can ! By God I can ! Why do you suppose I ran away ? To get free of it. Why do you think I loved Sanger ? "

He broke into a wild tirade against the people who would chain him and his labour to the chariot wheels of a social structure. He tried to urge his own conviction that beauty and danger are inseparable ; that ideas are best conceived in a world of violence ; that any civilization must of necessity end by quenching the riotous flame of art for the sake of civic order. But he could not say what he meant. He was not furnished with any of the right words for such a discussion, and used, moreover, so many inexcusably wrong ones that she lost the thread in her indignation.

"I can't stand this obscene language any more," she said, jumping up. "And I'm sure the world would be an unspeakably awful place if you could have your way in it."

"If you had yours, the only people who would enjoy themselves would be sick persons and young children."

"Well, why not? Lewis! I will not have it. Is it impossible to you to discuss anything without swearing? Very well then! We'd better let it drop!"

After preliminaries like these it was scarcely surprising, even to Florence, that the party was a failure. Jacob Birnbaum, reporting on it to his wife, said:

"Lewis is a fool! He does not take his opportunities."

"Was it very grand?" asked Antonia, who had stayed awake on purpose to hear all about it.

She supposed that she had not been invited because she was not grand enough. In many ways she was a very humble creature in spite of a pearl rope and fifty pairs of silk stockings.

"No," said Jacob. "The women were *comme il faut*, but they had no style. You in your chemise are worth all of them together. You are not invited because Mrs. Dodd is growing tired of the Sangers. She does not think that you are altogether a credit. Also, Lewis is not to be a second Albert, even though she is a little like Evelyn, you understand?"

"I don't think I do. I think she's fond of us. But how is Lewis a fool? Was he drunk?"

"Not so much. But he is throwing away all his good chances. These people might help him. He has insulted every one of them, I think, but old Dr. Dawson. There was this man there, Leyburn, who manages the 'Nine Muses,' does he not? He will produce 'Prester John' there, and Lewis shall conduct it. But Lewis! He would do nothing but abuse the piece!"

"Well, but it's very bad. Sanger was ashamed of it himself. He was very young when he wrote it. At home we thought it a joke. It was howled down in Paris, and quite right too."

"Still, it is foolish of Lewis. If his own work is to be heard later he should be glad to take these chances. And his wife is so very anxious, poor woman! I think she has arranged this party just for that. I wonder what she is saying to him now. There will be a terrible scene going on!"

But Jacob was wrong. Though the evening was an unmistakable disaster it led to no immediate quarrel.

Florence had known all day that she would not be able to control her husband; she was quite certain of it when, with a heavy heart, she went to dress. To encourage herself she put on a very beautiful new gown; and she needed all the spirit she could muster, for he was impossible from the first. Not that he succeeded in discomposing the guests, who were, for the most part, too well mannered and too fond of Florence, to show offence, even if they took it. But he forced her to be terribly ashamed of him. He interrupted Sir Bartlemy, contradicted Edward Leyburn, professed the blankest ignorance of any music save Albert Sanger's and his own, and played Millicent's accompaniments in such a manner that she was unable to get through a single song. Millicent was outraged past forgiveness and would not sing again, even when Edward Leyburn offered to play for her. Mrs. Leyburn, kind soul, filled the awkward gap by singing herself, though she had an audibly bad cold. Lewis listened for about ten bars and then left the room with a good deal of ostentatious noisiness, inviting the other men to come with him and have a drink. Jacob and Dr. Dawson followed him, and they seemed to be going to stay in the dining-room for the rest of the night. At last Sir Bartlemy went too, and by some unknown persuasions brought them back, but the evening, by then, was past retrieving. Everybody, in spite of themselves, looked glum. Florence could not suppose that there was any charm about her house and she trembled to think of the tale which Millicent might make of it all.

The Mainwarings did their best and so did Sir Bartlemy. They were very sorry for Florence because she had married Lewis. But she had not invited them out to Chiswick to be that.   Edward Leyburn, who adored her and had once wanted to marry her himself, made tremendous efforts.   He sat down at the piano and embarked upon a regular recital of songs to save them all the spasmodic difficulties of conversation until it should be late enough that they could decently go home. Florence, for a time released from her hospitable struggles, sat down with her back to the light, hoping that her wretchedness was not too bleakly apparent.   Her face felt quite stiff with the continued effort of smiling.   She listened sadly to German Lieder full of true lovers, forests and nightingales.

Her failure had crushed her so much that she was not even angry.   To-morrow, after a night's sleep, if she could get it, she might recover enough spirit to scold Lewis.   Just now she only wanted to crawl away into the dark and cry a little. Even the music unmanned her, for it brought to her mind the Spring and the Tyrol and all the little flowers that she had picked with her lover, as they wandered over the mountains. And she remembered her happy, confident schemes for their life together ; and the first days of her marriage when she had forgotten schemes and plans and lost herself, for a time, in the delight of being with him.   At last she turned to look at him, wondering if he too would remember.   She found his eyes upon her, strange, bright, questioning ; a glance which she could not interpret.

She glanced at the clock and saw that it was twenty minutes past eleven.   She had instructed Roberto to beat up some eggs at a quarter past that she might make zabaglione, a dish at which she excelled.   As quietly as possible she slipped out of the room and into the pantry, where he had put a tray with the Marsala, the powdered almonds and the little glass cups in which the confection was to be served.   Just for a moment, giving way to the exhaustion of disappointment, she sank down on a chair and leant her head against the pantry dresser.   She was thankful for the dark and quiet.

She felt shattered ; as though she could scarcely face the brightness of the kitchen.

"But taking in the zabaglione will make it easier," she said to herself. "They won't know what it is, and I can tell them about it. It's something new, anyhow !"

She heard herself saying brightly :

"It's only Marsala and beaten eggs, cooked ever so little, just to set it . . ."

She thought that Roberto had come in from the kitchen and was turning to tell him that she was ready when she felt herself lifted up from her chair and caught close in the arms of her lover.

"Lewis !" she whispered. "You oughtn't to be here ! Go back there and look after them."

"That's all right. They're busy singing. I've come to help you with the zabaglione."

But he seemed in no hurry to let her make it and she murmured in expostulation :

"Roberto is in the kitchen."

Lewis stretched out a hand behind him and shut the kitchen door.

"But we can't make zabaglione in the dark."

"We'll go in a minute. Why be in such a hurry ? You were sitting doing nothing when I came in. Tell me !"

She was lost again. When he was like this, he could do what he pleased with her. She sighed.

"Those songs," she said, ". . . they made me think of the Tyrol. Did they remind you of those times ?"

"Yes."

"Somehow . . . since then . . . Oh, my dear Lewis ! What has come over you ?"

"Don't you know ?"

"Oh, well. . . I suppose I do. But you're so. . .sudden."

213

"You're so beautiful," he muttered. "Florence . . . I wish all these people would go away."

"They'll go soon," she said soothingly. "But we must go back to them now. This is no time for dalliance. You're tearing my frock !"

"I'll get you another," he said grandly, forgetting that he had not a penny of his own in the world.

"That won't make me presentable at this immediate moment. Come along . . ."

And she slipped into the kitchen, where Roberto was looking quite pale and spent with beating the eggs for such a long time.

And so her ill-starred party did not end, as Jacob had supposed, in a scene. But it marked an epoch. From that day a subtle change came over the house at Strand-on-the-Green. This was in time perceived by all its inmates. But the first to feel it was Roberto, who had not, up till then, found himself entirely at ease in his new quarters. He discovered that they were suddenly becoming more home-like. In this clean, strange, frigid house, he recognised an atmosphere which he could not have defined but to which he was well accustomed. It spread rapidly from his cosy kitchen to the rooms occupied by his employers.

He first noticed a change on the morning after the party when he took to Mrs. Dodd her early cup of tea. Usually she would answer his knock or she would wake up when he put the tray on the little table beside her bed. While he drew up the blinds she would address herself with energy to the business of rousing her companion. Upon this morning, however, she continued to sleep, after the blinds were up and with the newly risen sun shining right into the room. Their slumber was so profound that discreet little Roberto paused and peered at them anxiously and saw that Madame's lovely hair, generally braided back at night into a thick rope, was loose and flung all across the pillow in a dark cloud about the still paleness of her face.

Roberto, who admired Madame above all women, approved of this ; he peeped at her with appreciation and with that strange, wordless pity which a sleeping person will awake in an observer, the compassion of a guarded spirit for helplessness. He stole out and stumbled over something on the floor ; it was the new dress, flung down as not even a petticoat should have been flung. Roberto, lately converted to neatness, was shocked. He picked up the gown and spread it over a chair ; next he rescued a silk shift. Then, realizing that the unaccountable disorder which had overtaken the room was something significant and past his mending, he smiled broadly and slid out on tiptoe. Down in the kitchen, as he fried the bacon, he sang Puccini and Verdi with a joyous heart.

Nor was his peace of mind shattered when, a week later, he was aware of a dispute, a quarrel so formidable that the house literally rang with it. This, too, was quite in order. He listened respectfully through the bedroom keyhole to two voices, a shrill voice and a surly voice, and he said to the children with many winks and nods :

" Lewis and Madame . . . dey fight . . . I tink . . . yes . . . "

To Florence, however, this quarrel was another step in the slow process of defeat. It was devastating to her, this sudden discovery that her temper could be ungovernable. For a few days she had abandoned herself to the reassurance of being loved, stifling her fears, doubts and regrets in that brief oblivion which was becoming for her, as it was for Lewis, a means of escape. Nothing had been done to reconcile their divergent points of view ; the issues were merely shelved, for neither was really prepared to yield to the other. And when a dispute broke out it was somehow the more bitter because of their recent intense preoccupation with each other.

Always they seemed to fight about such foolish things. This time it was the old, wretched question of Teresa's future.

Lewis was determined that the child should not go to school again. He spoilt her outrageously. For the other two a settlement seemed possible, but about Teresa there was no agreeing. The fight became unbelievably fierce, until Florence noticed an inflection in her voice which reminded her of the railings of Linda Cowlard. She fell silent, horrified and ashamed, and Lewis got in the last word.

" If Tessa leaves this house," he vowed, " I leave it. She's the only thing that makes life tolerable. So I warn you ! "

And he rushed out of the room and fell over Roberto, who was listening at the keyhole, so that the sound of cursing seemed to go on all across the landing and down the stairs. The absurdity of his last remark soon restored Florence to her normal serenity, but for a few minutes after he had gone she felt herself transported by a resentment so passionate that it seemed as if she had never been angry before.

CHAPTER XVII

" PRESTER JOHN " was produced at the "Nine Muses" in the course of the Spring with a success which justified all the risks taken by an enterprising management on its behalf. Charles Churchill, at his breakfast table, read a glowing account of it in the newspaper, the very same paper which had reported Sanger's death so bleakly a year ago.

"We've changed all that !" thought Charles, holding the column close up to his short-sighted eyes. ". . . 'a masterly performance' . . . hm . . . hm . . . 'surely the audience at the "Nine Muses" is the most intelligent in the world' . . . Why do they always say that I wonder ? I suppose because it's the sort of audience which reads the notices next morning . . . ' the enterprise of this undertaking' . . . dammit ! The whole column's about the 'Nine Muses' ! Ah, no ! Here we have it ! . . . Sanger . . . 'neglected too long . . . a national possession !' . . . Well, well ! 'A shattering message !' Heaven help us ! . . . 'and yet, surely, the most vocal music ever written . . . the second act one vast lyric !' . . . What's this ? What the devil's this ? 'Mr. Leyburn's conducting' . . . Leyburn ! . . . 'we venture to think that Mr. Leyburn a little mistook the subtle tempo of the first chorus !' . . . But where, I wonder, was my precious son-in-law ?"

Lewis should have conducted the opera ; Charles knew that. He also knew that Florence was building on its success ; that she regarded the engagement as a great thing. He scratched his head and read the column again and tried to suppose that

Leyburn was a printer's error for Dodd, but it would not do. Very much dispirited, and wondering if some untoward accident could have occurred at Chiswick, he went on with his breakfast.

By the second post came a short, sad little note from Florence to say that the Sanger opera had gone off quite well, but that Lewis had fallen out with the management at the last moment so that Edward Leyburn had taken his place.

"Edward did very well," she wrote, "considering the short notice."

"But she was set on it!" muttered Charles, looking at her letter. "Since when has she learnt to take a disappointment quietly? This is serious! I shall really have to go and see."

He had a horror of interfering parents. He had been determined, from the first, to let Florence manage her crazy marriage in her own way. He had said his say and she would not listen to him. She was old enough to know her own mind. But, on the other hand, he was very fond of her. He was sure that she was unhappy, and there was something in this note which read like an appeal for help. He thought he knew where he could assist her. She did not say so, but for some weeks he had guessed that she was growing rather tired of her young cousins. It was probably time they were removed from Chiswick. At least he could help her over that.

Soon after the production of " Prester John " he discovered that he could spare a week-end to his daughter, so he packed his bag, wired to Strand-on-the-Green, and set off.

He was received by his niece Teresa, who told him that Florence had gone into the country for the day, before his wire came. The children, she said, were out fishing, and Lewis had some men with him. Would Charles have tea with her, or would he rather sit with Lewis? Charles voted for tea promptly, whereupon she went to the top of the stairs and launched a flood of shrill, abusive Italian downwards at

Roberto. Then she came back into the drawing-room and sat herself down to entertain her uncle.

Charles looked her over sharply and with a sense of surprise that was faintly pleasant. He had only seen her once, just after her arrival in England. Since then she had grown a good deal and he rather liked her looks. She was plain, perhaps ; at least, she was not like any of the Churchills. But she was a friendly creature and seemed ready to be civil to him. He began at once on his mission and asked how long she intended to stay at Strand-on-the-Green. She said she supposed she would stay until she had to go.

" Oh," said he. " Then you are depending on my daughter to turn you out ? "

" You mean she doesn't want us ? " said Teresa, looking startled.

" I've never heard her say so. Still, as a guest, you must feel it a little . . ."

" A guest ! "

She opened her eyes.

" Aren't you a guest ? What is a guest, do you think ? "

" A person who's been invited . . ." she began, and pulled up, turning quite pink. Then she recovered herself and said : " But children, you know, are forced to be somebody's guest, if they have no home of their own. It's part of the undignified state of being a child."

" Do you call yourself a child, Miss ? "

" I do not. But your daughter Florence does, and on that account she has to keep me in her house."

" I see. Fourteen, aren't you ? "

" Fifteen. I've had a birthday since I last saw you."

" Dear me ! I'd forgotten. Very remiss of me ! "

" Let me give you some tea."

He recognized a slight inflection of Florence in the way she said this. But there was nothing of Florence in the meal which she had ordered; it consisted largely of a cottage loaf and a trayful of breakfast cups.

"I said the big cups," she commented, with some complacency. "Men always like them."

Charles beamed. He liked but seldom got them. He said:

"Fifteen! An uncle has no business to forget these things, has he? Yes! Two lumps if you please, my dear."

He pulled out his pocket-book.

"I think it's clever of you to have got it right within a year," said Teresa. "Bread? What is this for? Me? Oh!"

"Rather belated, I'm afraid. You'll be telling me you're sixteen before we've finished tea."

"What am I to do with it?"

"Get yourself . . ."

He could not at all guess what she would be likely to get for herself, so he said vaguely that it was to be something pretty.

"A pretty thing," said Teresa thoughtfully, looking at the note in her hand. "With all my heart; the next pretty thing I see. Have another cup?"

"And how did 'Prester John' go off?" asked Charles boldly.

"Really . . . I . . . couldn't say . . ." she answered slowly.

"Why? Weren't you there?"

"Oh, yes. We were all there. But we don't understand the people in this country. We thought it was very bad. It was only half rehearsed. And that Mr. Leyburn can't conduct, can he?"

"That I can't say. Why didn't my son-in-law conduct?"

"Lewis? Of course! He's your son-in-law. How funny! I never thought of you and him as being related. Well . . . no . . . He was going to do it, and then he couldn't."

"Why not?"

"Well, you know, 'Prester John' is such a very poor opera.

Sanger thought so himself ; my father, I mean. It was awful
that they chose just that one ; Lewis hated it. He was very,
very fond of Sanger. And at the rehearsals he got wild
because it was so bad. And at last he couldn't bear it and they
had a quarrel."

"So that was it ! Then it wasn't a success ? "

"But it sounded like one ! They clapped ! And cheered !
I've never seen Sanger's work better received, not even the good
pieces. Always it's been just a few people. But these were
all so enthusiastic ; and the papers next day didn't any of them
say how bad it really was. We couldn't help laughing at first.
It was so ridiculous. And Lewis laughed too, quite loud. And
then, when Florence told us to be quiet, I looked round and
saw that nobody else was amused."

"Where were you sitting ? "

"In the front ; in the stalls. And we got there late, so we
began badly, somehow."

Charles was getting a fairly accurate idea of the sort of
evening that Florence must have spent. She had admitted
beforehand that she should feel a trifle conspicuous, escorting
Sanger's children to hear a first English performance of Sanger's
music. The most intelligent audience in the world was largely
composed of her personal acquaintances. It was a pity if his
nephew and nieces had attracted even more attention by
behaving ill. And Lewis, too, had been told to be quiet. It was
monstrous ! Teresa got a severe little lecture upon civil
manners in public places, which she took very meekly. She
promised to do better another time.

"There won't probably be another time," Charles
told her. "I don't expect Florence will take you to
another."

"Oh, yes, but she will. Lewis is to conduct his Symphony
at the Regent's Hall in May. We are all going to that, and
I promise that we will behave."

221

"Oh?" he murmured, half to himself. "She's pulled that off, has she?"

"Oh, no," said Teresa quickly. "That has nothing to do with her. My brother-in-law, Jacob Birnbaum, managed that. He's Lewis's friend. When we want anything of that kind done he always sees to it."

Charles perceived that the word "we" indicated a community to which his daughter did not, presumably, belong. Teresa gave him to understand that the concert at the Regent's Hall would be a really important affair.

"Why can't she leave the fellow to paddle his own canoe?" he thought. "If he really has a pull with these Jew financiers, they'll do more for him than all her gentlemanly friends put together."

Aloud he said :

"So she's forgiven you, has she?"

"Not quite," said Teresa, after a little consideration. "But she will. She has so much . . ." no adequate English word arrived, so she shyly tried another language : ". . . so much *bonté* !"

Charles agreed. It was the right word for that particular benevolence with which Florence seasoned her obstinacy.

"But Uncle Charles !"

"Yes, my dear?"

"When you said about guests . . . Do you mean that we ought to go away?"

"Not yet," he said hastily. "Not until some suitable establishment is found for you."

"You know that Sebastian has got a scholarship in Dr. Dawson's choir school? He wants to go there. And Lina wants to go on the stage. Only in France, because she can speak Racine. Have you heard her? She can really."

"No. But Florence tells me that she shows promise."

"Well, but there's a school where she can go in Paris. Would that be a suitable establishment?"

" I daresay. I've come here, partly, to discuss it. If you children have professions that you want to pursue . . ."

" I know. I've none."

" Well. That's no harm. It's early yet."

" But Florence says that I'm to go to school again."

" Would you like that ? "

" I couldn't endure it," she said, with a quiet intensity which startled him.

" But my dear ! What's to be done with you ? I'd be quite ready to fall in with your views if you wanted to specialise. With your upbringing, it's late in the day to begin upon general education. I quite see that. I'm sure it's best for the other two to go their own ways. But you say yourself you've no . . ."

" I can't help it. I know what it is to have talent. I know that I've none. I love music. But that's not enough. I love apples, but I don't mean to be a greengrocer. It has to be something more than that ; something that comes so far first that there isn't any question of a second."

" And there's nothing that comes quite first with you ? "

She was silent and he wondered how anyone could be so misguided as to treat her like a child. The sad thoughtfulness of her face was old ; older, in its calm resignation, than any expression he had ever caught on the face of his daughter.

" Everybody has something that comes quite first," she said at last. " But sometimes, you know, it's complicated."

" Not always a thing," suggested Charles gently. " Often, especially for a woman, it's a person. That is more complicated."

At once he felt that he had been a little impertinent. He said hastily that she must not distress herself ; very few people had got a profession at fifteen. She must not let herself be hustled by the precocity of the rest of her family. But in his heart he felt that he was misstating her case. Her trouble was not the bewildered groping of adolescence for a goal in life, but

223

rather the sad finality of a woman who has beheld her destiny too young. His next attempt was towards another kind of consolation. Life, he suggested, was, after all, a very amusing affair. It was wise to cultivate a taste for it. There were so many entertaining things to be done. For a young woman, just entering upon the world, the opportunities of enjoyment were boundless. Didn't she think so ?

"Not in a girls' school."

"Well, no. Probably not. But education is a good investment."

"Is it ? Are you educated ? "

"Comparatively speaking . . . yes."

"Are you so very happy ? Happier than an uneducated man ? "

"I've been singularly fortunate in my life, Teresa. I've had remarkably little to bear ; less I daresay than you have had already. But I can honestly say that, in such trouble as has come to me, a philosophic outlook, which is the fruit, one of the fruits, of a good education, has been of use to me."

"Can't an uneducated person have a philosophic outlook ? "

"By the light of natural wisdom ? Yes. But it's harder and slower. And you must realize this, Teresa. Unhappiness is, to a certain extent, the sure lot of every one of us. We cannot escape it. We can only brace ourselves to endure it. But we have it in our power to do a great deal towards securing our happiness. That does lie in our hands. We can enlarge our tastes and interests and perceptions. That is the chief use of education, to widen the resources."

"Putting your eggs into a lot of baskets instead of one ? "

"It's safer, you know."

"Oh, safety ! I don't think we care so very much about it."

Again that odd use of " we " ; Charles remembered it later. He agreed that too much is sometimes sacrificed for security.

"Well, but you say that education helped you. What kind? What have you had that you value most?" she asked.

"A thorough grounding in the Classics," said Charles promptly. "For it's the key to the humanities. And, on top of it, a man should travel and see life . . ."

"Very well. I've travelled. And I've seen life."

"Pardon me! I disagree with you. I don't think you have seen much life as yet. Of its raw beginnings you may have seen something, but not of the finished product. To see life to any purpose you must be conversant, at least, with the ways of polite society. A polite society. I don't care where."

"Society at school was not polite. I could tell you tales that would curl your hair! Upon my word, I often thought there was more civility in my father's house. Have some more tea?"

"Thank you. I will have a third."

She did not tell him that he had had five, but pursued her theme, asking guilelessly:

"Could I have a thorough classical grounding?"

Charles told her, in some detail, that she certainly could. It was a subject very close to his heart; all his life he had hoped great things from the higher education of women. Nothing, he maintained, could form the mind of a young girl better than the study of Latin and Greek. He would teach her enough arithmetic to enable her to keep accounts neatly, the elements of geography, the dates of the kings of England, and then he would plunge her into classical literature. In her teens, she should read nothing else. He had meant to educate his daughter in this way, but had been defeated by the other educationists who surrounded her. At fifteen she had been so very anxious to form his mind that she gave him no opportunity of meddling with hers. For this he blamed Cleeve; he had a suspicion that Cleeve was full of earnest, cultivated women who read Robert Browning and wanted degrees. A dreadful type!

225

They had corrupted Florence. But the young female now so persistently supplying him with tea was virgin soil; none of these wretched, efficient governesses had been at her. And she seemed intelligent.

"I suppose," she said, "that I'd get a classical grounding at school?"

"Yes, I daresay," grumbled Charles, "in this disgusting new pronunciation that I can't make head or tail of."

"I don't believe that you have any more use for schools than I have."

"You must learn to get on with the other women."

"Must I?"

"Yes, you must. A boy goes to school for that, to find his level in a crowd of youngsters of his own age. And so does a girl, I suppose. But I declare it's all they're good for, these places!"

"Well, but which do you prefer? A woman who is very charming or a woman who knows a lot?"

"A charming woman can be very well informed . ."

"Yes, but would you rather have an ignorant woman with charm or a well-informed woman without?"

"You're driving me into a corner! Of course I admit that the world would come to an end if women weren't charming. But they'll persist in being that, thank heaven, whatever sort of education they get. And, Teresa, one of the most charming women I ever knew came to grief simply, so it seemed to me, for want of a wider education . . . a better regulated mind . . ."

He paused and sighed. Teresa looked at him and asked suddenly:

"Was that my mother?"

"Yes, my dear."

"Were you very fond of her?"

"She was our only sister. We were very proud of her."

"Did she go to a school like Cleeve?"

226

" Cleeve !   Not she ! "

She saw that he had no high opinion of Cleeve, and presently she began to tell him funny stories of the good ladies there and her adventures during her brief school career. He found her very entertaining. .Her way of talking had a turn that was at once innocent and shrewd, infantile and yet full of observation, adorned with a quaint, half literary idiom, and full of inflections borrowed from other languages. She was refreshing, after a long surfeit of cultured provincialism. He saw ignorance in her, and childishness and a good deal of untutored passion ; but of pose there was no trace and she was without small sentimentalities or rancours. He thought that he discerned the delicate beginnings of a noble mind, a grandeur of outlook which would well repay development. It struck him that the Sanger genius, driving all the other children to some practice of the arts, might here take the form of a particular aptitude for companionship, that rare touch on life which makes some souls so valuable to their friends. He could not imagine why Florence had not written more warmly about her. She was such very good fun. And if, as he half guessed, there was some tragedy behind her, that was her own business and she was perfectly able to deal with it herself. She was a courageous little creature. He wished that he could have asked her how Florence and Lewis were getting on ; it was a point upon which her opinion would have been useful.

It was an odd thing, but he had a queer sort of liking for his son-in-law. If it had not been for their unfortunate relationship he could have seen several merits in the young man. To begin with, it was enjoyable to remember that this was the son of Fulsome Felix. A great deal could be forgiven to him on that account. Charles was forced frequently to put up with the company of Sir Felix Dodd, who was always coming to Cambridge in some capacity or other which could not be ignored. He could endure now the atmosphere of a glorified

227

board school which always clung to that gentleman, remembering with inward chuckles the blot in the scutcheon. Lewis must have been too much even for the Dodd complacency.

And that night, when Lewis joined Charles and Teresa in the drawing-room, he was at his unusual best. He brought with him his two friends, Dr. Dawson, who was already known to Charles, and an obscure organist from somewhere or other. It was the first time that Charles had ever seen him in company of his own choosing, for his friends were a little nervous of coming to Strand-on-the-Green. He was talking of his work in a simple and modest way that showed how completely he was at his ease. Charles, by long habit, was quick to sift the cleverness of a clever young man for any grains of real gold that might lurk there. In this case he soon divined something more solid than mere promise. He knew nothing of music, but Dawson did, and he caught, now and then, a trace of something more than respect in the attitude of his old friend ; there were signs there of affection and a deep admiration.

" The fellow has real ability," thought Charles. " Dawson knows. Poor Florence ! She's right there, as far as I can see."

Presently it occurred to him, with a slight shock of surprise, how very well Teresa fitted into the picture. She seemed almost like Lewis's belonging. She had made one or two quite pertinent remarks ; that was natural, since they were on ground which was familiar to her. But her chief business was to minister to them and this she did rather nicely ; her hospitality had no polish but it was suitable, somehow, to the company. She made a fresh pot of tea and, finding that Dr. Dawson had missed his lunch, she fetched up some corned beef. Charles, watching how she slapped it down on the table with a kind of offhand geniality, thought that she would have made a very good barmaid. Then it struck him that it was her co-operation which had given Lewis the air of being so pleasant a host. He could imagine the pair of them entertaining with the greatest success, not in this house but in some queer, unmistakable house of their own. He told himself that no party can go well unless the host and hostess are inspired by the same social ideals. It is upon such occasions that the inner concord between man and wife is made most manifest. Only that Lewis and Teresa were not man and wife. For a moment he was almost thinking of them as if they were, because they ought to have been.

This idea grew upon Charles as he watched them, and it seemed strange to him that a thing so obvious should have occurred to nobody else. To his eyes it grew plainer every moment. The pair seen thus together, at a moment of unconscious ease, contrived to produce the united front, the pleasant assurance of a perfectly well-matched couple. Teresa was, probably, the only woman in the world who could manage this man ; she would respect his humours without taking them too seriously, she would never require him to behave correctly, and, if he annoyed her, she would reprove him good-humouredly in the strong terms which he deserved and understood. How could they have failed to see it ? Lewis was a fool ! If he had married little Teresa she would have made a man of him, whereas mated with Florence he was nothing but a calamity.

How much of a calamity was abundantly demonstrated when Florence returned, an elegant stranger breaking in upon them, the owner, one remembered, of a room which was not usually strewn with kitchen knives and corned beef. Immediately the party went to pieces ; a sort of constraint settled upon them. Not that she failed in hospitality ; she was most charming to everybody, and especially kind to the young organist because he was insignificant and had a provincial accent. Always she would be nice to her husband's friends. Charles thought she managed very well, for nobody made any attempt to help her out. Her manner to her husband was, he noticed, a little staccato ; she was nervous. He surmised that there had been a fine explosion after " Prester John," but of this there were only the faintest indications. He hardly knew how to diagnose the sense of a false note, a roughness, a want of decorum in her posture. Something very wrong was happening.

He watched her closely and at last discovered the flaw. It shocked him excessively. She was being, there was no other word for it, consistently nasty to her young cousin. In fact, she seemed scarcely able to let the child alone ; her sarcasms and her biting reproofs were so continuous as to sound almost mechanical, like a bad habit. She was exhibiting in that quarter a most lamentable failure of the " bonté," which used to be an integral part of her disposition. Circumstances were becoming too much for her natural generosity. She was not only jealous of Teresa's standing with Lewis but of her intimacy with all his friends. They had been, when she came in, a close convivial group ; she had tried to join in, talking cleverly, but they had not quite accepted her. She got homage for her beauty and her wit, but that was not entirely what she wanted. She wished them to consider her as one of themselves and this distinction they reserved for Teresa, an impudent chit, who had only to put in her oar, quote an opinion of Sanger's, to make them stop and listen to her. Florence was not going to be cut out, in her own drawing-room, by an unformed schoolgirl, and she was consequently a great deal too profuse in small snubs.

It was, in the father's eyes, pitiful that a beloved daughter should thus expose her sufferings in an exhibition of petty jealousy. But he had not observed the situation for very long before he saw that it held great dangers. Teresa bore it all well enough ; he could not help admiring the large, good temper with which she held her own in the contest. Perhaps she did not grasp the underlying spite of the attacks made upon her. It was for her friend to feel resentment on her behalf ; nothing of their byplay was lost upon Lewis. He seemed to receive all Teresa's wounds with a double bitterness. If

Florence had wished to drive him from her, she could not have chosen a better way.

"A pretty kettle of fish!" thought Charles wrathfully. "Does she want to bully those two into making a bolt of it? The sooner that little girl is packed off to school, the better!"

He had quite a good opinion of Teresa but, recollecting how she had been brought up, he had little reliance upon her principles or her prudence in such an affair. He was almost sure that she loved this undeserving wretch; when once he had suspected the thing every gesture that she made, every word that she spoke, bore witness to it. Should Lewis wake to his own need of her, nothing in the world could save her; her security lay in his blindness. She obeyed no laws; she knew none. She would inevitably follow the man if he beckoned to her; Charles could think of no possible reason why she should not. And here was Florence ordering her off to bed as though she were a tiresome baby, quoting some absurd doctor's order about bed at seven three nights a week. She was skipping out of the room when she caught her uncle's eye and came back to him.

"Good night, *Lieber Herr!*"

"Good night, baggage!"

"How long are you staying with us, if one may ask?"

"A week-end."

"Dear me! That's uncommonly short! I'd hoped you might stay long enough to give me a classical education."

"I'll begin to teach you Latin if you'd like. Then, later on, you can come to Cambridge and we'll begin Greek."

It seemed to him that any snare was worth trying with so wild a little bird.

"I know Latin!"

"You do, do you?"

"Some I do." She sang in a steady, poised little voice: "*Cum vix justus sit securus.*"

Lewis, across the room, stirred slightly and turned his head to listen. Charles thought :

"What's the good of school ? She'll run away."

"That," she was saying, "means that even good people will scarcely be safe, poor things . . ."

She kissed him and made off. Florence immediately called her back and reminded her that she had not said good-night to the rest of the company. Whereupon, she kissed them all rapidly but with much warmth, and was gone before any fresh reproof could fall upon her. Assuredly it was not easy to put her in her place. Florence had to laugh, though she offered quite unnecessary apologies for the manners of her young cousin.

"Not at all," said Charles. "We like it."

The obscure organist, whose name everybody forgot, had been greatly captivated. He quoted softly :

"Say I'm weary, say I'm sad . . ."

"Say that health and wealth have missed me," chimed in Dr. Dawson, with perfect truth, for he was a poor man and gouty.

"Say I'm getting old . . ." grumbled Charles rather glumly.

Lewis said nothing, having no idea what they were talking about. A good many of Tessa's kisses had already come his way so perhaps he regarded them as a commonplace.

232

CHAPTER XVIII

CHARLES, Florence, Lewis and Teresa sat together at break-fast. Sebastian, who always rose early, had finished his meal and could be heard in the music-room practising the Forty-eight Preludes and Fugues with precision and energy. Paulina was not yet down and a lecture on unpunctuality was awaiting her. Teresa was blowing on her tea to cool it in a vulgar way; Florence wearily told her not to.

"And why must you do your hair in that way?" she complained. "Dragging it all back! It's terribly unbecom-ing; your forehead is quite high enough as it is. Why don't you cover it?"

"If I did I'd look like one of those little girls in shops called 'Cash.' Wouldn't I, gentlemen?"

Charles and Lewis left off reading their letters and looked at Teresa's forehead. They liked it. Charles said:

"If you want to look pretty, hussy, you'd better grow a fringe and hide it."

Lewis wondered; he scarcely knew why it was that he found Tessa so beautiful to look at. He said:

"In a year or two, Florence, when you've fattened her, she'll look like that picture in your bedroom . . . that very startled lady with a towel round her head."

"The Delphic Sibyl? What nonsense, Lewis!"

"But she is," said Charles. "She's very like! I hadn't seen it before . . . It's on a smaller, slighter scale, of course . ."

" The Delphic Sibyl has a very noble face."

" So has Tessa," said both the men.

Florence pursed her lips and said rather acidly :

" I'm sorry, I'm afraid I don't see it.   Except that there's a sort of Michelangelo look about all the family . . ."

" My admirers," said Teresa complacently, " are mostly of the opposite sex."

" I think you had better do that entrance examination to-day," Florence retorted.   " If you go to Harrogate at Whitsun, they'll want to know how to place you.   You can do it in the drawing-room, this morning, where it will be quite quiet."

" I don't expect I shall be able," said Teresa gloomily.

" Oh, yes, you will.   It's quite easy.   Only the junior entrance.   Miss Cassidy thinks that, as you are under sixteen and very backward, you'd better be entered as a junior, till they have got you on a bit."

" How does she know I'm backward ? "

" Because I told her.   It's not your fault.   You'll pick up."

Teresa said nothing but gazed tearfully at her plate of porridge.   Florence exclaimed, with a little laugh :

" Oh, dear me !   I don't believe you like being told you're backward !   Funny, funny child !   She's getting quite pink ! "

" She's saying all this for your good," put in Lewis, leaning round the table to see how pink Teresa was.   " You should be grateful to her ; I've often thought it was a pity you had such a high-stomached opinion of yourself."

" I can talk three languages besides English."

" Yes, your languages are good.   But you know nothing else."

" I've read Shakespeare."

" I should hope you had," Florence told her crushingly.

" The juniors at Cleeve went to bed at eight o'clock.   And in recreation they did things for each other's albums.   And they mightn't get books out of the library. I'd sooner go to hell."

"You must work hard and try to get into the senior school as soon as you can. And you must grow up a little. You're such a baby for your age."

"Shall I have to play hockey? At Cleeve I didn't."

"You won't unless you're fit for it," put in Charles testily.

"Of course not," agreed Florence. "But by the Autumn term, when hockey begins, I daresay she will be able to play."

She knew this was not likely, but life would be unbearable if Teresa was allowed to make a fuss about her health. She needed bracing in every direction. Lewis asked gleefully how long she was to stay at this school.

"Three years," said Florence. "Yes, Father! It will be quite that, I should think, before she catches up."

"Well," muttered Teresa, "there are some things I shall know. At Cleeve we didn't know we had to pay to go to church. We thought it was free. We nearly died of fright the first time we saw that bag coming round. We thought we'd be turned out. I had to take sixpence belonging to the girl next me; she'd left it on her prayer-book and didn't see me pinch it."

"Stealing! You've no morals, hussy!"

"Not at all. The sixpence was going in the bag, anyhow. Poor Lina had to pull a button off her drawers to put in."

"I hope somebody told you that these things are not done," said Florence, with a frown at Charles, who guffawed.

"Quite a number of people did. That was what we disliked at Cleeve, being taught how to behave by five hundred people at once. It's the way they do things in this country."

"Well, if you run contrary to public opinion you must expect to suffer for it. But I hope you'll be wiser now."

Lewis passed his cup for more coffee and got his guns into position. He thought that his wife ought to be paid out for the way she was baiting Teresa, and he embarked upon a counter-attack.

"I think I agree with Tessa," he said to Charles. "This is not a country I like. I'm leaving it for good as soon as my concert's over."

Florence started and gave him a quick glance. In the heat of the scene she had made after "Prester John" he had declared that he detested England and would live with her no longer. But he had not repeated the threat, and she had come to believe that he had not really meant it.

"No," said Charles, blinking at Lewis over his spectacles. "Is that so?"

"Didn't Florence tell you we've almost agreed to part?"

"It is fortunate that you can agree upon such a delicate subject," murmured Charles.

"She, you see, can't live in comfort anywhere else, can you, Florence?"

"Not permanently," said Florence.

She was determined that he should not draw her into an argument at this time and in this company. He was probably only teasing her. If he really persisted in his desire to live abroad she would let the house and go with him, but not just yet. He might change his mind again, and she could do nothing until she had disposed of the children. She thought that it might be a wise plan to let him go alone, after the concert, and when he had seen how he liked it he might give up this foolish way of talking. In any case, nobody in the world should know that it hurt her.

Later, when she was alone with her father, she gave him her version of the affair. Lewis, she said, had got a temporary attack of nerves and was best out of England. She herself would follow him as soon as she had got rid of Teresa. Charles, at this, looked very thoughtful, and she was afraid that he was going to ask awkward questions. But at last he surprised her by saying:

"Do you know, my love, I'm not altogether sure that I think you're wise in your manner to that little girl."

Instantly she was up in arms.

"You encourage her, and it's not kind. That pert manner may be very amusing, but it will get her into trouble later on, and it shouldn't be laughed at."

He had spent most of the night thinking on this matter. It seemed to him imperative that Florence should be warned in some way. But he hardly knew how to begin. He ventured:

"Do you think this plan of school is really wise? Is she strong enough?"

"That's the only doubt. Otherwise, it's the very thing she needs . . . firm discipline and to have the nonsense laughed out of her by other children of the same age."

"She's old . . . in some ways . . . for her age . . ." he hesitated.

"On the contrary, she's a great baby for her age."

"That's where you are mistaken, I think. She would respond better if you treated her as a responsible person."

"How can I, when she behaves like a young hooligan?"

"This life, remember, is new to her."

"She isn't attempting to adjust herself to it."

"It strikes me that she's absorbing new ideas at every pore. Give her time and they'll bear fruit. But truly I don't think she'll have enough elbow room at school."

"These Sanger children seem to think that they have merely to say that they don't like a thing to be free of the necessity of enduring it. It's sheer unruliness."

"I thought that it would not take you very long to exhaust the charms of the Sanger children."

"I can do with the others. But I don't like Teresa."

"That's it!" Charles now spoke rather sternly. "You don't like her, and you make no secret of it. Is that just?"

"Oh, I've tried to be just. But she's so hard! She has such a forward, disagreeable nature."

"Try to see things from her point of view a little. Think how she's been brought up! Not only is she ignorant of all the finer shades of conduct, but she's grown up with no conception of the word 'ought.' She has only her instincts, her affections, and her quick wits to guide her. Fortunately, these are all singularly uncorrupted; at least, so it seems to me."

"Does it?"

"Yes, it does, when you think of the sort of life she's been used to. She's intensely receptive. And now, when she's almost formed, as far as intelligence goes, she is uprooted and brought here. She's pitchforked into a new world, and we expect her to conform at once to our standards, our very complicated standards, of existence. She discovers, piecemeal, the principles underlying our ideas of conduct. She has to assimilate, in less than a year, a number of social and ethical facts which were put into you before you were out of your cradle. At one moment she's scolded for telling a lie and at the next for picking her teeth. She has, by the light of her own wisdom, to sort out the relative values of these things. Can you wonder that she finds it hard?"

"It's the same for the other two."

"You are willing to make allowances for them. Besides ... they are children, and it's no insult to treat them as such."

"You think I'm unfair?"

"I think you are, my dear."

"So does Lewis," she murmured bitterly.

"Ah?"

"He encourages her." Florence flushed and broke out in a kind of dull anger: "I wouldn't have thought you'd take her part. But she will be that kind of woman; the kind that men always defend. The kind that men call 'a good sort.' Antonia is like that. You're a man and you don't see it."

" I think she has a good disposition ."

" You're mistaken ! She's not to be trusted. Those girls have bad blood in them, somewhere . . . something corrupt. They've never been innocent. She'll go to the bad, as fast as she can, unless she's watched. Sometimes I wonder if already , . ."

" Florence ! You are letting yourself get into a state of mind that does you no credit ! I couldn't have believed that you could speak so ! "

Charles spoke in great anger, though he was wrenched with pity for her, remembering the tolerant, unsuspicious creature that she used to be. She remembered too ; she had a sudden vision of herself going off to the Tyrol to fetch the Sanger children home, of her kindliness, of the thousand delicate scruples which, in those days, hedged and bounded every word she said. She had been so slow to think evil and so free from base imaginings. What had happened to her ? Life had become a shipwreck, a desperate, snatching, devil-take-the-hindermost affair. She began to think that she would leave this house, even if Lewis changed his mind about going abroad. It was an unlucky place. It had witnessed too much of the wreckage, the gradual disintegration of her old, civilized self, and the emergence of the untutored creature who talked as she had just been talking.

" Perhaps I'm unfair," she admitted. " I'll try to do better. Really, I will. But it angers me, the thoughtless way that you and Lewis egg her on."

" Lewis is very fond of her, I think."

" He is. He's fond of all the children."

" I know. I really think he is worried, when you threaten her with school. He is afraid she will not be happy. You should respect his feelings, my dear, if I may venture to say so. He is not, I imagine, a man who feels affection easily."

But there he went too far. She replied coldly that she quite

239

understood Lewis and his feelings. Charles hastily agreed; he was diffident and afraid of going too far; he did not think that he was justified in saying much more. But before they parted he had induced her to reconsider her sentence of school at Harrogate.

Meanwhile Teresa was busy in the drawing-room with her examination paper, and Lewis found her there, an hour later, sobbing distractedly over her sums.

"Oh, Lewis," she wailed, "do come and help me! I've done this sum about papering the room nine times, and . . ."

"Why on earth do you do it at all?"

"The answer comes out that it would take five million yards of paper to paper a room under twenty foot square, with a lot of windows! Well, that must be wrong, because rooms that size don't . . ."

"Let me look at it! Nothing would induce me to go to a school if I didn't want to. It's your own fault. My dear child! You've papered this room absolutely solid! You must find the surface space of the walls, not the cubic contents of the room. You'll run away, I suppose, as soon as she sends you?"

"Where could I run? I've nowhere. Look at this literature paper! And this : 'Say what you know about the retreat from Moscow.' Do you know anything? I don't. Could it be anything to do with that Empress Catherine, do you think, in Sanger's opera? It had some things about Moscow."

"I know some poetry about her," said Lewis hopefully. "It begins : 'In Catherine's reign, whom glory still adores, the greatest . . .'"

"Poetry is no use to me. There's a bit here quoted and I have to say who wrote it. It says : 'God's in his heaven, all's right with the world.' That seems a damn silly sort of a piece, doesn't it?"

Lewis agreed, with unnecessary violence.

"Though, mind you, some poetry is all right. Do you know a piece called 'Elegy, Written in a Country Church-yard'? It's lovely! I learnt it at Cleeve. It says :

> "For who, to dumb forgetfulness a prey,
> This pleasing, anxious being e'er resigned,
> Left the warm precincts of the cheerful day,
> Nor cast one longing, lingering look behind?
>
> On some fond breast the parting soul relies,
> Some pious drops the closing eye requires,
> E'en from the tomb the voice of Nature cries,
> E'en in our ashes live their wonted fires!"

She thought these lines so moving that her voice became quite tearful as she recited them. But Lewis was not listening. He had picked up from the table a penny exercise-book and saw that it was full of unformed writing. He had just read :

"Our early occupation exhausted us so much that we did nothing else remarkable this day of which there is nothing to report save that Sanger threw a bottle at Linda, thinking that it was empty. But it had Green Chartreuse in it and for this misfortune we are all smarting. We took some breakfast on a tray to our dear and beloved Lewis, who keeps late hours both ways. But he, lying in bed, said take it away, I don't want any, I have a little headache, rejecting us with many oaths, so that it took our most endearing persuasions to induce him to swallow. But in a little while he became more pleasant in his conversation, and I must confess that never, not even in his very worst moments, do we find him entirely disagreeable. We love him too well."

"What's this?" he asked, turning the pages.
She snatched it from him, crying :

"You mustn't look at that ! It's my diary."

"Let me, Tessa ! I was reading something about myself. Am I often mentioned ?"

"Sometimes." She grew very pink. "Let's get on with these sums !"

The next sum was about trains crossing each other on a bridge. At the sight of it she collapsed into tears again.

"Oh, dear ! Oh, dear ! What shall I do ? What shall I do ? I can't ! I cannot bear it !"

"Come with me !" The words broke from him before he knew that he had thought them. "Dearest, dearest Tessa ! My dear love ! Don't cry ! Don't let them make you cry ! Come with me !"

"Come with you ? Where ?"

"Anywhere ! When I go after the concert."

"Florence would never allow it."

"No," he said, more collectedly. "You'd have to do it without asking her."

"You mean . . really . . . that we should run away ?"

Yes. He discovered that he did mean that.

"Well," she said, after a pause ; "there are points in it. It's better than being like the cat in the adage."

"The . . . ?"

"Don't ask me what an adage is, for I don't know. But it's better than making—I dare not wait upon I would."

"I don't follow you. It's better than going to school."

"It's very good of you to be so concerned about it."

"I don't know that it is so very good of me," he said grimly. "You know very well why I want you to come."

"I'm not sure. Could you let me have it in plain English ?"

"In plain English . . . you're too dear to leave behind. I love you ; I can't do without you. And if you are going to be so unhappy at school, that settles it."

"Love me ? What do you mean by that ? There's a song :

242

'Away, false man, I know thou lov'st,
    I know thou lov'st too many.' "

"No, Tessa. This is a star part . . . a solo . . ."

"A duet you mean ? Looks to me more like a trio. Why did you marry Florence ? "

"You know why."

"Yes, I do know. It was unfair to both of us, if you loved me. That's what I'm complaining of."

"I know. But it's done now."

"And you want it undone ? Why couldn't you have thought of all this before ? You were so mad to get her that you forgot all about me. If you'd waited a bit you could have had me."

"Could I. Then . . . then . . . Oh, Tessa, say it ! "

"I loved you. I'd have had you. I promised myself to you . . . ever so long ago . . . When first I ever began to think about love. I thought then that I wouldn't ever have any man but you. I don't think I ever will. But it's too late now."

"No, it isn't. You still love me, don't you ? "

"What's that got to do with it ? I don't see that I can come now. I'd feel bad about Florence. I'd feel as if you were her belonging. And I'm her cousin, you know ; and I've lived in her house for months and months. She's been very kind to us, though lately she's been a little snappy, and I don't blame her with you going on the way you do. I should feel mean if I ran off with her husband. When first you said that you were going off after the concert, I thought of asking you to take me, but then I saw it wouldn't do. If you were anybody else at all nice, I'd go with you to get away from school. And if it wasn't for Florence, I'd rather go with you than anything in the world. But, as it is, I don't see my way to it. If I did, I shouldn't enjoy myself. The pangs of unappeased remorse would gnaw my vitals."

She looked at her diary as she said this, as if she admired her own language and would have liked to write it down. Lewis remonstrated with her scruples.

"I should have thought it was perfectly obvious that my marriage with Florence has come to an end. We practically agreed as much, the night after 'Prester John.' You heard me say at breakfast that we should probably part; she showed no signs of minding, did she? I expect she's very glad to get rid of me."

This sounded reasonable enough. Marriage, in Teresa's experience, did not last longer than was absolutely convenient to both parties. She had never supposed that the Dodd household was a permanent thing and lately it had showed every sign of going to pieces. Florence had made no protest, at breakfast, when Lewis proclaimed the state of affairs. Charles had accepted the thing quite conversationally. They had, of course, an unreasonable habit of concealing their sentiments; often they would not exhibit their anger. But in a case like this, Teresa calculated, they would surely speak up. She hesitated, and then said:

"I daresay that's so. But it's not my affair. It may be a very good thing that you should go; and if you go I suppose you'll have to get another wife. But I don't think she can be me. Everybody would know and they'd say we'd been carrying on in this house behind poor Florence's back. It would be awful for her, especially with the ideas she's got. She'd think I was a traitor. I really couldn't. I don't want to be a viper in anybody's bosom."

"Will you stop talking in that strain?"

"It's a very good strain. At least, it's got good intentions. A person must do what they think right, mustn't they?"

Lewis had nothing to say to this. His case was a little complicated in that he was not quite sure of his own wishes. Certainly he desired her company on his travels; he did not think that he could do very well without her. She was such a darling, and, now that he came to think of it, the only thing that had kept him so long at Strand-on-the-Green. But he wanted also that she should be happy and safe ; and he was not absolutely convinced of his own fitness to look after her. She had been evasive when he asked if she still loved him ; yet the crucial point of the whole matter lay exactly there. If she was still bound by that simple, uncompromising love of her childhood, to which she had just confessed, then nothing on earth must be allowed to hold them apart. But possibly she had changed. He questioned her, but could get no definite answer, though he saw that her eyes were full of tears. At last he said impatiently :

"Then you love Florence so terribly much that you'll put up with three years of school for her sake ? "

"Not three ; one," she explained. "Then I'll rebel and I think Uncle Charles will back me. I must, what do you call it, compromise ! That's a useful thing to do, Lewis. It shows you've got a well-regulated mind. I don't believe you know how."

"I don't, thank God ! "

"Well, I do."

"Then you've changed."

"Perhaps I have. It's not my fault. Nobody can help changing. Things are done to them and they change. If you think of all that's happened since Sanger died and we were brought here ! I seem to have had so many new things to think about. You can't forget anything that you've once learnt. You can't go back to being what you were. I wish you could. I'm sorry we came here, any of us ; we'd have been better to stay with the sort of people we were accustomed to. But as I am here I'd better see it through. I shall stay and be a lady."

"What's the good of being a lady if you're unhappy ?

245

"Unhappiness," she said, in the voice of Uncle Charles, "is bound to come to every one of us. I don't think we'd escape it in each other's company, Lewis."

"Nor do I. But I want your company."

"Then want must be your master, for I've said my say."

"There's been plenty of it."

"Well, you want to know such a lot."

"Only one thing, and I don't know it yet."

But she would not tell him. She knew that telling, for her, would be surrender. To say the thing would be so irrevocable that she could not then betray the truth by leaving him. To her, avowal and compliance went together. So she gathered up her papers and her diary and left him still uncertain. He was striding up and down the room, fighting it out with himself, when the face of Charles was poked round the door. It looked blank when it saw Lewis. Charles had stolen up, as soon as Florence was out of the way, to do Teresa's sums for her.

"Tessa?" said Lewis vaguely, in answer to his question. "She . . . she went away . . . I don't know where, I'm afraid."

Charles was just going to withdraw when he thought better of it. He came in and shut the door.

"I want to tell her," he said, "that she needn't stay very long at this school if she really dislikes it."

"She's got nowhere else to go," said Lewis defiantly.

Charles glanced out of the window and said :

"Look at that long line of barges the *Mary Blake's* got ! I've an idea that I want Tessa in Cambridge sometime."

"You want her ?"

"She can make tea. My housekeeper is a fool and can't. But I couldn't have her just yet. She wants petticoat government for a little longer."

"She might like that," said Lewis thoughtfully.

"You think so ? You've known her longer than the rest of us."

246

"Yes. She . . . she's . . . "

Lewis blinked and sought for words. Charles waited.

"She's different from anybody else," confided Lewis at last.

"I agree."

"School! You know it might spoil her."

"I don't think so."

"Well, if she stays," urged Lewis, "you'll see after her?"

"Stays?"

"Doesn't run off, I mean."

"You mean she might run off if we press her with school? My dear fellow, where could she run to?"

Lewis said nothing.

"She's taken you into her confidence?" suggested Charles.

"Taken! I've always been there."

"Quite so. And you think she will run unless we drop the idea of school?"

"No," said Lewis truthfully. "She says not. She says she'll try it for a year."

"Says not! And you say she will, is that it?"

"Yes," said Lewis absently.

"By all that's wonderful!" thought Charles. "The little creature's had the sense to turn him down. He's asked her and she's turned him down!"

Lewis, who had been conducting so fierce an argument with himself that he scarcely knew that he had been talking to Charles, now said:

"I want her . . . to do the best she can for herself . . ."

"She had better surely remain under the protection of her friends, of the people who love her?" suggested Charles.

Lewis shook his head at this and brought out a final melancholy statement:

"Nobody," he said, "could love her better than I do."

And Charles believed it. In the midst of his exultation he discovered that he was quite sorry for the young man.

CHAPTER XIX

" A BOWL ? " exclaimed Charles. " What bowl is that ? "

He had hardly attended to his daughter's conversation until something about a bowl arrested his mind.

" A sort of orange lustre. Very beautiful, isn't it, Lewis ? "

" What ? " said Lewis, without looking up.

He was reading an old exercise book which seemed utterly to absorb him.

" Tessa's bowl."

" Has Tessa got a bowl ? "

It seemed strange to Charles that Teresa should ever own anything so concrete as a bowl. Her very clothes seldom looked as though they really belonged to her.

" She bought a bowl with the birthday money you gave her. You must see it ; it's lovely."

" Fancy Tessa buying a bowl ! She'll drop it."

" I was surprised that she had the sense to hit on anything so good."

After her recent incredible demonstration of sense, Charles could not be surprised at anything in Teresa. He said that he would like to see the bowl, and Florence, going to the drawing-room door, called for it to be brought. Lewis looked annoyed. He had discovered Teresa's diary lying about, and he did not like to be interrupted until he had made himself acquainted with all its secrets. He was learning all that he wanted to know about the state of her heart. But he knew that if she saw it in his hands she would make a great scene and call public

248

attention to a proceeding which the others might consider a little ungentlemanly. So, when he heard her coming, he dropped it behind the sofa and joined in the conversation.

"What do you want a bowl for ? " he asked mistrustfully.

"He told me to buy a pretty thing, and it was the first I saw that I wanted."

"Admirable ! " said Charles, examining it.

"Not at all," stated Lewis. "Tessa doesn't want a bowl. She oughtn't to want one."

"Why on earth not ? " Florence was indignant. "It's really an exquisite thing."

"She has no house," explained Lewis, taking the bowl and balancing it on one hand. "People with no houses ought to know when they are well off."

"Take care ! You'll break it ! "

"Bowls lead to houses. Houses are mainly to keep bowls in. If Tessa had a house she could buy as many bowls as she liked. She'd be done for. As it is, she should beware. _C'est le premier pas qui coûte._ Oh ! There, Tessa ! I've broken your pretty thing ! "

Charles could never quite make up his mind if it was an accident ; but the lovely, brittle treasure lay in shivers on the floor.

"Lewis you wretch ! " cried Florence. "Never mind, Tessa dear ! We'll get you another."

"I'm a lady," said Teresa primly. "So I won't say what I think of him."

Lewis went on to his knees at her feet and began to collect the little bits. Florence told him that he might, at least, say that he was sorry.

"What shall I say ? " he asked, looking up at Teresa. "Shall I say that my peace of mind is shattered for ever ? "

"My bowl wasn't all that valuable, I'm afraid."

"It was rather valuable," Florence reminded her.

"No bowl," she stated loftily, "is worth the peace of mind of the lowest and the least, much less our ray of sunshine."

She got, in return for this, a look from Lewis which silenced her. She turned away and said :

"We must find a little coffin to put the remains in."

Florence caught sight of her face and mistook the blanched sorrow in it. She offered consolation :

"I'm sure we can replace it, my dear ; can't we, Father ? "

Charles produced a five pound note.

"Here you are, hussy ! The next pretty thing you buy give to me to keep. He's not to be trusted with them."

"He's too clever," she said darkly. "That's what's the matter with him."

"Are you coming to Chiswick Park station to see me off ? "

He was on the point of departure, after a very uneasy week-end, and he was anxious, if possible, to get a few words alone with her, that he might strengthen her resolution and temper her dread of school with promises of an early release. Florence had pleased him greatly by her obvious efforts to be more just ; the household, as a whole, had a tranquil air and he thought that things might do very well provided that Teresa stayed the course. In any case, he had said as much as he dared to all of them.

"I'd like to see you off," said Teresa, with a tentative glance at Florence, for she was not quite sure if she would be wanted.

"She can't come," explained Charles. "She has to go to Richmond. So nobody will see me off if you don't."

"I'll come too and carry your suitcase," offered Lewis.

Florence looked pleased at his civility, but a little surprised, for he did not often offer to carry guests' luggage.

"Sebastian will come too, and carry Uncle Charles's walking-stick," said Teresa, who did not want to walk home alone with Lewis if she could help it.

"Not I," said Sebastian, who was reading a score in a corner of the room. "I'm busy."

"Odd's boddikins!" exclaimed Teresa. "Don't you want to say good-bye to your Uncle?"

This oath was secret signal among the Sangers and meant a demand for help. They had found it useful during their life in England. Sebastian immediately pricked up his ears and loyally said that perhaps he would come to the station after all. Paulina, attentive to the password, asked Teresa if she should not also want to see her uncle off.

"No, I don't think so," said Teresa, who feared that, if four of them went, they might walk home in couples.

As it was, they went in couples : Charles and Teresa in front and Lewis behind with Sebastian and the suitcase. On the way Charles said what he could to his niece, and painted her future in the most amazingly attractive colours, if only she would be patient and go to school for a little time. She answered very sensibly and seemed disposed to do right as far as she was able. He believed that the worst struggle was already over for her, and he left her at Chiswick Park station in a fairly comfortable frame of mind.

He was no more ready to credit a young person with sense than are most men at his time of life ; but when he did so, it was with an almost over lavish generosity. Himself full of the garnered wisdom of years he was inclined to confuse Teresa's intuitive sagacity with that other more reliable article which can only be the fruit of experience. This was a mistake which he could not have made had she been a young man, for he knew all about young men. His experience of girls had been, on the whole, very small and his chief impression of them was that they were quite unlike boys, creatures of a weak, irrational temper, but without any great intensity of feeling. The women he had known best had been unreasonable rather than passionate. So that having made certain that Teresa was upon

251

the right course, he was not disposed to doubt her fortitude in pursuing it. Besides, he had observed the skill with which she had avoided another interview with Lewis. She was quite competent to manage the affair in her own way.

Lewis, however, had been reading her diary and had made up his mind. He was a little staggered by the history of faithful, ungrudging devotion which had been thus revealed to him. It seemed as though a final separation was not any more to be thought of ; as though all the love he could give was but a poor return for hers. He wanted to tell her about it, and he said, as the train with Charles in it rattled out of the station :

" I'm not sure that I want Sebastian just now."

" Well, I do," said Teresa. " His opinion is always sound."

She explained that she had taken Paulina and Sebastian into her confidence. Paulina had advised her to go with Lewis, but Sebastian was very much against it.

" Most officious of him," complained Lewis.

" I don't understand what you're after," said Sebastian. " Do you want her for your wife ? "

" Yes," said Lewis.

It was exactly what he did want. It seemed to him that Tessa was all that a wife should be : tender, loyal, his other self, the only creature in the world to whom he would turn for prudent counsels.

" But that's just exactly what she can't be," Sebastian pointed out. " You've got a wife already. She'll be your . . ."

" Hold your tongue, Sebastian. And you, Tessa, mind the traffic ! "

The question was suspended until they had got themselves across Chiswick High Road. Then Sebastian began again :

" But what will she be ? "

Lewis threw a glance of rather shamefaced appeal at Teresa, who suggested that, as she was not coming, it was of no consequence.

"Well, I don't approve at all," said the boy firmly. "It wouldn't be suitable for you, now that you're almost a lady really. Why can't he get somebody like Linda."

"I would suit him better than Florence does," mentioned Teresa, as though anxious to be fair to both sides.

"Well . . . could anybody suit him worse ? "

"I know him so well."

"All the more reason for knowing there's no sense in it."

"Of course, I never could make out what she saw in him."

"I daresay she thought he would improve."

"Improvement wouldn't hurt him."

Lewis did not like this. They talked across him as if he was not there. The interview was not turning out according to plan, but what could he say, in front of Sebastian ?

"I wish," he said, "that you wouldn't talk about me as if I was some awful fate that either you or Florence had to endure."

"Well, so you are," retorted Sebastian. "I heard Ike say once that he always pitied Sanger's women, but that he was a great deal sorrier for yours."

"You see, Lewis, you don't always know your own mind," complained Teresa. "Sanger at least knew that."

They had an unsatisfactory walk. Teresa and Sebastian teased Lewis all the way until they got to Kew Bridge ; but this baffling strategy only made him all the more obstinately determined, and quenched his last scruples. At last, when they were leaning on Kew Bridge watching the tide, he succeeded in taking her by surprise.

"Well then," he flung at her, "go to your school ! But I happen to know that you consider it a damnable charnel house, and that you would rather fling yourself into the smoky abyss of Etna if it were handy."

She recognised the quotation and grew livid with fury.

"Of course . . . if you've been reading my diary . . ."

" You shouldn't leave it about."

" I know it was foolish of me. One doesn't expect, in Florence's house, to have people like you wandering around . . ."

She abused him for several minutes without ever repeating herself.

" All this Billingsgate," he said, " only tells me one thing."

" And anyhow the bit about the charnel house was poetic licence. I wrote it to relieve my feelings."

" Oh ! Is all your diary poetic licence ? "

" Most of it."

" Still . . making allowances for that . . . I'm sure now . . ."

" If you'd had eyes in your head you could have been sure before, without going and reading my private diary."

" Still I was modest. I didn't like to be sure."

" What weren't you sure of ? " asked Sebastian puzzled.

Lewis and Teresa were silent ; he wanted to hear her say it, and she was afraid. Sebastian looked from one to the other, and exclaimed in immense surprise :

" Do you love him, Tessa ? "

" He thinks so," she said rather sternly.

Lewis looked embarrassed, as though he had been accused of a fearful indiscretion. He had nothing to say for himself. The long silence which followed was broken by Sebastian, who said that he thought he should like to go to Camden Town. He considered that the conversation had taken a difficult turn, impossible for three people to sustain, and an omnibus for Camden Town was just coming across the bridge. Teresa, deciding that flight was the only remedy for her situation, exclaimed that she would come too.

" You've no money," said the prudent Sebastian. " And I've only enough for myself."

" I've a five pound note."

254

"He'll give you the change all in halfpence."

"Well, Lewis must have some. Here, Lewis ! Lend me half a crown !"

Lewis, dazed, produced a handful of silver. She snatched a coin and jumped up on the 'bus which had stopped beside them.

"Wait a minute," cried Lewis. "I haven't finished."

"I have."

She was whirled away from him. Lewis stood on the curb gaping after the 'bus and saw her climbing up to the top, her long plaits slapping her back and her little brother at her heels. Away under the bright April sky she went, past the houses and the busy shops, down to Hammersmith Broadway.

At last he pulled himself together and started back to Strand-on-the-Green. But before he got home he changed his mind. He would endure no more of her mockery; she must not be allowed to return from Camden Town and find him ignominiously there. He would go away; without a word he would disappear, and she could see how she liked it. In any case he hated the place and would live there no longer. So he returned to Chiswick Park and took the train for town. Strand-on-the-Green saw nothing of him for a week, and Florence went about the house looking as if the world had come to an end.

As for Teresa, she jolted along on the top of her 'bus and was at first very unhappy. It had been hard to leave Lewis so; but it had, at least, been final. She cried a little into a clean handkerchief, which she unexpectedly found in her coat pocket. Sebastian looked at her with compassion but said nothing until they were past Turnham Green Church. Then he asked :

"But are you really going to this school ?"

"I suppose so. I don't care what I do."

"I expect you'll learn a lot there," he said.

"I don't feel as if I'd much more to learn. There's nothing left remarkable beneath the visiting moon."

"That's nonsense," quoth he.

"I daresay. But it's how I feel."

"Uncle Robert," said Sebastian, after a long pause, "says that the young can't know what real sorrow is."

"Does he? Silly old donkey! Look, Sebastian! What's that funny place?"

"That's Olympia, where they have the Military Tournament that Ike was telling us about."

"Oh, I should like to see it! Do you think we could get Ike to take us before we go to school?"

"We might ask him. I can't see what you want to call Uncle Robert a silly old donkey for, Tessa. He may be right. We can't know. We haven't been old yet. When you are grown up you may have worse times than you've had already."

"Oh, no," said Teresa, decidedly, craning to get a last look at Olympia, which she thought an admirable building. "I'm sure I never shall."

In this her wisdom had instructed her, for she never did.

256

BOOK IV
THREE MEET

CHAPTER XX

It was nearly a week before Florence could bring herself to go in search of Lewis. To begin with she would not admit that there was anything strange in his absence. He had wild ways. He would come back. She resolutely banished from her mind the tormenting suspicion that he had deserted her. It was bad enough, it was horrible, to know that such a thing should so easily seem possible ; it could not really happen.

When, after three days, her fears became more clamorous and insistent, she clung desperately to her dignity. She had said of Evelyn Churchill that it was degrading for a wife to pursue her husband. She would do nothing. She would take no notice. But she wandered about the house with a feverish, mechanical energy and a look as though she were always listening for something.

She had plenty to do, for Paulina was to be despatched to Paris, with a suitable outfit, at very short notice. A convenient escort having turned up, the child was being got ready in a hurry. There was no peace for anybody until the morning when, howling loudly, she was handed over to her disconcerted travelling companions at Victoria.

Florence had refused to take Teresa and Sebastian upon this final expedition, fearing a scene upon the platform. They were very sulky about it and she was not surprised to hear, when she got home, that they had run off somewhere. Roberto thought they must have gone up to town, because Teresa had on her best hat.

"Oh, well," sighed Florence, "it doesn't signify. They'll come back, I suppose."

It was too much to hope that they had gone for good, but she was glad to get them out of the house for a little while. They were a trial, poor children, though she had come lately to better terms with Teresa, who was more civil and tractable in consequence of a sort of promise that she should not go to school before the Autumn.

There was a pile of letters for Lewis in the hall ; some of them looked quite important. It was most inconvenient not knowing where to send them. They could, of course, go down to the hall where he would hold his Sunday rehearsal ; Florence thought that she might send, with them, a courteous note, apologising for the delay in forwarding and suggesting that he should give her an address. That would not look too much like pursuit ; it was the merest commonsense. At present the ridiculous pile, which grew larger every day, advertised to everybody in the house her ignorance of his whereabouts. To Millicent, who called that afternoon, she felt compelled to offer an explanation :

"Look ! Isn't it stupid of Lewis ? He's gone off and forgotten to leave me an address. What on earth am I to do with these ? Unless he writes or comes I can't get hold of him before the Sunday rehearsal."

"Gone off ? " said Millicent blankly. "Where ? "

"That's what I'd like to know," complained Florence, with a laugh which she hoped was convincing. "He went off on Saturday, while I was out. He's the vaguest creature. I rather think he may have gone into the country. He does, sometimes, when he's working, you know . . ."

"But my husband saw him last night . . ." began Millicent, and broke off, gaping excitedly.

"Saw him ? Where did he see him ? "

Millicent looked her over for a second and then said :

" Having supper at the Savoy. Doesn't look as if he was out of town, does it ? "

" N—no. Only it's funny he doesn't write or telephone about his letters."

" Very funny."

" Was he alone, do you know ? "

" Oh, no. Jewish-looking people, Hope said they were. At least, the men were Jewish-looking . . ."

" Oh, yes. He knows a lot of Jews," said Florence at once. " Come out and sit in the garden. It's quite warm."

She felt that she might conceal her unhappiness better in the garden. She had been so wretched lately that she could almost believe that anxiety and depression were stamped all over the walls of her charming house, like the damp coming through. This prying young woman would be sure to smell it out. They went into the garden and sat under the mulberry tree and she tried to re-establish the pose of the serenely confident wife.

She had come lately to feel that Lewis was not entirely to blame for his attitude towards his sister. Millicent could be very disagreeable sometimes. This afternoon she was unbearable. Nothing would interest her. She sat playing with her pearls and staring in front of her with a little smile, while Florence ploughed on through politics and the arts and even descended to social small talk in order to avoid family discussion. At last, after a prolonged silence, she said :

" I hope you put it across Lewis for the way he behaved over that Sanger opera. You don't mind my being frank, do you ? He ought to be made to understand that he can't behave like that. The whole of London is talking about it."

" Oh, are they ? " thought Florence viciously. " You mean that you are talking about it to the whole town."

Aloud she said that Lewis was apt to display his opinions a little too frankly.

" A little ! You should hear the Leyburns ! Of course,

rudeness sometimes pays. But it should be discriminating rudeness, not to the wrong people. He's so wholesale. He always was. When he was seven weeks old, he was sick all over his rich godfather. That's been his line ever since."

And Florence learnt that the Leyburns were never going to ask him to their house again ; that a set was being made against the performance of the Symphony in Three Keys ; that even old Sir Bartlemy said that half an hour was the utmost that he could stand of young Dodd at a time. All this was said in a tone of superficial raillery very difficult to answer ; Millicent was careful not to pass the limits permissible to a plain-spoken sister. It was not until she touched upon non-professional scandals that Florence was able to protest.

"You know," she said, "he shouldn't go about with these awful Jews. Or with the awful ladies that the awful Jews go about with. It gives a wrong impression. Of course, one knows why he hesitates to introduce his friends to you, in fact, you simply couldn't meet some of them, but it all gives a sort of confirmation to the ridiculous things people say. There again, I'm bound to say . . ."

"Why are you bound to say ? "

"Oh, I always say what I think. But if you won't hear the truth . . ."

"I won't hear idle gossip."

"Gossip ! My dear ! I wouldn't dream of repeating gossip to you. I know you are so much above these things. Believe me, I don't tell you half I hear. Not a quarter ! Still, we'll drop the subject, if you find it painful. I see in the paper, by the way, that little Mrs. Birnbaum's baby has arrived."

"Oh, has it ? I missed that. When was it ? Sunday ? And I ought to have enquired. I must ring them up."

"Married a year now . . . isn't she ? "

"Very nearly," calculated Florence.

"Hm ! Rather stupid of people to say that the child is

none of Birnbaum's, don't you think? Because I think you told me that they are rather a devoted couple."

"Do they say that?" cried Florence indignantly. "It's the most cruel, scandalous nonsense. Wicked! She's my cousin, you know; one of the Sanger children."

"I know. That's it. People have got hold of the name. He's such a legend nowadays. Nobody can believe that a daughter of his can be quite . . . The general idea is that he kept a sort of harem at that Austrian place. And you know, the rumours about that Birnbaum set . . . well! . . . they have to be heard to be believed. Not that I mean that quite, do I?"

"I don't know what you mean. I can't believe there's much amiss with Antonia. She was a wild little person before she married, but she has quite settled down."

"Of course! You went out there with your uncle, didn't you? And you found no harem, I take it?"

"N—no," said Florence, and then firmly: "Oh, no."

"Ridiculous what people will say, isn't it? And you married your little cousin off at once to Birnbaum, didn't you? Did you find him there already, or where did he spring from? And of course you met Lewis there too. I'm sure we ought to be very thankful it was you Lewis married and not the cousin. I don't know that we'd have welcomed Sanger's circus into the family with the *empressement* which we showed to you, my dear!"

Florence was too angry to answer, and Millicent presently asked if she had seen the baby.

"I shall tell everyone that you have," she said, "and that it's as like Birnbaum as possible. We must uphold the family reputation. By the way, have you got rid of the other girl yet? The plain one."

"Teresa?"

"Yes, Teresa. What have you done with her? She hasn't gone to Paris with the little one, has she?"

"I don't know what will be done with her. She's delicate:

263

I doubt if she ought to go to school. She has queer faints
. . ."

"That's a pity. I should send her and take the risk, if I
were you. What is it? Heart? They take very good care
of them at these schools."

And as Millicent pulled on her gloves, she observed thoughtfully :

"She wouldn't be as easy to find a husband for as the pretty
little Birnbaum. Well! I must be off. So nice to have
seen you, my dear !"

She got up and Florence followed her through the house,
explaining how childish Teresa was for her years, how
undeveloped.

"Nearly sixteen, isn't she?" said Millicent, pausing on the
doorstep. "I shouldn't wonder if she knew a thing or two, in
spite of all you say, Florence. Good-bye! Next time you
lose Lewis, I should advertise. You know . . . the agony
column . . . 'Come back! All forgiven and forgotten !'
Or you might try the Birnbaums, mightn't you?"

And she was gone, walking lightly down the river path, while
Florence, gazing after her, reflected upon the squalid complexion which Sanger affairs took on in retrospect. The
Karindehütte, after London gossip had been busy with it, really
sounded no better than a . . . than what Linda had called it.

She turned into the house and looked again at the letters, and
decided that really she had better try the Birnbaums. Not
that there was the smallest atom of truth in Millicent's odious
suggestions ; but if he was dining with Jewish-looking people,
it was very possible that Jacob might be able to trace him. She
would go and take some flowers to Tony and sit with her a bit ;
that was no more than an obvious duty. And she would just
mention that she had no address for forwarding letters, and
Tony would tell Jacob and Jacob would tell Lewis and Lewis
would write perhaps.

She set off for Lexham Gardens with a large bunch of iris ;

but Antonia's room seemed to be so full of flowers already that there was hardly space for more. It was a peculiar room, eloquent of luxury and wealth, and yet dirty and untidy, with the kind of sluttish disorder in which the Sangers felt most at home. Even the monthly nurse had not succeeded in making it look like a sick room. There was a piano in it, and several decanters and a mixer stood among the medicine bottles on the chimney piece, while cigar ash was spilt about everywhere.

Antonia, looking very well and incredibly beautiful, lay in an enormous bed, her satin counterpane perfectly strewn with the books, fruit, sweets, cigarettes, and gewgaws which Jacob bought for her every time he went out of the house. She exclaimed joyfully, when she saw Florence :

"Oh, my dear ! Why didn't you come before ? Have you seen my funny baby ? "

"Dear Tony ! How are you feeling . . ."

"Have you seen my little boy ? Oh, he's ugly ! Ho there ! Rachel ! Bring in the *bübchen !* "

"Vait a little," responded a guttural voice from an inner room. "In tree minute I bring him . "

"Oh, Florence, I've been longing to show him to you. He's the ugliest thing you ever saw. Ike says he doesn't think he can be mine, he's so ugly. I think he's uncommonly like his dad, but I'm too nice to say so. Push those horrid garments off that chair and sit down."

"My dear ! How are you ? "

"Oh, I'm quite all right. Never felt better. But I felt very queer on Sunday. You know, I never expected it would go on so long ; I began to feel very funny just after breakfast, and of course I thought the *bübchen* would turn up then and there. And old Rachel hadn't come because she wasn't fixed to come till Monday. And Ike was out. And, you know, I'm so shy of all the servants in this house, they're so grand. I didn't like to tell them what was the matter with me. And there was nobody I could tell but Lewis."

265

" Lewis ! "

" Yes, he was still in bed because he had a headache, because they'd been out late the night before. And I went wandering round the house in the most awful state of mind. And then I felt rather better, and I wondered if it would do me any good if I went out and took a ride on a 'bus. And then I felt funny again ; really awful ! And I got so desperate, thinking that my baby would be born before Ike or anybody came to help me, that I went up and woke Lewis. Oh, and he was so nice ! You can't think how kind he was ! He got up at once and dressed in two seconds and sent off one of the maids running for Rachel, and another for Ike, and another for the doctor, because we didn't know any of their numbers, because Ike threw the directory out of the window at a cat two nights before. And then he went down and made me a cup of tea, wasn't it clever of him ? And he told me funny stories about how Ike once tried hiring a Chinese cook. Oh, he can be kind, when he likes ! I was a bit frightened, but I couldn't help laughing. And then Ike and Rachel and all the servants came tearing in. And the thing didn't finish till late in the evening ; I was ever so much worse later on, only luckily I didn't know I was going to be. And Lewis and Ike sat with me a long time to cheer me up, and sang bits out of " Otello." And Rachel sang too. She's got a nice voice, though she is a monthly nurse. She's Jacob's first cousin, you know. He has some very funny cousins. Her brother keeps a pawnshop in the Old Kent Road, but he's quite rich."

They were interrupted by the entrance of Rachel with Antonia's baby. She was a frowsy, elderly Jewess, who looked as if she had got into a nurse's uniform by mistake. But she was, none the less, at the top of her profession, and Jacob had known what he was about when he secured her services.

" Look at him, Florence," crowed the little mother. " Isn't he a horror ? "

He was certainly a plain child and so ridiculously like Birnbaum that Florence wanted to laugh. She prodded him gently, with a grudging, awkward tenderness. In the abstract she did not like babies until they were old enough to crawl and prattle and be amusing. Very young ones she found a little monotonous. Of course, she wanted one herself, but that was a different matter.

"He's got a lot of hair," she said.

"Yes. But Rachel says it will all come off," said Tony sadly. "He'll be worse still when he's bald."

And she pressed him to her heart and kissed the top of his threatened head and whispered some inaudible, loving remark into his ear. Plainly she thought him the world's wonder. Something in her face stung Florence almost unbearably; she could not watch it. She got up and wandered about the room, looking at the Gainsboroughs that Jacob's friend had collected. Presently she asked:

"But is Lewis staying here?"

"Lewis?" said Antonia. "Oh, yes. Didn't you know?"

"My dear Tony! Lewis is a most trying man. He walked out of the house last week and forgot to leave an address. I've been left without the slightest idea where he could be."

"Florence!" Antonia opened her eyes very wide. "You didn't know? But when Tessa and Sebastian came here this morning, surely . . ."

"Did they come?"

"Oh, yes. Didn't you know? They've gone out now with Lewis and Ike to Stavgröd's recital. They'll be back any minute."

"I'm sorry they came. I'd no idea of it. I hope they didn't tire you."

"That's quite all right. I see stacks of people, don't I, Rachel? I had a dinner party here last night. But how like Lewis to forget to tell you he was here! Surely Tessa and Sebastian knew, didn't they?"

Florence could not tell her. Privately she believed that

they did and that the whole Sanger family was plotting against her behind her back. But in truth they had known nothing of it. Their visit to Lexham Gardens had been pure impulse and nobody could have been more surprised to find Lewis there than was Teresa, who wished genuinely to keep out of his way.

Florence made an attempt to retreat before the return of the concert party; she felt as though she could hardly trust her temper. But she could not get away in time. A joyous hubbub was heard in the hall while she was bidding Antonia good-bye, and in they all burst in the most remarkable spirits. Jacob came first, vainglorious, swelling with pride over his lovely wife and ugly son, flinging down a fresh armful of gifts upon the already loaded bed, kissing Tony, kissing the baby, kissing his cousin Rachel, almost kissing Florence when he discovered that she was there. Behind him came Lewis, Teresa, Sebastian, Nils Stavgröd, and some odd friends with raucous voices and jocular manners. Florence was quite bewildered by all the noise and laughter, and began to be concerned about Antonia. But she need not have troubled. Tony was more than equal to it. She pulled a shawl a little way across her white breast and her baby, shook hands with everybody, and called on Jacob to furnish them with cocktails. To Lewis she said severely :

"Why didn't you tell your poor wife that you were coming to us ? She didn't know where you were."

Lewis explained that he had left home to get away from his wife. He had shot one look at Florence, as he came in, a gleaming, baleful, sullen look, and now he seemed determined to ignore her. She said composedly :

"I only wanted to forward his bills. There are a good many waiting for him. Come children ! I think we'd better go. Antonia oughtn't, I'm sure, to have such a crowd in the room."

"That is no matter !" cried Jacob. "She adores company, do you not, my angel ? "

"I do not forbid it," put in Rachel. "A little barty is cheerful, *nicht wahr* ?"

So Florence stayed because she saw that she could not get her family away. But she sat a little apart from their circle and succeeded in looking as if she did not belong to them. With an increasing disgust she listened to their conversation. Tony jested with the men, while old Rachel, with hoarse chuckles, supplied occasional anecdotes which always smacked of her calling. Even in the impudent, childish remarks thrown in by Teresa and Sebastian, there was the same complete want of decorum. There was, lavishly displayed, the serene, enthralling beauty of Antonia's motherhood ; it was the only good thing in the room. But no one seemed to have any reverence for it ; their language profaned it. Florence marvelled that she should ever have found their speech naïve and amusing ; nowadays it nauseated her. And there was Tony giving Stavgröd a detailed account of her confinement, apparently in explanation of her absence at his concert ! They were all loud in their regret that she had not been there. Stavgröd had played the Kreutzer Sonata quite well. According to Lewis he would never play it better.

"Oh, dear ! And shall I never hear it ?"

Antonia turned her enchanting wild eyes upon the fair-haired young man, who instantly became pale with admiration.

"I shall be most happy . . ." he muttered. "Any time . . . now . . . if Madame is not fatigued . . ."

Madame rewarded him with another of her disturbing smiles and Jacob opened the piano. Lewis and Sebastian wrangled a little over which of them was to play, but Lewis prevailed because he said firmly that he knew this piece.

It was surprising music ; Florence, for a time, could not help listening in spite of her troubles. But it was Lewis rather than Stavgröd who claimed her attention. He did not often play the piano and she had never heard a performance like this from him before. He certainly knew the piece. There was a peculiar passion and sadness in it which plucked at her very heart strings, as though she was herself an instrument for his cruel, clever fingers. And he gave her besides a conviction of restrained power; she felt that he had mastered all emotion and turned it to his own ends. It was outrageous that he could do it. She knew him to be hard, lustful, and unstable; he had no business to command so much effortless beauty. Playing like this required noble thoughts and unflinching aims. But then, this was his real life.

And it was so with all of them. She watched them as they listened; even old Rachel, gross and ugly though she was, had a strange light on her face as she leant against the door, smiling and watching the violinist. Teresa and Sebastian were fixed and intent. Jacob had forgotten wife and child, had turned away from them and was staring through the room, all dim with smoke, as though he could see some lost vision beyond the window among the dark trees of the garden. And Tony, though she pressed her baby in her arms, had wandered in her mind elsewhere. Her lovely eyes had an inward brooding look. Music, with all these people, came first; that was why they talked about it as if nobody else had any right to it. Once Florence had liked them all too well; now that she understood them better she was frightened of them. She wanted to challenge them, to make a demonstration of her power, to call them back to that world of necessity and compromise which they so sublimely ignored, but with which they would have ultimately to reckon. After all, she was the strongest. She had order and power on her side. They were nothing but a pack of rebels. But she must do something immediate that would prove her strength over them. When the music was finished she rose to her feet, and it was as if they had all grasped something of her emotion. They were silent and watched her curiously as she made her farewells to Antonia. Only Lewis, on the piano-stool, kept his back turned to her and went on strumming softly. But she knew that he was listening.

"Good-bye, Tony," she said. "I'll bring Teresa round to see you again before she goes. She's our next departure, you know. She's going to school at Harrogate the day after Lewis's concert."

This was the earliest day that Teresa could possibly go. Florence finished buttoning up her gloves while her bomb took effect. Teresa turned very pale but made no protest. Lewis stopped playing, swung round on the piano-stool, and asked his wife :

"Is she really going so soon ?"

His look disturbed her, but she managed to reply firmly :

"As soon as I can get her off."

"When did you settle it ?" he asked very low.

"Just now," she answered, meeting his glance.

"She always speaks the truth," he said, turning to Teresa with a grin.

He got up and came into the hall with them. He took down his hat and Florence asked in surprise if he meant to come back to Chiswick.

"To the Silver Sty," he said. "Yes. I've no time to lose."

They went down the steps, out of the heat and haze of the smoky, untidy room into the sharp Spring evening. Florence said in an undertone :

"You don't think that by coming back you can alter my plans for Tessa ? I warn you, it's no use."

"Tessa !" He smiled a little and glanced over his shoulder at Teresa, who was dragging along listlessly behind them with her young brother. "Oh, it's all up with her now, isn't it, Tessa."

"What ?" she asked blankly.

"It's all up with you now, isn't it ?"

She said nothing. She shook her head in a kind of dumb fright, looking at the pair of them as if she would ask how much more she would have to endure at their hands. She felt rather

271

sleepy and yawny, walking along after them, and paid very little attention to where she was going. At a crossing she narrowly escaped death beneath the wheels of a taxi. Instantly the stored exasperation of her elders was poured out upon her. She walked between them, blinking mildly at their furious, frightened rebukes.

"Why can't you look where you are going?" stormed Florence.

"There are prettier ways of committing suicide," Lewis told her.

"It's pure carelessness."

"You seem to know nothing at all about self-preservation."

"A child of five should have more sense!"

"And so inconsiderate! Spoiling our pleasant walk!"

CHAPTER XXI

THE young Sangers could never quite accustom themselves to the immense importance attached to concerts at Strand-on-the-Green. This was because they had, as yet, hardly learnt the difference between private and public life; the transitions between the two had been, in the old days, much less abrupt. They had been used to live, as it were, without reticences, transferring themselves noisily from the racket of their home to the racket of the Opera House without an appreciable change of atmosphere. There had been none of these secret toilets and preparations, these studied issuings forth into the larger world.

Their cousin, on the other hand, possessed a special concert room demeanour—a still, serious, attentive carriage which sometimes, on special occasions, showed itself quite early in the day, as though she were practising inwardly. Traces of it were apparent for a whole week before the performance of the Dodd Symphony, which was, of course, the most important thing that had ever happened. An extreme solemnity hung over the actual day, a suspense which damped even the hardened flippancy of Teresa and Sebastian; they went off of their own accord, at an early hour in the evening, to wash their faces and put on their best clothes, a business to which they generally required to be driven.

Florence had told Teresa to put on her new white frock. It was a maidenly garment of embroidered muslin with sleeves to cover her sharp elbows and a high yoke which hid the hollows in her young neck. A white ribbon spanned the broad middle of the dress in that region where it was to be

hoped she might some day have a waist, and other white bows
tied up her tail of fair hair. Also she had new patent leather
shoes, with steel buckles, and thick, black silk stockings. All
this gear was designed for school parties and concerts, and
became her almost as little as it would have become that Delphic
Sibyl whom she so closely resembled. Its infantile scantiness
emphasized everything that was out of scale in her person : the
lanky awkwardness of her rapid growth, and the shy, abrupt
grandeur of some of her gestures. She peered at the glass rather
dismally and could not help feeling that she looked foolish.

"God in His wisdom gave you that face," she informed her
reflection, "and Florence in her wisdom gave you that dress.
But they don't understand the value of team work. And
neither of them consulted your feelings very much. It's not
your beauty, my girl, that will get you into trouble in this
world."

She had reached a pitch of wretchedness when all evils
looked very much alike. Her detestable clothes, the forlorn
certainty of school before her, the effort of decision behind her,
the loss of her home, the separation from the people she loved
and understood, the reverberation of that terror and bewildered
shock which had haunted her ever since the night of Sanger's
death, all these oppressed her with an equal weight. To
thrust her love out of her heart and life had been so monstrous,
so unnatural an effort, that all vital feelings had gone with it.
The impulse of protest had died ; she had no wishes left and
felt, with an odd, surprised relief, that it would be quite easy in
future to do what she was told and go where she was bidden.
Desiring nothing, she was afraid of nothing save the bodily
pain which so often assailed her. To endure this without
complaint was now her chief care, for, though its onslaughts
were appalling to her mind, she could not bear to think that
anybody should know. Illness of any kind was, in her eyes, a
little shameful ; in Sanger's circus it had never been tolerated,
and Kate was the only person there who sympathized with

aches and pains. This illness especially, this unsparing enemy that took such complete possession of her, that conquered her spirit and turned her into nothing but a tortured body, seemed base to Teresa, as though there was something indecent in the ugliness of such a contest. She tried never to think of it, but she could not help being rather frightened when she thought of school where she would be running about all day. Really nowadays, when she had to run, she felt almost ready to die.

Two buttons at the back of her dress proved to be beyond her management, and she did not like holding her arms up, so she went downstairs to demand aid. In her cousin's room she found Lewis, with all his red hair standing on end, submitting to a toilet. He was to leave the house before the rest of them, but it seemed likely that he would not be despatched in time. He had been got into his boiled shirt and was standing, palpitating but patient, while his wife dealt with his tie. Both were looking distraught but on better terms than they had been for months. The excitement of the moment was such that they had no time to think of their grievances.

In moments of animation Florence always appeared to advantage. Her fine silver dress, with a brilliant Chinese shawl, was flung on the bed, and she was running about in a little silk petticoat, a narrow sheath for her slender, supple beauty. Her hair, tossed back from her face, hung all soft and cloudy over her white arms and shoulders. Self-forgetfulness was, in her, as rare as it was delightful ; both her companions were conscious of its charm. They stared at her in dumb but unconcealed admiration, moved to that immediate pleasure in beauty which was the strongest impulse in their natures. Lewis, especially, could not take his eyes away from her ; he was nervous and preoccupied, secretly dreading the night's work before him, shrinking from the effort, and she was like a reassurance, a solacing repose. There was a sort of dim grati- tude in the looks which he cast at her. Teresa saw that he was half bewitched again and wondered if another period of reconciliation was due. She gauged in her mind the command over his senses which Florence so palpably possessed, and balanced against it the inevitable rebellious reaction in him, the rancour, the protest against domination, which had made the history of these two so stormy. She thought :

" Does she want him back ? She could get him for a little while, when he's resting after the concert . . ."

She felt no personal concern in the idea that they should come together again ; such thoughts would trouble her little in the careful, safe grave she was digging for herself. It was not in her disposition to be jealous of her cousin's beauty ; she could never grudge a quality which so enriched the world. Nor was she afraid, now, of any failure in her own resolution, since she would not see Lewis again. He was not coming back to Chiswick after the concert ; he would sleep that night in town and next day he was going abroad. He said that he did not know where he was going and the implication that he would not, at any rate, come back had been perfectly understood by the whole household. Florence had seemed to acquiesce. Nobody seriously believed that she was going to join him later, and this sudden tender cordiality was, therefore, very puzzling to Teresa, who could discover no cause for it. On no grounds could she explain the generosity with which Lewis, in spite of his amazing faults, was always treated, unless as an exhibition of that forgiving quality which she had once described to Charles as *bonté*, the persistent, noble benevolence which she firmly believed her cousin to possess.

" There you are," said Florence, finishing the tie. " Flatten down your hair and make yourself neat. What do you want, Teresa ? "

" My frock."

" Can you really not fasten your own frock ? Come here."

" Is this neat ? " asked Lewis, after dealing with the brush that had been given to him.

" Passably," said his wife.

"You look like a calf going garlanded to the sacrifice," Teresa told him.

Immediately she was sorry she had said it. It was a great deal too true. He did have very much the look of a dumb beast driven to the shambles, and all this festal preparation only made it worse. She exclaimed encouragingly :

"It'll be over quite soon, you know."

"Very soon," he agreed, with an unamiable expression. "Where shall we all be this time to-morrow ? You'll be saying the multiplication table along with the other young ladies, Tessa. And I shall be . . . God knows where ! "

This was not quite true as Teresa knew where. He had told her privately that he was going, by the early boat, to Brussels, in case she might feel disposed to slip out of the house next morning and join him ; a communication which she had received with that mute obstinacy, that sulky demeanour of resolution, which was her last line of defence. But she did not point out his inaccuracy. She saw that the allusion to the garlanded calf had stung him, and she felt that he was perhaps justified in giving her an unkind reply. She merely made a noise of melancholy assent and retreated in good order. It was not until she had shut the door behind her and Lewis was half-way into his coat that the truth flashed across his mind. His wits that night were not at their best. He could hardly believe that he had said good-bye to her, that an incredible, impossible thing had really happened, that they would never speak to one another again. For a few seconds he stood petrified ; then he turned to Florence and said :

"I shan't see Tessa any more ! "

"No," she said easily. "Except, of course, across the Regent's Hall. You can give us a special bow if you like. You . . . you won't be seeing me again either, you know."

She glanced at him sideways. He was wrapped in thought and replied absently :

"No, I suppose not."

277

He wanted to tell her about it ; she had been so nice all day. He was seized with a strong, sudden impulse to deal openly with her, to lay the whole truth before her, and to trust that the truth might mend matters. The truth, to him, was the story of Tessa's goodness, her sweet, staunch loyalty. There had been some baseness and enmity between the three of them, but none of it had touched Tessa, and he scarcely believed that it could live if it was brought into the light. He was going away. He had to leave his love behind him. It seemed to him that he might endure that if Florence would but comprehend her. He turned round and said to her, with a new, grave friendliness :

"I wish that you would be better friends with Tessa . . . that you would love her. She deserves to be loved. Everybody must, I think, that really knows her. If you could hear how she speaks of you, how she admires you, you . . . you couldn't help it. I don't think you quite understand how . . . how good she is."

"No . . . I don't quite understand," she said, with a bitterness which, in his eager appeal, he failed to remark.

"I can't bear to go away and leave her with people who don't know that," he said simply. "Do try, Florence ! I know I'm a bad advocate. I know I've behaved very badly to you. This has been a wretched business and it's best that I should go away, for I've only made you unhappy, and I should go on making you unhappy. But I feel that the worst thing I've done is that somehow I've put you and Tessa against each other. Because you ought to love each other. My fault, that is ! I've not spoken plainly. You see . . . I love her so much . . . so much ! I want to know that she'll be happy. And now I have to leave her with you and you treat her as if she was an enemy. She's not. What can I say ? You are so much better fitted to love each other, you two, than I am to have anything to do with either of you. Oh, Florence, can't you see it ? If you'd only see it, I could go away and say God bless you both."

278

She had not thought it possible that he could speak like this. In all their life together she had never heard these tones in his voice, or met that look of unreserved appeal, save once in the Tyrol, when he first spoke to her of the little girls, and begged her to take them to England. She had loved him from that hour. And now she knew that it was all for Teresa, the gentleness which she had divined in him then. She had given her heart to Teresa's lover.

"Since when have you loved her so terribly?" she asked.

He didn't know. Always, he supposed.

"Why, then, did you marry me?"

"I was a fool. Oh, Florence, be angry with me, not with her! She's done nothing to deserve it. She loves you."

"Have you told her? Does she know?"

"Yes, she knows. And you knew it too, didn't you? Didn't you? You've known it for a long time. That's why I'm speaking of it now, because you know it already, and you're a person one can dare to speak the truth to. And you were angry because I didn't tell it; weren't you? You thought you deserved straighter dealing. And now you see that it isn't her fault. You're too generous to do anything else . . ."

She would not look at him. Instead, she looked at her watch, and said that it was time for him to go. But the crazy fellow would not go; he still pleaded, hoping absurdly that this appeal might somehow make things easier for Tessa.

"Florence, don't put me off like this. Can't you see . . ."

"I can see no good in discussing this business now."

"If I could make you understand what she is really like," he cried despairingly. "I think she never could have a vile thought about anybody. She couldn't do a base thing. She . . ."

At that she cut him short, flinging at him abruptly the question which for weeks had tormented her, returning to her mind as often as she banished it. It burst from her.

"You may as well tell the whole truth now. What, exactly, has there been between you?"

"I've told you. I love her."

"And what does that mean? Is she your mistress?"

Though she would not look at him, she could feel the shock of his sudden anger. But he tried to control himself.

"No, she's not. I tell you, she'll have nothing to do with me because she loves you."

"I don't believe you."

"It's true. She would never be as unjust to you."

"What am I to believe? I've seen enough of the whole pack of you to know that you can't be trusted."

She went across to the dressing-table and began rapidly to pin up her hair. Glancing furtively into the glass she was surprised to see that this mortal wound had, as yet, written no history on her face. Only her eyes had an alarmed look. She said to herself that it was too soon. Lewis, watching her, was passing rapidly to a pitch of extreme fury, baffled by his helplessness and the necessity of leaving his friend in the power of a woman who hated and maligned her.

"Supposing you were right," he said, "what would you have done?"

"I should never forgive you."

"Her, you mean. But you won't forgive her now, when I swear she's done you no wrong; you're making a wicked mistake."

"There's no question of forgiveness where she is concerned. I have no very strong feelings about her; I think she's too . . . too contemptible. She's no better than Tony. She's wanton. This sort of thing was bound to occur sooner or later, I suppose. And it happened to be you, because you haven't the decency to respect your wife's house. I should have foreseen it. No, it's you I shall never forgive."

"Oh, yes, you would, my dear! You'd forgive me anything."

He said this with as much insolence as he could muster, only desiring to punish her for speaking so ill of Tessa. He flung in her teeth the numberless occasions when she had allowed him to cajole her into submission and forgiveness. And when she would not turn round he crossed the room and seized her by the shoulders, wrenching her round and whispering :

"Always ready to forgive me you've been ! Always so generous ! Tessa thinks you're an angel. She doesn't know how easy you are to manage."

"Never . . . after this . . . never again . . ."

"Oh, yes ! As often as I like. You would ! You would ! "

"I hate you."

"Women like you are fond of saying that. It means nothing."

"I pray to God I may never see you again . . ."

"I've heard that before too."

"Is this how you treat her ? I hope it is. I hope you make her suffer as I do . . ."

"Oh, no ! "

He flung her away from him and repeated :

"Not at all. It would be impossible for her to suffer as you do. She has some pride. And then she's not like any of the rest of you. If I tried my fascinating ways on her she'd give me a black eye ! "

And he took himself off.

Florence stood where he had left her. She hardly moved until, a few minutes later, she heard the front door clap after him and the sound of his footsteps hurrying away down the river path. Then, with a kind of hasty, mechanical precision, she finished doing her hair and put on her dress. One clear thought remained in her mind. She must hold herself undefeated until the concert was over ; for to-night she must pretend that nothing was amiss. And to-morrow she would go back to Cambridge, to her father, and never so much as think of

Lewis again. And she would tell her father the truth about this betrayal, so that Teresa's evil name might never be spoken to her.

Nothing in her life, not even her love, had been so absorbing and powerful as was this hatred for her cousin. She was glad to be so angry. At last she had a justification for the gathering suspicion and resentment of months. Passion held her together under the shock which had snapped her life in two. It gave coherence to her thoughts and enabled her to master herself sufficiently for the business of the evening. Of Lewis and the atrocious things he had said she would not allow herself to think; it was enough to know that Teresa was responsible for it all.

She was almost calm again when a knock at the door startled her. Sebastian stood there, remarkably respectable in a new Eton jacket, demanding smelling salts or sal volatile.

"What for? Are you ill?"

"Tessa is."

"What's the matter with her?"

"I don't know. She's lying on her bed. She looks very funny."

"Oh, indeed! Then she had better not come to the concert."

They went upstairs to Teresa's room and found her sitting on her bed, wiping the sweat from her face, in a spasm of nervous sobbing. Her pain had been bad for a little time after she heard Lewis leave the house, but she was better now and declared that nothing was the matter. Florence became very stern and efficient, administered sal volatile, dismissed Sebastian, and said firmly:

"You had better not come to the concert if you feel like this, Teresa. Did you have those palpitations?"

"I'm quite well, really."

"Still, one can't have these ways. If you stay quietly at home to-night you'll know how to control yourself another time perhaps."

"There won't be another time. I'm coming, Florence."

"I shall not take you."

"Then I shall go by myself. You can't stop me. I have money. I shall go the minute you've left the house."

"Oh, very well. There won't be, as you say, another time. You can't disgrace yourself more than you've done already."

"What do you mean?" asked Teresa mildly.

Florence hesitated, but her feelings got the better of her. She must speak, even though she might be sorry afterwards. She would speak now, because prudence might stop her later on. She explained, in a dry, gentle voice:

"Because I've never spoken of it, you don't think I haven't seen .. what's been going on all these months? I've seen it, and I've tried to ignore it, because it was so . . . so odious. I've tried to make excuses to myself; to tell myself that you are too young to know what you are doing. I'd meant to say nothing of it. I knew you'd learn to be ashamed when you are older. But . . ."

"Ashamed?"

Teresa was really astonished. If Florence knew all, it was natural that she should be annoyed, but nobody, surely, need be ashamed of themselves.

"Yes! Ashamed! Because I'm ashamed for you. And now I feel that it's only fair that you should know one or two things before you go away. So I'll speak now, and then we'll never mention this again. Teresa, you must know that among decent people a woman who openly pursues a man is considered to have lost all her dignity and self-respect. She's despised and degraded and condemned by everybody. Especially when it is a man who doesn't particularly care for her. I can't . . I can't tell you how contemptible she makes herself. And to see quite a young girl doing it is horrible."

"Yes, but what has that to do with me? I haven't been pursuing a man that doesn't particularly care for me. It's a mug's game; I agree with you."

"You know perfectly well that you have. It's been almost impossible for me to say anything, since the man has been my husband; but now that he has gone, now that you will not see him ever, ever again, I can say it. You've thrust yourself upon him. You've thrown yourself at his head in a perfectly uncontrolled way. It's been quite obvious to everyone."

"I love him. I always have. And perhaps anybody could see it. But it's not true, what you said."

"It's quite true. He's spoken of it to me himself."

"He? Oh, no! You must have made a mistake, Florence. He would never . . ."

"It's odious, as I've said before, to have to take you to task for your manner to my husband, but for your own sake . . ."

"I'm afraid I must take you to task for your manner to me. I don't think you mean it, really, Florence! But I will not have these things said to me. It's not my fault that I love him. I did long ago, before you came to the Tyrol. It isn't a happy thing at all; it's brought nothing but sadness to me. Only it has been so much all of my life that I couldn't want it to be different, any more than I could want to be changed into another person. And I've come to see, since I've been here, that we can't all be together now that he is your husband. That's why I agreed to go to school. I wouldn't otherwise. You know I said at first that I wouldn't. But ever since I saw that I ought to go, I've not said a word against it, now have I? All these weeks! I wanted to write to Uncle Charles, often, to get him to let me off. But I never did."

"You'd better not write to him. I shall have to tell him how difficult all this has been, and then he'll see, as I do, that you are better at school."

"If you tell him untrue things about me, I shall tell him the truth myself."

"Which of us do you think he'll believe?"

Teresa was silent. She was becoming frightened of Florence. Yet she was accustomed to associate anger with hard words and

violence, and she could hardly believe that deadly insults are
sometimes spoken gently. Florence, so lovely and dignified,
could not really hate her, could not really mean to deny her the
right to love and to suffer. This controlled animosity was
something quite new, and it alarmed her terribly. She said,
backing away :

" You are making a mistake. You don't mean these
things. Something funny must have happened . . . What's
the matter . . ."

But Florence would not stop. She went on, low voiced and
relentless :

" You speak of love ! What can you know of it ? I wonder
that you dare. When you are older perhaps you'll be ashamed
. . ."

" I know all about it," interrupted Teresa sombrely.

" What do you mean by that ? "

The question was rapped out with a rising shrillness, and
Teresa exclaimed in a panic :

" What's the matter with you ? Florence ! Don't !
Don't look at me like that ! Don't speak like that ! I've
done you no harm. What did you think I'd done ? "

Before her eyes the woman was turning into a Medusa ; she
shut them, to escape from that stony, vindictive head, thrust
close into her face. She felt her shoulder grasped and the hard,
hoarse voice whispered again into her ear :

" Tell me what you mean."

" Don't ! I won't." She sobbed and struggled. " Let
me go ! "

With a scream of terror she got herself free and ran from the
room and downstairs and out of the house. Florence, left alone
in the little bedroom, drew a long breath of relief. In five
minutes the accumulated venom of many months had found a
vent. She was glad now, though she was aware that she might
repent later. She was triumphant. It was even satisfying to
know that she had hurled a rank name after her flying enemy.

To-morrow she would probably blush to think that she could have screamed such a word out through the house, but filthy language was the only sort of speech which the Sangers understood.

"Thank goodness! I've put the fear of God into her!" she thought. "She deserved every word of it. How frightened she looked and how shocked! One would think she'd never heard anybody swear before. But I suppose it must have been rather a shock to hear me swearing!"

The first chill of doubt fell upon her exaltation, and she hurried off, back to her room, to put on her shawl.

Teresa was, indeed, nearly shocked to death. Her fear was like a nightmare, she did not know where to turn or how to protect herself from this horrible woman who looked like an angel and talked like a devil. Uncle Charles might prate about the merit of a civilized life, but there was no safety in it. If Florence, who had seemed so beautiful and so good, was really like this, there was no safety in it. Only she could never get away; they had trapped her now. Lewis, the only friend she had in the world, was lost to her. He was gone beyond her reach. He would have taken her and shielded her, and though he might be a little rough sometimes she would always know where she was with him. Besides, she loved him. And yet she had made him go away. She had been mad.

Still gasping with indignation and fright she ran a little way in the dusk along the river path and then, looking furtively around her, came to a standstill. There was nobody on the path and all the houses seemed quiet. A couple of swans paddled lazily over the dim water, up past the island, but otherwise the river too was deserted. She could hear the tide, which was almost high, gurgling against the barges moored to the island. She debated with herself the practical difficulties in the way of a quick escape and came to the conclusion that it would be no use to jump off the wooden embankment at the edge of the path. She would merely stick in the shallow mud.

She must go farther down, where it was deeper at the edge. She started back towards the bridge and collided with a person hurrying along to the station.

" *Scusa !* " said the person.

It was Roberto going to the concert, in his bowler hat, with his going-to-Mass umbrella under his arm. He always took his umbrella to concerts in the old days. She must get back there somehow. She must get to Lewis.

" It's you, is it ? " she said. " You'll be the last person to speak to the deceased. I hope they won't hang you for murdering me, Roberto. They might do anything in this country."

" *Scusa !* "

" Remember me, but . . . ah, forget my fate ! " she said impressively.

" *Subito !* " said Roberto obligingly.

He said this when injunctions were laid upon him which he did not understand; it testified to his willingness. Teresa laughed. She knew that she could not possibly jump into the river. There was still too much to laugh at. She would go to Lewis and they would get away from it all. She asked Roberto if he had pencil and paper. He had, and she scrawled a message to Lewis telling him that she would meet him by the early boat train to-morrow. This note was to be given into his very hands, as she impressed upon Roberto in two languages.

" Take it into the artists' room," she insisted. " You must get there somehow."

" *Subito !* "

Roberto had spent most of his life in artists' rooms and had no doubt of his capacity to get there. He trotted off down the river path. Teresa sauntered back to the house, kicking little pebbles sideways into the water as Lewis was apt to do. They had many identical gestures.

CHAPTER XXII

THEIR places were in the first circle, well at the side and almost above the orchestra so that they had a good view of the house. Sebastian and Teresa, having wrangled a little over the best seat, devoted themselves to a scrutiny of the packed masses in the gallery in order to discover Roberto. They waved excitedly when they found him. Florence looked down at the arena below her, and observed the sort of people who were coming in, and was confirmed in her estimation of the evening's importance. Whatever Millicent might say, they were coming. She saw friends who never went to concerts unless they were important, people who were not even musical but whose opinions were universally respected ; all the people who had gone to hear " Prester John," and another choicer group which would not, apparently, listen to Sanger but which was curious about the Dodd Symphony. She had got them all, sitting below and around her—all that world which she desired to conquer. The applause and recognition of this audience would, in her eyes, justify to the world her belief that she had married a great man. It would be her defence against Churchill criticism, and now that her life had come so entirely to grief she badly needed a defence.

She nodded to her friends, here and there, in a leisurely way. Her concert room demeanour was in full force. She held her round, dark head very high over the glowing, lavish folds of her shawl, and she was sparing of any gesture with her hands. She was determined not to be agitated and voluble ; she would not twitter as so many women will when their men are on trial before the world. To be serene, assured, beautiful, that was her part of the business, and if she had not always managed it in the past it was because she had been forced to appear in public with a train of strident young Sangers. In future . . . but there would be no future. Lewis had passed all permissible bounds, and they were to part. But she must forget that until after the concert. The orchestra was trickling in.

The children, hanging over the edge of the balcony, were exchanging salutations with a few odd-looking acquaintances.

Old Sir Bartlemy Pugh, having seen them from the opposite side of the house, came round to speak to her. She was glad, for she had caught sight of Millicent coming in with Lewis's father, who was looking more than ever like a civic portrait. Both he and his daughter were staring up at her companion with interest, nor were they the only people in the Regent's Hall who would notice that the old gentleman had hobbled all the way round the first circle to make himself agreeable to young Mrs. Dodd. She talked calmly and without undue animation, but a little flush of pleasure glowed in her cheeks.

" All the world and his wife seem to be here," said Sir Bartlemy. " It's a long time since I dragged my gouty limbs to an affair like this. And I hear that they've put the Symphony after Jansen's horrid little bit of work. I needn't have hurried over my dinner. I've a good mind to go home and finish my coffee ! "

" But I'm most anxious to hear the Turkish Suite," declared Florence, who was secretly delighted at the intimacy of these remarks.

Very seldom did Sir Bartlemy permit himself to speak slightingly of a contemporary, and then only in the company of close friends. She had never heard him call anything horrid before ; she felt that she had graduated in his friendship.

" Mawkish ! Mawkish ! " he complained, shaking his head. " Turkish Delight, we call it, down at Greenwich.

How are you, Dawson ? Do you realize we are in for the Turkish Suite ? "

Dr. Dawson was making his way to a seat behind Florence. He was accompanied by a group of pale young women, members of his celebrated choir, who escorted him everywhere. One of them carried a railway rug to wrap round his knees if he found the Regent's Hall draughty. He grinned at Sir Bartlemy and scowled sideways at Florence with a hasty :

" How are you ? I've just been round back there, and Lewis is here all right. I congratulate you, Ma'am, on producing him at the right hall on the right evening. It takes a clever wife to do that. It was a good idea sending him here in charge of the butler."

" The butler ? " said Florence, a little puzzled.

" Your Italian fellow . . . He seemed to be chaperoning Lewis when first I went in down there. I don't know where he disappeared to."

" Roberto ? " Florence gaped. " I didn't send him. Are you sure ? He's up in the gallery . . ."

" Quite sure. Have you met Baines ? "

And he introduced her to a little old man who had come in with him, an almost legendary person who had trained more great singers than any three men of his generation. He was now so ancient that most people thought he must be dead. He lived at Wimbledon, took a few pupils to amuse himself, and turned up once a year at the opera in order to remind the world that he was still alive. Hardly ever did he attend a concert and his appearance for the Dodd Symphony was unexpected and sensational.

He twinkled at Florence a rheumy eye which had ogled four generations of pretty women and talked away to her, in a high cackle, above the confused din of the tuning orchestra, the booms of double basses beneath, and the short, sudden brays of clarinets. He told her that he had met Lewis in Vienna, ten years ago, at a supper given by Sanger.

"We have Sanger's circus with us still," exclaimed Dr. Dawson. "This is one."

He stretched an arm, caught Sebastian by the back of his jacket, and turned him round. Branwell Baines looked a little surprised at such cleanliness and order, and commented:

"Well, well, I wouldn't have guessed it! I was sorry to miss 'Prester John,' Mrs. Dodd, but I'm getting on, you know, and I don't go about very much. Saving your presence, I had a little chill on the liver, and these east winds . ."

Here there was a great outcry from the children that Ike and Tony had come and was it not very soon for Tony to be out? Florence and her three cavaliers turned to look downwards, and saw that eight out of every ten people were glancing curiously their way. Antonia, still a little frail but regal, in black velvet with the most amazing pearls, was leaning upon Jacob's arm, receiving the compliments and obvious congratulations of a number of Semitic-looking gentlemen, who most of them found it necessary to kiss her hand. She looked up to where Florence was sitting between Sir Bartlemy and Branwell Baines, with Dawson leaning over the back of her chair, and waved gaily. Florence smiled serenely back and bowed to Mrs. Leyburn and a good many other people.

The lovely ladies who were to play the harp in Jansen's Turkish Suite were proceeding to their lone post in front of all the forest of music stands and shirtfronts. The noise of tuning was beginning to subside and Sir Bartlemy, with a hasty farewell, ambled back to his seat on the far side of the circle. Florence, settling herself and her trappings comfortably into her seat, felt that Teresa, beside her, had stiffened and was sitting bolt upright. She looked down and saw that Lewis was making his way up on to the platform. There was a little applause, not very much, not enough to call for acknowledgment, and he took no notice of it. A moment later he had mounted the *estrade*, and his back was turned upon them all. He tapped on the rail and the hum of the hall behind him sank to a rustle. The rustle was silence.

Music stole out like a mist into the great spaces of the building. It hung in the air in front of Florence, an almost visible fabric, a flowing pattern of strings cut through by the sharp notes of horns, blurring the piled tiers of faces which went up, and up, to the dark, high gallery. Down below, the orchestra was a chequered tapestry of black and white, across which the slender white bows moved all together. Only Lewis stood out clearly, and Florence discovered how very well shaped his head was, when seen from the back, a thing which had been long known to Teresa. Standing thus, he looked a different man altogether. She examined him curiously through the pleasant measures of the Turkish Suite, which seemed nice music, if a trifle saccharine. His carriage as a conductor pleased her enormously, but she wished that she could see his face. He was very still and there was, to her eyes, almost too much gravity in his pose, considering the work in hand. The orchestra, sweating their way through the Caucasian dances of the second movement, must be finding some source of energy in his expression for he did almost nothing, and his immobility contrasted strangely with their manifest toil. Then, as a crescendo swelled on a faint quiver of his baton, she wondered what sort of a noise would be heard if he should take it into his head to exert himself. The Symphony in Three Keys had plenty of noise in it. She began to get excited.

The thing was over unexpectedly soon and the applause was considerable. Florence found herself a little enthusiastic; it was better music than she had thought. More people were coming in. The clapping went on. Lewis, pale, wild and unconcerned, came back and bowed unsmilingly to the gangway between the stalls. The clapping went on. They wanted Jimmy Jansen. He came and bowed energetically to everybody, but he did not look very pleased. Dr. Dawson leant across his railway rug, and poked Florence in the back, and whispered :

"Good man ! Jansen wrote that last *allegro ma non*

troppo, and he took it *presto*. 'Pon my word, it's a vast improvement ! "

' " I expect he thought he'd written it himself," said Teresa with a little chuckle. " It's a mistake he often makes when he's conducting a piece. He stops and says, ' Now why did I do that ? ' "

" That's nonsense," said Florence coldly.

She had almost succeeded in forgetting Teresa, and it was necessary that she should. To be married to a man like Lewis was not easy ; there would be, always, so much to forget. But she did not think that anything in the future would be as difficult as this estrangement for which Teresa was responsible. Almost she felt that she could not pardon it ; it was too outrageous. The only way was to banish the whole episode from her mind, to send the girl away, out of their lives, to think of her, if possible, in a spirit of tolerance and pity. It was unjust to hate her, for she could not help being what she was, an unfortunate little animal without training, without very much intelligence, so ignorant as to be almost blameless, obeying blindly the instincts which commanded her. But she had been, unwittingly, the cause of much grief ; it was her fault that Lewis had said those heart shattering things. Really, he was too cruel. It was impossible to live with him. The scene to-night must have ended it. Only that they were all like that ; some of them were much worse. Sanger used to beat his wives. Lewis never did that.

All these thoughts were flashing through Florence's mind as she told Dr. Dawson that she had liked the Turkish Suite.

" Very noble, he made it sound," agreed Dr. Dawson. " It's a trick he has."

She remembered how he had played the Kreutzer. It was certainly a trick he had, if nobility, grandeur of interpretation can be called a trick. Her mind roved over their life together, as she tried to decipher in the man she knew the features of the artist thus revealed. He displayed, as a musician, a largeness of spirit which she had never divined in the man. She confided to Dr. Dawson that she had never known that he was so good a conductor.

" Very few of us knew," was his reply.

He was with them again, looking different, looking more collected, mounting the *estrade* with a sort of brisk determination which took her by surprise. The silence, under his lifted baton, was complete and sudden like the flash before a thunder clap, a soundless shock, a pause. The baton fell and the lordly racket of his Symphony was let loose on them. An astonishing pandemonium it was, written at a time when Sanger dominated all his ideas, yet with a shape and contour which passed perpetu-ally beyond the purely revolutionary formula invented by his master. Its long, striding intervals, its violent rhythms, fell upon the ear, at first, like an outrage, and Florence felt, as she had always felt when she heard this Symphony, that her powers of criticism were failing her. She was helpless under the force of ideas stronger than her own ; her musical idiom, generally so crystal clear, was losing shape, growing dim, crumbling. She was transported into a region of wide spaces, formless ether, mist and the flames of lost stars, where the imagination, suddenly enlarged, grasped ultimately the idea of order, the slow procession of the glittering worlds weaving a pattern in the void.

" I wasn't mistaken," she thought. " It's wonderful. He's a great man. I don't care what anyone else thinks."

She looked down and watched him, as he directed this uncharted storm which he had willed, his baton darting and flickering in a great wind of sound, his red hair pushed away up on to the top of his head. Then she looked at the hall and saw no more planets, but Jacob and Antonia listening with their mouths open. Tony did not like it ; she hated loud noises and the drums, of which Lewis was making lavish use, frightened her as much as a thunderstorm. Jacob was patting her hand to soothe her. Jimmy Jansen and the critics, just behind, were grinning broadly. Florence scanned more faces anxiously ; a good many people looked amused. She found herself growing resentful of their impenetrable stupidity ; she could better forgive those who looked horrified. Then she fell to listening again, wholly lost in the delight of the second movement and its theme for strings. The drums had died away ; they could just be heard, the faintest heart beat, through the dying cadences of 'cellos and violas. Clarinets and horns were silent. Lewis, having bludgeoned his audience into submission, having broken down their powers of resistance, that defence against dangerous beauty which the sane mind will preserve, was prepared to play them a tune. He could do what he liked, now, with those who had accepted his art. And even to those who did not, his theme was beautiful, for he could, for all his self-denying, write those inevitable tunes of which there are so few in the world. This interlude, heightened to a supreme simplicity by contrast with the din which had gone first, was so short as to be little more than a reprieve, an illustration of the peculiar effect of melody heard after a shock. It passed, and the beat quickened to the fury of a last movement and a return to Sanger's methods. Teresa and Sebastian, who loved Lewis when he was tuneful and loathed his work with the drums, sighed deeply as the respite ended.

Florence, coming out of her dream, remembered suddenly that she had been upon the point of parting with this man, she could not clearly remember why. But she had actually thought of going back to Cambridge, of allowing him to go away without her. She had nearly lost him, and yet he had been hers. He should be that again. All her charm, all her wisdom should be used to win him back. He was a great musician ; he was worthy of all the love and devotion she could give. If he wanted to live abroad, she would go with him. If he was difficult, she would bear with him. If he was cruel, she would steel her heart to endure it. But she would never, never never let him go.

The storm swept on to its climax, ending with a crash, and
Lewis, frantic, distraught, leapt into the air, as though he would
dive head first off his little platform into the midst of his
perspiring orchestra. The shattered audience pulled itself
together and applauded doubtfully. A few enthusiasts shouted
a little and somewhere, at the back of the house, there was an
attempt at hissing. An atmosphere of disorder hung over the
hall, as though it had seen lately some deed of incredible violence.
Many people took their departure, and others hurried off to get
a drink somewhere. Listening had been thirsty work. Dr.
Dawson pulled himself up, handed his railway rug to one of
his ladies, and stumped off to bed, snarling, as he passed the
benevolent Baines :

"What d'you make of it, hey ? Never heard such a filthy
hullabaloo in your life, did you ? "

But the kind old man merely waved a deprecating, benignant
hand complaining :

"Ah, these young men ! These young men ! He'll
change everything, will he ? Why should he ? I don't want
it changed. And why, when he can write a second movement
like that . . . but," turning to Florence, " I trust I may tell you
that his conducting is . . . like nothing that I've ever watched
. . . and I've seen a good deal in my time. The most
triumphant . . ."

Millicent came up and said :

"I'm afraid it's been rather a failure, my dear. You like it,
I suppose ? Of course, these polytonic things don't seem ugly
to some people. Personally, I thought those drums were like
having the plumbers in. And what instrument in the world is
it that makes those queer, yawning noises ? "

Florence could not tell her. But Sebastian, who could,
explained it all very lucidly, to the amusement of Sir Bartlemy,
who had come round to sit in Dr. Dawson's place.

"Well, Florence," he said, " it's a little like an ogre at a
tea-party ; your husband's Symphony after the Turkish Suite

296

Why has Dawson gone? Isn't he going to listen to the Concerto? Silly fellow! Why that's the crux of the whole affair."

"I don't feel up to it," said Millicent. "I feel as if I'd fallen down several flights of stairs. And where's the sense of putting a weighty classic after a thing like this. How can people be expected to listen? It's too late."

"That's it! That's it!" chuckled Sir Bartlemy, rubbing his hands. "That's a little joke our friend Dodd has got up his sleeve. Listen! Lord bless you, of course they'll listen. They won't be able to help it, now. That's his doing. Nothing makes you listen so well as a good shaking up. They'll find it as easy as falling off a log, you see!"

"They like it better," said Millicent vaguely.

"Like it better? Of course they do. We all do. We like it so much that we don't listen to it. We miss half. To-night we'll miss nothing; he won't let us."

Florence wondered, later, if this was indeed true. Although she was herself moved, as never before, by the next item, the overpowering applause surprised her. To many people present its success was a vindication of the old music against the new. The Press, next morning, hailed Dodd as a conductor and laughed at his Symphony. But Jacob Birnbaum, down in the stalls, was discussing with his friends the details of the next concert, with much guttural joviality. It must be very soon, said Jacob.

Lewis, however, never gave another concert in London.

CHAPTER XXIII

THE train, running over points near Ashford, changed its smooth rhythm for a succession of loud, clanking jerks. Lewis roused from an uncomfortable doze. He opened his eyes at the morning sunlight shining in his face and discovered confusedly that the night was over.

He tried to think. It was one of those bad days when everything is out of gear, and he could not put two ideas together. He was aware of the slowness of mind, the extreme lassitude of spirit, which always overtook him after a concert. He was listening for some coherence in the noise of the train and could find none. The sun in his eyes gave him a headache. He blinked at it angrily.

The person opposite leant forward and pulled down a blind so that his face was shaded. Looking towards her, in a sort of dumb gratitude, he was not much surprised to discover that it was Tessa. But it took him a little time to remember why she was there and that they were on their way to Dover. He recollected slowly how Roberto had brought him her message, the night before, and how he had nearly missed the train. He had bounded down the platform at the very last moment and she was waiting for him, steadfast but a little pale, by the barrier. And as they slid clear of the murky station, into the sunlight, he had fallen asleep, only rousing for a second when they crossed the bridge because Tessa opened the window and hung out, taking a last look at London and the glittering river. Now, as far as he could see, they were deep in Kent, rushing southwards through a bright, windy morning.

It was lovely to be with her. She was the only person in the world with the wits to draw blinds without being asked. He found his tongue and enquired if she had breakfasted. She shook her head.

"Nor have I," he said. "We'll get something on the boat."

"You can ıı you like. For me to eat on a boat is simply a waste of good food. I've a queasy stomach."

The other people in the carriage looked at her with a sort of wondering, dull resentment, and Lewis said :

"It's inconsiderate of you to talk in that way. We've all got to go on the boat." Then, vaguely : "Are you ill ?"

He hardly knew why he asked this ; but she did not look right somehow.

"No. It's all the fuss yesterday, and the concert, and not sleeping, and getting up early, and having no food."

This catalogue of hardship almost reassured him. Perhaps, after all, she did not look so very queer. He told her to wake him up when they got to Dover. Then he shut his eyes, but opened them again a moment later to take another look at her. She had put on, for this expedition, a new serge school suit, very neat and brief, and she had a brown paper parcel by way of luggage. It occurred to him, for the first time, that she might be unhappy and frightened at the step she was taking. He smiled at her and she returned his look a little dimly, like a person a long way off. He tried to think of some very protecting, comfortable thing to say but could only manage to demand if she was quite all right. She nodded, and he reflected that she ought to know how to look after herself, having been brought up to it. The blessed peace of being with her stole over him again and he drifted off into sleep.

She sat staring out of the window at the long rows of hop poles, spinning like the spokes of a wheel. These had interested her, she remembered, when she came first to England, less than a year ago. And now, so unexpectedly soon, she was off again, having learnt in this short time a number of things which would be in future of no use to her whatever. She had an idea that, for her peace of mind, she had best forget everything that had happened since Sanger's death. She was going back to the ways of her childhood, not because they seemed admirable to her but because there was no place for her elsewhere.

She was profoundly happy, but a little bewildered at this sudden change in her life. It was such a miracle to find herself alive and with Lewis instead of dead and at school. It seemed to her now as though she had escaped annihilation by the merest chance and she could hardly believe in her recovered safety. Having chosen life instead of death, she was secure for ever. She sat very still with her hands folded, watching her friend as he slept. He was all huddled up in his corner, and his face in repose looked young and weary, the harsh lines which scored it in his guarded hours seemed now painful and innocent. She saw that he was tired out, and she felt sorry when they flashed in and out of the chalk cuttings by the sea and she knew that she must wake him.

The morning air at Dover was very cold and her paper parcel, though not large, had grown so heavy that she nearly dropped it as she followed Lewis up the gangplank on to the boat. A chattering crowd pushed her this way and that and she could see no place where she might sit down and rest herself.

"Oh, dear," she gasped, "I'm so cold! I'm so tired! Couldn't we get a chair or something? There are some men with chairs."

"Those are for the first-class passengers, my dear. Let's walk about a bit and get warm."

She shivered so much that he opened his bag and pulled out his old yellow muffler to wrap round her throat and shoulders. It brought back the old times very suddenly, for in the Tyrol he had worn it on all occasions and she had never seen it since. Florence had suppressed it. It smelt of a good many things, chiefly tobacco. She snuggled into it gratefully and they found a sheltered place where they could watch the great, rattling crane which heaved up endless loads of luggage and plunged them into the hold. Teresa thought of all the clothes in all those boxes and looked at her own parcel and felt glad that she had kept so free of possessions during her English sojourn.

Even her lustre bowl was broken ; she was as free as the sea-gulls flashing through the sunlight over their heads.

Presently the bell rang and the siren hooted and the long line of porters ran back the gangplanks. The boat drew away from Dover quayside and the blank wall that hides the trains, and the grey, terraced town with its white cliffs, and all the ramparts of the English coast, getting lower and smaller. Teresa waved good-bye to it and to Uncle Charles's niece, a shadowy person, the creation of his persuasive fancy, and once, for a short time, almost convincing. It was not a difficult farewell, for the capacities of this dimly apprehended young woman had been so unripe, her destiny had lain so very much in the future, that she might never have come to life. Teresa had lost faith in her.

They had not gone far into the windy morning before she was compelled to go down into that Limbo where Belgian stewardesses in dubious aprons ply their grim trade. She felt desperately ill, but not so bad that she could not enjoy the antics of her fellow passengers. In an undertone she rehearsed their complaints, announcing her condition in every sort of accent, Glasgow, Kensington, Cambridge, Dublin, Leeds, Wapping and New York. But before the end of the crossing, which was a bad one, she lost interest in life. Time had ceased to exist for her, when a voice penetrated the chilly fog of exhaustion which shut out the world.

" Mademoiselle is alone ? She has no friends ? "

Two stewardesses were looking at her in evident anxiety Their faces floated in the fog above her head. One of them said that she was blue and they asked again if she was alone, this time in French, and very loud, blaring at her like a couple of trombones.

" *Toute seule . . .*" she replied weakly. " *. . . non . . . un monsieur . . la-hàut . . . on arrive dèja ?* "

" *Nous sommes en retard . . . Mademoiselle est vraiment malade ? Elle se trouve mieux à présent ?* "

"Woirse and woirse !" said Teresa, with a recollection of the lady from New York in the next bunk. If she could survive this crossing she would make Lewis laugh, telling him about all these ladies. She said in a stronger voice that she could do with some brandy if they had any.

They gave her brandy and she found the strength to struggle to her feet. All round her the battered wrecks of women were gathering themselves and their possessions together. She looked in her purse and found half a crown and three halfpence. She gave the half crown to the stewardess and climbed rather uncertainly up the steep ladder. She noticed that the woman stood at the bottom watching her anxiously as if afraid she might fall back suddenly.

"I must look frightful," she thought.

Outside, the cold air did her good. She found that they were nearly in, slipping past the endless Ostend Plage, with its fringe of hotels and casinos. It was a boisterous, changeable afternoon and the enormous sky seemed to be full of clouds, all sailing at different speeds, speared through with brilliant, watery shafts of sunlight. Behind them was a grey forbidding waste, already blurred with rain.

A dense crowd was lined up for the gangplanks and she could not see Lewis anywhere. But, as they began to stream off the boat, she thought she caught sight of him, well ahead of her, going into the Douane. Thither she followed him and got an official to deal with her parcel, after a long interval of pushing and shouting. She had to untie the string, and as she was doing it up again she was appalled to hear somebody call out that the Brussels train was just starting. Gathering her possessions in her arms, she ran, strewing articles of toilet over the railway lines. Lewis, hanging out of a carriage window, hailed her :

"Here you are ! Jump in ! I nearly went without you !"
She jumped in, and the train started.

"Your tooth brush is on the line," he said, taking a last look out of the window. "What made you cut it so fine? Were you changing your money?"

"No," she replied, at last getting her breath back. "I didn't like to change such a large amount in a hurry."

She showed him her three halfpence and he laughed.

"You'll have to buy me another toothbrush," she said.

"On the contrary, you must do without one. Many most admirable people do."

She raised her eyebrows and asked sweetly :

"Were you sick on the boat, my turtle dove?"

He said not, but she scarcely believed him for he looked very yellow. They were going along through the flatness of Belgium and he would not tell her what any of the towns were. Whereupon she made all her enquiries of an impudent looking young Belgian beside her, explaining that her husband, with a gesture at Lewis, had never been abroad before and was recovering from the effects of sea sickness. The youth, with a broad stare at her swinging plaits and school clothes, asked pointedly if Madame had never been abroad before either. Madame replied with some aplomb that she had ; she was still sustained by the brandy she had taken on the boat, and talked a great deal to all the people in their carriage, giving much uneasiness to Lewis, who knew that their appearance was odd and might cause comment. He was relieved when they reached Brussels and got out of the train unmolested.

They walked a little way and then took a tram. Teresa was silent now and docile. She sat beside Lewis, as they rumbled along towards a distant suburb, leaning against his shoulder and watching the stormy sunset behind the houses. It was a menacing sky : rags and banners of red cloud hung above the noisy streets and lit the faces of the people with an angry flame. The cries and shouts of the city sounded in her ears like cries of danger, warnings called forth by the wild light. Her dim remembrances of Brussels were not like this. When she had been there as a little girl it had seemed rather dull ; this was a town imagined in a dream, a flaming adventurous place where anything might happen. She looked up at Lewis to see if he too found it exciting. He was gazing at the bright sky with the extreme concentration of purpose which he used for all important things ; it was the first time that he had looked really awake since they started on their journey. He seemed to be gathering in that noisy radiance and stowing it away in his mind. An idea came to her and she asked :

" Where are we going."

He removed his light, steady eyes from the fiery clouds and blinked at her, as if trying to remember. Then he said :

" To Mdme. Marxse. She'll put us up. You remember her ? You all stayed in her house once before, didn't you ? "

" I think I remember," she said slowly.

When she was a very little girl Sanger's circus had spent some months with Mdme. Marxse. Only she seemed to remember an old woman who was unbelievably fat. Oh, but monstrous ! At that age one sees things out of scale.

" Is she fat ? " she asked.

" Fat ! We call her *Reine des Fées.* You see ! "

Teresa remembered now that that was what they did call her. Yes, and she had a bust like a broad shelf, buoyed up by a much boned corsage ; it was with some awe that the young Sangers had watched her eat, so impossible was it that she could see her plate. The same idea had occurred to all of them— that it would be much better if she would put the plate on the shelf just under her chin. And like a lurid picture stood out the day when Sanger had said it. Suddenly he had leant forward in the middle of a silent meal and said persuasively :

" Reine, why don't you allow your plate to repose on your bosom ? It would go better. You are dropping your food on your best gown."

Another memory dawned ; Evelyn, the beautiful mother who was so difficult to remember, had reproved the children for giggling, in case Mdme. Marxse might be mortified.

"Must we go there?" asked Teresa, rather reluctantly.

"She knows us all," explained Lewis. "She'll . . . she'll hold her tongue . . if anybody comes asking for us . . ."

"I see. I've quite forgotten Brussels."

But when they stood on the door step of Maison Marxse, she recognized the house opposite which used to have a birdcage with a canary in it. The smell of the entresol, a mixed smell of onions, stale scent, dirty black clothes and dust, carried her back more entirely into childhood. The door shut behind them like a trap and the meagre boy who had let them in went shuffling down the passage in front of them. An overpowering odour of the past rose up and clutched at her in the little room where Mdme. Marxse, larger even than memory had painted her, wheezed upon a sofa amid sacred reliquaries, pampas grass and cats. It was such a small room, far too small for its occupant; it must have been built round her for she could never have got in at the door.

Lewis was greeted with a cascade of asthmatic chuckles and many shrill questions. Teresa had time to look about her. She remembered the picture over the stove, a puzzling group of a much curved, nude lady and a swan, which recent study of a classical dictionary enabled her to identify. But in spite of this piece of information she felt very much like a little girl, as she stood shyly clinging to her lover's hand, while he bargained with *Reine des Fées* for a room. Presently she was pulled forward and introduced. The old woman remembered her, and she was folded in an odious, flabby embrace spiced with a whiff of strong waters. Enquiries were made after the other brothers and sisters. Caryl and Kate? How were they?

"I don't know," said Teresa vaguely. "When Sanger died we were all separated."

"Ah, that man! That man!" wheezed Madame. "So many children he had! It is unknown how many! And now all scattered? Here we have one. Thou knowest Mignonne? A brother of thine. My grandson."

305

"Yes," said Lewis. "I'd forgotten Paul. How is he, Reine?"

"But ill! We shan't keep him long. He is at school now, with the Jesuits. Many days his cough is bad and he cannot go. But still he wins all the prizes."

"Takes after his father," commented Lewis. "They all do. They're all too clever to live."

Teresa remembered the narrow-chested boy in the hall; she felt no enthusiasm on hearing that he was her brother. But it was probably true that he was intelligent; Sanger seemed to have scattered the curse of intellect most lavishly about the world. She got an uneasy glimpse of life's continuity; it appeared that these things could have no end. She wondered how many of the children called to life by Sanger's lust would thank him for it. Her next thought caused her to tell Madame that Tony had a baby. Madame remembered Tony perfectly. A pretty little bitch! And a mother already? Well, well! Teresa it seemed had also got a man. The little black eyes leered round at Lewis. Sanger's daughters were not likely to die old maids. Well, well! Lewis would teach her.

"For he's the first, isn't he, *petite ange?*"

Teresa nodded, still clinging to his hand.

"Thou couldst scarcely have begun younger," commented the old woman. "How old . . say . . . fifteen? Mother of God! What a hurry the girls are in nowadays! Still, I was no older . . ."

She plunged into grimy reminiscence. Lewis, who had scarcely listened to the conversation, became at last attentive and said impatiently in English:

"A bawdy old thing, isn't she?"

Teresa laughed. She thought Mdme. Marxse as good as a Shakespeare play at the Nine Muses, a rich entertainment, better even than the sea-sick ladies. That was because she and Lewis were together; their completeness shut them off from the world. They were like people watching a comedy from a

306

box, seeing more significance in life, savouring its humour more soundly, because in their hearts they were remote.

Mdme. Marxse had, it appeared, a room for them on the third floor. A fine room with a good bed.

"That will do, I think? If you wish you may sleep well. Myself I often think that a good bed is wasted on a pair of lovers. They never notice. But she looks tired, the *gosse*; tired and pale. Thou hast been ill lately, my child?"

"Only on the boat, Madame."

"The boat! Ah! Ah! One understands. Will you go up and see the room? Myself I cannot take you; I never climb these stairs. For five years now I have lived *au rez de chaussée*. But my daughter shall take you up. You remember Gabrielle, *petite?* No? Ah, your father would, I think, remember."

She screeched for her daughter, who answered in a deep bellow from the next room and presently joined them, wearing a petticoat and underbodice, protesting angrily that she was just dressing to go out. She was a handsome slattern with small black eyes, a sallow skin and a sumptuous figure. Teresa seemed to remember her little, lascivious mouth, which was almost lost in the ample curves of cheek and chin, but the face which memory recalled was younger, more animated, and framed in cloudy black hair, very different from the short, woolly tufts which hung over Gabrielle's brown neck. This, it seemed, was the mother of the intelligent Paul.

Gabrielle greeted Lewis with a spurt of sudden laughter and a brief warmth in her hard eyes, but she refused to recollect anything about Teresa.

"One of Sanger's children," cackled Madame. "A little sister for thy Paul."

"I'm sorry to hear such a poor account of Paul," put in Lewis.

"*Est poitrinaire*," Gabrielle told them indifferently. "What good are his brains to me? He will never earn a sou. Always he will be an expense to us, if he lives . . ."

307

And she asked Teresa abruptly if her mother was dead.

"Yes," said Teresa, in an annoyed voice, "and I was born in wedlock."

She felt somehow that Gabrielle had once been a trial to Evelyn and that a little rudeness from Evelyn's children would pass as an expression of loyalty. Madame screeched with laughter and called Teresa a "*type original.*"

"Which means," said Lewis severely, as they climbed the stairs behind Gabrielle, "that you are a very rude little girl."

Teresa pinched his arm and murmured an aphorism which she had learned from Aunt May, the wife of Robert Churchill :

"It all goes to show that you can't be too careful."

And they arrived at their lofty bower quite breathless with giggling. Gabrielle threw open the shutters and flounced out of the room, shouting over her shoulder, before she banged the door, that they must come down soon if they wanted food. It was a small, dingy room with a large, dingy bed in it. Other furniture was hard to find. The strength which had thus far supported Teresa went from her ; she sank with a little gasp on the bed, too much exhausted even to take her hat off. Lewis took it off for her, moved to some compunction, and vowing that they should go down directly and get something to eat. Then he began to unpack his bag, strewing things about the room. Soon there were sheets of music everywhere, and these, with the yellow scarf that hung over the end of the bed, made the place look exactly like every other room which had ever belonged to him. To Teresa it was home ; she saw in her mind's eye all the funny rooms which they would share and they were all like this one, half smothered in music, with a pair of boots on the mantelpiece and a big, hard, untidy bed. She wanted to tell him about it but instead she discovered that she had said :

"Lewis . . . I do feel so very ill . . ."

He looked frightened and then said that it was no wonder. She had fasted for nearly twenty-four hours. She would be quite restored by food and a good night's rest. Urgently he demanded that she should agree with him, which she readily did, surprised at herself for having been so plaintive.

"Though I doubt the night's rest," she said. "I wonder if this is really Old Greymalkin's idea of a good bed."

"Old what ? "

"Old Greymalkin ; the hag downstairs. She made a point of it that this was such a good bed and everything . . ."

"Did she ? It'll be our bridal bed I suppose, so it's a pity it shouldn't be comfortable. Let me feel it ! Oh, Tessa, it's not so bad. I've slept on worse."

"Feels to me more like a stone quarry. But this is a very odd place altogether. I'm surprised at you for bringing me here. Will you look at the stove-piece with that indecent little china ornament next door to a statue of the Sacred Heart ! How Uncle Charles would laugh ! "

"Would he ? "

"I'm sure he would. That's why I do. A year ago I wouldn't have seen the joke of that. I'd have thought it a perfectly natural thing for those two to be side by side. Oh, dear ! There's no getting away from it ! You can never get quite back."

· Lewis was looking round the room, taking it in, with an immense effort of imagination, through the eyes of Uncle Charles. He examined the torn curtains and the flyblown paper and the gas-jet and the incongruous ornaments ; finally he looked at Teresa, exhausted but intrepid, stretched upon the bed. He clapped his hand to his head in a sort of seizure and announced :

"Call me a fool ! We'll go away to-morrow."

"Dear heart ! Why ? Are we the wandering Jew ? "

"Filthy place ! "

"It can't hurt us."

"Can't it, my blessing ? I'm not so sure. There must be other places . . ."

309

" I think you'll find they all look pretty much the same."

" I ought to have thought . . . it took me so much by surprise when you changed your mind like that, at the last minute . . . I never thought . . . Tessa ! "

" Um ? "

" You haven't told me yet, why you did change so suddenly."

" No. And I shan't ever tell you."

" Why not ? "

" It isn't . . . . a suitable subject for people to talk about."

" Dear me ! "

He was surprised. He could not imagine the subject which would appal Tessa into silence. He came and sat on the bed beside her and said in a low voice ·

" Tell me ! "

" Blest if I do."

" Tessa, you must ! You must let me have everything . . . now . . ."

" Not a bit of it. You'll never know ; you can keep on guessing till the cows come home, but I won't tell you."

" I don't need to guess. You've got a face like a cinematograph. He who runs may read. I know what it was."

" Bet you don't . . ."

" Something frightened you."

" Aren't you clever ! "

" What was it ? I always know when you're frightened ; there are two funny little lamps in your eyes, right in the very middle of your eyes, and they light up when you're frightened. I can see them now ; you're frightened still. Tessa ! Don't hide away from me ! Tell me what it is ! "

She had twisted herself away from him, and was hiding her tell-tale face in the pillow. But he could see a deep blush spreading over her cheek and the back of her neck. His astonishment grew. What in the world could ever make her blush ?

" Are you ashamed of anything," he demanded sternly.

310

A muffled voice bade him leave her alone.

"Well then, look at me ! "

She sat up and looked at him, straightfaced and rather indignant, the pink slowly ebbing from her cheeks. He saw that she had been ashamed, but not for herself. Some one else had been at her. But who ? After he had left Chiswick . . . Oh, it was obvious !

"It was something Florence said," he stated.

"Lewis ! Please . . ."

"Did you have words ? "

"I shan't tell you."

"And she made you frightened and ashamed ? Why can't you tell me ? "

"Because . . . women oughtn't to . . . to tell men . . . about each other . . ."

"I see. Then we'll leave it. But you're an astounding creature, Tessa. You'll listen to Reine's conversation without turning a hair, and yet a genteel person like Florence . . ."

"Please ! "

He laughed. He could quite imagine the sort of thing that Florence had said ; it was probably enough to make anybody blush. Whatever it was, he blessed her for it, since it had sent Tessa to him. He went on teasing for a little while, but he did not press the point.

"I don't believe that you really understood half that Reine said," he insisted.

"Perhaps not," she murmured, her cheek against his. "But I know what she thinks. She thinks a funny thing about you and me. She thinks I'm your fancy lady."

"So does Florence, as a matter of fact."

"Does she ? " Tessa sheered away from all thought of Florence. "Well, but Lewis, I've a hard thing to ask you. If I'm not . . . what they think . . . what am I ? "

He sat for a long time silent, holding her carefully as though she was something precious and easily broken. Then he said :

311

"You mean, what would I call you if I wasn't your lover?
That's a tight place! Listen! Will this do? I won't . . .
I couldn't . . . ever again, in all my life, call any woman by a
name that sounded too hard for you. I would think of any
woman that she could be to some man, perhaps, what you are to
me."

"That sounds all right. Don't look so worried. I only
just wanted to know. It's . . . completely unimportant . . ."

He had lost himself a .ittle, quite carried away by her passion
and the fiery intensity of her mind. Almost he believed himself
capable of a love like hers. They sat watching the swift fading
of daylight in the sky, while sounds of distant traffic floated up
from the street to their high, hidden retreat. He discovered at
last that she was very cold; her little fingers, locked in his, were
icy, and she shivered so often that he again offered to lend her
his muffler. He lit the gas, a bare, noisy jet which threw a
green light upon the disorder of the room and turned the
window panes from sapphire to black. She looked more wan
and frail than ever and he exclaimed:

"You look very mouldy. Come down to supper."

"I couldn't really. I don't want anything. I'm too tired."

"Well then I'll go down and bring something up."

And he left her, treading lightly from the room and shutting
the door behind him with caution. Outside, in the closeness
of the dark landing, the evil of the house seemed to pounce upon
him and he was faced with the knowledge that he had brought
her there. He would take her away. He groped his way
downstairs past shut, secret doors, ranging the world in his
mind, seeking a suitable shelter for the pair of them. No place
offered itself to his imagination. As she had said, all places
seemed so very much alike. Their safety lay only in themselves, and she had no doubts about it. Why should she? But
for himself it was different; he had not that constant and
unswerving love which would shine like a torch in dark,
unfriendly places.

He interviewed Gabrielle and induced her, with some bribery, to prepare and bring up a tray of food. He told her that they would be leaving in the morning. Then he started up again, still wrestling with the problem of the future What in the world was he to do with her ? They had, unfortunately, no friend whom they could consult. Nobody appreciated Tessa, unless it might be that old gentleman, her uncle.

Confronted by the idea of Charles Churchill, Lewis became very thoughtful.

He found Teresa upon her feet, struggling with some labour and difficulty to take off her frock. He sat down and buried his face in his hands, trying to clear his mind, still distracted by the lethargy of thought which had disabled him all day. At last he said :

" Suppose I wrote to your uncle . . ."

" Uncle Charles ? What do you want to write to him for ? "

" I don't know.",

" I'll send your love when I write, shall I ? " she jeered.

" Oh ! You'll write, will you ? "

" I thought I'd send him a picture postcard now and then."

" Well, when you do, tell him . . ."

" What ? Damn these buttons ! "

" I must think."

What, indeed, was he to say to Charles ? It was more easy to guess what Charles would say to him. And yet Charles was the only person in the world who had a proper value for Tessa.

" It's very stuffy in here," she said suddenly, in a choked little voice.

He told her to open the window. In his mind he had begun a letter to Charles. He was never very good at writing letters. He could not at all plan one that explained the nature of his passion for Charles's niece—a thing so delicate that words seemed to hurt it, a thing so beautiful that it must somehow be preserved, a thing so strong that nothing in the world could stand in its way

313

" I can't open it," said Teresa, who had been tugging at the window. " It's stiff."

" Try at the top," he advised, without looking round.

She stared up at the top, clutching her breast for a moment, where pain was alive and threatening. Then she braced herself for another effort.

Lewis gave it up. There would be no sort of good in writing to Charles. The only result would be a separation ; they would come and take her away from him. That was not to be thought of. The alternative was to succomb to Maison Marxse. He wished that Gabrielle would hurry up with that food. Not that he would let her in. This room was Tessa's stronghold. He would go out and fetch the tray in from the landing.

The noise of the flaming gas seemed to have grown very much louder. The room was frighteningly quiet. Teresa had stopped pulling at the window ; she had stopped moving. He looked round and saw that she had slipped down on to the floor.

" Have you fainted ? " he asked, jumping up.

She made no reply.

He picked her up and put her on the bed. There was no water in the room, but he found a damp sponge among her things and began anxiously to sponge her face in the hope of bringing her round. Her colour disturbed him. Presently a gleam of consciousness returned to her eyes.

" Light the light ! " she whispered.

" It's lighted."

She stared fixedly at the soaring green flame. He began to think that she could not see it.

" Tessa ! " he protested. " Dearest love . . ."

He went on sponging her face. The hissing of the gas grew so loud that he could hardly be sure that she breathed. And all day she had been cold.

He heard the tray clinking outside and cried to Gabrielle for help. She opened the door with a bump, pushing the tray in front of her. But when she looked at the bed she exclaimed, and came quickly forward. She put the tray on the floor and came to Lewis and took the sponge away from him.

"What's the good of doing that ? " she asked in tones of anger and alarm.

He saw, then, that there was no sort of good in it. His heart's treasure was gone ; she had eluded finally both his love and his folly. He became, in an instant, so certain of his loss that he gave up the defenceless thing in his arms to the rude, untender handling of Gabrielle ; she could do no harm now to the living Tessa. He stood watching while she made a hasty, indignant examination and at last he explained, stupidly :

" She has got away . . . she's dead . . ."

" That is evident," agreed Gabrielle. "Still, a doctor must be fetched. I will send Paul."

She hurried off and soon there began to be noises of footsteps, the cries of alarmed people, lower in the house.

Lewis, discovering in his turn that the room was very airless, went to open the window. It would not move and he found a wedge at the top. When he had taken this away the sash slid up easily. He stood holding the wedge in his hand, looking at it and thinking, with a kind of slow amazement, that it had killed Tessa.

The night wind blew in, swaying the dusty curtains, and all the sheets of music on the floor went rustling and flapping like fallen leaves. A chill tempest, it blew over the quiet bed, but it could not wake her. She slept on, where they had flung her down among the pillows, silent, undefeated, young.

Lewis leant far out of the window, as if to hail a departing friend. Down in the street he saw a long, long double row of lamps burning steadily in spite of the gale. People moved like shadows over the bright pavements. Above the houses, very high in the sky, a small, pale moon raced through the clouds as though some enemy pursued her

CHAPTER XXIV

FLORENCE had been forced to seek help from the Birnbaums. She had not meant to tell them of her fears when she hurried round to Lexham Gardens in search of Teresa. But Antonia had exclaimed immediately :

"Tessa gone ? Himmel ! I knew they would."

And Jacob said :

"We must follow them. She shall be brought back."

They took it for granted that Lewis and Teresa were gone together. It seemed to Florence as though the whole family had been awaiting this calamity ; they must have known of it all the time. And, though they were kind to her and sorry for her, she could not help a certain distrust of them, for she had an idea that their sympathies were upon the other side.

They were, however, quite obviously distressed and anxious. Teresa, they said, must be pursued and recovered. Jacob was sure that they would have gone to Brussels, and Tony suggested that they might be staying with Reine.

"We always do, when we go to Brussels," she explained.

Jacob, who knew Mdme. Marxse by reputation, was inclined to agree with her. He said that he would take the early train upon the following day.

"You ?" cried Florence in surprise. "Did you think of going ?"

"It is better," he said, "unless your father . . ."

She had not realized that he would take the affair so personally. But he had a good deal of clan feeling. Teresa was Tony's belonging and he was not going to have her lost.

"I must go," said Florence. "I'm responsible."

"I think," he suggested nervously, "that it would be better that I should go. There is no necessity . . ."

"It's good of you. But she was my charge. I can manage it alone."

"Mrs. Dodd, you must let me come with you. Or your father. But I, perhaps, would be better than he. You do not know these people. You could do nothing with them."

"Reine is an old devil," supplemented Antonia.

Florence did not want him. She loathed the idea of travelling with him. But she saw that she might, indeed, require his help. She really could not present herself at the house of this Mdme. Marxse, clamouring for her husband. It was horrible. She thanked Jacob and compromised by accepting his escort. He grumbled about it to Antonia afterwards, declaring that he could have managed the business and brought Teresa back perfectly well by himself.

"Can't you see," said Antonia, "that she's going after Lewis? She doesn't care in the least what becomes of Tessa. She hates Tessa. But she won't let Lewis go."

"You are wrong," said Jacob positively. "She will leave him after this. She will not, naturally, endure such behaviour. This is the end of that affair."

"Not at all. You think she's proud? She isn't a bit. She'll follow him about anywhere. She won't let Tessa have him, even though everybody knows that he loves Tessa and not her."

"Does he love Tessa? I think he loves nobody but himself. I'm afraid to think what will happen to that little girl."

"They're all right," she insisted comfortably. "They love each other . . . well . . . like we do."

"I see little safety in that," he said rather grimly. "And we are probably going too late. But it is clear that she must be brought back. I wish your cousin did not come too. She frightens me, that woman. She is always so correct; and I

317

. . . am not always correct, you understand. What a journey we shall have ! "

" Poor Florence ! "

" Why do you pity her ? She should not have married him. She is not very young and it is to be supposed that she knew the world. It is all her own fault."

" She was very kind to us last Summer."

" To you perhaps. To me she has never been kind. I am a very wicked man ! What, I would ask, does she call Lewis ? You are mistaken, Tony. She will never forgive him. She must hate him."

" Perhaps. You can hate a person and want them."

He agreed, with a nervous glance at her, not daring to ask what she meant precisely. Always he lost himself when he made an attempt to explore her deeper mind.

The journey proved no better than he had expected. He did his best to be inoffensive to his companion, but his behaviour, when travelling, was too ornate for her taste, and embarrassment did not improve it. Beside her quiet elegance he was monstrously out of place. He handed her in and out of first-class carriages, ordered sumptuous meals, bullied officials, and made himself and his wealth generally intolerable. It was a relief when they got to Brussels.

He selected their hotel, a large, noisy, expensive place which she detested, and left her there while he went to make enquiries after the fugitives. This most odious part of the business was, at least, to be spared her ; he would do it all, as he had carried her wraps and tipped the porters.

She sat waiting for him to come back, in a chilly, magnificent bedroom. Her spirits sank as the moments passed ; she became the prey of a kind of despairing lassitude. She wondered, miserably, why she had come. Yesterday she had been strained and anxious to be off ; all through the night an implacable, goaded imagination had kept her from sleeping. Now she felt as though nothing mattered. Time pressed no longer. She hardly cared whether they traced Teresa or not. She was sure that they had come too late.

"Why did I come?" she muttered to herself. "I won't see him."

She took off her hat and veil and smoothed her hair. Then she fell to pacing the room, up and down, up and down, while the long minutes dragged. At last she flung herself down on a couch by the window and closed her eyes. Immediately there floated before her that vision which had haunted her mind for forty-eight hours—the dim, chequered pattern of an orchestra and the white bows moving through the air all together. The themes of the Dodd Symphony had run in her head, maddeningly, through all her other distractions. To the memory of its rhythms she had made her preparations for this hurried journey, she had heard it in all the trains and in the Brussels traffic. Now, as she dozed, the music swelled and grew louder, thrilling through her tired brain; the violins took on the sweet, piercing quality of dream sounds; the drums, hammering ominously, frightened her. They grew so loud that she started up. Jacob was knocking at her door, asking if he could speak to her for a moment. She came out, and stood talking to him in the passage.

"Well?" she asked.

He was pale and disordered. Agitation quivered in his large, opulent person and kindly face. He looked past her into the room and asked if he might come in. He said that it was a bad business. She opened her door wider and let him in. Her aversion was so great that she disliked having to do so, despite the unintimate atmosphere of the room.

Once inside he hardly seemed to know what to say. He stood looking at her, tongue-tied and miserable. She asked whether he had found them.

"Yes," he said. "They went to Mdme. Marxse."

"Did you see them?"

"I saw Lewis. Mrs. Dodd . . . it is terrible . . . I hardly know how to tell you . . . I . . . she . . ."

319

"You mean . . . he's ruined her . . " she helped him.

"She is dead."

He almost shouted it, in the effort to get it said. Florence started away from him, growing very pale, crying out :

"No ! Oh, no ! Impossible . . ."

He thought that she would faint, and was relieved, as then he might put an end to a painful interview and summon assistance. But she collected herself and asked, in a low voice :

"When did this happen ? "

"Yesterday."

"I can't believe it."

"I know ! I know ! I could not."

"Yesterday ! When ? After they got here ? "

"I think so."

He gave her such details as he had been able to collect. After the first she showed little agitation and a great anxiety to know everything.

"Where is Lewis ? " she said at last.

"Here."

"Here ? "

"In the vestibule. Downstairs. I thought that perhaps you might wish to see him. Shall I send him away ? "

"No. No, don't do that."

She reflected for a moment and then asked :

"Does he . . . does he want to see me ? "

"I think so. He has sent a telegram for you this morning."

"Telegraphed for me ? Why did he do that ? "

It appeared that he had sent for her. He had told Jacob that she would take charge of affairs. There were complications ; a doctor had not been summoned until too late and there would have to be something in the nature of an inquest. Lewis, utterly bewildered by all the responsibilities thrust upon him, had sent for his wife.

"She's been ill for some time," said Florence thoughtfully. "Growing too fast, you know. And you say the crossing

320

was bad. It could easily be accounted for. Did you see her ?"

" No. They had taken her away, to the mortuary I think."

" But Lewis was there ? "

" Yes. He hardly knows what he is doing. He says that she belongs to you now."

" And he wired for me this morning ? Yes ! " she tapped her foot pensively. Then she resumed, with energy : " He was quite right. My arriving here to-day will make all the difference. I represent her guardians, if there is any fuss. There's more chance of the thing being hushed up. We could say that they came on ahead . . . This woman, Mdme. Marxse, she'll help us out ? She'll tell the same story as we do, if we have to invent something to put a good face on it ? "

" Rcine will swear to anything that keeps her out of trouble with the police," Jacob assured her. " She is half mad with terror. She will be quite easy . . ."

" I'll have to see Lewis," Florence decided. " It's going to be difficult. The whole thing looks so bad. She was under sixteen, you know. The law . . ."

" It depends on you," said Jacob, staring at her curiously. " It is for you to say whether he persuaded her to leave the protection of her friends . . ."

He broke off. He was amazed and a trifle shocked at her composure. He found himself wishing that she would be a little grieved. She seemed to view the business simply in the light of a threatened disgrace. He saw it like that himself, though he was very sorry for his young sister-in-law ; his mind, as he hurried back to the hotel, had been full of uncomfortable possibilities. He had dreaded the scene with Florence, supposing that his shocking news would utterly prostrate her. He had seen himself, the only practical person at hand, dealing with doctors and policemen, and persuading his lofty-minded companion of the necessity for some sort of compromise. But it had seemed so impossible that Reine and Florence could ever be brought to any concerted action. Now, finding it perfectly possible, beholding the young woman no less anxious to avoid a scandal than the old one, meeting cold competency where he had expected distress and indignation, he was relieved but not happy.

She asked him if Lewis was likely to be reasonable, and he said in a lugubrious voice that he did not know. Not to anyone, not even to Tony, could he have described the impression which Lewis made upon him. If Florence was showing too little sensibility, Lewis, as usual, was showing too much. Jacob, a plain man, was harassed between them. Florence went on speaking in her quiet, dry voice, mentioning steps that must be taken. How could he describe to her that little, untidy room where Tessa had died, and where Lewis had sat all day, after they took her away, in a dazed and timeless trance among the strewn sheets of music ? There had been something in that rigid petrifaction of grief which frightened Jacob. He said to Florence :

" He should not stay at that place."

" Would he come here do you think ? "

" Perhaps. I believe he will do what he is told."

" Well then, bring him here. We shall have to stay in Brussels evidently, till this business is settled. I must send for my father. Can you get Lewis a room ? "

" Certainly, Mrs. Dodd. Will you see him now ? "

She thought not. She did not feel quite prepared, yet, for that interview. But Jacob was to look after him. And his letters ! They had better be taken down ; they were on the dressing-table. Jacob went to pick them up and saw beside them several notices of the Dodd Symphony which she had contrived to collect on the preceding day, in spite of its disorganisation.

" I suppose he won't have seen those," she said with a slight blush.

" I think not," said Jacob rather grimly. " He left England less than ten hours later."

" Perhaps you'd better take them down then," she suggested.

" *Du lieber allmächtiger Gott !* " thought Jacob as he put them in his pocket and left her. " Perhaps I had better not ! All women are wonderful, but this one . . ."

He was not a tactful man and he had a great regard for Press notices, but the civility of showing these to Lewis seemed to him, at the moment, hardly well chosen.

Florence, left to herself, was also a little surprised at her own calm detachment. It was as if she had always foreseen this resolution of events, so instant was her response to the call for prompt thought and action. She sat down and mustered her powers, that she might lay her case before her father, and make him understand that Lewis, now so unexpectedly given back to her, was the most precious thing on earth. She had him completely in her hands, and for the sake of a securer future it was imperative that she should dismiss the past as though it were something irrelevant.

" You'll think I'm hard," she wrote to Charles. " But you must see that I have to be. Try to think of it as I do. Don't be so sorry for her that you forget me. It's not her death but my life that matters. I *cannot* live without him. And I have the future still to think of."

Teresa had had her chance and had lost him. And she had escaped from life so easily. Florence could not, really, even pretend to pity her, just now. To go on living, to be confronted every day with the necessity of thinking, to look forward into the empty years and make plans for them, to build up upon wrecked love a monument of worthy achievement, this seemed to her a much harder thing.

Jacob, going down, found Lewis in the vestibule, waiting, withdrawn in a secret, shocked meditation, while streams of people pushed past him into the hotel restaurant. He looked as if he had been there for ever. Jacob tapped him on the shoulder and commanded him, with awkward compassion, to come in and have something to eat. They went into the restaurant, where a band was playing and much food was displayed. Jacob, despite the gravity of the occasion and a real pity for the man beside him, could not help brightening up a little. He glanced richly round and a table was at once found for them.

" Your wife," he said to Lewis, " is resting. She will see you later.'

Lewis looked at him vaguely and nodded.

" All right," he said.

" She thinks that you had better come to this hotel."

Lewis said all right again and added, as an afterthought, that he had no money. He was given to understand that he need not concern himself on that point. Jacob ordered a meal and they began to eat in silence.

Presently Lewis said :

" Sanger never liked him either."

" Who ? " asked Jacob, rather startled.

" Trigorin."

" Trigorin ! Oh, yes. We were speaking of him ? "

" No." Lewis frowned and explained, with an effort, " they're playing the ballet music from ' Akbar.' "

" Ach ! So they are. And Trigorin did the dances. Yes ! "

Both men listened to the vigorous measures which, since Sanger's death, had become so popular. Jacob thought that he should produce " Akbar " at one of his places. He began to estimate in his mind the risk and the probable vogue which was just beginning. He thought of the immense volume of work left by Sanger and still unproduced, and exclaimed :

" That man ! His influence, as yet, is scarcely felt. He has left so much behind him that is vital ! "

Lewis did not hear. He was thinking of Trigorin and had escaped for a moment into the mountain Spring. He was breakfasting with the absurd creature in the little inn at Erfurt

324

He breathed again the heavenly air as the train panted up through the pine woods; he heard the cow-bells in the high pastures. And again he teased Trigorin as they steamed across the lake to the landing-stage where Tessa waited. Here the memory turned to present anguish, for at the end of it, as at the end of every thought, lay the discovery of Tessa dead. He had got there before he had quite done smiling at Trigorin on the boat, and Jacob asked what the joke was.

" I was thinking of our loss," he explained. "Tessa . . . I mean . . . loss . . ."

He whispered the word to himself once or twice as though he was trying to get accustomed to it. Jacob, who supposed that he would feel like this himself if Tony were dead, attempted diffident consolation.

" It will pass," he said. " You will forget. Everything, in time, becomes easier. We do not continue to suffer."

" No," responded Lewis.

But he looked rebellious, as though he could not endure the thought that we do not continue to suffer, as though he would have liked to insist that our memories are immutable. He did in truth detest that pliant, slavish adaptability which enables the human race to survive. He cried out, in a sort of horror, to Jacob :

" I shall forget her."

Certainly he was not showing much disposition to be reasonable. Jacob, remembering the inordinate reasonableness of the lady upstairs, was inclined to sympathize with this mood. Still, he was harassed between them, and he understood how it was that the young Teresa, bewildered by two such monitors, had relinquished the problem.

Sanger's ballet crashed to a final chord, and above the din of plates and knives, the babel of conversation in many languages, there rose up a faint crackle of applause. "Akbar" was a favourite number. Jacob sighed heavily and looked with a rare indifference at the red mullet on his plate. He wished himself at home and thought with a little stab, half pleasure and half pain, how Tony, when she heard his news, would sob and cry and turn to him for comfort. She needed him so seldom, and her tears were so beautiful, and it was fitting, in his opinion, that tears should be shed by somebody over this heavy day's work.

VIRAGO MODERN CLASSICS

The first Virago Modern Classic, *Frost in May* by Antonia White, was published in 1978. It launched a list dedicated to the celebration of women writers and to the rediscovery and reprinting of their works. Its aim was, and is, to demonstrate the existence of a female tradition in literature, and to broaden the sometimes narrow definition of a 'classic' which has often led to the neglect of interesting books. Published with new introductions by some of today's best writers, the books are chosen for many reasons: they may be great works of literature; they may be wonderful period pieces; they may reveal particular aspects of women's lives; they may be classics of comedy, storytelling, letter-writing or autobiography.

'The Virago Modern Classics list is wonderful. It's quite simply one of the best and most essential things that has happened in publishing in our time. I hate to think where we'd be without it' – *Ali Smith*

'A continuingly magnificent imprint' – *Joanna Trollope*

'The Virago Modern Classics have reshaped literary history and enriched the reading of us all. No library is complete without them' – *Margaret Drabble*

'The writers are formidable, the production handsome. The whole enterprise is thoroughly grand' – *Louise Erdrich*

'The Virago Modern Classics are one of the best things in Britain today' – *Alison Lurie*

'Good news for everyone writing and reading today' – *Hilary Mantel*

'Masterful works' – *Vogue*

www.virago.co.uk

To find out more about Margaret Kennedy
and other Virago authors, visit
www.virago.co.uk

Visit the Virago website for:

- News of author events and forthcoming titles
- Features and interviews with authors, including
  Margaret Atwood, Maya Angelou, Sarah Waters,
  Nina Bawden and Gillian Slovo
- Free extracts from a wide range of titles
- Discounts on new publications
- Competitions
- The chance to buy signed copies
- Reading group guides

PLUS

Subscribe to our free monthly newsletter

ELIZABETH AND HER GERMAN GARDEN

Elizabeth von Arnim

Introduced by Elizabeth Jane Howard

'May 7th – There were days last winter when I danced for sheer joy out in my frost-bound garden in spite of my years and children. But I did it behind a bush, having a due regard for the decencies . . .'

Elizabeth's uniquely witty pen records each season in her beloved garden, where she escapes from the stifling routine of indoors: from servants, meals, domestic routine – and the presence of her overbearing husband, the Man of Wrath.

'She has a wild sense of comedy and a vision – continually thwarted though it was – of potential happiness'
Penelope Mortimer

'Marvellous . . . about love and affection, spring and picnics on frosty afternoons, and the leisure that we have forgotten ever existed' Miriam Rothschild

'A gem of a book: rare, simple, innocent and charming'
Susan Hill

THE SOLITARY SUMMER

Elizabeth von Arnim

With an Introduction by Deborah Kellaway

The companion volume to *Elizabeth and her German Garden*

'I want to be alone for a whole summer, and get to the very dregs of life. I want to be as idle as I can, so that my soul may have time to grow. Nobody shall be invited to stay with me, and if anyone calls they will be told that I am out, or away, or sick . . . Wouldn't a whole lovely summer, quite alone, be delightful?'

This charming companion to the famous *Elizabeth and her German Garden* is a witty, lyrical account of a rejuvenating, solitary summer filled with books and Elizabeth's reflections on her beloved garden.

Descriptions of magnificent larkspurs and burning nasturtiums give way to those of cooling forest walks. Yet the months aren't as solitary as she'd planned: there's still her husband to pacify and the April, May and June babies to amuse.

'Recreates a Wordsworthian sense of rapturous awe'
Deborah Kellaway

MRS PALFREY AT THE CLAREMONT

Elizabeth Taylor

Introduced by Paul Bailey

On a rainy Sunday in January, the recently widowed Mrs Palfrey arrives at the Claremont Hotel where she will spend her remaining days. Her fellow residents are magnificently eccentric and endlessly curious, living off crumbs of affection and snippets of gossip. Together, upper lips stiffened, they fight off their twin enemies: boredom and the Grim Reaper.

Then one day Mrs Palfrey strikes up an unexpected friendship with Ludo, a handsome young writer, and learns that even the old can fall in love . . .

'The unsung heroine of British twentieth century fiction'
Rebecca Abrams, *New Statesman*

'Jane Austen, Elizabeth Taylor, Barbara Pym, Elizabeth Bowen
– soul sisters all' Anne Tyler

'Elizabeth Taylor had the keenest eye and ear for the pain
lurking behind a genteel demeanour' Paul Bailey, *Guardian*

MARY LAVELLE

Kate O'Brien

With an Introduction by Michéle Roberts

Mary Lavelle, a beautiful young Irish woman, travels to Spain to see some of the world before marrying her steadfast fiancé John. But despite the enchanting surroundings and her three charming charges, life as a governess to the wealthy Areavaga family is lonely and she is homesick. Then comes the arrival of the family's handsome, passionate – and married – son Juanito and Mary's loyalties and beliefs are challenged. Falling in Love with Juanito and with Spain, Mary finds herself at the heart of a family and a nation divided.

'She writes with almost poetic intensity of the ecstasy and anguish of love' Val Hennessy

'A superior type of romantic novel . . . colourful and unorthodox' *Times Literary Supplement*

A LOST LADY

Willa Cather

Introduced by A. S. Byatt

Marian Forrester brings delight to her husband, an elderly railroad pioneer; to the small town of Sweet Water where they live; and to Niel Herbert, the young narrator of her story, who falls in love with her as a boy and later becomes her confidant. He witnesses this vibrant woman in all her contradictory facets: by turns faithless and steadfast, dazzling and pathetic, invincibly charming yet dangerously vulnerable to the men she charms. All are bewitched by her charisma and grace – and all are ultimately betrayed.

'This classic has the striking economy of Hemingway, and is as poignant an elegy for the pioneer West as I have read. The vivacious Marian Forrester stands as a romantic paean to the pioneer's reckless abandon, counterpointed by the narrator's prim decency' *The Times*

'A poised and perfectly shaped novel' *Daily Mail*

'Her finest novel . . . The portrait of the nervy, alive Marian Forrester as a woman determined to survive remains unforgettable . . . This wonderful performance displays Cather's narrative technique at its sharpest, as well as her understanding of the eloquence of the slightest gesture, the simplest statement . . . A masterpiece' *Irish Times*

INVITATION TO THE WALTZ

Rosamond Lehmann

Introduced by the author's grandson, Roland Philipps

A diary for her innermost thoughts, a china ornament, a ten-shilling note, and a roll of flame-coloured silk for her first evening dress: these are the gifts Olivia Curtis receives for her seventeenth birthday. She anticipates her first dance, the greatest yet most terrifying event of her restricted social life, with tremulous uncertainty and excitement. For her pretty, charming elder sister Kate, the dance is certain to be a triumph, but what will it be for shy, awkward Olivia?

Exploring the daydreams and miseries attendant upon even the most innocent of social events, Rosamond Lehmann perfectly captures the emotions of a girl standing poised on the brink of womanhood.

'A novelist in the grand tradition, and, more than this, an innovator, the first writer to filter her stories through a woman's feelings and perceptions' Anita Brookner

virago

To buy any of our books and to find out more
about Virago Press and Virago Modern Classics,
our authors and titles, as well as events and
book club forum, visit our websites

www.virago.co.uk
www.littlebrown.co.uk

and follow us on Twitter

@ViragoBooks

To order any Virago titles p & p free in the UK,
please contact our mail order supplier on:

+ 44 (0)1832 737525

Customers not based in the UK should contact
the same number for appropriate postage
and packing costs.